D1292187

A Garland Series

Foundations of the Novel

Representative Early
Eighteenth-Century Fiction

A collection of 100 rare titles
reprinted in photo-facsimile in 71 volumes

Foundations of the Novel

compiled and edited by

Michael F. Shugrue

Secretary for English for the M.L.A.

with New Introductions for each volume by

Michael Shugrue, *City College of C.U.N.Y.*

Malcolm J. Bosse, *City College of C.U.N.Y.*

William Graves, *N.Y. Institute of Technology*

The Golden Spy

or a Political Journal of the British Nights Entertainments of War and Peace and Love and Politics

by

Charles Gildon

with a new introduction
for the Garland Edition by
Malcolm J. Bosse

Garland Publishing, Inc., New York & London

1972

Bibliographical note:

This facsimile has been made from a copy in the Yale University Library (IK G389 709)

Library of Congress Cataloging in Publication Data

Gildon, Charles, 1665-1724.
The golden spy.

(Foundations of the novel)
Reprint of the 1709 ed.
I. Title. II. Series.
PZ3.G3886Go 8 [PR3478.G3] 823'.5 77-170519
ISBN 0-8240-0526-0

Printed in the United States of America

Introduction

During this literary period writers often used for their narrator an alien observer who looks upon a nation's customs with a fresh eye and as a consequence reveals evils unnoticed by members of the society. This method of narration was encouraged by the success in the late seventeenth century of Letters Writ by a Turkish Spy, which was an English translation of Giovanni Paolo Marana's Espion turc. In 1708 appeared an English translation of Le Sage's Le Diable Boiteau, a satirical novel which featured a non-human spirit instead of the foreign observer used by Marana. A year later Charles Gildon's The Golden Spy added a new dimension to the method by making his commentator an inanimate object.

Throughout the rest of the century practically anything that could move or remain in proximity to human life was used by writers of satire to tell the story: among others, a bedstead, a black coat, a cork-screw, an embroidered waistcoat, a gold-headed cane, a gold ring, a goose-quill, a hackney coach, a mirror, a pin, a pincushion, a silk petticoat, slippers and shoes, a sofa, a stage coach, a watch. An especially popular inanimate narrator was money: a bank-note, a guinea, a "bad" guinea, a half-penny, a rupee, and a shilling were chosen for narrators of satiric tales.

Gildon was the first writer who recognized in the chief characteristic of money, its mobility, a way of getting a fictional observer from place to place logically *and rapidly. By emphasizing the moral relationship between the story teller, gold, and the human sin, greed, which is associated with money, he developed the potential of such a narrator for judging the behavior of man.*

The Golden Spy *begins with a long preface which in its bitter criticism of the moral temper of the day sets the stage for a satirical treatment of eighteenth-century life. The story opens with an unnamed narrator waking from sleep at the call of a voice from among some gold pieces lying on the table. This coin, "a half Louis d'Ore," explains that it has had access to human secrets, lust, and greed, "from the Prince to the Peasant" (14), then tells a story of seduction and revenge which culminates in a stated moral: "Unlawful Love is generally attended with Infamy and Ruin" (27). Having established its ability to give accounts of human life, the coin further explains its own character, because in this literary age even such a fantasy must carry with it an assertion of authenticity. The coin claims that actually it is an immaterial substance, a spirit lodged in gold; though it possesses great knowledge and like the genii of Arabian folklore can change shape, it is afraid of coming under the control of greedy, deceitful human masters. The coin's next story illustrates the proposition that the lust for gold and for flesh are essentially the same, one lust calling forth the other. The "Story of the Mercenary Gallant" ends the first section, entitled "The First Night's Entertainment."*

"The Second Night's Entertainment," subtitled "The Court; or, the Male and Female Favourites," introduces three other coins, an English Guinea, a Spanish Pistole, and a Roman Crown, all of whom tell stories of lust and

greed, the events which they relate conforming to the national character each coin represents. The Italian coin, for example, describes an avaricious woman who by a life of licentiousness is able to make her son a Cardinal.

The third section, subtitled "Gaming," deals with the fate of men whose greed turns them to games of chance. The Guinea suggests that although the English are not as violent as the French and Italians, they are as conniving and may well exceed all peoples in their love of gambling. In one of the stories in this group Gildon shows a penchant for writing fabliaux-type tales; he describes in explicit salacious detail how a woman gambler pays off her debts by selling herself to brutish rakes.

"The Fourth Night's Entertainment" begins with a sharp criticism of life in the city:

> *Take warning by me, quit the Lewd Town, which contains nothing worthy the Residence of a Man of true Sense: the Men are Sharpers, the women Whores; Religion is Hypocrasie; Friendship Design; Knavery thrives, Honesty starves; Fools pass for Wits and Men of Sense are contemn'd and in Raggs (147-48).*

The ensuing tales follow a pattern: those with an Italian setting are rife with dark intrigue and revenge; the French stories are written in a lighter vein and emphasize the cynical acceptance of immorality in Gallic society; the narratives set in English describe lowborn women and boyish rakes who openly exhibit an exuberant sexuality. Gildon brings this section to a close by heaping opprobrium on the Irish, whom he accuses of being a race of gigolos: "These Stallions invade other Mens Rights, and put their own Spurious Issue in the Room of the Right Heir of the Family" (237).

In the fifth section Gildon attacks the English judicial system by affirming with Swiftian fervor that often the law corrupts rather than protects mankind. In one story a constable ruins the life of a lady and her entire family; a greedy cleric in another tale acts as a marriage broker; and in a third a young woman is unfairly jailed by an old lecher who has her released only to drug and debauch her.

The sixth and final section is subtitled "Of Peace and War; or, the Trade of the Camp" and opens with a long discussion in a coffee house between men holding different views on the problem of the Spanish Succession. The question of a standing army, an issue hotly debated in Queen Anne's reign, is introduced; one speaker cynically observes that people want peace for their own selfish economic ends rather than for the nation's good. When the unnamed protagonist returns home from the coffee house, his spirit-coins take up the discussion of politics and war. The French coin points out that gold rather than iron determines victory in war. The other coins join in to discuss the military success of Louis XIV, their conclusion being that the French fight dishonorably, using bribery and dissimulation rather than arms and courage. The narrative ends abruptly on this chauvinistic note, with Gildon's human speaker stating merely, "I shall take care often to Consult my Golden Spy*" (304).*

The impact of this book ultimately suffers from repetitiveness; too often one story of a woman duping her foolish husband is shortly followed by another story on the same theme. There is, however, a breadth and vivacity to the work that anticipates the fiction of Smollett and Fielding. Gildon's narrative method reveals an early eighteenth-century writer's impressive attempt to create a coherent framework for wide-ranging satirical vignettes.

Malcolm J. Bosse

THE GOLDEN SPY, IN THE Courts of *EUROPE*.

THE

Golden Spy:

OR, A

POLITICAL JOURNAL

OF THE

British Nights Entertainments

OF

WAR and PEACE,

AND

LOVE and POLITICS:

Wherein are laid open,

The Secret Miraculous Power and Progress of GOLD, in the

Courts of *Europe*.

Intermix'd with

Delightful INTRIGUES, MEMOIRS, TALES, and ADVENTURES, Serious and Comical.

LONDON:

Printed for *J. Woodward* in St. *Christopher's Church-yard, Thread-needle-street*; and *J. Morphew* near *Stationers-hall*, M DCCIX.

THE
Epiſtle Nuncupatory,
TO THE
AUTHOR
OF
A TALE of a TUB.

SIR,

T*His Addreſs is not to let you know that the Author ſent the following Sheets to viſit the World at the frequent Importunity of learned and witty Friends; or to explain to you the drift and deſign of the Preſent I ſend you, for indeed it is purely to follow the Mode; for there is, Sir, you know, a Faſhion in Books, as well as in Dreſſes, and to be out of it in either, gives an ill Grace to the Perſon or the Book: And my Author having ſent me his Copy without inſcribing it to any living Creature, and you, Sir, having engroſs'd* Prince Poſterity, *I was affraid, that shou'd my Book be out of the Fashion of an Epistle Dedicatory, in an Age so prodigal to Flattery, it wou'd look so naked and bare, as to fright all the modish Buyers, whom I always desire to be my best Customers; since a plausible* Title Page (*the Booksellers Art*) *and a good* Gilt Back, *seldom fail to please them.*

Being therefore come to this Resolution, my next difficulty was to find a Patron. I had indeed a very long Debate in my self whose Flag to Advance, under whose Banner to enter the Battel of Criticks, *a formidable Generation, that have no more Mercy than Hunger, Necessity, or a Clergy-man's Revenge. I look'd over the Catalogue of all my Customers, of* White's Chocolate House, Tom's *and* Will's Coffee-house, *and the* Temple, *to say nothing of my* City Chaps, *who sometimes deal in Wit, and are as terrible* Criticks *as any of the former: Nor did I neglect the consideration of the Ladies, but cou'd not find one of all my Roll fit for my purpose. For, said I, how can* WIT *ever hope for a Patron among those who subscribe so profusely for* NONSENSE; *or Art find a Friend where Ignorance and Impudent Pretence are receiv'd; or that Satyr shou'd please the* Piquet *and* Back gammon *Players of* Covent-Garden; *or that* Cook upon Littleton *shou'd defend the* Belle Railery; *Or that the Ladies wou'd be favourable to a Man that can produce his* Witnesses, *when they are so fond of Eunuchs that have none?*

Con-

Considering therefore that WIT *was banish'd the Court, the Great Men's Studies, and the Ladies Closets, the* Chocolate-house, *and* Playhouse, *my old Acquaintance Mr.* Britain *the Smallcoal Man made me turn my Eyes towards* Clerken-well Green *for Refuge; hoping, that the Neighbourhood of the* Bear-Garden, *where now are the most natural Judges of* Wit, *wou'd afford the best Patrons.*

'Tis true, had I fix'd on the ingenious Mr. Britain, *People wou'd have thought, that I might have found a difficulty in some of the laudable Topics of Dedication; as the* Ancient Family, *and* known Generosity *of the Patron; yet to shew them their mistake, I protest sincerely, that had not the least influence on my rejecting his Patronage, since I do not at all doubt, but that I might have spoke as much Truth on both Heads, as generally has been spoken by most of our Modern Dedicators; Who often run the Pedegree of their Patrons up to the* Conquest, *(and we are beholden to them that they stop there) tho' perhaps they wou'd be puzled themselves to tell their Forefathers in the Pious Days of good Queen* Bess; *tho', it may be, the first of them, that made any Figure, was only a* Court Pimp; *or favourite* Valet de Chambre *of some antiquated Lady, whose salacious distemper made him a Gentleman, by getting him a Place, in which, by Cheating the Queen and Country, he might raise an Estate, and leave his Posterity the*

Title of Right Honourable. *For as that Sage* Donn *and Holy Father,* Pope Pius *the second, judiciously observes,* Few Great Families have had a very honourable Rise. *Besides,* Poets *and other* Dedicating *Authors can make Pedegrees, as well, as any* Herald, German, *or* Welshman *of them all. His very Name wou'd have afforded many pregnant Conjectures in his Favour. For several Persons eminent in their Stations have born it; which in the Memory of our Fathers, has been thought sufficient to make old* ROMANS *of some honest* Saxons, *never heard of in the World till these later days. As, first, Mrs.* Britain *has been a Lady very useful in her Generation, and furnish'd the* Quality *with many a Maidenhead both Real and Artificial. Nor has this Name been unknown in the Kingdom of the* Beaux, *and* Gallants; *and if we wou'd pursue the Advantages of the* Name *to its Antiquity, How easie a matter wou'd it be to make it as ancient as the Nation it self? And so with a little of our Modern Author's Address in fine* Panegyric, *I might have deriv'd it from old* Brute *and the* Trojans; *tho' that perhaps I might have left to Mr.* Samms, *and the rest of the most profound and Learned Antiquaries of this Nation, especially to* Geofry *of* Monmouth, *and about a Thousand* Welsh *Manuscripts. But if all this had not been sufficient to vanquish his* Modesty, *and make him quite forget his* Small-coal

coal Bagg, *I cou'd have told him, that in pious Times of* Yore, *a great while ago indeed, and a great way off, before the barbarous Inundation of* Goths, Vandals, *and* Lombards, *Men were distinguish'd from the Mob only by their Virtue, their Valour, or Knowledge or Excellence in some* Science *or* Art; *and have prov'd it by a* Latin *Quotation:*

Nobilitas sola est atq; unica Virtus.

Tho' that perhaps might have been look'd on as a Satyr on the Quality *of these Times; and by the* High-flyers, *for a rank piece of* Republican *Malice.*

Thus with much ease I cou'd have proclaim'd the Wonders of his Generosity, especially to Men of Art; *a Virtue so uncommon in this present Age, that a* Fidler *shall draw* Hundreds *out of the Purse of a* Lord, *who wou'd not give* Sixpence *to all the* Sense *of Mankind; and when the Noblemen's* Valets *take* Brokerage *for* Dedications.

Purely *therefore to avoid the Imputation of a* Maligner *of our Men of* Quality, *I laid all thoughts of addressing to Mr.* Britain *aside, and cast my Eyes on you, Sir, who being perfectly* unknown *for your* Quality, *or* Virtues *to the World, wou'd not administer Matter of* Envy *or* Abuse *on my present Address: Besides, Sir, to you All manner of* Tales

Tales *lay a claim most peculiar. You led the Dance of* Tales *to the Town, which yet is not weary of following the Humour. The* Arabian *and* Turkish Tales *were owing to your* Tale of a Tub; *And the last was Midwif'd into the Press by the eminent Bookseller of the* Wits, *and* Chairman *of as* eminent *a Club: The* Devil on two Sticks, *and many more* Ejusdem faraginis: *Nay, even* Histories, *having long been a sort of* Tales of *so many* Tubs, *easily pass'd on the Town for your Productions. But, Sir, one of the chief Motives of this Address to you, is that the World might be sensible, that I have too much Modesty (tho' a* Bookseller) *to* palm *the following* Treatise *upon you; The heighth of my Ambition being to send it abroad under the advantageous Circumstances of* your *Patronage: For tho' I cou'd never find that a* Lord's *Title or Name to the* Dedication, *sold me a Book, or excus'd the Dulness of my* Author; *yet I am in Hopes that yours will do both; since I have seen many a* Blockhead *pass for a* WIT *by keeping good Company; and* John Dryden, *and* Will Wycherly familiarly *pronounc'd, and with an Air of* Intimacy, *has rais'd a Reputation, that Nature never design'd.*

Besides, Sir, at a Time when all the Fine Arts *are so visibly discourag'd by both the* Great, Vulgar, *and the* Small; *when the first*

have

have run down Poetry and Plays for Ballads *and* Operas; *when the latter from a Zeal of* Reforming *of* I KNOW NOT WHAT, *has not only ſuppreſs'd the Antient* Fair *of St.* Bartholomew, *ſo that we may ſooner expect to ſee there a* Bonner, *than a* Pinkethman; *when the more* Modern Fair *of* May, *and that Celebrated one of* Greengooſe, *are Reform'd of all their Ornaments as of ſo many* Popiſh Ceremonies, *to the great decay of the Conſumption of* Pigg *and* Pork, *and* Greengeeſe; *where the Noble and Antient Art of* Rope-Dancing *is almoſt aboliſh'd as* Ancichriſtian, *becauſe the* Finnambuli *were offenſive to one of the Plays of Old* Terence, *the poor Remnants of theſe nimble Artiſts being forc'd to find a Hoſpitable Retreat at* Sadlers Wells, *where Mrs.* Buſhel *ſhows her Plump Thighs to the* Sober Saints, *their Pious Wives and Daughters, and hopeful Young Sons too, without the leaſt fear of* Scandal. *When the Facetious* Jack-puddings *are ſilenc'd for fear of* Prophane Wit, *or forc'd to content themſelves with a* Mountebanks Stage, *to Joke off their Pills, Potions, and Plaiſters, to the detriment of many an Honeſt, tho' Credulous* Cit. *When the Ingenious* Puppet Shows *ſuffer a greater Perſecution in this Land of* Liberty *and* Moderation, *than once they did among the* Wiſe *and* Religious Switzers, *who zealouſly burnt a Maſter of a* Puppet Show *for dealing with the Devil; from whence, our* Godly *and* Wiſe Reformers, *have ever ſince taken*

taken it for a most Diobolical Entertainment. *When the Spirit of* Hypocrisy *aims at Reforming us into* Solitude, *by Politically destroying all* Publick Meetings *and* Recreations; *at least, when they have left no place free for our Diversion but the Markets of* French *Commodities, the* Taverns; *and when no body is like to be suffer'd to thrive but* Vintners, Victuallers, Justices Clerks, Reforming Constables, *and* Informers; *for Godliness is now not only a* Gain *but a* Trade, *for which Men quit their old Employments as less* Beneficial, *and serve their end in* Reforming: *When* Usurers, Extortioners, *nay,* Debochees *and* Drunkards, *Piously set up for* enlarging the Kingdom of HEAVEN; *and while that they serve the* Old Gentleman in Black *in all the deeds of their Lives, are* Canoniz'd *by the Pulpit Gentleman in Black for their Zeal against* Common Drabs, *and Demolishing* Puppet Shows.

At a Time, I say, when all these fine Arts *lie under such a Pressure, what* fitter *Patron cou'd I choose, than the* Darling *of so* Judicious *and* Pious *an Age; who have discover'd so peculiar a* Genious *in* Merry TRIFLING, *as cou'd never want* Success; *when to Write* Serious, *is to be* Dull; *and to Think* Rationally, *to be* Pedantick *and* Enthusiastick. *I confess, that there have some other* Worthy *Gentlemen appear'd of late, who have*

had

had no unhappy Talent this Whimsical *way, among which our new* Philosophical Transactions *are a Masterpiece in their Kind, especially the Author's* Facetious *and Witty* English Epigrams *in a* Greek *Character. The* TATLER *has likewise lately taken up this* Taking Mode, *and crept like the Fops of the Times into the Closet of the* Great *and the* Fair, *by a* Modish Impertinence; *so that if a Peace* shou'd *come, I know not, but out of excess of Joy, we may not endure any thing but* TATLERS *these Ten years to come; which might prove as surprizing to your good Prince,* Posterity, *as our Military advantages over the* French Bully; *for we do now in* Writing *as in* Building; *if* Light *and* Gaudy, *'tis no matter how* Lasting; *and, indeed, it is but dealing* fairly *with* Posterity *to leave them the Liberty of building their own* Houses, *and writing their own* Books, *according to their own* Whims.

But, Sir, these are both far short of your Excellence, *and meer* Imitators *of it. The former redicules only meer* Humane *Arts and Sciences; while* You, *Sir, go farther, and Burlesque* Religion it self; *while speaking and thinking of it in a* Good Humour, *you have brought it to be no more than an* Old Coat, *leaving to the Good Friend honest* Moderate MARTIN, *scarce so much as a* Lappet *to cover his* Nakedness. *You have indeed done*

greater

To the AUTHOR of

greater Wonders in Controversie, *than* Guy of Warwick, Bevis of Southamton, *or* Amidis of Gaul, *in the performances of* Chivalry. *While* Stillingfleet, Tillotson, *and the other Champions of our Cause, have brought whole Armies of Authorities and Reasons against the* Whore of BABYLON, *you with* a JOKE *confute the Obstinate* Bellarmine *and* John Calvin *at once, and have certainly discover'd the* Shortest way with CONTROVERSY.

Yes, Sir, You put me in mind of the Merry Philosopher Democritus, *who thought the World only worth Laughing at. And perhaps you may be in the Right on't when you see every thing turn'd* Topside Turvey (*as they say*) *When* Divines *turn* Buffoons; Sharpers *turn* Cullies; *Men of Quality turn* Sharpers; Irishmen *turn* WITS; *Lawyers turn* Arbritrators; Tallymen *and* Paunbrokers *turn* Reformers; Whiggs *turn* Tories; *and* Tories *turn* Whiggs; Nonjurers *turn zealous defenders of the* REVOLUTION; Polititians *turn* Gamesters; *and* Coblers *turn* POLITITIANS.

Were I the Author I should here tell you Wonders of the Book *I Dedicate to you; That like* Homer, *according to the* Criticks, *it contains* all Arts *and* Sciences; *but speaking for another, I shall let him shift for him-*

himſelf, only informing you, That in the next Volume you will find Wonders indeed perform'd by GOLD, *ſuch as wou'd ſurprize ev'n a* PRIEST *or a* COURTIER; *who are generally ſo well acquainted with its Value and Force. And ſo, Sir, I Subſcribe my ſelf,*

Your

Humble Servant, the

BOOKSELLER.

THE

THE Golden Spy.

The INTRODUCTION; or, *The First Nights Entertainment.*

AMONG the many great Advantages we have of those who groan under the Tyranny of the *Inquisition*, that of the *Liberty of Philosophizing*, and making free and noble Enquiries into the hidden Secrets of Nature, is not the least valuable; since by that the modern Times and more free Nations have made many and inestimable Discoveries, which have been both useful and entertaining to the World. But it was the ill Fate of *Campanella*, who seems to have had a peculiar Genius this way, to be born a Subject of those Princes who with a great deal of ill Policy suffer a Tribunal in their Dominions, that denies any dependance on them: For *Campanella* was thrown into the Inquisition for Writing of things that were above the Understanding of an ignorant Age, and more ignorant People.

None of his Writings ever pleas'd me more than his Book *de Sensu Rerum*, which made me often wish that Chance or Industry might furnish me with some Experiment, that might with sufficient evidence confirm his Speculations. But when my Endeavours had prov'd fruitless, and all my Enquiries had left me not the least Light into my Desires, Chance supply'd one beyond Controversie, and which produc'd an Instance not only of the *Sensibility of Things* which we generally not only esteem mute but inanimate, but ev'n of their Rationality, and discoursive Faculty, Observation, Memory, and Reflection. Of this Nature was some Pieces of coin'd Gold, that Fortune had thrown into my Hands, from whose Conversation I learn'd many Secrets of Policy, and Love, part of which I shall relate, the rest I shall reserve for a more private Conference. I confess this Adventure, in a more Superstitious Country and Person, might have pass'd for a first-rate Miracle; but here, where Enquiries into Nature discover e'ry day such wonders, and with me who have read of the *Soul of the World*, and Maxims that hold ev'ry part of the Universe to be compos'd of animal sensible, and perhaps rational Particles, the Wonder rose not above the Power of the Operations of the secret course of Nature.

Were it not a receiv'd Maxim, that nothing is more Powerful than Gold, in War, and Peace; in Courts, and Camps; in Church, and State, with the Great and the Fair; yet

our

our present seeing and feeling of this Truth in the *French* Management were sufficient to establish it. For by this they have made all *Europe* tremble, and rais'd *France* to that height of Empire, which She has obtain'd, and yet struggles to preserve, with a Force almost equal to the rest of the World. I have indeed often thought what noble and diverting Discoveries might be made, could any of the *Louis d'Ore's* or *Guineas* reveal by discourse what Affairs they have negotiated, and those secret Intrigues, which have produc'd strange and terrible Effects in Kingdoms, and Families. But whilst I thought these Reflections but vain Amusements, as I lay awake one Night, I was agreeably surpriz'd with a proof of their Solidity. I heard an odd sort of humming noise like one strugling to speak, or not awake enough to give his Words their true Articulation; this was the more alarming, by being just under my Pillow, or somewhere about the Head of my Bed; yet I was so far from imagining this to be any Ghost, Hobgoblin, or Fantasm of the Night, that I suspected some Rogue had privately got into my Chamber, and hid himself till he found his opportunity in the Night to accomplish his Ends in Robbery or Murther. Leaping therefore from my Bed, I call'd for my Servant, who coming with a Light, search'd e'ry place with all imaginable Care and Exactness; but finding nothing, I kept the Light, and bid him retire to his Rest.

I was no ſooner laid down again, but I heard the ſame ruffling Noiſe, but it ſeem'd ſtronger than before, and directly under my Pillow, where yet I could find nothing but my Breeches, and in my Pockets a few *Louis d'Ores* and *Guineas*, with ſome *Dutch*, *Spaniſh*, and odd *Italian* pieces of Gold, which my Curioſity that day had prevail'd with me to purchaſe. Conſcious of my wonted Fate, which would never let me ſleep while I had any Money in my Pocket, I took them all out and laid them on a little Table juſt by my Bedſide; ſecure now of Repoſe, I found all quiet about me, and the Noiſe remov'd to the very place where I laid all my Gold. But that which now added to my Surprize was, that I plainly perceiv'd, that the former Noiſe began to aſſume a Tone extreamly like that of the Humane Voice, arriving at laſt to a Murmuring Articulation, ſome broken words of which reach'd my Ears, and ſeem'd to come from a Perſon juſt breaking from a profound ſleep, and yet not conſcious enough of Reaſon to make Senſe of what he utter'd.

Tho' I am not naturally Superſtitious, or very Credulous of Apparitions, yet the fruitleſs ſearch that I had juſt made, having ſatisfy'd me that I was my ſelf the only viſible living Creature in the Room, I found within me a Concern, of which, (till then) I thought my ſelf incapable. But reflecting, in the midſt of my Fear, that this could be no Spirit of Darkneſs, ſince it ventur'd into the Light, I grew more couragious, in which I was confirm'd by by ſeveral Pious and Religious Conſiderations which are proper and uſeful on ſuch Occaſions. Drawing therefore aſide my Curtain, I directed my Eye by the guidance of my Ear to the very Place whence this Sound ſeem'd to ariſe; but my wonder encreas'd when I diſcover'd nothing in Sight, but what us'd to be there, (except my Gold) which, tho' of ſeveral Intereſts and Countrys, I could not but ſuppoſe would lie together without quarreling.

I had heard, and Experience had taught me, that Gold would make the Silent ſpeak, and the Loquacious dumb; but I little ſuſpected that any of that Metal could ſhake off that natural dumbneſs which the Opinion of the World had ſo long fix'd upon it. But I had not gaz'd long e're I found to the contrary the ſame Sounds were renew'd, and I plainly heard a ſmall Voice among the Gold, which ſtruck me with an Amazement not to be expreſs'd; and yet it was an Amazement, that ſtruck more on my Curioſity than my Fear; for I immediately ſnatch'd up the neareſt piece to me, which happen'd to be a *Spaniſh Piſtole*, and clapt it to my Ear, and ask'd it many Queſtions; but all in vain, for it remain'd as ſullenly ſilent, as if it had no more power to ſpeak than the World generally imagines.

On the top of the Heap lay a half *Louis d'Ore*, which obſerving my uneaſie Curioſity, with a true French Briskneſs familiarly call'd to me, and bid me not give my ſelf a Labour ſo vain, as to loſe my Time in ſolliciting the Dumb to ſpeak, ſince of all that Heap He (for after what paſs'd betwixt us I may, with the Grammarians leave, call it *He*) only could yet a while comply with my Deſires. 'Tis true (continu'd he) ſome of theſe have had the Power of Speech, but by proſtituting that Faculty, have for a time quite loſt it; but that the reſt neither ever had or ever would enjoy that Prerogative. I my ſelf have now for ſome time (purſu'd my talkative Monſ.) been ſtrugling to recover a Power, of which I have long been depriv'd, and juſtling the reſt, to rouſe them from their long and drowſie fit of dumbneſs, but have not yet been able to prevail.

This Declaration of my dapper piece, gave me full ſatisfaction about the odd Noiſe that had given me ſo much diſturbance, which yet I thought amply rewarded by ſo wonderful a diſcovery. In ſhort (purſu'd he) I will not trouble my ſelf any longer with my dull languid Companions; but ſince we are in this Solitude, without any Witneſs, I ſhall addreſs my ſelf wholly to you. Tranſported with ſo engaging an aſſurance, I took him up in my Hand, gave him a thouſand kiſſes, and hugging him cloſe in my Boſom, full of Pleaſure as great as if I had got the beautiful *CÆLIA* in my Arms —— *Go on*, (ſaid I) *my Charmer, go on, and bleſs me with a Converſation, which ſure no Man ever enjoy'd before! Why art thou ſilent my adored? Why doſt thou delay thoſe Joys, that are as enchanting as uncommon?*

It

It was a considerable time e're he would vouchsafe to utter one Word, which threw me into a very painful Fear that he had lost that happy Faculty, which, I found by his Confession, was not always in his Power. In the midst of my impatient Expectation, now almost in despair, he began again to speak, but in a much weaker, and a sort of upbraiding Tone, which made me something uneasie. I ask'd him, however, the reason of a Change so sudden; and the hated Cause of a Silence, I found my self unable to endure.

You your self (said he, something angrily) are the only Cause, who by your fond Actions and Caresses, seem to confess the Miser, a Creature to whom we have the utmost aversion; his Love is as troublesome to us, as odious to all the World besides; for, shut up in his Coffers, we lose this agreeable Quality, which is only mantain'd by an absolute Freedom of circulating with the Sun about the World, where we make far greater Discoveries than that glorious Planet; for we are admitted to those Secrets which are industriously conceal'd from his enquiring Eye; and made Confidants of those Intrigues of Love and Politicks, which he would only disappoint or destroy. Whether we go in Bribes to tame troublesome Zeal of the *Patriot*; to betray the *Statesmans* Trust; or purchase the Honour and Chastity of the Matron or Virgin; for we, like the sage *Ulysses*, accomplish most of our greatest Exploits in the dark.

I aſſur'd him, that Curioſity alone had betray'd me into the odious Suſpicion of a Guilt, of which I had the utmoſt Abhorrence, Avarice being a Vice the moſt remote of any from my Nature. I begg'd him therefore, by his hopes of perpetual Liberty, to proceed without any ſuch Fear, and ſatisfie me in thoſe admirable Secrets of his Eſſence, which it ſeems were ſo very different from the Common Opinion.

Pacify'd with theſe repeated Aſſurances, reſuming his Courage, he thus again began:

I will not entertain you with an Account of the Generation of this Metal in the Bowels of the Earth, both becauſe that affords but little Diverſion to any but a profeſs'd Virtuoſo, and becauſe owing my Origin to another Cauſe, I am little acquainted with that terrene Gold by which you form your Idea of the whole Kind. I, Sir, am part of that famous *Golden Show'r*, diſguis'd in which *Jupiter* penetrated the ſtrong Brazen Tower, to poſſeſs the Charms of the beautiful *Danae*, which Story to look on as a meer Fable, favours too much of a Modern Incredulity; ſince, ever ſince that time, you find that there is no place ſo ſtrong, or guarded with that Vigilance, to which *Gold* will not gain Admittance and bring to a Surrender ſooner, and with more Safety, than the Batteries of Cannon, and the Valour of Heroes. I confeſs (continu'd he) all *Gold* is not of this nature, as will be plain from an Inſtance which I will preſently give you. But all the *Gold* of that Show'r is ever

ir-

irresistible. This is plain from daily Experience; for if we only look into the Affairs of Love, we shall find some Lovers at a vast expence, without being able to obtain the least Favour of their Mistresses; whilst others with a little of this, and a tolerable Address, easily get into their Arms, in spight of all the watchful Eyes of Husbands and Spies never failing to gain the strongest Fort, if they vouchsafe but to set down before it. This Truth I shall convince you of, in a Story of a certain Lady who had me once in her Possession, as soon as I have premis'd a short Account of my self, and the various Transmigrations I have pass'd, by that Means to remove your Incredulity or Doubts of whatever I shall reveal.

Since I came down from Heav'n in that *show'r* with *Jove*, I have had multitudes of Masters, and Shapes full as various. Much Time I have spent in the Service of the Ladies; have been the Ornaments of the Swords and Weapons of ancient Heroes and modern Generals, and perfectly know what those acquir'd by their Valour, and these by their Money. I can tell you their Conduct and Government, show you the Art of rising in the Camp without Valour or Sense, and all the dark Mysteries of husbanding a War to Years, that might be decided in a few Months. I have been lock'd up in the Cabinets of Princes, great Kings, and mighty Emperors, and am perfectly acquainted with their most secret Intrigues, private Vices, and Follies. I have belong'd to several great Politicians, Favourites and Courtiers,

and

and know all their Principles and Maxims. I have been too often in the Coffers of the Clergy, and many times in their Studies and Closets, which has brought me throughly acquainted with their Vicious Inclinations, Irreligion, Hypocrisie, Cruelty, Ambition, Avarice, and Pride. I have likewise adorn'd the Fingers of the greatest Favourites, Male and Female, seen all their Bribes, told over the Price of the Extortion and Robberies they have committed, and seen the Plunder of Nations cram'd into their private Coffers. I know the cause of the Fall of *Sejanus*, that great *Roman* Favourite, and could give them all such good Advice, as might secure them from the like Fate.

From the Courtiers I easily pass'd to the Gamesters; those, tho' never such Scoundrels by Birth and Parts, are admitted to the Tables of Lords and Princes: nay, this very one thing has brought the Lacquey from behind his Lords Chair, to the Table with him. And the Ostler from rubbing the Horses Heels, into the Bed with a Dutchess. The Metamorphoses of this Mystery are greater than those of *Ovid*; for here Footmen, Porters, Butchers, Tapsters, Bowl-Rubbers are transform'd into Gentlemen, and Companions for Ministers of State, and Princes themselves; and on the other hand, Lords, Knights, and Squires into Scoundrels, excluded the Conversation of the Chambermaid; Porters, Pimps under Sharpers, Setters, and the like. I have belong'd to Pimps and Bawds of all Nations, and know the

the ſecret Amours of all the Great Men, when they careſs falſe Beauty in their Arms, as they do falſe Merit in their Favour in their Poſts. I have ſeen the moroſe ſow'r Miniſter of State hug the rotten Remains of Footmen and Porters under the ſpecious Names of Virgins and Citizens Wives; and the Matrons of Quality, when they have been inſenſible of the Adreſſes of Wit, and Accompliſhments of Perſon and Qualifications, melt luxuriouſly in the ruſtic Embraces of Brawny Coachmen, and Tinkers. I have ſeen the falſe Modeſty hide her Face in public at a double Entendre, yet riot in ſalacious Enjoyments in her Cloſet. In my Travels thro' *England* I have not eſcap'd the Gripe of the *Godly*, where I have made notable Diſcoveries of their Hypocriſie; for while their Pretences would raiſe them above Men, their Practice lays them lower than the Wickedneſs of Devils: for indeed, they endeavour to ſeem better than moſt Men, to get it into their power to be more abandon'd than all Men. The canting Reformer, who buſily pretends to alter the courſe of Nature, and ſend the poor Whores to *Bridewell*, I have ſeen reeking in Adultery with his own Neighbours Wife. Others who have look'd on a pint of Wine in a Tavern as an unpardonable Profanation of the Lord's-Day, I have ſeen get Drunk in their own Houſes, to the Edification of the Godly. I have ſeen others that have with a Gogle of Deteſtation damn'd all the Frailtys of Nature and Youth, ſwallow the Eſtates of Widows and Orphans with more eaſe than a Glaſs

of

of Whitewine, and Bitter in a Morning, without the leaſt remorſeful keck of Conſcience, and then by the Tub-thumper tranſlated to *Baxter*'s *Saints Everlaſting-Reſt*, without any Reſtitution to the poor ſuffering Victims. The Stock-jobbers I have been throughly acquainted with, and know all the ſlights and cunning of their Tricks, and all the familiar Cheats of the honeſt Traders of the City.

I can tell you the Scandal and Impertinence of the Ladies *Viſiting-days*; the Machinations of all the political *Juntoes*: for I have been of all Parties and Factions, and am perfectly acquainted with all their Rogueries; their ſham Pretences to the Good of the Public, to bubble the People into their meaſures, for their own private Intereſt and Advantage. I can let 'em into the Secret of *High-Church* and *Low-Church*, and point out all the *Fools* and *Tools* that manage and are managed by the Demagogues of each. I can ſhew you a Scene of the uſeful *Doctors-Commons*, where Proctors without Religion exclaim on the Danger of the Church. I can inform you in the Art of making a *bad* Cauſe *good*, before a Judge that weighs the Merit of Plaintiff and Defendant by ounces of Gold, not Witneſſes or Right. I can teach you the Art of bribing Parliaments and public Aſſemblies, who, drunk with this *Aurum potabile*, diſembogue the Rights of the People while they vote againſt Arbitrary Power, and boaſt of *Magna Charta*.

As I have had ſuch various tranſmigrations thro' the great World, ſo have I taken a ſhort

turn

turn to its Miniature the *Stage*. I know all the Intrigues of the Ladies of that Romantic Region; their wonderful Conſtancy, exact Fidelity, and uncommon Generoſity: I've been Witneſs of the *Utopian Felicity* of their Lovers, free from the *Anxieties* of Rivals. I have div'd into the Myſteries of the Management of that politic State; for they, like the greater World, conceal Self-intereſt and Injuſtice under the ſpecious Name of *Arcana Imperii*. I can give you the Characters of their *Hero's*, their Honour, Capacity, Judgment, and Knowledg in the Art they profeſs; their Juſtice to each other and to the Poets; their illuſtrious Birth and learned Education, by which they are qualified for ſuch great Poſts as they frequently enjoy. I have likewiſe been converſant with the Kingdom of *Sounds*, the *Opera's*; can tell you all their wiſe Subſcribers, with *their* Merits and Characters. I can paint in as lively Colours as they uſe, the bright *Female Songſters* and the as-famous neither *Male nor Female Singers*. There I have ſeen a *Switz* Trumpeter paſs for a great Maſter of Muſic, and Eunuchs palm on the Town Grimace, and Action for Harmony and Voice. And tho' theſe may ſeem Trifles not worth your hearing, yet ſince the Fools of Figure have given them the Air of Importance, they may perhaps afford you variety of Diverſion.

From theſe two *Fairy Orbs* I have ſometimes eſcap'd to the Pockets of the Poets, with whom tho' my ſtay was generally very ſhort, yet they being Men without Diſguiſe or Deſign, I can draw

draw you a perfect Scheme of their Virtues, Capacities, Learning and Genius.

In short, Sir, I have been in every station of Life, from the *Prince* to the *Peasant*, and can unfold all the Mysteries of Iniquity, that in all Nations have always enrich'd Knaves, impos'd on Fools, and baffled Men of Sense.

I have frequently pass'd the Chymist's Furnace, and been tortur'd for the Alchymist's Projection; have seen the Bubbles who spent their present Fortune for a future Chymera. I have also many times pass'd the Physician's Hands in the form of a Fee, and so am perfectly acquainted with the Skill and Method of the Faculty in Practice in regard of the *Patient* and the *Apothecary*.

But, to come to an end, Sir, I am the eldest Son of *Time*, and may justly say, that I know the Transactions in all the Climates of *Europe*, and Ages of the World, in War and Peace, in Love and Politicks.

Having thus given you sufficient Proof of my Experience and Knowledg, I hope what I have to say will find a perfect Belief; for assure your self, Sir, I am not so fond of talking as to throw away my Words where I meet with any Doubts of my Veracity.

My *little Piece* here pausing a while, I gave him all the assurance imaginable of a Mind ready to receive, as Verities undoubted, all he had to tell me. Pleas'd with what I said, and the manner of my uttering it, he immediately went on to the Story; which was, to prove the different Force of this *Gold* of Heavenly birth

birth from that which was drawn from the Bowels of the Earth.

The Story of Count Guido, Bernardo, *and Donna* Biancha.

COunt *Guido* (ſaid he) was of the City of *Fano* in *Italy*; his Father was a Gentleman of a good Family, yet, according to the Cuſtom of the *Italian* Nobility, he ſcrupl'd not to improve his Fortune by Traffic. But Avarice growing on him with his Age, and his Wealth finding an abundant encreaſe, he became ſo doating a Lover of his Mony, that he never durſt truſt it out of his ſight: So living moſt miſerable, he died moſt odious and contemn'd. His Son in the mean while (the Subject of our preſent Diſcourſe) with a ſmall Allowance rais'd himſelf by his Valour and Parts in the Emperor's Service, to the Dignity of a Count of the Empire: But his Father's Death ſoon recall'd him from the rugged purſuit of Glory in the Field of *Mars*, to make a more conſiderable figure in that of bright *Venus*. He came home therefore from the Campaign to take poſſeſſion of Riches ſo immenſe, as fall very ſeldom to the ſhare of any one Man.

A large Eſtate was the leaſt part of his Wealth; for the Sums he found hoarded up in his Coffers and other ſecret places, were ſufficient to have purchas'd him an *Italian* Principality. But theſe heaps of Treaſure having been ſecluded from the Light ſo many Years, the young Count had the misfortune either to have

have none of his lucky Gold I have mention'd, or its Vertue was lost by so long a confinement.

The Count was of a quite contrary temper to his Father, being naturally as profuse as the other was niggardly: He immediately set up a magnificent Equipage, and wanting a Palace fit for his reception, he resolv'd to pull down the old House of his Father, and erect a noble Pile, answerable to the Riches he was now Master of, designing in the mean while to travel, and show his Magnificence to foreign Nations. He therefore left the overseeing his Building to the care of a grave Relation, whose Knowledg and Honesty he thought he could best confide in, and so set out for *Venice*, to take the Diversions of the Carnival, and show his splendid Equipage, where many Nations might be Witnesses of his Pomp and Magnificence.

He had not been long at *Venice*, but the Figure he made recommended him to the Acquaintance of the *Great*, and the Eyes of the *Fair*. For, besides the dazling Beauty of his Riches, which gave Charms, Wit, and Honour where Nature gave none, he had really those of Person to a degree of perfection; his Stature was tall, his Shape neat, his Mien great, and yet graceful; his Eye full, black, and spritely; his Hair hung down to a length very uncommon; he danc'd and sung finely, and talk'd with a great deal of Vivacity and Wit, so that the Men were mightily taken with his Conversation, the Women more; for the Liberties of the Carnival had made him more known to

that

that Sex than at another time he could have been. Tho' he was not extreamly prone to Intrigues with the *Fair*, yet was he not ſo cold, but that Donna *Biancha* found ſuch a paſſage to his Heart, as render'd him entirely her Captive. What other Affairs he had with the Ladies of *Venice*, as they have nothing to do with my preſent Deſign, ſo did they never come to my Knowledge, I being at that time a ſort of wandring Foliage round a Bracelet, which Donna *Biancha* always wore on her Arm.

Biancha was Wife to the younger Brother of an Ancient *Magnifico*, who had as few Qualifications of Merit as any Nobleman in *Venice*. His Age was above Fifty, his Temper Coveteous, Froward, and Jealous, and his Perſon was fully as diſagreeable as his Mind, for he was Crooked, and Paraletic; and all his Conjugal Happineſs (if the indifference of a *Venetian* Husband and Wife can merit ſuch a Name) depended on his Authority as a Huſband, and the Vigilance and Fidelity of his Spies. *Biancha* on the other Hand was perfectly beautiful in her Perſon and Face; but in her Mind as ſilly and inſipid as moſt of the *Venetian* Ladies are.

Count *Guido* had taken particular notice of her in the *Piazza* of St. *Mark*, where her very ſhape and mein had made ſo great an Impreſſion on his Heart, that he could not reſt till he knew the cauſe of his Deſires: He therefore employ'd his Spies, whom he paid very well, to watch her home; tho' the Task was difficult as well as dangerous, Gold made them accplifh their work, and inform the Count who his Miftrefs was, and where fhe liv'd. By the fame means he had notice wherever fhe went, fo following her one day to Church, he plac'd himfelf as near her as poffibly he could, in hopes either of throwing in a word of paffion in the intervals of her heavenly Ejaculations; or, that fome lucky Accident or other would difcover whether her Face were of a piece with the reft of her Body, which was entirely charming. But he might have pray'd and watch'd in vain for fuch an opportunity, had not an almoft fatal Chance laid open that Countenance that coft him fo many fighs and fuch dangers as rob'd him of his Life in the end. They knelt before an Image of the *Virgin*, which had the Character of fo compaffionate an Idol, as never to deny any Suit that was prefer'd to her, and it was this day adorn'd in a moft pompous manner, and furrounded with great illuminations; and if it had been known that the Count had pray'd to this Miraculous Image for the fuccefs of his Defires in that particular, the Event had certainly made no inconfiderable figure in the Legend. For the crowd being great, and *Biancha* very near the Rail of the Image, part of her Veil, in turning, fell over it, and caught fire from the Candles, and in a moment burft out in a Flame. The Count was the firft that, alarm'd with her Danger, call'd to them about her, who before he could make way to her, had tore it from her Head; which at once difcover'd a Face, that would have turn'd *Jove* into all thofe Forms to enjoy her, which he us'd

in

in his Amours with the Heroines of Antiquity, and a ſhort Death invading it, and cloſing her Eyes, which yet ſet the Count's Heart in a greater Flame than that of her Veil, and much harder to be extinguiſh'd; for hers, by the care of her Attendants, was ſoon put out, but his could not expire by any thing but its Cauſe.

The Lady being in a ſwoon, the Count and ſome others made way through the Crowd for her Servants to carry her into the open Air, where ſoon recovering, ſhe open'd ſuch Eyes as eaſily compleated a Conqueſt, that was ſo far gain'd before.

The Count was not the only Man, that was wounded on this occaſion; for there happen'd to be by another, who tho' he deſerv'd her much leſs, was yet far more ſucceſsful in his Endeavours; for *Bernardo* ſoon obtain'd all thoſe Favours for which the Count ſigh'd, and labour'd long in vain.

Bernardo was juſt the Reverſe of the Count, in Perſon, in Temper, and Fortune. His Perſon was low, and ſomething diſtorted, his Hair black as a Raven, his Eyes almoſt white, and his Complexion ſallow; his Age about forty: As he was far from being generous in his Temper, ſo his Fortune was but the ſhatter'd Remains of a Prodigal Father; which yet he manag'd to the beſt Advantage of making a tolerable Appearance in his own degree of Quality. This Gentleman was by at this Accident, and ſhow'd himſelf not leſs officious than the amorous Count, in aſſiſting *Biancha* in this fiery Misfortune, and found ſome gracious Regards from the Fair one, which

Guido was not able to engage by all the Harmony of his Parts and Addrefs, fuch wild Caprice fits Sovereign in the Appetite of Woman.

By this time it was no Secret who the Lady was, nor where fhe liv'd; fo that both her Lovers knew the ftrict Guard fhe was under, and therefore that Gold was abfolutely neceffary for every Approach. This gave little pain to the Count, who valu'd his Mony only for its Ufe, and Subfervience to his Pleafures, and he therefore refolv'd to facrifice his whole Fortune to an Enjoyment without which his Life muft be an infupportable Burthen. *Bernardo* on the other fide was as fenfible that Mony was neceffary to bring about his Satisfaction; but his Exchequer was then at a low ebb, and not many pieces of Gold could be drawn thence for an affair of this Importance: yet he was fo fortunate as to have all his Gold tinctur'd at leaft with this noble Kind of which I have fpoken. He therefore gave fome, and promis'd infinitely more, fo that whatever Hand it came to, had no Power to refift its force, but was entirely brought over to his Intereft. He happen'd to have his Picture in Minature chac'd in the fame Gold, which coming into the poffeffion of *Biancha*, by a ftrange kind of Witchcraft, made him appear in her Eyes the moft defirable of Mankind; and was refolv'd to run the rifque of all, to gratifie their mutual defires.

Count *Guido*, in the mean while, had made very large Prefents to all her Guard, and receiv'd as large Promifes of their Affiftance; and the Lady dy being made acquainted with his Suit, receiv'd what Jewels he sent her, and resolv'd to improve this Affair to the Advantage of her Favourite Lover. To this end she discovers all the Count's Pretensions to her Husband, insinuating at the same time, that Mony might be got by the descreet management of so wealthy a Lover; and that he could not doubt a Fidelity, that had voluntarily sacrific'd so handsom and accomplish'd a Person to his and her Honour. Avarice had a great Ascendant over the Husband, so that being thus admitted a Confidant, he easily allow'd of the Conduct. Thus as the Count gave largely, all the Spies encourag'd him, took what he gave, and deliver'd his Letters and Presents to their Lady; so that Hope brib'd by Desire confirm'd him in his Folly.

The Count, to improve Opportunity, caress'd the Husband extreamly, and lost his Mony to him freely, to render himself the more agreeable to his covetous Humour. But all he got by what he did, was only fair Words from the Spies, and a transitory Look now and then from *Biancha* at her Window, which only serv'd to heighten his Desire and Impatience.

In the vicissitude of his Gaming, it was his luck to win a few pieces of the nobler Metal, and with the same luck presented them to the most powerful, because most trusted of her Guard, who was so entirely gain'd by this powerful Bribe, that the Count was promis'd admittance on the first Opportunity of the Absence of the Husband; which the Count took care soon to supply, by making a Friend engage him at play by losing his Mony to him. But alas! the Count did not imagine that all the happy Minutes he furnish'd, *Bernardo* enjoy'd; for when the Count detain'd the Husband to engage his Familiarity by losing his Mony to him, *Bernardo* was admitted to the Wife, and rifled all those Charms at ease, which *Guido* took all those pains, and was at so vast an Expence for in vain. Thus on the present occasion, *Bernardo* was before-hand with him; and whilst he was attending at the Door, was admitted to his Mistresses Arms.

Count *Guido* being at last convey'd up to an Anti-Chamber of *Biancha*'s Apartment, by the Spy he had thus gain'd to this Interest, he attended there a while with trembling and impatience at so near an approach to the Person that only by her Pity and Charms could give his perpetual disquiets any cessation or ease. But Fate, that disposes us and our Affairs with an arbitrary sway, soon gave a melancholly turn to all his Hopes, for listening to every noise, he thought he heard from the adjacent Room the hoarse sound of two murmuring Voices, of so different a tone, that the difference of Sex was easily discover'd. So that now fir'd with Jealousie, he stole closer to the Door, and putting his Ear to the Key-hole he plainly heard the following Words—*My dear* Bernardo, *your Power over my Weakness is but too plain, to you have I sacrific'd my Honour, and my Husband, nay, to you I have sacrific'd the handsomest, richest, and most accomplish'd Gentleman*

of

of Italy, *my Husband, that I might be the more free and secure in the dear Happiness of thy Embraces.* Love, *my dearest* Biancha (reply'd the Man) *is the chief, nay, the only Merit, that can deserve thee, and Love is what I possess in a far greater degree than any of Mankind; I therefore deserve thee more than all the rest of my Sex.*

Words like these were sufficient to drive such a Lover into such a Rage and Madness, as to produce a fatal Consequence; nor could the Count bear the Indignity of being made a property for the benefit of another; but bursting open the Door, he drew his Dagger, and rush'd in with a Resolution at once to put an end to the Life and Happiness of his Rival. But the noise he had made, had alarm'd the Lovers, so that *Bernardo* by the help of *Biancha* slipt out at another Door, and made his escape; while *Biancha* (being pleas'd that it was not her Husband, as she fear'd, but a Lover without Power) stopt the Count from pursuing him, upbraiding him in this manner. *Whence Sir, this Insolence in my Apartment, where your very Being deserves Death! which for my sake you ought to expect; yet in regard of a Passion you have so often troubl'd me about, I might pardon this rude effect of it, because tho' we do not value the Sacrificer, the Sacrifice is not always disagreeable. But your only way to let my Pity take place of my Resentment, is to retire this moment, and never more to think of a Passion so injurious to my Honour.*

Your Honour (reply'd the Count with a smile expressing too much of disdain) *I hope is safer in my Hands, than in those of that Wretch, who is fled from my Resentment. He that wants Courage, Madam, can never boast much of Love; and since you have once made so ill a Choice, permit me to hope that you will now take the Opportunity of a better. Tho' I know no Ground* (assum'd *Bianca*) *for an Insolence that is not to be born without a speedy Revenge, yet, Sir, I can see plainly that you mean to insult me, or which is as bad, to press me to that criminal converse with your self, which you would insinuate I have been guilty of with some other; yet assure your self, that whenever I shall be so weak to make the choice you mention, I shall never think him worthy of it, that can see any fault in my Conduct, which betrays as little Love as Respect: begone therefore with thy fruitless Hypocrisie, as unavailing to thee, as disagreeable to me, unless you resolve to suffer that Punishment your Intruding Boldness deserves.*

The Count was struck dumb with her uncommon Assurance, and confounded with her Rage, and Indignation; but this knowledge of her Guilt to both her Husband and him could not make him bravely to quit the pursuit of so worthless a Creature; but throwing himself on his Knees, and clasping her Hand, he open'd his Bosom and presented her his Dagger; *Here Madam* (said he) *transfix the most loving and tender Heart in the World, revenge your self upon me, and deliver me by a speedy Death from Pains and Agonys that are infinitely more terrible. I can endure any thing but your Fury; and tho' my Fidelity deserves a milder Fate, yet if I*

must

must dye to atone the Follies of my Tongue, let this fair Hand be my Executioner.

In short, he argu'd so pathetically, look'd so dejectedly, as would have rescu'd his Life from any Woman besides, if not have gain'd a farther Advantage in her Heart; but she only seem'd to be pacify'd, and with the height of Dissimulation grew calmer and calmer, till she admitted him to kiss her Hand, and talk of Love in so free a manner, as bred that Confidence of her sincerity in him which she desir'd to accomplish his Ruin in a more barbarous manner. But she had a double design in her Complaisance, to revenge her self on the odious Disturber of her private Pleasures, and secure them for the future by the Credit she should get with her Husband, by making the last Sacrifice of a Lover she did not care for, for one on whom she doated.

By this means she took an Opportunity to send away a Servant with all speed to her Husband, to let him know, that the Count was got into her Apartment without her knowledge; and that she would amuse him there till he came to punish him in Purse or Person, as he should think most convenient.

In the mean while, to delude him the more, and get to the place most fitting for her purpose, she led him into her Bed-Chamber, to raise his Mind to hopes and eager desires which she determin'd never to satisfie. Poor Count *Guido* now thought himself in the very direct Road to Happiness; and the Lady did all she could to confirm his fatal mistake by al-

allowing him all the Freedoms he could wish, except the last; till now word was brought, that her Husband was coming, and would not be long from her Apartment; that all the Avenues to the House were beset, and that Revenge seem'd glaring in his Face. She express'd all the Confusion in the World, and the utmost Concern both for his Life and her own. He advis'd her to fly with him; that, she told him, was now impossible; but the exigence admitting no debate, she advis'd him to go out of Window by a Cord that she found, and while both Ends were fix'd to the Bars of the Window, to sit in the middle till he were gone and yielded a better opportunity for his Escape. Necessity made him take hold of the only way of a Respite of his Fate, tho' he declar'd he had rather die, than have her expos'd to her Husbands barbarous Cruelty. When he was seated, and the Casement clos'd, his Head was so near it, that he could both see and hear all that was done in the Room. The first amazing thing he saw, was *Biancha* flying into the Arms of her Husband, and he as kindly receiving her, and then she drawing him near the Window, spoke aloud to him in these Words. *I have, my Dear at last got into our Pow'r that troublesome Invader of your Honour and mine, use your own discretion in the Punishment of the sawcy Intruder, tho' I think as Death is his due, so nothing else can perfectly secure my Reputation, since by the Treachery of some of your Family, he has been admitted into my Apartment, and by his own violence he has forc'd himself into my Bed-*

Cham-

Chamber. What Scandal may he not raise; to the Death of my Repose and yours! 'Tis true, the Rights of your Bed are yet not contaminated, but had you staid much longer all my Arts could not have protected me from his Madness.

The Husband in a great fury ask'd where he was? what she had done with him? and whether she did not dally with his Fury? She replied, *Turn your Rage against a just Cause, and let the Count feel your Anger, not me, who have with an artful address fixt him where he can neither help himself nor hurt you; approach that Window, and you will find him ready to receive your Chastisement, without any possibility of escaping.*

The Count observing them coming to his place of retreat, he with a Penknife cut one of the ends of the Rope, and sliding down by it as far as he could, chose rather to venture such a mighty fall, and trust to the clemency of the Waters, than to the pity of such a Wife and such a Husband; so leaping into the great Canal, he was toss'd about: And now almost spent with swimming, he met with a *Gondola*, (as we afterwards were inform'd) which conveying him to shore, he immediately left *Venice* in that condition, and died, as Report went, on the Road to *Ferrara*.

Thus, Sir, (said my little Piece) this Story makes out what I have told you of the different nature of *this* and the *common Gold*. You may likewise learn this Moral from it, That *Unlawful Love is generally attended with Infamy and Ruin.*

Pleas'd

Pleas'd infinitely with this Story and its Moral, I ask'd him if there was any great quantity of this valuable Metal now in the World: he assur'd me there was, since the Tow'r of *Danae* and all its Avenues were almost fill'd with it; but that *Jupiter* being in indignation at the Father, for slighting him as a Gallant for his Daughter, and locking her up close till deliver'd, and then throwing her and her Child into the Sea, he scatter'd it all round the face of the Earth. *One grain of this Gold is sufficient to compass the extent of your Ambition or Love; for there is no Fortress so strong, as to be impregnable to it; nor any Heart so hard, that it will not soften at its touch.*

But, said I, since so small a quantity is able to compass all our Desires, how comes about that when we offer but *a little* to bribe a *Judge*, corrupt a *Governour*, or suborn a *Confidant*, we seldom or never succeed, and yet seldom fail when we *double* the Dose, and raise it to the Constitution of the Recipient? I find (said my Piece) you have soon forgot, or little minded, what I told you, That *this Metal is scatter'd over the whole World in grains*; and that, *perhaps, one grain may not fall to the lot of a thousand pieces of lesser excellence. Belvoir* is worth perhaps a million, and yet is not Master of a drachm of this; whereas *Boufoy*, who has not the *fortieth* part of his Wealth, may be much better stor'd with this Omnipotent Gold: Thus the former meets Success in *few* things, the later in *all*.

The Positions you advance (said I) are so uncommon and surprizing, that you'd infinitely ly oblige me, if you'd but discover the Secret of distinguishing this sort of Gold from t'other. *This Gold*, said he, *is like the* Materia subtilis, *the wonderful Effects of which are reveal'd by Time and Experience, tho' it entirely fly the cognizance of all the Senses.*

But pray (interrupted I) are not you, who now hold this wonderful conversation with me, of this admirable Species? No, (said he, in a sort of surprize) the thousandth part of me at this time can't claim this Honour. But I begin to smell your Design, and ought immediately to put an end to our Converse, by a Silence that may prevent your putting me under a confinement that is equally my Fear and my Aversion. But should you so deceive me, the Punishment would soon reach your self, since contrary to common Opinion, by our Liberty, not Bondage, we bring Wealth to our Owners. And this I take to have been the cause of my so often changing my Masters and my Shape; whether they discover'd my Talent by my Countenance, or that it is my Fate to be a perpetual Knight-errant, I know not; but let the Cause be what it will, *Pythagoras* himself, who remember'd so many different things in as many different Bodies, never had so great a variety of Shapes as my self.

I could entertain you with abundance of the Secrets of Antiquity, as the Impostors of the Priests of *Apollo*, having long been a piece of the golden *Tirpod* from which they pronounc'd all their Oracles; but modern Cheats have put those ancient Frauds so much out of countenance,

nance, that my Diſcourſe upon the former would ſeem too inſipid to entertain you. 'Tis true (anſwer'd I) my Curioſity rather leads me to know the Myſteries of modern Iniquity, in which I am ſo much a ſtranger, that all you ſhall tell me will have the Charm at leaſt of Novelty.

In that, aſſum'd he, I can give you an entire ſatisfaction, from the ſcepter'd Monarch to the humble Shepherd, that walks with his Crook on the Plains; but I muſt tell you, Sir, this is a point ſo very nice to touch on, that if it ſhould be known whence the Intelligence came, ſome of the diſoblig'd Great ones (who hate Truth more than Merit) would certainly compleat my Ruin and Miſery, by ſhutting me up where I ſhould never more behold the glorious Light of the Sun. *Your Fear*, replied I, *ſeems to me altogether groundleſs, ſince the Stamp you bear is common to ſo many thouſands, and the peculiar Mark of your Excellence ſo inviſible to human Eyes.*

Being ſatisfied with this reaſon, he laid aſide all Caution, and diſcover'd ſuch private Intrigues of the *Fair*, the *Great*, and the *Godly*, as were as ſurprizing as new: He gave me a full account of all the Particulars of the Intrigues of the Biſhop of —— with the Lady * * * *, and ſeveral of the fair Sex: The Adventure of the Bell was pleaſant enough, tho' to the mortal diſappointment of the Biſhop and the Lady. Nor was the Miſtake of the Summer-houſe leſs diverting, than an Argument of his Lordſhip's Vigour and Good-nature, extending his Bene-

volence

volence to the loweſt as well as the higheſt. I could likewiſe tell you by what means the Dean of —— got the rich Biſhoprick of——, for which he was more beholden to the fair Eyes of Mrs.—— , than his own great Learning or Piety: but theſe are things of an invidious nature, and I dare not yet reveal 'em, leſt I ſhould be thought to wound that Venerable Body thro' the ſides of ſome of its looſe Members; tho', I confeſs, 'tis hard that thoſe who ſhould have no liberty of ſinning, ſhould be the only Men ſecur'd from all Reflections, when moſt abandon'd in their Actions; but I ſhall not, as matters ſtand, venture to provoke a ſort of People that are more famous for *teaching* than *practiſing* Forgiveneſs: Beſides, they have been ſo often on the Stage, and ſo long the Anvil of Satire to no purpoſe, that 'tis hard to produce any thing new on ſuch a Subject.

I preſs'd my little Piece to give me a full account of the *Camp* and the *Court*, which were places I had but little acquaintance with. You muſt not (replied he) expect to find Princes and Great Men ſuch Gods as their Flatterers and Idolaters make 'em, or ſo exalted in Wiſdom and Virtue as in Riches or Degree. Alas! their Failings and Follies, as well as Vices, are as numerous as thoſe of other Men: Nay, I who have been admitted into their Cloſets, have been Witneſs of ſuch Tranſactions as the meaneſt of their Subjects would have bluſh'd at. Theſe Demi-gods, whom ſome Men reverence as things of a ſuperiour nature in many par-

particulars, in all Ages, have diſcover'd themſelves to be much leſs than Men.

But 'tis too late to begin with ſo ample a Subject, when the Night is ſo far waſted, that you muſt neceſſarily require ſome hours of Repoſe; wherefore I will diſmiſs you with a Story much more light and airy, and which will not diſturb you with any unpleaſant Remembrances.

The Story of the Mercenary Gallant.

IT hapned lately that I was in the Service of a Lady of Quality and Figure, who was full as amorous as beautiful; but tho' ſhe lov'd her Pleaſure much, yet ſhe lov'd her Money more, and therefore choſe often to eaſe her Inclinations with her Husband, rather than part with her Gold to her Gallant. It was her Chance to be in love with a young Gentleman of a ſlender Fortune, tho' he liv'd to the height of a bulky one.

This Lady's Husband being involv'd in many Law-ſuits, was oblig'd to be much in Town about the Inns of Court. This furniſh'd the young Gentleman with frequent Opportunities of preſſing an Amour, in which he had a view not only to the Perſon of the Lady, but her Wealth, from which he hop'd a ſeaſonable Supply to his importuning Occaſions; but the Lady on the other hand, tho' liberal of her Favours, was always careful of keeping her Purſe, juſtly believing her Charms ſufficient to purchaſe Lovers, without being at the expence of buying

buying them with her Gold. His aſſiduity in Addreſs ſoon got him free admittance at all hours even to her very Cloſet, where he had frequently revel'd in her Arms, and by a vigorous Embrace ſatisfied her moſt ſalacious Deſires; but he had attempted all Ways and Arts in vain, to move her Generoſity to grant him a little Supply, which was ſo very neceſſary to ſupport his Equipage: But one day entring her Cabinet, he found her extended on the Couch, with her Neck and Breaſts quite bare, and few Charms hid from the Eye; but he had been too often ſurfeited with Beauties he had not now ſo ſtrong a reliſh of, as of a more charming rich Necklace which encompaſs'd the Ivory Tower of her Neck, and hung down in little Croſlets on her Lilly-white Boſom.

The Gallant lik'd the Prize too well not to have thoughts of ſecuring it, as a Pledge at leaſt of a Reward of his amorous Services, which he thought was his due. Sleep was his Friend on this occaſion, for that held her faſter in its embraces than ever; ſo that undoing the Locket, (which I then was) he took it from her Neck, and, to make a clean conveyance, ſwallow'd the Pearls one by one, like Pills, till the whole Doſe was compleated: Then making a little noiſe, as if juſt enter'd, he wak'd the fair Lady, who expreſs'd a ſmall reſentment for his diſturbing her Repoſe; but turning that to Raillery, ſhe ſmiling told him, he ne'r took any Favour but what was preſented him, and that ſhe now perceiv'd he made a Conſcience of his Doings.

I'm not ſo conſcientious (replied he) *Madam, as you are pleas'd to imagin, nor are there many who make a better uſe of an Opportunity than my ſelf; I always endeavour'd to ſteal thoſe Favours that were refus'd me, and ever valued them moſt which I obtain'd in that manner: Nor can you, Madam, be poſitive to my Conduct with you at this time; nor do you know but that I have ſtole ſome dear Favour while you were in ſo deep a Sleep, and ſo eaſily gain'd what you would not have granted had you been awake. Alas,* ſaid ſhe, *you are too ſenſible I can deny you nothing, and that makes you ſlight thoſe minutes of Happineſs of which Fortune ſeems to be prodigal to you: I thought you had known our Sex better, who are pleas'd to loſe that by an agreeable Violence, which they refuſe to grant on other terms.*

Her Words were ſuch a pleaſant double Entendre on what he had done, that he could not forbear burſting into a laughter; this provok'd her to accuſe him of an unpardonable Indifference, with ſuch a tone of reſentment, that he thought himſelf oblig'd to appeal to her to decide how well he had improv'd the time of her ſleep, by that means to try whether ſhe really knew any thing of the Theft he had been guilty of. *Either* (ſaid he) *you are ſenſible of all that has now paſt betwixt us, or you are not; if you are, you muſt know that I have not miſimploy'd my Time; if not, you can't juſtly reproach my Indifference and Neglect of an Opportunity, which you know not how I have improv'd.*

No Sir, (ſaid ſhe with a languiſhing Air) *you have done nothing; and as I can't enough admire your Modeſty in your Conduct, ſo whenever I fall ſick*

be

be sure you shall watch with me, because you are not likely to disturb my Repose.

Being with this Reproach touch'd to the quick, he began to offer those Civilities she seem'd to upbraid him with the omission of, but she repuls'd him with Disdain; however a little gentle pressing soon reconcil'd her to his Embraces, by which having appeas'd her, and sitting both on the Couch, she related a Dream she had in the Sleep in which he found her.

I saw, said she, *a wanton* Cupid *in the same figure he is drawn by the Poets and Painters, with Wings on his Shoulders, and his Bow and Quiver by his side, and in his Hand a Girdle, which he call'd the Girdle of* Venus; *methought I was sufficiently appriz'd of the power and vertue of this Girdle, and then was desirous to know what the young Wanton design'd to do with it; when, to my surprize, he tied it about my Neck, not my Waist, and told me, whilst I wore it I should never want Admirers, then vanish'd out of my sight. Assoon as he disappear'd, the Image of a Man presented it self to me, whose Mein and Person were extreamly agreeable to my Fancy, and who seem'd to have much of your Air and Countenance; he made some attempts on my Honour in vain, and more on my Girdle, which whilst he strove to untie, I wak'd, and found it only a Dream.*

But (said the Gallant) *if I have really acted all these Parts of which you only dream'd, I hope you'll allow that all your Reproaches were unjust. True,* said she, *but since what I have told prov'd a Dream, I shall very much suspect the reality of your Pretensions.* So rising up to adjust her self in the Glass, ſhe found her Necklace was gone, and looking about the Couch for it in vain, ſhe was not uneaſie, ſuppoſing he had only put that Trick upon her to teaze her a little, and therefore went on in this manner: *You had reaſon* (ſaid ſhe) *to ſtand for the Reality of my Dream, ſince the laſt Man I had to do with has robb'd me of that which encompaſs'd my Neck; and, to come to the point, it is you that have untied my Necklace; but the Jeſt being over, I pray return my Pearls.*

He deny'd the Accuſation, but ſhe thinking he had a mind ſtill to carry on the Diverſion, ſaid, *I prithee reſtore me this Girdle of* Venus, *ſince without it* Cupid *told me I ſhould loſe all my Lovers. I will prove the little God a Liar,* (anſwer'd he) *for I my ſelf will love you as long as I live.* This profeſſion would have pleas'd her at another time, but now being intent on her Loſs, ſhe deſir'd him to reſtore the Jewel which he certainly had. With an Air of reſentment he deſir'd her to ſearch him, and clear him from an Imputation ſhe could not in Juſtice lay on him, after ſo intimate and long a correſpondence as they'd had. She was ſurpriz'd at his Aſſurance, and would once more have examined the Couch, but he oblig'd her to ſearch him all over; ſhe finding nothing about him, lookt round the Cloſet, but could meet with nothing but the Ribbon and Locket, which he could not ſwallow, all ſhe could do to recover the reſt proving in vain; which he perceiving her extreamly concern'd at, in a gay manner thus addreſs'd her:

Madam,

Madam, I believe that your Necklace is become a Prisoner of War, and that you have no way to retrieve it, but by paying the Ransom according to the Cartel: To be short with you, tho' you have search'd me all over, I have 'em conceal'd about me, if you can but discover the place, they are yours; if not, Two hundred pieces must redeem 'em. To save her Money she renew'd her search, but that proving vain, she promis'd the Money on delivery of the Pearls; he desir'd till the next day, but could not obtain it, till he told her whither he had convey'd 'em.

The next day he brought 'em in a fine embroider'd Purse, and she deliver'd the Ransom agreed on, assuring him, That were she but assur'd of his Fidelity, she could not repent a Present that his Ingenuity deserv'd. Vows and Oaths were not wanting, and other Proofs of his Flame, which were very pleasing to a Woman of her Inclination.

This may shew to what Inconveniencies Ladies expose themselves, when they trust their Honours to young Fellows who make a Trade of Love, and have a greater Passion for the Vanities of Show, than for the Charms of their Mistresses.

My little Piece having finish'd his Story, I laid him down with his Companions, and went my self to Rest, which I found very welcome to me, but I fell not to sleep without a Wish for the speedy passage of Time betwixt this and our next Entertainment.

THE

Second Nights Entertainment.

The COURT; or, *The* MALE *and* FEMALE FAVOURITES.

BEing fully refresh'd with Sleep, I got up, and passing away the Day in reading, I amus'd my impatience of the Nights return, by seeking now for Reasons from the Philosophers for such Events as they never dream'd of. At last the welcome Shades of Night began to spread over the Hemisphere, and a universal Silence in a few Hours succeeded, when having dismiss'd my Servant, and fasten'd my Chamber-Door, I set all my Gold at Liberty on my little Table, and threw my self into my Bed in my Night-Gown for my more easie Conversation with my Golden Discoverer of Secrets, that I was extreamly desirous of having a perfect Account of.

I had not lain long, but I heard first one, and afterwards three other pieces began to talk; the Adventure was so surprizing, that I resolv'd not to interrupt their Conversation, but to listen to their Discourse, whence I might perhaps

haps learn ſome things that one might conceal. But it was not long before I was oblig'd to interpoſe my Authority for the preſervation of the Peace. For there was a *Guinea*, a *Spaniſh Piſtole*, a *Roman Crown*, and my little *Louis d'Ore* engag'd in a deep diſpute, in which, as the Terms went very high, ſo neither would yield to the other the preheminence, or even allow an Equality of Merit either in War or Peace.

But the moſt poſitive in this, was my little *Louis d'Ore*, who made extravagant Encomiums on thoſe many Advantages that *France* has over all other Nations; the Politeneſs of its Natives, and the Valour and Conduct of its King. This made me imagine, that my little piece had been converſant with Monſ. *Boileau*, and heard what he had wrote of the Life of *Lewis* with all the exquiſite Art of Flattery; and indeed I could not but ask him if he had not been admitted to his Counſel? No (ſaid he) but I ſhould be the moſt ingrateful of all things, if I paid not the ſame deference to *Lewis le Grand*, which he pays to us.

As he was reſuming the praiſe of the *grand Monarch*, he was interrupted by the *Spaniſh Piſtole*, and with that Air of Haughtineſs which is ſo natural to the *Spaniard*, ſaid, that all other Nations were but the ſweepings of the *Spaniſh* Monarchy; the ſupream Lord of which was deſign'd by Nature for the Empire of the World, and having already the Title of *moſt Catholic*.

A bare Name and empty Title, interrupted the *Roman Crown*, is of little importance without something more substantial to support it. But you must all own (continu'd he) that all Nations submit to ours, for what we held in the Time of the old Romans by the Sword, we now maintain by the Power of the Keys; the greatest Kings and Princes of *Europe* still paying their Duty to *Rome*.

Not so fast, (said the *Guinea*) that time is now past, for Kings are no longer the Bubbles of the Pope; and since the days of our good King *Henry*, his Holiness has been taught, that the Subjection of other Princes is very precarious. But if conscious Worth may have leave to boast, what Nation can compare with the *English*, who are not content to be rich and free themselves when almost all the World is in slavery, but extend their Power to the Relief of the distress'd on the Continent; shewing themselves as dreadful to the Enemy by Land, as on the Seas, which is their proper Dominion; and tho' it be a little World of it self, yet it is able to strike a Terror by the force of its Arms and the Valour of its Natives, into the greater.

You have all spoke very well (said I) on the Excellence of the several Nations whose Arms you bear, let us therefore adjourn this debate, and proceed to a discovery of those Secrets of the Court, and the Camp, which I have been promis'd by my little *Louis d'Ore*.

All agreed to the Subject, but none agreed to yield the preference to any other in beginning

ning of his Account; but the matter coming naturally before me as Maſter of them all, I ſoon gave it to the *Roman Crown*, as being much the greateſt Stranger in the parts; and it being now the Mode of being fond of e'ry thing that comes from *Italy*, even to their moſt ridiculous Follies and moſt abandon'd Vices, I was willing to be in the Faſhion.

The *Italian* more full of himſelf than the Favour which he look'd on as his due from *Tramontani*, began in this Haughty Air.

I am not ſurpriz'd that the other Pieces, who diſown the Grandeur of *holy Rome*, ſhould contend with me for Preference; but I am very much ſcandaliz'd at the Catholic Gold for ſo impious an Uſurpation, eſpecially the *Louis d'Ore*, whoſe Maſter pretends to be the eldeſt Son of the Church, and its preſent defender againſt all its Oppoſers. Nay, 'tis a ſort of Ingratitude not very common, ſince had it not been for Cardinal *Mazarine*, an *Italian*, there had been no ſuch thing as either *Lewis le Grand* or *Louis d'Ore* in *Rerum Natura*.

The Monſieur could not forbear bluſhing at the Reflection, but told him that *Mazarine* convey'd vaſt Sums of *French* Gold into *Italy*, but never any thence to *France*. That is not the Queſtion, reply'd the *Italian*, my Aſſertion is, that *France* ow'd its brighteſt *Lewis* to *Italy*, that is, to the Manhood and the Inſtructions of Cardinal *Mazarine*.

I was apprehensive of the ill Consequences of Reflections so severe, I therefore by my Authority bid the *Italian* proceed while the rest waited their Turns.

Before I come to the extraordinary Actions and Adventures of the Courtiers and Favourites of the Court of *Rome*, where I have been conversant (for Gold is more brought to *Rome*, than from thence) I must say a word or two of a Court in general, in which I shall show the Excellence of that Life above all others, the necessary Qualities of a Courtier, and the prudent Maxims by which the skilful move in that slippery Sphere.

I have been in the hands of many besides Courtiers, and therefore I am acquainted with the Common-places of those, who have not been able to arrive at the Happiness they rail at; they tell you, *exeat Aula qui volet esse pius*, *He that would be pious, let him avoid the Court*; but no Body has said let him avoid the Court who would be great, rich, and happy. Now which is the most valuable State let the majority of Mankind determine; the pious are few and miserable, their opinion therefore is of small weight with the many who aim at Wealth and Grandeur. The desire of Happiness is natural to all Men, and the surest means of attaining that can never be justly condemn'd. The Speculative Notions of vain Philosophers, who never so far believed their own Precepts as to put them in Practice, may serve to lard the Discourses and Harangues of those poor Wretches who want Genius and Power to raise themselves

ſelves above the Vulgar. But Men of Spirit will rather purſue a Subſtance which in her Enjoyment yields them all, they can deſire in this World.

Virgil diſtinguiſhing the Greatneſs of the Romans from other Nations, ſays,

Excudent alii ſpirantia mollius Æra
Credo equidem, vivos ducent de marmore vultus,
Orabunt cauſas meliùs, cœliq; Meatus
Deſcribent Radio, & ſurgentia Sydera dicent:
Tu regere Imperio Populos Romane, *memento*
Hæ tibi erant Artes, &c. ——Virg. *l.* 6.

ſhewing, that the height of Humane Perfection was to be able to know the Art of Government. Now 'tis evident, that this Art is only known to the *Courtiers* of every Country; the ſtate therefore of a *Courtier* is the moſt excellent of any, even by the Confeſſion of a *Poet*; a Creature incapable, by a natural diffidence and neglect of Induſtry, of attaining that Happineſs.

Beſides, vulgar Minds are always in pain by Tortures of their own creating; or at leaſt that ſmell ſo ſtrong of the Nurſery, that a Boy of Senſe would be aſham'd of them; theſe are Terrors of Conſcience, the Vanity of Immortality, as if the Soul were to be carry'd from the Body to feel Torments unſpeakable, for following the dictates of Nature in a higher degree than others; as if an Immaterial Being could be ſenſible of material Puniſhments, or that it were a Crime to obey the Soveraign

Law

Law of Self-preservation, by the Directions of that *Self love*, which is founded on Reason, and implanted in all Mankind in a greater or less degree of Perfection. But a Courtier is free from all those Bugbears of the Priests, they act by a Spirit so much above the Vulgar, that they have nothing common with them. Not but they have some Appearances that hold a sort of likeness to what the Vulgar call Virtues. For *Friendship* they have *Complaisance*, *Assurances*, and *mighty Professions*, by which if any one be deceiv'd, it is the fault of his own Ignorance or Pride; Ignorance, in not knowing that this is only *Mode*, on which no Man ought to look with a serious and credulous Eye; Pride in fancying himself an Exception to the only general Rule that has none. For *Fidelity* they have *Self-Interest*, a much surer Tye than the Airy Notions of Honour and Probity; for as long as it is their Interest to be true to Prince or Acquaintance, so long is their Fidelity to be depended upon, and no longer; It is therefore the Duty of the Prince, and Acquaintance, in regard to themselves never to trust or imploy those whose Interest they cannot make to be true and faithful.

For *Religion* they have sometimes *Hypocrisie*, that is, where it may be prejudical to their Interest to confess the Atheist, and there their Parts are so fine, and their Address so admirable, as to impose on the Credulous the very Works of Infidelity, for the Effects of Grace, and so while they play the Devil, pass for Saints. Instead of that foolish Principle of forgiving your Enemies, which makes a Man only the Anvil of Affronts, those who are resolv'd to thrive, hold it for a Maxim never to be dispens'd with, that the least Opposition to their Aims is never to be forgiven, but reveng'd to the last degree: this makes them tremble, and all others afraid to engage them, want of Success in the Attempt being certain Ruin. There have indeed been some Fools in Post, who have believ'd it the best way to take away Opposers by Obligations; but they are but woful Politicians, not to know that most Men are more influenc'd by Fear than Gratitude, or a sense of Merit.

What some have argu'd about a Prince, some good Statsmen hold will reach his Ministers, and so by degrees all his Court; and that is, whether it is safe in these great Posts to be lov'd or fear'd? both indeed seem very necessary, but since it is a matter of great difficulty to know the Advantage of both, it is safer to be fear'd than lov'd; for we may with justice affirm of Men in general, That they are Ingrateful, Inconstant, Dissemblers, Fearful of Dangers, Coveteous of Gain: While those to whom they are oblig'd are Prosperous, and out of all Danger, all are observant of them, assiduous, offering to sacrifice their Lives and Fortunes, and Children for their Service; but as soon as ever Evil Fortune shows her Face, and frowns on their Benefactor, they all fly away, as from Infection and Ruin, and almost forswear they ever knew the hopeless Victim, so little will they own their Obligations. Besides, Men make less scruple of offending those who aim to be belov'd, than those who endeavour to be fear'd. For Love is constrain'd into

some

ſome Law of Duty; but Mankind being infected with all manner of Diſhoneſty, makes no Scruple of breaking that Law on the very ſlighteſt occaſion of gratifying his own Profit or Intereſt.

But on the contrary, Fear is retain'd in its Deference by placing perpetually before its Eye the Image of the Puniſhment certain, and impending over its Head: yet is there a Medium in this too, both for Prince and Miniſters, that this point be not puſh'd ſo far as not only not to conciliate Love, but alſo procure Hatred; for it is not inconſiſtent that a Man ſhould be at the ſame time fear'd, and yet not hated. That is, the Executions muſt be few and ſeldom.

This being thus pretty well prov'd, it will be no wonder that the moſt compleat Stateſmen have their Bravo's, their Inſtruments of Fate to Poiſon, Stab, or Suffocate whom ever they pleaſe, and that ſtand in the way of their Pride, Luſt or Ambition. Theſe things may ſeem ſtrange to you, Sir, who have not been converſant with Courts; but you muſt all know and conſider that Books eſpecially have fram'd a ſort of Men who never in Reality exiſted in the World, that is Men of Virtue and Honour, Probity, Sincerity, without Self-Intereſt, and the like. For it is certain that the manner of Mens living is ſo very different from what the Moral Rules preſcrib'd for the Model of their Lives, that whoever ſhould neglect what is done to purſue what ought to be done, pulls on himſelf a certain Ruin inſtead of conſulting his own Intereſt and Happineſs, which is a Sin againſt himſelf, and by Conſequence a Sin againſt Nature; for, for any Man to be be an Honeſt Man among ſuch a number that are Diſhoneſt, muſt find himſelf in great danger of Perdition. 'Tis therefore, a neceſſary Maxim for Princes and Courtiers to conſider how they may be in the number of the later, and turn it to their own Advantage. It may be ſaid that it is to be wiſh'd, that all thoſe virtuous Chymera's made by Speculation were in Courts; but ſince thoſe are not to be had, nor maintain'd againſt the very Grain of Humane Life, that Prudence ſupplies all their Places, which can ſo far diſguiſe their Vices as to avoid their Infamy, and ſecure their Intereſt. For it is a great Accompliſhment, nay, perhaps the very ſupream Perfection of a Courtier, to know how to put on ſuch Shapes as may be conducive to his Intereſt. For Men are generally ſo ſimple and ſo obſequious of their preſent Neceſſities, that whoever is a Maſter in the Art of Diſſembling, will ſoon find a Bubble, who will ſurrender himſelf to be deceiv'd by him.

I ſhall only name *Alexander* the ſixth Pope of *Rome*, in whoſe Cuſtody I was all his *Popedom*. He was all Impoſtor, and apply'd his whole Study and Exerciſe in all the Arts of Fraud and Malice, by which he might deceive all, with whom he had to do; nor was he diſappointed in finding Subject matter enough to work on. No Man was ever more officious in his Aſſeverations; nor had any one ever a more ſpecious and plauſible way of taking a ſolemn Oath; nor did ever Nature produce a Man that ever perform'd leſs of either; yet all his Deceit ſtill turn'd to his Account, in bringing him that Succeſs which

which he always propos'd; for he was perfectly Master of the Manners and Nature of Mankind, and of the *Art of Deceiving*.

There's still a greater reason for all of my kind to speak well of Courts, since there is still the *Golden Age*. Gold governs there with an absolute sway, and with that you may compass whatever you desire, and by your Address and Management there, you may obtain that Gold which obtains all things; nay, it is remarkable, that whereas in all other stations of Life you get Wealth by Labour, and Exchange of one Commodity for another, here you sell nothing but Words for it, or Trusts, or Dignities, or other Titles, which tho' of little value in their own nature, yet have such advantageous Perquisits annext to them, that they are very well worth the Purchase. In Traffic or Trade you deal with a few, and in Things that are inanimate; but at Court you deal in Mankind, you sell and buy Nations, and make the People your Property, while their Seed-time and Harvest flow all into your Pocket. 'Tis true, all have not an equal share of the Crop, yet things are generally so manag'd, that few but find it worth their while, and chuse rather to be a Door-keeper there, than a *Major Duomo* elsewhere.

Not to detain you longer in generals, I shall give you one instance of the amazing things done by a Lady in Power in the Court of *Rome*, who wanting the Prudence of a Man, let her Desires aim too far, and by robbing all, made every one her Enemy: Whereas if she had set any Bounds to her Avarice, she might have had Power

Power and Wealth with ſecurity. For if any Favourite be ſo wholly devoted to Coveteouſneſs, to have no regard to any thing, he only heaps Riches together to ſet other ſucceeding Favourites to employ their Power to raviſh from them thoſe enormous heaps from which their ill Conduct has baniſh'd all Defenders. For a Courtier minds not whom he plunders, and he that is likely to yield the loweſt Spoil, is the moſt likely to be made a Sacrifice to others.

The Hiſtory of Donna Olympia, *Siſter-in-law and Favourite of Pope* Innocent *the* Xth.

IN the Time of *Innocent* the Xth, I was part of the Chain which Donna *Olympia* wore when ſhe was yet under the Circumſtances of no extraordinary Fortune, and was therefore hung up in her Cloſet when ſhe got Jewels more rich in her Adminiſtration of the Popedom. By which means I became a Witneſs of many of her ſecret Intrigues of State and Amour. She was of the Family of *Maldachini*, that made but a little Figure in *Rome*, till ſhe rais'd it by her Intereſt in the Pope. She was marry'd young, and diſcocover'd from her Childhood an Ambition of Rule, in her Childiſh Plays always giving Laws to her Play-fellows. Being come to Age of Marriage, ſhe refuſing to turn Nun, was marry'd to Signior *Pamphilio*, Brother to *Gio-*

vanni Baptista Pamphilio, who was afterwards Pope *Innocent* the Xth. By him having had ſeveral Daughters and but one Son, her Affections grew weak to her Husband, but ſtrong to his Brother the Abbot, afterwards Biſhop, and Cardinal, and Pope; for the Husband would maintain his Prerogative as Maſter, never conſulting her in any of his Affairs, but the Brother never did any thing without her Advice, which made him in her Eye ſeem beautiful and charming, tho' the moſt forbidding and ugly of any Man breathing; and her Husband diſguſtful and loathſom, tho' a Man of tolerable Appearance. She oftner went in the Brothers than Husbands Coach, and was more often with him in the Cloſet, than her Husband in Bed; ſo that he frequently could not tell where to find either Brother or Wife, they being perpetually together.

Nor can this appear ſo extraordinary, if you do but conſider that moſt of the Prelates of *Rome* oblige the ambitious Ladies, by admitting them into their Council, and following their Directions in the moſt holy and important Affairs. But the Abbot *Pamphilio* being too ſenſible of his forbidding Face, could not be very engaging with a Lady of ſo many fine Qualifications as to Shape and Perſon as Donna *Olympia*, preſented her with a Charm more powerful than Youth or Beauty, the entire diſpoſal of his Will.

Perhaps it will not be ingrateful to you to give you a ſtretch of the Character of the Nature of this Lady, before I give you an Account of of her Story, and ſhow her in that Power which was ſo formidable to *Rome*, and had like to have been ſo fatal to her ſelf at the laſt.

In the Company of the Ladies ſhe ſpoke little, but ſhe abundantly retriev'd that Taciturnity by her Loquaciouſneſs among the Men. She us'd to ſay, that ſhe had not Words enough to throw away on that Sex, from which ſhe could learn nothing of Conſequence or Value. Among the Men, her Diſcourſes were always ſupported by Reaſons of State, and embelliſh'd frequently with ſome Maxim or Sentence. Her Memory was ſo happy, that by reading or hearing any thing once over, ſhe would never forget it. She could not ſubmit to the Opinion of another, without doing her Temper the laſt violence, deſiring rather to periſh with her own Opinion, than live and proſper by the Advice of another. She was covetous to a degree, ſo abandon'd, that ſhe could not endure to hear any body ſo much as talk of or mention the Bounty of others; nay, ſhe made a Virtue of her Vice, by this Maxim, *that Women were made to gather together, and not to diſperſe.* She often chang'd her Servants, that they might not by long continuance with her grow too familiar with her Conduct; ſhe ſeldom went to the Balls, Feaſts and Entertainments of the *Roman* Ladies, that ſhe might not be oblig'd to make the like. The Oſtentation of her Charity to the Poor Religious, got her ſome Reputation of Devotion, tho' the meer effect of Vain-glory, never doing any Charity that had not firſt been carry'd round the Palace in Proceſſion in the Eyes of the People; but even thoſe ſhe laid aſide as ſoon as ſhe was got into the *Vatican*. She gave her Son no Education, ſo that he could ſcarce read at Twenty, leſt Learning ſhould rouſe his Spirits, and make him interfere with her in the management of the Houſe of *Pamphilio*. Her Table was penurious, and yet ſhe made her Steward bring in his Accounts every day to a farthing. She was prodigal of Compliments, and gave larger Promiſes than any one could deſire of her, being admirably dexterous at evading all ſhe had ſo promis'd, with Excuſes adapted to the Perſon and Circumſtance of the matter.

The Abbot *Pamphilio* is now made a Cardinal, and all his Favours diſpens'd by Donna *Olympia*, who firſt taught him the Art of Diſſimulation, tho' it be as ancient as principal Cuſtom of the Court of *Rome*. Toward the later end of *Urban* VIII, ſhe thought every moment an Age, ſince from a calculation of his Nativity ſhe found he would arrive at the higheſt Dignity of the Church in the 70th Year of his age: when *Urban* dy'd, and the Cardinals were going into the Conclave, ſhe took leave of her Brother-in-law thus; *Perhaps I ſhall ſhortly ſee you Pope, but never more Cardinal. Were you but Popeſs*, replied he, *I would willingly relinquiſh my Claim*. Being contrary to expectation choſe, ſhe threw open the Gates of her Brother-in-law's Palace, to be rifled by the People, with a great deal of ſeeming ſatisfaction, having firſt ſecur'd the beſt and moſt valuable of the Goods,

tho'

tho' ſhe had ſaid but a few days before, That *on condition her Brother-in-law were choſe Pope, ſhe would not only ſacrifice the Palace, but her ſelf, to the People.*

So known a Favourite ſoon drew all the Viſits, and all the Addreſſes of every Pretender, to Donna *Olympia*; and the firſt thing ſhe procur'd at Court, was the Ruin of the *Barbarini*, Favourites of the former Pope, getting their Abbeys and other Revenues into her own poſſeſſion, imprudently ſhewing an Example how ſhe ſhould be us'd her ſelf on the deceaſe of the preſent Pope her Protector; for ſhe exceeded all the *Barbarini* had done, and diſpos'd of all the Court Affairs, public and private: And to ſecure 'em the better, ſhe got her Son *Camillo* made a Cardinal, and (as firſt Nephew to the Pope) declar'd *Cardinal Patron*, not out of Affection to him as her Son, but to wreſt the management of Affairs out of the hands of *Pancirollo*, and put 'em where ſhe ſhould naturally diſpoſe and direct 'em at her pleaſure.

The Amours of Camillo *and the Princeſs of* Roſſana.

CAmillo was a very young Man, as much unqualified for, as little deſirous of the Dignity; he had a Soul more inclin'd to affairs of Love than affairs of State; his Heart was already on fire, by the Beauty and Perfections of the young Princeſs of *Roſſana*, whoſe Huſband being old, was not thought ſo agreeable to her Inclination as a Prince ſo young as *Camillo*,

millo, and whose near Relation to the Pope gave a Prospect of all that a moderate Ambition could desire.

The Prince of *Rostana*, besides his Age, was more infirm by an old Paralitick Distemper, which had some time confin'd him to his Bed: He was very fond of his young Wife, and she very complaisant to him, and being Mistress of a *Roman* Dissimulation, disguis'd her Disgust so artfully, that it pass'd with him for a sincere Tenderness. She never stirr'd from him but when she went to Church, where *Camillo* was always ready to receive her; so dividing her hours of liberty betwixt Heaven and Love, she always return'd home in so short a time, that the old Prince could have no suspicion of any other cause of her absence than Devotion.

But these frequent meetings had made Love spread his Empire in both their Hearts, *Camillo*'s Person was extreamly charming, but his ignorant Education denied him those few Qualities of Mind that are more valuable. The Princess, besides a beautiful Person, was Mistress of a sprightly Wit, and a Spirit equal at least to the degree of her Dignity.

The old Prince proving worse, she was more confin'd, till at last she could not stir out at all; and her Prudence had strictly enjoin'd him to send her no Letters, not doubting but the old Prince's Death would soon set her at liberty to do what she pleas'd.

While she was thus confin'd, and *Camillo* in pain for an Absence he could only support by the hopes that it would be ended soon, by having

ving her in his Arms as his own, his Mother's Ambition interfer'd with his Paſſion, and, unknown to him, has him aſſum'd to the Scarlet Robe and Hat, and declar'd *firſt Nephew* and *Cardinal Patron.* This made ſo much noiſe in *Rome*, that the Princeſs of *Roſtana* could not long remain ignorant of a Change ſo fatal to her Repoſe; the Rage and Fears it gave her were beyond expreſſion, but had the good fortune to be happily cancel'd by the Death of her Husband, ſo that they were all taken for Offerings to his Monument, where ſhe ſoon after plac'd him in a magnificent manner, he having added all his to her vaſt Fortune.

Notwithſtanding her green Widowhood, ſhe could not refrain upbraiding the new Cardinal with his Fickleneſs and Infidelity, wherefore by a Confidant ſhe ſends him this Letter:

THo' Contempt is more your due than Anger, yet I can't but let you know my Reſentments; the form would have me defer my declaring them till the Prince has been longer in his Grave, yet Anger cannot liſten to the cold remonſtrances of cautious Formality. You Men are ſtrange unaccountable Animals: I pray what did you propoſe to your ſelf by amuſing me with your Vows of Affection, when you had none, nay, when you deſign'd to diſclaim all manner of honourable Pretenſions, by preferring Ambition to Love? Did you think me ſuch a Trifle, that you might abuſe my Credulity without any Puniſhment, becauſe I'm a weak Woman, you a Pope's Nephew, and exalted to the ſacred Purple? Miſtake not your ſelf or me, you are not above reſentment, nor I unable to revenge. I confess, I would willingly hear what you have to say, before I utterly condemn you. Farewell.

He soon return'd her this Answer, not a little pleas'd that she was now a Widow, and at liberty to dispose of her self according to her Inclinations.

My charming Princess,

THO' *I dread your Anger more than that of all the Powers on Earth, yet at this time I had much rather cause your Anger to write, than that your Indifference should keep you silent: There is a Charm in your dear Anger, that makes me see I am not indifferent to the most beautiful Princess in the World. Believe not, Madam, that I think my self out of the reach of your Revenge, if I could be voluntarily guilty of any thing, that could justly provoke your Indignation; for, Madam, you'll alwaies have it in your power to punish me, because you'll ever be able to make me miserable with a Frown; but I beg you to suspend your Anger till I am able to convince you by an Interview, where I may tell you what is not so convenient to commit to Paper. Appoint your Time, and I will commit my self to you, to punish or absolve as you shall find me guilty or innocent. Adieu.*

The Princess was not a little appeas'd with this Letter from Cardinal *Camillo*, and took care to appoint him to come the next Evening after it was dark to her Palace, where she order'd all things for his private reception. The

Room

Room ſhe receiv'd him in was all hung with black, and illuminated with ſome few white Wax Tapers, where ſhe attended him on a mourning Couch, in a dejected poſture, from which ſhe aroſe as he came near her, in a very humble and ſubmiſſive manner: *Ha! my Lord,* ſaid ſhe, *is this the Habit of a Lover? My adorable Princeſs,* (replied he, kneeling down and taking hold of her Hand, on which he fix'd a thouſand burning Kiſſes) *this is not indeed the Habit of a Lover worthy you, but of an unhappy Creature made a Victim to the Ambition of a cruel Mother, who has no regard to the tender Sentiments of an amorous Soul. Ambition and Avarice take up all her Thoughts, and Nature gives her no conſideration for my Youth; Inclinations abhorrent of the Dignities to which ſhe has (againſt my will) compel'd me to wreſt from the hands of* Pancirollo, *the managing of all Affairs. But* (interrupted the Princeſs) *muſt we now put an end to all your Vows, and cancel all thoſe Aſſurances you have given me of a Faith inviolable? Muſt all be ſacrific'd to a Mother? That will indeed be a Proof of your Obedience, but how agreeable to your Honour, I leave to your ſelf. Alas, Madam,* replied *Camillo, if you can yet credit a Man you have but too much reaſon not to believe, ſince any thing could make him take a ſtep that was not anſwerable to that Love which you have inſpir'd, yet believe me, I will have no regard to her Impoſitions; I am not yet bound in Prieſts Orders, I can but throw up all theſe foreign Dignities, and lay aſide the Purple, theſe Trappings of proud Titles, if you would but receive me into your Favour, which I confeſs I have forfeited. Aſ-*

ſure

ſure your ſelf, Madam, that it lies wholly in you to direct my Actions, and I am either Camillo *your Adorer and Husband, or elſe the wretched* Cardinal Patron, *whom all his Power can afford no ſatisfaction, while it gives you any Pain, and deprives me of all that can make me eaſie. Can you forgive me? Can you receive me again into Favour? Can you give me any Hopes, that I ſhall not alwaies ſigh in vain, but be at laſt permitted to call you mine, without fear of Separation? Speak, my Goddeſs, on you only my Fate depends; you alone can make me happy or miſerable.*

After a little pauſe, with her Face cover'd with Bluſhes, at laſt ſhe made this Reply. *If you, my Lord, can quit this Grandeur for my ſake, I cannot be ſo ungrateful as to diſtruſt the ſincerity of your Profeſſions; and as I then ſhould with reaſon believe that you lov'd me above all things, ſo I do not find any Diſpoſition to make you a Return unſuitable to your Deſerts. Do therefore as your Love prompts you, keep not my Heart in ſuſpence, nor urge me by Diſſimulation to betray my innocent Sentiments, ſo as to yield you matter of Triumph, and me of Diſgrace; for as I cannot reſiſt your Tenderneſs, ſo I will not bear your Neglect.*

This Converſation ended with mutual Aſſurances of inviolable Love; and a convenient time for the decency of Widowhood being now over, *Camillo* lays aſide the Purple, to the ſurprize of all *Rome*, the joy of the Princeſs, and the indignation of the Pope and Donna *Olympia*, when his Marriage to the Princeſs follow'd very near his renunciation of the Cardinal's Cap. The Pope and his Mother, after a long

long debate, resolve to banish both *Camillo* and the Princess, Donna *Olympia* fearing the Wit and Beauty of the Princess would win so on the amorous Heart of the old Pope, as to be a dangerous Rival of her Ambition; making no manner of doubt, but that the Pope would be better pleas'd to have to do with a young Niece, than an old Sister-in-law.

This Resolution being taken, Donna *Olympia* sends for her Son, and in her Closet accuses him of Folly and Undutifulness, where he gave her a full account of all the Progress of his Love, as I have told you, and beg'd her mediation with the Pope, to forgive his following the Dictates of his Passion, since it had directed him not only to one of the finest and most accomplish'd Ladies of *Rome*, but also one of the greatest Fortunes. But Reason and Nature were of little force with a Mother to her only Son; for, redoubling her Reproaches, she bid him be gone and never see her more, but retire to his sloathful *Grotto's* with his fine Wife, and leave the World to be manag'd by those of greater Genius: So she flew out of the Closet, and left him to reflect on his Fate.

But Donna *Olympia* return'd to the *Vatican*, and set her self entirely to make the best of her Market, and to ingross all she could scrape together, either by Raillery, Extortion, or Oppression. She reduces the Pope's domestic Expences, that she might pocket all she could; no Judge Criminal was made, but by her recommendation, to whom she gave inhuman Instructions to gratifie her Avarice, ordering them

them to regard not the Blood, but the Purſe of the Guilty, commonly ſending to 'em for the Redemptions, pretending ſhe would lay 'em out for the benefit of the Poor; ſo that the Judges aiming to make ſome advantage to themſelves of their Poſts, brought Extortion and Oppreſſion to its utmoſt extent. In fine, whatever Office at Court fell, Donna *Olympia* diſpos'd of it; the Officers of the Datory were to keep thoſe in ſuſpence who pretended to Eccleſiaſtical Benefices, till ſhe had fully inform'd her ſelf of their value; and thoſe who offer'd moſt, without any conſideration of Capacity or Deſert, were made Biſhops, Abbots, *&c.* but they muſt firſt bring the full value of the Place, her rates being, that an Office of 1000 Crowns a Year, that laſted but three, ſhould pay her one Years Income; if ſix Years, double; and ſo in proportion: but if it were an Office for Life, ſhe would not bluſh to ask the Moiety of the Revenue for the firſt twelve Years: Some Biſhopricks lay vacant more than five Years together, (ſhe receiving the Profits all the while) becauſe ſhe could not meet with a Chap that would come up to her rate.

An Abbot of *Naples* to raiſe 20000 Crowns for Donna *Olympia* for a Biſhoprick in her Gift, perſuaded his Brothers to joyn in ſelling all the Paternal Eſtate; which, with all their Credit, could juſt come up to the Purchaſe; but the Abbot dy'd before he was well ſettled in his Seat, which by that means return'd to Donna *Olympia*, and ſhe ſoon ſold it again

for

for the ſame ſum, while the Abbots fooliſh Family was ruin'd by his Ambition.

The fair Princeſs her Daughter-in-law had by this time a luſty Boy, but her Malice gave out to the Pope and many others, that Don *Camillo* was incapable of Generation, and that the Princeſs muſt have found ſome more ſubſtantial help to impregnate her. This was believ'd by the Pope, becauſe ſhe ſaid it, but it did not influence *Camillo* to a Jealouſie he was otherwiſe apt enough to entertain,but in pique of honour it reviv'd his now languiſhing Love, and made his Princeſs have a ſhort ceſſation of thoſe ill Humours which Poſſeſſion had ſuffer'd at laſt to appear. Tho' ſhe gain'd nother point in embroiling the Happineſs of ſo near a Relation, ſhe purſu'd that of her Avarice ſo impetuouſly, that the Priſons were full of Innocent Perſons, and the Streets of the Guilty, theſe preventing their Confinement by a Bribe, and thoſe conſtrain'd to remain in Cuſtody till they could purchaſe their Enlargements.

But there was a Roman Gentleman, confident of his own Integrity, ſwore that Donna *Olympia* ſhould never touch a farthing of his Money; and to ſecure this, took his Son from a Clerk's Office, which he was in, leſt he ſhould be oblig'd to make any Petition to her: But all in vain, Donna *Olympia* was not ſo eaſily to be avoided, for ſhe hearing his Reſolution, ſoon drew him into her Net. She order'd a *Sbirro* to pick a Quarrel with him, and give him opprobious Language, which the Gentleman being unable to bear, corrected him

him with a Box or two on the Ear. He was upon this ſeiz'd, carry'd to Priſon, and condemn'd to dye for contempt, and ſtriking a public Miniſter; ſo that to ſave his Life, he was oblig'd to preſent Donna *Olympia* with a Purſe, and pay a conſiderable Sum into the Exchequer.

You may perhaps wonder, Sir, at a Woman paſt threeſcore years of Age toiling night and day, without allowing her ſelf any Reſt, when ſhe could not make uſe of what ſhe had already attain'd. But, Sir, if you meaſure the Conduct of Courtiers and Favourites by common Senſe and Reaſon, you would make them mad People. But they have a Pleaſure peculiar to themſelves; for great Power and great Riches are things that yield more Pleaſure and Satisfaction than the reſt of the World imagine. What tho' the People were ſo provok'd by her Thirſt of Gold, that when they ſaw her Coach paſs by, they came up rudely to't, and call'd her Whore, and were ſo rude, that ſhe was fain to make her Eſcape to a Monaſtry, and ſo to the Palace, and have his Holineſs to qualify their Indignation with a Daub of a quantity of Bread. Nor did ſhe mind the ſcurrilious Ballads ſung of her about the Streets all the Nights; thoſe diſagreeable Thoughts being loſt in her Power, ſince there was no talk in the Palace but of Donna *Olympia*; Donna *Olympia* here, Donna *Olympia* there, all Letters were deliver'd to Donna *Olympia*; Memorials were no longer given to the Pope, but to Donna *Olympia*. Preſents were daily

mount-

mounting the Stairs of the *Vatican*, whence none ever return'd. These Glories made Donna *Olympia* an ample amends for the hate of the People. In short, she got in the Ten Days before Pope *Innocent* dy'd, half a Million of Money; e'ery one making hast to purchase while yet Donna *Olympia* could sell. Among the rest, there was a Canon who had made above an hundred Applications for a Bishoprick in vain, proffering Donna *Olympia* but 5000 Crowns, whereas she demanded eight, and tho' he advanc'd to 6000, she would by no means abate the two thousand, till now the Pope was dying, she sent for him to come to her, and ask'd him if yet he continu'd in the same mind, but finding him a little cool in the matter, assuring her, that through a violent Temptation of the Flesh he had spent two thousand on a fair Lady for the Favours she had granted him. Well, well, (said Donna *Olympia*) then you have four thousand left, make haste and bring them to me, that you may not lose what I have thus long kept for you, for I would not lose the Satisfaction of having presented so worthy a Man to the Bishoprick, while the Church wants such able Pastors as you. Thus he was declar'd Bp. the minute he gave into Donna *Olympia*'s hands the 4000 Crowns.

The Pope dying, after three months contest *Alexander* the VIIth was chose, he began to prosecute her on millions of Complaints, but the Plague interrupted the Cause, by carrying off Donna *Olympia* at *Orvietto*.

Here

Here my little *Roman* Piece made a ſtop, and I expreſs'd my Satisfaction at an Account, which contain'd ſo odd a Story as that of *Olympia*, valuing my ſelf on my own Happineſs of being no Subject where ſuch arbitrary doings might take place.

Your *Roman* Courtiers (began the *Louis d'Or*) is ſomething different from any of *France*, you have nothing in chace there but Money and Power; we have often more gay Purſuits; at leaſt we mingle a Gallant Air with our ſevereſt Politics. Monſ. *Fouquet* was a very great Favourite, and Intendant of the Finances; he had Ambition enough, and made uſe of the Happineſs of having his Maſter's Ear to the Advancement of many of his Creatures. For it is natural for all Miniſters of State and Favourites to place their Friends and Creatures about the Prince, becauſe they are Spies on their Enemies, and fortify their own Intereſts. It is true, that it is dangerous for a Prince to have the Creatures of any one Favourite only about him, they looking more on the Intereſt of him that immediately rais'd them, than the Service of the Prince, who was but the diſtant Cauſe of their Advancement; they only ſerve for Watchmen about the Soveraign, caſting Nets, Chains and inviſible Hands upon him, ſhutting up his Prince by this means. This Method gave Monſ. *Fouquet* ſecurity in all the Extravagance of his Amours. There was no Lady at Court, that had any ſhare of Charms, but he felt a Tendre for her; nor any one

one whom he fancied, but he attempted; nor attempted any one, but he conquer'd: Not by the Beauty or Comlineſs of his Perſon, for that was very diſagreable; nor by the Vigor of his Youth, or Fineneſs of his Addreſs, for he was above fifty, and unhappy in a very Unharmonious Utterance: But having the whole Exchequer of *France* at his command, he was Maſter of many pieces of this excellent Gold of which I have already diſcours'd. Nor is the Wonder extraordinary, that *Court Ladies* are ſo complaiſant, to proſtitute their Bodies to the moſt powerful Man of the Court, who could uſe ſuch prevailing Arguments as *Piſtoles* to compaſs his Ends.

The Story of Monſ. Foucquet *and Madam the Counteſs of* ——

BUT what was now extraordinary, was his Amour with Madam the Counteſs of ——, a Lady of a great deal of Beauty, and no leſs renown'd for her Virtue than her Wit and Underſtanding. She never came to Town, but liv'd in a Country Seat with her Husband, who was a Gentleman of an ancient Family, and had long held his Title, but his Eſtate was very much ſhatter'd, and ſcarce ſufficient to keep 'em in that Splendour which his Quality requir'd.

It happen'd that Monſ. *Foucquet*, in his Progreſs, came to her Husband's Chateau, as the only place fit to receive him in thoſe parts; his

Reception was anſwerable to his Dignity, and the hopes the Count had that this Opportunity might be ſo improv'd, as one day to put him into a Poſt that might ſupply the defects of his Eſtate: (tho' in that he might have been deceiv'd, had not his Lady's Eyes brought ſtronger Arguments for his Service than his Merit, ſince Merit is a thing little minded by Courtiers.)

By that time the Count had a little refreſh'd the Stateſman, Supper was ready; and, to make the Entertainment Compleat, Madam the Counteſs was at the head of the Table. Monſ. *Foucquet*, tho' ſomething tir'd with the fatigue of his Journey, yet he was extreamly ſenſible of her Charms; every Look he caſt on her, and e'ry Word ſhe utter'd, encreas'd his Flame; ſo that by that time Supper was over, and his Appetite ſatisfy'd with eating, his Heart was fuller of Love. He had not been us'd to ill Succeſs in his Amours, and therefore had the leſs doubt of the like in this. He only contriv'd to find ſome means of delaying his departure a little while, till he could either perſuade the Husband to Court, or the Lady to his Bed. And he was not long about the matter; for walking after Supper with the happy Pair in the Garden, he pretended to ſlip and ſprain his Ankle, ſo much that he was carry'd to his Chamber, and there attended both by the Count and his Lady, they hoping by Aſſiduity at this Occaſion to lay ſome Obligation upon him to have a favourable Eye to their Affairs.

This

This pretended illneſs kept him there ſome days, while the diligence of his fair Hoſteſs gave him frequent opportunity of telling her his Paſſion,and that he was the greateſt wretch alive without her immediate Compaſſion. Gallantrys of this Nature, tho' not ſo common in the Country as City, yet enough eſtabliſh'd e'ry where in *France*, made all his Addreſſes paſs for Compliments of that Nature. But the Counteſs being left with him one day, and no body by but his own Servants, they had the wit to withdraw by degrees till they left him alone. When he preſs'd his Paſſion with all the Eloqence he had, he ſeiz'd her Hand,and gave it a thouſand Kiſſes ; nor ſatisfy'd with what but enflam'd him more, he raviſh'd ſome from her roſie Lips, which ſhe receiving with the utmoſt diſdain, was leaving theRoom,but ſhe could not diſengage her ſelf from his Arms in a minute; which time he us'd to mollifie her back with aſſurance of a preſent of 20000 *Louis d'Ores* for the Favour, which would be a Profit not Injury to her Husband, whoſe Eſtate ſtood in need of ſo powerful a Relief. She by this time had got free from him,and left the Room,which Monſ. *Foucquet* did not at all endeavour to hinder, aſſuring himſelf that he had ſhot ſuch a golden Dart at her Perſon, that the more ſhe reflected on it, the more favourable Effects her Thoughts would produce.

The Count returning, found his Lady in Tears, and with no little difficulty got out of her the Cauſe. The Count had been at Court, and knew what a latitude was there allowed in Addreſs to the Ladies, and was not therefore much ſurpriz'd or diſpleas'd at the Adventure. The Twenty thouſand *Louis d'Or's* are perpetually in his Head, and he began to reaſon a little Philoſophically on the Subject. My Eſtate is eating out with a deep Mortgage; I have not hopes of any Redreſs in a Redemption, I am out of all ways of Preferment; here are 20000 Piſtoles in ſubſtantial good Gold, an Army enough to drive away all my Neceſſities; the obliging the only Man that can make my Fortune, and raiſe me to what height he pleaſes. And what he ſeeks, what is it? a pleaſing Theft of an imaginary Treaſure, for which he pays me with a real. It is what I may loſe whenever my Wife pleaſes, to ſome Scoundrel for nothing. I have no other Tenour of it but her Will or Humour. 'Tis true, ſhe has yet been very virtuous; at leaſt I have not been able to diſcover the contrary; and that is all the Ground I have for my Satisfaction. But if ſhe has hitherto been Chaſte, how can I be ſure but my Page or my Chaplain may find an opportunity of pleaſing her ſome time or other, and if a wanton one likes her Man, ſhe will deny him nothing. Since therefore the trifle is ſo ſmall, that *Foucquet* would give ſo much for, and that very trifle depends on a ſecurity ſo much more trifling, a Womans Virtue, that is Humour, I think it is the white ſpot of my Fate, and not to make uſe of it to my own happineſs, would be a ſin againſt my ſelf.

Arm'd

Arm'd with theſe good Reſolutions, he charg'd his Lady to be as complaiſant as ſhe could, and to raiſe his Deſires, and by that means his Price; and let her know, that if ſhe ſhould liſten to the Stateſman's propoſals ſo far as to ſurrender her Perſon into his Arms, provided ſhe ſecur'd the Sum, he ſhould count it rather an Obligation than an Offence. She expreſs'd her Reſentment at his Baſeneſs to a very high degree, and could not be brought into his Company while ſhe ſtay'd, except at Meals, whence ſhe always retir'd as ſoon as they were over.

The Count in the mean while addreſs'd to *Foucquet* for ſome Poſt of Honour, that might put him into a capacity of retrieving his ſinking Family; and the Courtier having an Eye to his own happineſs, gave him ſuch Aſſurances, that he did not doubt of Succeſs at his coming to Court. It was now time for Monſ. *Foucquet* to leave the Counts Houſe, which he did with all the Regret in the World, aſſuring the Count, that he ſhould no ſooner come to Court, but find Preferment ready for him.

The Count ſtay'd no longer after him than to ſettle his Affairs, for an Abſence he had ſome Reaſon to hope would not be very ſhort. He and his Counteſs being come to Town, Monſ. *Foucquet* provided him a Regiment for the firſt Step, which pleas'd the Count ſo well, that he allow'd him all the free acceſs to his Houſe that he could deſire; but ſtill found the Lady obſtinate. The Count was now gone to the Campaign, and *Foucquet*

F 3 try'd

try'd all the means the Invention of Desire could prompt, but could not master her obstinacy. In the midst of this contest, News is brought her of the Counts being kill'd in the first Encounter he was in. The grief of her Widowhood, and the decency of Religion put a Necessity on Monf. *Foucquet* to forbear his Visits. But the Mourning was not quite over for her Husband, e're ill news was brought her out of the Country, that the greatest part of the Estate left her by her Husband was seiz'd by the *Mortgagees*. This news was not unwelcome to *Foucquet*, he therefore having advanced his Price now to 60000 *Louis d'Or's* she sent him this Letter, which was found among his Papers when he fell into Disgrace.

Your Person I hate, your Money I have occasion for, wherefore if you bring the 60000 Louis d'Or's *with you, you shall not depart without your odious Satisfaction.*

The next Evening Monf. *Foucquet* was admitted, and having given her in Bills, Jewels, and Money the Sum agreed upon, the Countess conducted him up to her Bed-Chamber, and with a great deal of Reluctance surrender'd her beautiful Person into the Arms of the only Man in the World she had an aversion to. But she stay'd no longer in *Paris* than to take one to discharge the Mortgage and return her Money into the Country; Where she led a very pensive and solitary Life, till she was vanquish'd by the vigorous addresses of a jolly young Chevalier, who marry'd and bury'd her in a few years Time.

But

But that you may not outdo me in a Female Favourite (purfu'd my *Louis d'Ore*) I fhall not omit the Marchionefs *D'Ancre*,to whom I belong'd from her Rife to her Execution.

She was a Lady of the Bed-Chamber to *Maria de Medicis*, and fo very much in her Favour, that marrying *Conchini* an *Italian*, as fhe likewife was, fhe rais'd him to the dignity of *Marfhal* of *France*, and thence by her Intereft with the Queen, over whom fhe had an abfolute Afcendant,to be prime Minifter, and to have in his Power and Gift all the great Offices of the Court and Kingdom, which are very numerous, and capable of making a great train of Dependants; which difquieting the Princes of the Blood, more provok'd by the Infolent Carriage both of him and his Wife, they ftrove in vain to put them out of the Favour of the Queen Regent; fo that they fhot him in the very Palace, and try'd, condemn'd and beheaded her.

While yet fhe was in her Profperity, fhe was extreamly foolifh in her Avarice; encreafing by her Oppreffions and fordid Deeds that Envy which naturally great Power and Favour produce. There was no Degree of Men but felt the Effect of her Covetous Temper. Tradefmens Bills were never half paid, tho' all reckon'd to the Queen: Whatever Gifts the Queen beftow'd, two thirds fell fhort into her hands, and the Receiver thought himfelf well dealt with, if a third came to his. There was a young Gentleman that had got together five or fix hundered *Louis d'Ores*, and apply'd to her Laquey to purchase a Place for his subsistance. He was told, that the best way of presenting, was, to buy some fine Diamond Ring, in which having laid out 300 of his *Louis d'Ores*, he brought it to the Marchioness *d'Ancre*, who having survey'd it, gave it a thousand Praises, and told the young Man, that he could not have given less for it than 500 *Pistoles*: he willing to magnify his Present, assur'd her, that she had guest the Price most exactly. This was what she desir'd, so praising the Jewel again, she return'd it, and told him, that she had much rather have the value in Gold, since she had so many Jewels already, that she did not know what to do with them. The young Man was free to dispose of his Ring to some loss, and so making up the Sum, deliver'd it to her in Gold, and he had the Place he desir'd.

The Fatal Rape.

THere was another young Gentleman, all whose Revenue depended on an Office in the *Parliament* of *Paris*, in which he had a quarter-share, and on another Man's Life; however, he joyns with all the Patentees, and undertakes to solicite a fresh account of more Lives in Reversion. He applies to the Maquess *d'Ancre's* Agent, and agreed for 500 *Pistoles*; but his Lady in the mean while having notice of the matter, and finding she could get more Money for it, makes a Creature of his beg it of the Queen in her Name.

The

The bargain being thus made, the young Gentleman was surpriz'd at the disappointment, and soon finding whence the Blow came, very boldly wrote the Marchioness *D'Ancre* the following Letter, which coming to her in the Church, as she could not forbear reading of it, so could she as little forbear tearing it in pieces when she had read it.

I wish you, Madam, a long continuance of those great Favours you possess in her Majesty, and that by Acts of Goodness and Kindness you may perpetuate your Memory to Posterity. But it has been the Misfortune in all Ages of Persons of your exalted Station, never to hear the Complaints of the Injur'd, till they became so universal, that nothing but their Displacing or Ruin could appease the abus'd People. That you may not be ignorant, Madam, in a piece of Injustice lately done to me, I must inform you, that I had absolutely agreed with the Marshal's *Agent, and with his Consent, for the Place that Madam* de **** *has for your Lady begg'd in her name. I desire you would do me Justice, and not prostitute your Character for a Trifle below your pursuit.*

This Gentleman had a beautiful young Wife, whom he had not long marry'd, who by a Relation being introduc'd to the *Mareschal*, so pleaded her Case, that she at once convinc'd his Judgment of the Injury he had done her, and his Heart, that he should attempt yet a greater. For being struck with a violent Passion for the young Lady, he was resolv'd to gratify his Inclinations at the ex-

pence

pence of the Happineſs of the Lady and her Husband. He therefore gave her hopes of ſucceeding in her Petition, and order'd her to come again when he had made a full enquiry into the matter. The time being come, and the *Mareſchal* having prepar'd all things in order to the ſatisfying of his laſcivious Deſires, ſome Ladies were ready to receive the poor Victim, and amuſing her Innocence with pleaſant Railleries and Stories, took her inſenſibly from thoſe that came with her, and had her into the Lady's Apartment; Where having refreſh'd her with a noble Collation, they took care to ſpice ſome of her Glaſſes with a ſoporiferous Potion that would not work immediately. Thence therefore they went to bath in a *Bagnio* ſtrow'd all with Flowers, and ſcented with delightful Odours, they waſh'd her with rich Waters, and having all done the ſame, they lay down each on a Couch for a few moments in looſe Linnen Garments, fit for the Heat of the Seaſon and Place. The Opiate now working, the Ladies withdrew, and the *Marqueſs* all undreſt came, and eaſily takes poſſeſſion of the unreſiſting fair one. But he was not eaſily ſatisfy'd with viewing ſuch naked Beauties, which nothing could equal among Womankind, and repeated his Embraces till he found the Potion gave way to the Power of Nature, and that ſhe in the midſt of his Careſſes gave him a Return that he did not expect. But the fury being over, he found that ſhe was not well awake, and ſo left her to come to her ſelf.

When

When ſhe was now perfectly awake, ſhe found her ſelf in a poſture that was ſomething unuſual, and was ſenſible by ſome Remains and Tokens, that foul play had been offer'd her. However, hearing ſome-body coming in, ſhe diſſembled a while as if ſhe yet was aſleep; when the *Marqueſs*, not yet ſatiated with Enjoyment, aſſaults her afreſh, and tho' ſhe ſtrugled ſufficiently and cry'd out, yet he gain'd his lewd will, and had the pleaſure of ſeeing her Eyes, tho' full of Rage and Indignation, while he felt ſuch Tranſports that none but happy Lovers can gueſs at; ſtrugling, at laſt ſhe flew from his Arms, but knew not what to do with her ſelf. She curs'd her Fortune, call'd him all the treacherous Villians ſhe could think of, and thoſe abominable Women who had betray'd her thus to Ruin. No Ruin, my Dear, (reply'd he) can come near the Woman whom the Marqueſs *D'Ancre* ſecures in his Embraces. May all the Curſes of the Injur'd overtake thee (interrupted ſhe) and mayſt thou fall by the Hands of ſome Aſſaſſine, or rather Common Hangman. He preſs'd to kiſs her and renew all his Dalliances, in hopes to appeaſe her Grief by making her Guilty by her own conſent, but all in vain; ſhe was inexorable, he as outragious; tearing off her looſe Garment, and leaving her beauteous Form all naked to his Eyes, ſhe fled into the Bath to hide her ſelf; he throwing off his Garment, purſues her into the Element of Waves, but there with ſtrugling with him ſhe was ſtrangled in the Waters, and he in a fright

re-

retires, and comes to the Instruments of his Villany, bids them to try if there were any Relief, but in vain, the poor Lady was stone dead, and in the Night thrown into the *Sein*, and being so found, was thought to have been murder'd for her Chastity. But the Husband having in vain sollicited for Justice, had nothing to trust to but Patience, till the Crimes of all had brought 'em to a fatal and ignominious end.

My little Piece, with a true French Loquaciousness would have gone on, but that the *Guinea* now urg'd his Right and Turn of Discourse, and that since I had out of Civility to Foreigners given them the preference of speaking, that they on their side should have so much Moderation and Manners, as to be content with what they had said without taking up too much of the Night in their own Relations. This bluff Reproach made all be silent, when I encouraged my *Guinea* to go on, and let me know what powerful things this Gold had effected in this our World, as well as in the Greater of the Continent.

I shall first (reply'd the *Guinea*) say something of a Court in General, as the *Signior* has done, tho' I shall differ with him in my Sentiments of the Excellence of either the Conduct or Principles of most Courtiers. This other World of *England* is as much distinct from the Continent in Happiness and *Liberty*, as in Situation. The Name at least yet remains here, and the Thing, tho' often invaded in almost e'ry Reign, yet has ever triumph'd

in

in the end, and brought its Enemies to Shame and Confusion. A Court therefore here is of a different Nature to what it is in an arbitrary Government; for here the Courtier or Favourite has a harder part to play to come off with Credit and Success, than in *Italy* or *France*, where they need only the Art to wheedle and impose on the Prince, and they are Masters of their Desires. But here the Courtier, Statesman or Favourite must have as careful an Eye to the Good-will of the People, as to the Favour of the Soveraign, or their Prosperity will be of a very short date. 'Tis true, the *English* Favourite may not be one jot honester than the *Italian* or *French*; may believe as little in God, and the Duties of Religion or Morality; may be as voracious and as insolent as either; but then he must endeavour to assume Popular Principles, declare for the Laws and Liberties, put on the Vizor of the Patriot, to win the People into a Credulity of the justness of his Designs and Actions, and then he works with safety, because his Miscarriages and Rogueries, if discover'd, will be turn'd on the Malice of the contrary Party; and he will have the Party that is strongest forget his Crimes in his Misfortunes, and clear him of all Imputations he atchiev'd for a Popular Name.

I would not, Sir, have you imagin that I have been so little acquainted with our Court in all Ages, as not to know that *Avarice*, *Treachery*, *Dissimulation*, *Ingratitude*, *False Promises*, and *Poysonings* too, have had place here as well as in *Italy* or *France*; but I can say in general, that

that our Courts have been freer from *Blood* than those, and outwitting or undermining a Man has often been the extent of the Revenge of the most inveterate of our Favourites; nay, the People have generally been satisfied with the meer displacing of evil Ministers, without punishing 'em for Crimes which naturally deserve the worst of Deaths, but leaving them to enjoy in a Retreat what they have spoil'd the Public of when in Office. Whether this be an Argument of their Goodness or Folly, I leave to your Judgment. But if Reward and Punishment be the life of good Disciplin, certainly the *English* have always wanted it most of any People alive.

I shall not detain you here with a Discourse I heard once spoke to a great Prince in this Realm, to prove to him, That it was directly contrary to the very Duty of a King, to hear any particular *Favourite*, since the Prince being made for the Peoples Good, that's the only End he ought ever to pursue: For 'tis impossible that any Favourite, who has so many by-Ends of his own, should ever lay before the Prince the Real Good of his People; that is only to be known by leaving his Ear open to all, to the public Representations of the People, and to all those whom Birth and Dignity have brought to a Right of Admittance to the Prince's Ear, as well as his Peers.

This does not exclude a King from imploying one Minister more than another, because 'tis certain one Man has a greater Capacity than another, and by consequence more fit to be im-

imploy'd. Diſmiſſing therefore theſe nice points, I ſhall only give you ſome account of the Power of *Gold* in theſe Nations.

And firſt, I ſhall ſhew you not only a Female Favourite of this Nation, as voracious as your *Olympia* or *d'Ancre*, but whole *Parliaments* ſelling their native Liberty for Gold and Favour with the Prince. What is it for a Woman to ſurrender her Honour for a Bribe proportion'd to her Wiſhes? But for Men of Eſtates to part with the Security not only of them, but their Lives, for a Bribe, which very Bribe is not ſafe in their hands by that means, is a Miracle that only *Engliſh Gold* can perform.

But to make a right progreſs, I ſhall begin with my Female Favourite.

Edward III. was a Prince who for many Years made the moſt glorious figure in the World of any that ſate on the *Engliſh* Throne ſince *William* the *Baſtard*, yet in his declining Years a Lady had the good Fortune to captivate his Heart, in ſo powerful a degree, as to ſully his paſt Glories, and gave the State ſome Diſturbances, which were complain'd of in Parliament till ſhe was baniſh'd the Kingdom.

I was then part of a Gold Ring which ſhe always wore on her Finger, and ſo I had the opportunity of being a Witneſs of all her Actions. In her Perſon ſhe was graceful beyond any equal, enclining to tall; her Skin white as the driven Snow, her Hair Jet, her Eyes a languiſhing Hazle, her Teeth even as Pearl, and of that very colour; her Cheeks vermilion'd lion'd o'er with Nature's moſt exquiſite Paint, her Lips as ruddy, and her Breath as fragrant as Roſes; her Hand ſmall, her Fingers taper, her Foot little, her Leg exactly turn'd, her Waſte ſlender, her Boſom full, and Breaſts hard and round, her Neck proportion'd; in ſhort, her Features were perfect, nor any Blemiſh to be found in any Part about her; ſo that if any thing could excuſe the old King, ſuch an Angel as *Alicia Perrers* might, but Kings are not Maſters of their own Actions nor Paſſions, they ought to be more mortify'd than we ſuppoſe the *Carthuſians*, or than the *Stoic* would be thought; at leaſt, if they yield to a Paſſion, it ought to be bounded with ſuch Caution, as not to reach the Public. But King *Edward*'s Dotage of Reign grew more ſtrong, as his Body grew more weak; and the leſs he was capable of pleaſing a fair Lady, the more he was fond of retaining her. But tho' this Lady had all theſe Charms of Perſon, yet her Mind was wholly diſfurniſh'd of all thoſe Graces, which ſhould have confirm'd her Merit, and made her truly deſirable. She was a very Female *Cataline*, profuſe of her own Riches, and voracious of others; as ſhe could give Wounds to others, ſo was her Heart extreamly capable of receiving an amorous Impreſſion; nor would ſhe ever diſappoint her deſires by needleſs Scruples of Honour, or Fear that the King ſhould ever hear of her Intrigues. Yet this it is to be Whore to a King; her Viſits were admitted by the moſt virtuous, and ſhe was careſs'd by all the La-

dies

dies of Quality. The King in honour of her had proclaim'd *Justs* and *Tournaments* in *Smithfield*, and this Lady being made Lady of the *SUN*, rode from the Tower of *London* through *Cheapside*, attended by many Lords, Knights, Squires and Ladies, every one of the other Ladies leading a Lord or a Knight by his Horses Bridle till they came to *West-Smithfield*, where as soon as the *Lady of the SUN* arriv'd, the Tournaments began, which held for seven days together. There was at the upper end of the List a sort of Semi-circular Theatre or Throne, adorn'd with fine Tapestry, and various Seats in the midst of which, on a sort of Throne above the rest, sate the *Lady of the SUN*, adorn'd with Beams more piercing and burning than those of the fiery Planet it self, on each side sate two rows of Ladies sparkling as the Galuary or fixt Stars, behind each Chair stood her Knight. But all the Eyes of the Assembly were bent with desire and admiration. Happy above Measure (sigh'd each to himself) the Man that can gain the Good Graces of so Angelic a Creature. But as her Beauty was able to inflame all Mankind, so was her Bounty of that Beauty able to satisfy all her Adorers; tho' that part of her Character was not known at this Time, perhaps scarce discover'd by her own dear self, who till this fatal day had not thought of any other Person but the old and feeble King, and on him only for her Profit, for the Gold, Jewels and Grants she got of him, not for the amorous Pleasures he gave her. But this Tilting in her Honour, under the Title of *Lady of the SUN*, as ſhe appear'd in greater Glory, and more conſpicuous than ever before, ſo did many a martial Knight exert himſelf both in Feats of Arms and Addreſs, much more than ever they had done, without hopes of being gracious in her Eyes. But Woman, like Fortune, ſeldom chuſes by Merit, but by the blind impulſe of her own Fancy, influenc'd by ſome odd, ſecret, inviſible Charm, which no-body elſe can diſcover.

Thus the *Lady of the SUN* took little Notice of any of the Noble and the Brave, who had perform'd their Parts to admiration of all that beheld them, but had ſoon fixt her Eyes on one *Michael de la Pool*, a Merchants Son of the City of *London*,(afterwards in *Richard* 2d's time Earl of *Suffolk*, &c.) This Gentleman was very young, and *guiltleſs of the Razor was his Chin*, the Doun ſcarce yet appearing there; his Hair was flaxen, his Complexion clear and ruddy, his Stature pretty tall, his Air and Mein bold, yet agreeable; his native Aſſurance was fortiſy'd with his native Ignorance, (wonderful matter to make a Favourite of) and that had plac'd him on the Theatre among the People of Faſhion, and ſo luckily as to be wholly expos'd to the View of the *Lady of the SUN*, who found her ſelf as much ſurpriz'd with his Charms, as all the Men were with hers.

There

There were others there who would have given many a lavish Present to have made such a progress in her Heart as *Michael* had done, but in vain; among the rest was Sir *Edward Hunsfield*, a Man of considerable Fortune, and one, tho' Nature had given him not one generous Quality, had Folly and Extravagance enough to squander it away in a few Years, without the Imputation of having done the least good with any Part of it. Sir *Edward* knew nothing of the finer Sentiments of Love, but only the brutal Enjoyments, which like a Brute he had rather come immediately to, than heighten his Desires and Pleasure by all the decent and charming Approaches the skilful Managers of Pleasure make use of on these Occasions. Having therefore seen the *Lady of the SUN*, found an impatient desire of lying with her, and letting his Confidant know his Distemper, he reply'd in this Manner: *Stay, dear Friend, Sir* Edward, *since your Ambition is mounted so high as the Mistress of a King, you have this comfort, that her Temper is such, that you may buy her Favours with Gold, to which she sacrifices all things.* The Knight was well pleas'd that any way was cut out to a Pleasure that had rais'd his Desires to a greater stretch than ever before he had experienc'd, and gave his Friend or Pimp full Power to treat with the Lady's Agents in this Affair, which with some difficulty was concluded for 10000 Nobles; and he being admitted to her Apartment, found the Lady in Bed, ready to receive him and his Money. But the Knight's misfortune was such, that when he had enter'd the Lists of *Venus*, and the willing Fair one ready to surrender all her wonderful Charms to his Arms, the Knight prov'd less than a Man, and spent the whole Night in fruitless Attempts at a Happiness his Stars had depriv'd him of the Power of possessing. The time of parting is come, the Knight full of Dispair and Rage, curs'd his Stars, and whatever had disabled him from reaping the Benefit of his Purchase; yet Apologizing in as tender a manner as he could to the Lady, begg'd that she would allow him another time of Tryal. But she smiling, told him, that she fear'd it would be to no purpose, but that if he pleas'd to bring the other 10000, she would give her self the Mortification of his Embraces another Night, but on no other Condition. So departing with Shame, Sir *Edward* never after solicited so vain and expensive a Suit.

De la Poole in the mean while found his Stars more propitious, arriving at greater Happiness with less Charge. For before the days of the Tournament was over, he had found some favourable Glances from the *Lady of the SUN*, to which his own Vanity gave such an Interpretation, as to raise his Endeavours to improve the Imagination to a Reality. For as soon as the Sports of the day were at an end, he took care at the rising of the Company to press among the Crowd, as close to her as possible; and Opportunity offering, in the hurry, seiz'd her fine Hand, and press'd it with Ardour: She first suffer'd his Assurance, and then

then encreas'd it by returning his Advances, till he found out the way of being admitted privately to Closet; and where the Man that knows himself belov'd is alone with the Woman he desires both by Ambition and Love, there is no time left before he secures his Aim, by seizing all that the Lady could give. Her Resistance was not great, and she perhaps discover'd more fire in the Encounter than the happy Man she bestow'd those Favours upon, that so many sigh'd for in vain.

These amorous Thefts had been sometimes repeated when the Negotiation with Sir *Edward* was finish'd, and Five thousand of the Nobles she received from her Bubble she gave to her favour'd Gallant, with which he purchas'd an Annuity of 500 Nobles a year, which he possest till his Disgrace and Ruin in the succeeding Reign.

De la Poole, tho' he had a mixture of Love in this Intrigue with this Lady, yet Self-Interest was the charm that preserv'd his Constancy so long, that some of the Enemies of the *Lady of the SUN*, by their Spies, had some notice of the Affair, and did what they could to put an end to the Dotage of the King, by making a discovery of her Infidelity. It was with all the Address of Cunning that they could insinuate so much Suspicion into the King, as to make him agree to a tryal of finding him in her Apartment alone with her, as she promis'd to show him. Information was brought, and the King and his Friends pass'd by a Master-Key into her Lodgings, at the very Minute that *la Poole* was happy in her Arms. The King, I suppose, out of a desire of not being undeceived, making some noise at the last Door, the Lovers had just turn'd to disengage themselves, and by her dexterous Address she hid him under her Petty-coats, and sat down upon him, and feigning the Collick, receiv'd the King and his Attendants without the least surprize; discovering all the while the Agonies of those sharp Pains to which she pretended. The Room being search'd, and every place examin'd, the King look'd on her with a pleasing Eye, but frowning on those that had accus'd her, led them speedily from her Apartment, begging pardon for their unseasonable Intrusion.

The Company being gone, she immediately got up and deliver'd the Prisoner from his confinement and pain, and throwing him on the Bed to recover his fright, she goes and fastens all the Doors, to prevent any farther surprize; when returning to him, she could not forbear laughing at the happy Event, and the woful Condition her Lover had been in while he bore all his burden on his Shoulders, almost stifled with the very Heat of the Empyrean of Love. Having rally'd a little, and lightned his Spirits, they ventur'd into the Bed, and there revel'd in the very Luxury of Pleasure, till the Mornings approach gave him notice to retire, which he did with all the safety imaginable.

Tir'd

Tir'd with the Pleasures, not the Pains of the Night, the Lady kept her Bed to a very unusual hour, which serv'd for a confirmation of the reality of that Illness she had only pretended: for when a Man has a mind to be deceiv'd by a Woman, the very things that should discover the Imposture confirm him in the belief of its being a Reality. Thus the King, almost afraid to see her, after he had betray'd a Suspicion, without being able to justifie it by a Proof of her Infidelity, approach'd her Bed with a visible fear of her Anger. She was not insensible of her Power, but was resolv'd to turn it to her own advantage, and therefore receives him with a seeming Disdain, and (in short) makes him pay dear for doubting her Honour, when he could bring no proof of her Guilt.

Her imagin'd Innocence in this, gave her such an Ascendant over the King's Soul, that he could deny her nothing: This Advantage she was resolv'd to make use of while the King was alive, and the Death of the *Black Prince* had remov'd all her powerful Opposers. She was possess'd of this Maxim, That *if she got but Money enough, she could be guilty of no Crimes but 'twas in the power of that to stop the Prosecution.* She first engross'd all the profitable Places to her self and her Creatures; every thing that would bring in the *Gold*, she took care to dispose of at the best Market Price. If there was any Suit in Law depending betwixt her self (or any of her Creatures) and any other, she would her self appear and sit in *Courts of Judicature*, by her Presence and Influence to wrest Justice from its byass: And there were such Judges in Commission, as would endeavour to gratifie a Lady, from whom they might hope so much.

Virtue is not naturally (or at least customarily) the Growth of Courts, or any of the Avenues to 'em; so that 'tis no Wonder that most, if not all those who had any dependance there, or any Views that way, were ready not only to submit to her Exorbitances, but even to flatter 'em with the specious Name of *Prudence*, and an *innocent Care of her Interest*. I will not so much condemn her for fleecing such as apply'd only for the Means and Power of fleecing some others, that might have a Dependance on the Offices they purchas'd, since those would else have made use of her Power only for their own advantage, while the Infamy of their Actions would reach up to her who had prefer'd 'em; but by making them pay for what she did for 'em, she prostituted not her Character to the Hate of the People for nothing. Yet she can never be forgiven, in suffering her mercenary Temper to vanquish all Considerations for the Frailties of Love, to which she found her Heart always very much inclin'd: For, from the King, she try'd most Degrees of his Leige-people, even to Rope-dancers and Players, or any Man whose robust Appearance promis'd a vigorous satisfaction of her salacious Enjoyments. Yet she prov'd an implacable Enemy to a young Lady, call'd *Matilda*, and her Lover *Gotofre*, in the Misfortunes which attended 'em on the discovery of their Intrigues.

The

The Story of MATILDA *and* GOLOFRE.

M*Atilda* was a Relation of this Favourite *Lady of the* SUN, and all her dependance was entirely upon her Father and Mother, who were very nearly related to her. In hopes of Preferment, *Matilda* was ſent out of the *Country* to *Court*, to be under the Eye of *Alicia*, the *Lady of the* SUN: On the Road ſhe and her Company were overtaken by a young Gentleman about the age of Twenty, and his Servant. It hapned the Waters were extreamly out in many parts of the Country, eſpecially in that part which they were yet to paſs, between the place where they joyn'd company and *London*. After ſome hours Converſation, the young Lady and Gentleman found themſelves ſtruck with a mutual Paſſion for one-another, and every moment improving it, they came to a Lane overflow'd with Water, and in it was a Bridge that was to be paſs'd, but was entirely cover'd by the Flood, which to miſs was to hazard in a great meaſure their Lives: Young *Golofre*, in pain for his Miſtreſs, rode before her, to direct her Horſe in the way, but in the midſt of the Water, juſt by the Bridge, her Horſe by ſome ſtrange Accident ſtartled with ſuch vehemence, that he threw the Lady from his Back, who ſcreaming out as ſhe was falling into the Water, ſhe ſoon ſank; the Lover immediately leap'd from his Horſe to ſave her, and as ſhe roſe a ſecond time, caught hold of her Arm, and drew her cloſe to him. There

was

was, about a Bows shot off, a sort of Island in the Water, that held its Head a little above the Stream, and attended by two or three Trees and a small Hutt or House, the only hopes of Life to the despairing Gallant; thither he steer'd his Course, supporting his dear *Matilda* with one Hand, in his cumbersom Accoutrements, now almost spent with getting to the desir'd place.

Scarce was he able to get either himself or his dear Lady up the Bank, which at the place they came to was somewhat more steep and slippery than in any other part; yet, unable to venture farther, he exerted himself and with no little difficulty got her ashore, and by degrees into the Hovel that was there. It had been a Receptacle of some Wretch that us'd in the Summer-time to live there on the Alms or Expences of Travellers, by selling a Dram, or some such thing, as they pass'd; but in this Season it was left desolate, as unable to afford any Benefit by being in such a solitary place. There was in it a sort of a thing like a Chimney, a broken Stool, and two or three Hurdles that might supply the office of a Bed: There were likewise some little pieces of Sticks, that might make a Fire, could they find any means of lighting the Fuel; but Industry overcomes all things. *Golofre* more concern'd for his Mistress than himself, gently placed her on the Hurdles, and bending her Head down, would have made her bring up the Water she had swallow'd, and by good Fortune having a Bottle of Cordial Water in his Pocket, he gave her some, which produc'd new Life and Vigour to support her under this Misfortune. Searching

about,

about, he found a Flint and ſome Touchwood, and by the help of his Knife he ſtruck fire, which he improv'd ſo far, as to light the Sticks which Fortune had thrown in his way: By this means they dry'd themſelves, expecting their Servants would bring 'em ſome Relief. But they by good Luck having eſcap'd the Danger, and *Golofre*'s Man having got his Maſter's Horſe, ne'r deſign'd to proceed in ſo dangerous a Road, but by the firſt opportunity got up into the higher Ground, and made his way over Hedge and Ditch to the firſt Houſe he could ſee. The Lady's Horſe was drove down with the Stream, and her Servant with much ado getting back again, never ſtaid to examin whether his Miſtreſs were ſafe or no, but return'd home to his Maſter with the News, that ſhe was drown'd.

Golofre's Man had found his paſſage ſo difficult, that when he came in ſight of a Houſe it began to be duskiſh, and almoſt dark by that time he had reach'd it: It fortunately prov'd to be a Mill that ſtood on that Rivulet, which the Rains had now made ſo dangerous a Torrent. The Miller had a little flat Boat, which he us'd to paddle with on the head of his Mill-pond, and was ſoon perſwaded by the Man to venture down the Stream with that Boat, to fetch up his Maſter and the Lady, but no Price could win him to ſo dangerous an Attempt in a Night that afforded not one glimering Star to direct ſo uncertain a Courſe, but as ſoon as the Day began to peep they ſet out on their Voyage, and in three hours time arriv'd at the place, where they found the poor Lovers in deſpair of all Relief; for having throughly dried

dried themſelves by the Fire, and again reviv'd themſelves with a Dram, they had leiſure to conſider their diſmal Circumſtance; yet could not all the Danger they had paſt, or that which they were now in, reſtrain his declaring his Paſſion, and preſſing her ſo far as to confeſs, that by Gratitude and Inclination ſhe was inclin'd to reward a Love ſo agreeable to her Wiſhes.

Vows of eternal Love and Friendſhip being paſs'd, he began to conſider how he ſhould find Means for her to get ſome Repoſe; he renew'd the Fire, pull'd off his Coat, and wrapping her in it, laid her on the Hurdles, her Head lying in his Lap, to his no ſmall pleaſure and ſatisfaction. Tho' *Matilda's* Fatigue had compel'd her to yield to ſome ſhort Slumbers, yet *Golofre* had a mixture of too much Pleaſure and too much Pain, to have the relief of a wink of Sleep all that Night, but often in the Tranſports of his Paſſion hug'd *Matilda* ſo eagerly, that he wak'd her from her Repoſe.

The Miller and his Man being come, they all went on board this noble Veſſel; and the Miller being as skilful as *Typhis*, they arriv'd ſafely at his Mill, and there with what the Miller's Stock could afford they refreſh'd themſelves, and *Matilda* went to reſt in the Miller's Bed, and *Golofre* in his Man's; and tho' neither of 'em were Beds of Doune, yet they ſlept heartily, being warm and ſecure.

But the Convenience the Miller had was not ſufficient for the Condition of the Gueſts; and no Town was nearer than four or five Mile; and the Lady found her ſelf in a very bad

bad Condition, very feaverish and weak, but made shift by the help of the Millers Wife to dress her self, and get on Horseback, and by a gentle pace to reach the first Inn of a tolerable Accommodation, where she immediately took her Bed, and he sent for a Physician, the best in the Country, but she grew worse and worse, becoming lightheaded; so that *Golofre* who never was from her, thought fit at last to send his Man away to her Fathers House to inform him of her Condition; this was two days Journey at that Season, and before her Mother could come, her Feaver had left her, and she was in a fair way of recovery.

Matilda took care to give a large and pathetique Account of *Golofre*, and the Services he had done her, and that owing her Life to him, she could do no less than comply with his Importunities by a promise of Marriage, if she could get her Friends Consent. The Mother had view'd him with Eyes that persuaded her to think kinder of him than of a Son-in-law; and considering that their stay was not to be long together, she made several advances to the young Man, which he would better have met, had his Heart been free from the Charms of the Daughter; for the Mother was not above Thirty four, and very Youthful both in Appearance and Thoughts, she had Beauty enough to render her desirable, and provocation enough from a fumbling old Husband to wish that others might think so, especially young *Golofre*, whom every moment she lov'd more and more. She had Address

enough

enough to put off his Demands and her Daughters to the decision of her Husband, to whom it was necessary that she should return, till her health was confirm'd, and the Fathers determination in that particular receiv'd.

Being therefore now able to sit a Horse, an easie one was got, and the higher Roads chosen to return to her Fathers, whither young *Golosre* was invited on what he thought the Happiness of his Life, but indeed only for the use of the Mother, who had attempted by broad sides often to let him know her Mind, of which he having inform'd the Daughter, she took care to allow as few moments of Persecution to her Love as possible; but it was impossible always to prevent some opportunities, when a Mother that govern'd the Family made it her Business. *Bertha* (that was the Mothers Name) had manag'd the old Man so, as to give Denials to the Pretender, telling him, that should he yield to his Suit, it was only to deprive himself of those Honours which he had coveted, by seeing her marry'd to a Man of the first Quality, by the Interest of Madam *Alicia* their near Kinswoman; That he had now, thro'. her Interest, a fair prospect of arriving to the Dignity of a Lord and Peer of that Realm. These were Arguments strong enough to secure her Husband from granting a Boon, that must deprive her of the Happiness that she esteem'd the greatest in this World.

Golosre began to be weary of doubtful Replies, and therefore press'd the old Gentleman

to

to be plain with him; and let him know what he had to depend on in a point of that concern to his Repoſe; and found at laſt, that the Father, unable to put him off longer, let him know that his Deſire was not in his Power; that his Couſin *Alicia* had taken her for her own, and demanded the entire diſpoſal of her Perſon, that in Gratitude for the Life he had ſav'd, he would write to her in his behalf. This being all the Anſwer he could get, *Golofre* having inform'd *Matilda* of the matter, reſolv'd to go immediately for *London*, and try by ſome means or other to get into the good Graces of her who had the diſpoſal of his Happineſs in the Perſon of *Matilda*. The Evening before he was to depart, *Bertha* at her wits ends, was reſolv'd to put all to the hazard of a tryal of Skill. When, therefore, *Golofre* was in Bed, and aſleep, as ſhe had taken care her Huſband ſhould be, by a private Door ſhe let her ſelf in her Shift into the Chamber where her Beloved lay, and gently got into the Bed without waking him, ſhe having taken care that the old Gentleman and he ſhould have both their Load, *Bacchus* over-powering *Venus* and all her Night Torments, Languiſhments and Watchings, *Golofre* ſlept moſt profoundly. How *Bertha* manag'd the matter I can't tell, but being a Woman of Addreſs, ſhe did not entirely loſe her Satisfaction; which eagerly purſuing, the Gallant awak'd, and ſurpriz'd betwixt ſleeping and waking at a Woman in Bed with him, and in ſo familiar a poſture, he was removing away from her, but ſhe claſ-

ping

ping him about the Waſte, cling'd too cloſe to be eaſily ſhook off. *Whether, my dear* Golofre, *doſt thou flee from the languiſhing* Matilda *(*ſaid ſhe*)? My Parents deny me thy Lawful Embraces, but not being able to live without them, in my Night of Deſpair I have thrown aſide my Virgin Modeſty to poſſeſs them without the Ceremony of Law. What has paſt betwixt us in thy ſleep was but a half Satisfaction, while I was depriv'd of thoſe Tranſports thy Love for* Matilda *muſt give thee to find her in thy Arms, ſuffering thee to rifle all her Charms. Why thus cold, thus indifferent? Spare my Modeſty, while darkneſs hides my Bluſhes, and thy ſelf a Man in Reality, as well as in Appearance.*

Golofre had too noble an Idea of *Matilda* to think, that ſhe could either act or ſpeak in this matter, and believ'd, that it was no other than her Mother, and thus reply'd, ſtriving to get looſe from her hold, while ſhe twin'd her ſelf about him like a Snake, not to be ſhook off. *Madam* (ſaid he) *diſmiſs me, ſuch Impudence unmans; me while you kept your Virtue you had Charms, now you act like the moſt abandon'd Proſtitute, you have none: Diſmiſs me, or I ſhall raiſe the Houſe and expoſe you to your Parents, who as I find they do not love you, ſo have they Reaſon.*

Baſe Man, reply'd Bertha, *too well thou know'ſt in whoſe Arms thou art;* Matilda *would have found thee more warm; yet know, thou canſt never enjoy her without Inceſt, and I will take care, if poſſible, that you never ſee each other more.*—— *Yet you ought to conſider the Injury you have done me, for my Virtue wounded me with a Paſſion that muſt*

render

render my Life ever miserable. If thou hast sav'd my Daughters Life, wilt thou murder me for her sake? No, I know no Reason but that she should die for her that gave her Life, not I for doing it. Do not struggle thus, I cannot hold thee long: Am I not fair? I'm daily told of a thousand Charms that yet smile in my Face, have I not one to touch thy obdurate Heart? Not enow to move thy Compassion, if not Love?——— As she would have gone on, he broke from her, and she in her Agony could not help reproaching him, so loud, and in terms so vehement, that he was afraid the House would be disturb'd. She apprehended his fear, and following him out of Bed—*No, no,* said she, *if I cannot live in Happiness, thou shalt not live beyond me, here I will fix my self till my Husband come and transfix us both, that will be some Pleasure, to dye with you, and hinder any other from enjoying the Pleasure that is deny'd to me.* She urg'd him with that vehemence, that he perswaded her to go into the Bed, and that he would come to her, and do what he could to acquit himself of what she expected from him.

Perswaded by these fair Words, nor yet willing to be caught in that condition by the Family, she return'd to the Bed, supposing some necessary Occasion might oblige him to stay a little; but he making to the Door, with much ado got it open, and flying to his Man's Chamber, she pursu'd him; he had scarce got in e're she was come to him; but being thus excluded, she vow'd Revenge, and so left him.

But all this had made ſo much noiſe, that not only *Matilda*, but ſome of the Servants were rouz'd; and coming out with Candles, found *Goloſre*'s Door open, tho' all his Cloaths there, and preſently *Bertha* full of Rage and Tears, in her Smock: She could not bear the ſight of *Matilda*, but giving her ſome blows and ſcratches on her Face, ſhe drove her to her Chamber, and had it not been for the Servants, had certainly deſtroy'd her. This rouz'd the Old-man, who miſſing his Wife, and hearing his Daughters Voice, gets up, runs to her Chamber, and examines the matter, interpoſing his Authority: *My Dear*, (ſaid *Bertha*) *lying awake, I heard* Matilda'*s Chamber-door open, and ſhe trip away, as I imagin'd, to* Golofre'*s Chamber; fearing the worſt, I immediately went after thus in my Shift, to prevent what I fear'd: I heard her open his Door and ſteal in; I follow'd and purſu'd her even to his Bed, where ſeizing her, her Gallant roſe in her defence, threatning me in a vile and ſcandalous manner; but, unable to move me, I got her out, and my Paſſion prevailing, beat her and ſcratch'd her Face, but am ſorry I proceeded ſo far, ſince I had happily prevented the Miſchief.*

This rais'd the Old-man's Indignation, and taking his great Sword, would have gone immediately to his Chamber, and made him pay his Life for his Attempts on the Honour of his Family; but being a little pacified by his Lady, and deſir'd to defer it till the morning, he was led back to his Chamber and Bed by his falſe Spouſe. The Servants and *Matilda* knew that all *Bertha* had utter'd was entirely falſe; and

and *Matilda*, who knew her Mother's Paſſion for *Golofre*, was ſatisfied that ſhe had made ſome fruitleſs Attempt on his Virtue, nothing elſe could have put her into ſo violent a Rage.

Golofre's Man in the mean while got up, dreſt himſelf, and coming down, found the Servants with Lights, by the help of which he gather'd his Maſter's Cloaths together, and carried 'em up to his Chamber, where he dreſt him, and told him what he heard from the Servants below. *Golofre* was mightily touch'd with the Misfortunes of his dear *Matilda*, and choſe rather to expoſe himſelf and *Bertha* to the Reſentment of the old Gentleman, than to leave *Matilda* expos'd to the Malice and Revenge of ſo barbarous a Mother: He therefore reſolv'd not to ſtir till he had ſeen the old Gentleman, and ſet things in as good a poſture as he poſſibly could. The old Man was up before his uſual Hour, full of Reſentment for the ſuppos'd Injury *Golofre* had done him; his Wife puſh'd him on, hoping that one or both would fall in the Quarrel, and that if either ſurviv'd, it might be in her power ſoon to ſend him after the other; to ſuch dangerous Extreams do our Paſſions drive us, when we give our ſelves up to their conduct, without regard to Virtue or Honeſty.

Matilda had lock'd her ſelf up in her Chamber with only her Maid, full of Tears and Deſpair both for her ſelf and her Lover. And now the old Gentleman and *Bertha* came into the Hall, where they found *Golofre* and his Man ready to take Horſe as ſoon as they had ſeen

 him.

him. *Bertha*, to amuſe her Husband, immediately falls on the young Man, calling him baſe and treacherous Villain, a Spoiler of their Honour and Peace, and thunder'd out ſuch a Volley of abuſive Curſes, that the old Man was fain to command her to be ſilent, and leave the righting his Honour to himſelf.

Madam, ſaid *Golofre*, *I am ſorry your Madneſs and Folly have put me under a neceſſity of declaring to your Husband, that your Rage at me is becauſe I would not be the Spoiler of the Honour of your Family, and not becauſe I had in vain attempted it: but the Preſervation of your Daughter's Life, and the clearing mine own Honour, oblige me to a Courſe I tremble to take.*

Theſe words alarm'd both the Husband and Wife, but ſhe, who had only Impudence to bring her off, began to ſcold again, but her Huſband told her, that a method ſo prepoſterous would more confirm him in his Doubts than all the Evidence *Golofre* could bring. Silence being therefore made, *Golofre* in as modeſt terms as poſſible let the old Gentleman know how ſhe had perſecuted him with her Love, and that if he had that Night but yielded to have broke the Bands of Hoſpitality, there had been no Diſturbance, but he had departed in Peace, and done a Villany, which his refuſing to be guilty of has involv'd him in. He then oblig'd the Servants to give an account of all they knew, and by comparing all together, the Husband was ſatisfied of his Wife's deſign of making him a Cuckold, but not of the Matter of Fact, ſince he eaſily believ'd that *Golofre*'s Heart

Heart being prepoſſeſs'd with the Love of the Daughter, he might eaſily reſiſt what could be therefore no Temptation to him. Commanding his Wife to her Chamber immediately, he took his leave of *Golofre*, and at his deſire ſent his Daughter to a Relation ten miles off, till her Face was recover'd, and ſhe got to *London*, there to undergo as heavy a Perſecution for Love under the *Lady of the* SUN.

What became of *Bertha* and her Husband I know not, having only heard what I told you related by *Matilda* and *Golofre*, to *Alicia*, in hopes by that means to ſoften her Heart to pity a Love that aroſe in Misfortunes, and yet never met with any Smile of Succeſs.

When *Matilda* was come to *London*, ſhe was graciouſly receiv'd by her Couſin the *Lady of the* SUN; and the more, becauſe ſhe found in her Charms that might be able to engage the Heart of ſome Man of Power to ſtrengthen her Intereſt when the old King ſhould die, and when ſhe muſt expect the Aſſaults of her Enemies, for all the Irregularities which ſhe had committed all the time of her Power.

She try'd the King's Sons, but there ſhe was too much hated to hope for Succeſs, or any tolerable Terms: ſhe at laſt conſider'd of her old Gallant *de la Poole*, by a ſort of Prophetic Spirit foreſeeing his Power and Intereſt in the next Reign, tho' then there was not the leaſt appearance of any ſuch mighty Fortune attending him. *De la Poole* ſaw her with admiration, and had he ſuppos'd that *Alicia*'s Power would have been of any long continuance, he had ſoon gorg'd the Bait; but as Matters ſtood, he kept her in ſuch a ſuſpence, that ſhe had no reaſon but to think that he thought the Match very honourable as well as advantageous to him.

Golofre had made ſuch an Intereſt with a Privado of the *Lady of the* SUN, that he was admitted with *Matilda* to make a full relation of all that had paſs'd between them, which they told in ſo moving and pathetic a manner, as muſt have mov'd any one who could be ſenſible of any thing but her own Intereſt; ſhe was too much a Courtier to diſmiſs 'em without Hopes, tho' ſhe reſolv'd to diſappoint their Deſires.

Golofre was no ſooner gone, but *Matilda* was order'd to be ſtrictly guarded, and all Admittance (even Letters to or from *Golofre*) entirely forbidden: And *de la Poole* growing colder as the King grew weaker, ſhe applied to another young Spark, who was very great with all the King's Sons, had a Place about the Prince of *Wales*, and was therefore likely to ſecure her the better when he came to be King. He ſaw her, liked her, and immediately agrees with the *Lady of the* SUN, who acquaints *Matilda*, That ſhe muſt prepare to marry this Gentleman in two days time, becauſe ſhe would not leave ſo uſeful a Match to the hazard of Fortune.

Matilda was ſtruck dumb at the News, and diſtracted with Deſpair, reſolv'd not to outlive the violation of her Faith. With ſome Induſtry and more Gold ſhe brib'd one of her Guards,

Guards, (for Courtiers can't resist Gold on any Consideration) who convey'd a Letter from her to *Golofre*, by which she inform'd him of all that was design'd against his Happiness and hers; promising, if he could contrive any way, that she would flee with him from the hated Court, to the farthest part of the habitable World. It was the good Fortune of these Lovers, that the Messenger who brought *Golofre* the Letter was the Son of a Neighbour of his, who had formerly been supported by his Family Time out of Mind; and enquiring his Name, took care to let him know his Obligation, and with Prayers and more Gold agreed to help her to escape to him the next Night.

Golofre got a Priest and every thing in order to fix Matters so fast, that it should not be in the power of Fate to separate 'em any more. All things being therefore done with Diligence and Care, *Matilda* was convey'd to an Apartment provided, and immediately married to him; and the Hour of the Night, and further security of their Love requiring it, they immediately went to Bed; where I leave 'em to those Joys true Lovers find in each others Embraces, and return to the *Lady of the* SUN, who was soon inform'd of her Escape, and of the Servant that convey'd her away. Her Rage being highten'd by the disappointment of that Refuge she promis'd her self, she imploys all her Creatures to make strict enquiry after 'em, who at last lighting on the House, search'd it, and found 'em in Bed together. *Golofre* told 'em she was his Wife, and that no Man had power to ſeparate 'em, which now could only be done by that God who joyn'd 'em.

Build not on that, ſaid one of the Leaders of thoſe who ſearch'd for 'em, *for the Court can do as much as he that made you, in this or any thing elſe, when it pleaſes: However, ſince I have not yet Power to do any thing in this, we ſhall only ſecure you here till we inform our Lady what diſcovery we have made.*

Alicia was more enrag'd that ſhe was diſappointed, than if ſhe had allow'd him a Favour for Friendſhip; but reſolving not to loſe the means of her future Security, ſhe determin'd to deſtroy him by the force of Law if poſſible; if not, by more clandeſtine means. She eaſily obtains a Warrant to ſecure him for ſtealing a valuable Jewel at the ſame time he carried off her Couſin; ſhe had thoſe that on his Tryal would ſwear it, and doubted not of the Kindneſs of the Judge to wreſt an Evidence to her ſide as far as he could. *Matilda* was forc'd from her dear Husband by the violence of the Meſſengers, and born to *Alicia* at the ſame time that *Goloſre* was carried to Priſon. The poor Lady *Matilda* ſuffer'd, tho' not in ſo nauſeous a Priſon, yet in a fine Room, all the Perſecution ſhe was capable of from the *Lady of the* SUN, whoſe Rage was proportion'd to the Diſappointment ſhe had given her: She upbraided her with Folly and Ingratitude, proteſted that her favour'd Lover or Husband ſhould be hang'd, and that ſhe would turn her out to Miſery, if ſhe did not comply, and marry the Perſon ſhe had choſe for her.

Thus

Thus was ſhe for ſome time perſecuted, and *Golofre* by the unwholſom Damps of the Priſon became ſickly, when the very Perſon *Alicia* planted for his ruin, deliver'd him. The *Lady of the* SUN had charg'd *Matilda* to receive her Friend kindly, and to make no diſcovery of her being already married, or ſhe would take care, by the next Viſit, to remove her pretended Husband out of the World; and ſo introducing her Friend, left the young Couple together. He preſs'd his Love, ſhe diſcover'd nothing but Deſpair, till affected with her Grief, he began ſeriouſly to enquire into the Cauſe; and having work'd her into a belief of his Sincerity by his Proteſtations both of Secrecy and Service, ſhe told him the whole Story of her Amour and Marriage, and the cruel Event of it. *Now, Sir,* (ſaid ſhe) *if your Pretences of Love are real, you will not ſee me miſerable, but bring me ſome Relief; yet no Relief can be of any force with me, but the Safety of my Dear* Golofre; *aſſiſt in that, and you'll oblige me in ſo ſenſible a manner, that any thing in both our powers will be ever your Due.* The young Courter, tho' touch'd with the Story, was yet ſo much a Courtier as to do nothing without a Bribe, where it could be had, and therefore preſſes thoſe Favours ſhe could grant, without depending on any one elſe: She reſiſts ſo vigorouſly, that even Force was offer'd, till ſhe deſir'd a Parley; the Articles were, That when he had ſet 'em both at liberty, and done ſomething worthy ſuch a Favour, he might demand without fear of a Repulſe. Tho' *Matilda* never de-

ſign'd

ſign'd to comply with his lewd Deſires, yet ſhe had found, that Sincerity was of no uſe in a Court, where falſe Promiſes are current Coin.

All the young Man could do, was to find out *Golofre*'s Priſon, and remove him to better Lodgings, which he had no way to do, but only by threatning the Goaler with ſevere Puniſhment, if *Golofre* miſcarried under his cuſtody; telling him, That Madam *Alicia*'s Reign was very near an end, when not only ſhe, but all her Creatures, would be brought to anſwer their illegal Practices.

Golofre being remov'd into a more wholſome Apartment, began to mend apace; and the *Lady of the* SUN hearing by her Spies of the Goaler's ſudden Kindneſs to the unfortunate Priſoner, ſent him a ſevere Reprimand, letting him know, that ſince he had remov'd him from a place that would have diſpatch'd him to their hands, ſhe expected he would now take care himſelf to ſend him to another World. In theſe Streights, on both ſides, the Goaler knew not what to do; but conſulting with his Wife, (a notable Baggage, and one who had taken ſome liking to *Golofre*) ſhe advis'd him to ſend to *Alicia*, that he ſhould be diſpatch'd the next Night, and at the ſame time to convey him away to ſome place out of Town till the King was dead, which was hourly expected.

Tho' this News was agreeable to *Alicia*, it ſtuck *Matilda* to the Heart, who was juſt expiring with the News: When her new Lover came and found her in that condition, he was extreamly ſurpriz'd at an Account of the Cauſe, and going
ing

ing to the Goaler, assur'd him of a severe Punishment as soon as the King was departed, who could not hold out a day longer. The Goaler at last taking him aside, under the assurance of Secrecy, told him what he had done, and where he might find him. He comes back to *Matilda* with this good News, which immediately reviv'd her, and made her desire that he would take her out with him, and convey her to her Husband, since by his Authority she might go out, tho' not without it; and, that it was now a proper time, *Alicia* being confin'd to the King's Chamber, he being now on his Death-bed.

The Gallant, who could deny her nothing, comply'd with her Desires, and convey'd her to her Dear *Golofre*, delivering her into his Arms, with an assurance of all the Service in his power at any time. The Gallant being gone, *Matilda* and her Husband resolv'd that moment to retire far from the Court, and to live on that pretty Fortune he had, where neither Lust nor Ambition should ever interfere with their Love.

In the mean time it was now the turn of the *Lady of the* SUN to grieve for the King, there were manifest Tokens of Death, yet did she still flatter him with Hopes of Life, so that he neglected making that Provision for his Soul which a dying Christian should, till he was taken quite speechless: Mean while the *Lady of the* SUN took care to make use of her Time, purloining away the most valuable things in the Palace, stealing the very Rings off his Fingers as he lay expiring, and then, like a true Harlot and Favourite, left him gasping for Life, not capable of speaking a Word.

Word, and with only one poor ſimple Fryar in the Room.

The old King being dead, and the young one proclaim'd, as there were many about him who wiſh'd for their ſhare of the Plunder of the *Lady of the* SUN, either by Bribes or Grants, ſo they let her not long continue unmoleſted, bringing a Proceſs againſt her: Yet ſhe on her ſide had ſo well imploy'd her time, that with her Money ſhe had corrupted many of the *Lords*, and all the *Lawyers* of *England*, who did not only ſecretly ſollicite her Affair, but publickly pleaded her Cauſe, and us'd all their Intereſt in her behalf: Yet ſhe was ſo much and generally hated for her rapacious Avarice, that ſhe was ſo vigorouſly proſecuted by the Parliament, being by her own Mouth convicted, that ſhe was baniſh'd the Land, and all her Eſtate, movable or immovable, forfeited to the *Exchequer*, from whence (by the late King's Favour, or rather Dotage) it had been unduly taken.

On her departure ſhe gave the Ring, in which I then was, to *Michael de la Poole*, in hopes that if he arriv'd at the good Fortune that had been foretold him, he might do her ſome Service as to recalling her into her own Country, from a Baniſhment ſhe abhorr'd; but he, like a true Courtier, before he was ſo, ſoon forgot her; nay, made it his buſineſs to joyn with all that rail'd againſt her.

I hope, by what I have told you (ſaid my *Guinea*) of the *Lady of the* SUN, I've been equal with

with the *Seignior* and *Monsieur*; but what is to come shews my Power more than any Instance they have produc'd; it was in the next Reign after my Lady *Alicia's* dominion that this Experiment was made.

The Grandson, yet a Child, succeeded *Edward* III, and tho' he reign'd 22 Years, yet without the Glory of his Grandfather, he had all the Dotage of his Age; for never Prince had more Favourites, and those more unworthy of his Favour, and whose cursed Advice at last brought him to an ignominious End in a private state. E're yet he was of age, this *Michael de la Poole*, made Earl of *Suffolk*, *Robert de Vere* Duke of *Ireland*, with an Archbishop of *York*, had led him so astray, that the Parliament did threaten to depose him if he would not surrender those Misguiders of his Youth, and come to them; which being oblig'd to do, his Favourites fled: *De la Poole*, before he was set at liberty by the King, to make a second Escape after he was taken at *Calice*, gave me to the King, as a Token to remember him, assuring him I once belong'd to the finest Lady in the World; and that as he believ'd he should never see His Majesty more, so, as his last Advice, he recommended the E. of *Nottingham* to him for a Man of Judgment, and one who could put him in a good way of managing the *Parliament*, who had hitherto been such a Curb to his Inclinations.

The King took his Advice, and being now One-and-twenty Years of age, assum'd the Government himself, and by the Advice of *Scroop* Earl

Earl of *Wiltshire* and the Earl of *Nottingham*, made many alterations. And the time of Parliament coming on, he advis'd with his new Favourite *Nottingham* how to order that point. *My Leige*, (said my Lord *Nottingham*) *some of our Princes have taken very wrong Measures for the Ends they have aim'd at; they have taken it with Disdain, that they could not do what they pleas'd without being accountable to any among Men; and have on those Notions grown so unpopular, that if they have not lost their Crowns, they have considerably shaken 'em, and had a Reign perpetually disturb'd with Tumults and War; whereas if they had but consider'd matters justly, they might have been much more absolute, and much more secure in all their Arbitrary Proceedings, if they had but studied the Art of bribing the Members of Parliament. Your Majesty has a great number of Places in your Gift, which ought to be distributed among the leading and active Members of your House of Commons, to others you must give Pensions, which will never be a Farthing out of your Pocket, for they will not scruple to give Taxes, so long as by your Gifts they have an Encrease and Interest for their Money: Nor will they be over-nice in examining into Accounts, when their own Receipts must be found amongst 'em. By these two Articles you engage another numerous Party of Gentlemen, who are in hopes of the same Advantage, and these will go a greater length than those already in Pay, since they will perswade themselves, that the more they do to merit a Reward, the greater the Pension or Place will be. When this Method is fix'd, you need advance but one or two in a Session, and you carry all before you; all your*

Actions

Actions are stamp'd with Jure Divino, *and you can do nothing that can be found fault with, since you have then the whole Power of the Nation to back you.*

The King seem'd well pleas'd with the Advice, and resolv'd to put it in execution. The time for Election coming on, his Agents went to all the Boroughs, and spar'd no Bribes to get Men fit for the turn, and capable of being manag'd by the Court; so about *Lady-day* the Parliament meets, and care was taken to have Sir *John Bushy* chosen Speaker, and Sir *William Maggat* and Sir *Henry Green* were the chief Managers of the Court Cause; Men who were ignorant, covetous, and ambitious: Nor must we leave out their Flattery, Sir *John Bushy* in his Speeches not being contented to give the King his due Titles of Honour, but such as were fitter for the Majesty of the Almighty, than for any Earthly Prince.

Such a Power had Gold and this Method with the Parliament, that meeting in the beginning of the Year 1398, at *Shrewsbury*, the King, by the Interest he had made among 'em, caus'd not only all the Proceedings of the Parliament in the tenth of his Reign (which were great Asserters of Liberty) to be condemn'd and annull'd, but even obtain'd a Concession of 'em, That after the present Parliament should break up, its whole Power should be confer'd upon, and remain in certain Persons by them particularly nam'd, or any seven or eight of 'em, who by vertue of such Power granted

granted did afterwards proceed to act and determine many things concerning the publick state of the Nation, properly the Business of a Parliament.

Yet, in confidance of this Method, the Earl of *Nottingham* lost his Country, and the King himself his Crown; for there is such a Love of Liberty fix'd in this Nation, that no Court yet has been able to overthrow it; as most Courts (except this present, where Patriots only prevail) have made it their fruitless Endeavours to do.

The *Guinea* perceiv'd by this time that I grew sleepy, and therefore excusing himself for the length of his Entertainment, after two others had spent some Time in it, hop'd the Variety of the Matter would make Amends for the long tediousness of the Narration; and so we all committed our selves to Silence.

The End of the Second Nights Entertainment.

THE

THE

Third Nights Entertainment.

GAMING.

THO' much of the laſt Night was ſpent in the Accounts my GOLDEN SPIES had given me, yet I loſt good part of what re-main'd, in ruminating on what I had heard. I that had falſly abus'd my ſelf with an Opi-nion, that none were worſe than my ſelf, was ſtrangely ſurpriz'd to find Men guilty of ſuch Crimes as would never enter into the Heart of Man to act or imagine: Is it poſſible (ſaid I to my ſelf) that all thoſe Maxims of Right and Wrong, of Virtue and Vice, which I have learnt from my Childhood, and read confirm'd in the Commonwealths of old, ſhould be no-thing but a vain Speculation, that only ſerves to miſlead him who believes it into Ruin and Perdition? Can it be, that what ſeems to be founded on the Criterion of Truth, Evidence, ſhould indeed be only Matter of meer Scepti-ciſm? And, that thoſe who ſeemingly govern the World, and direct the ſecret Movements of the State Machine, ſhould lay thoſe things down as Maxims of *Wiſdom*, and the ſacred Rules of *Prudent Conduct*, which bear all the Marks of a Conſummate and moſt Diabolical Villany? This ſtill rais'd my Wonder to a greater height, to conſider how they could keep Human Society together, or that any Government could live, much leſs flouriſh, under the Direction of ſuch Maxims as are deſtructive of the Public Good and all Particular Happineſs.

The Confuſion of my Thoughts upon this intricate Subject turn'd my Brain ſo, that giddy with the View, I tumbled at laſt into an uneaſie Slumber, which held me till the approach of Day: Soon after ariſing, I put all but my *Guinea* into my Scrutore, and retiring into my Cloſet, taking it out, and laying it on my Table, I thus addreſs'd my ſelf to it.

The Relations you all gave me laſt Night have not a little diſturb'd my Repoſe: 'Tis true, I was not much affected with the Villanies of *Italy* and *France*; the Miſery of Slavery both in Church and State, under which they groan in a different degree, would make one eaſily ſuppoſe they can renounce all the Duties of Religion and Humanity: But when you came to advance the ſame on the Great ones of our Nation, I confeſs, I was in hopes that having receiv'd ſome Diſobligation at Court, you dealt with it as moſt Grumbletonians do. Therefore ſince we are alone, pray be candid, and ſet my Judgment right in this Particular; Is not our Court always free from thoſe Villanies of the firſt magnitude, which are ſo well known to prevail in all other Courts?

I am

I am ſorry (replied my *Guinea*) you ſhould doubt my Veracity, who could receive no Advantage from impoſing a Falſity on you in any thing of this nature; but I am willing to believe this Incredulity, from the charitable Opinion you have of your Countrymen, imagining them free from all the Vices of other Nations: But that's a very great miſtake; I've been in many Countries and Courts, and know that the Magnitude of Vice is varied ſometimes by different Modes and Kinds. The *Engliſh*, it's true, ſeldom make ſo little of Murder in their Revenge as the *Spaniard* or *Italian*, but then they find to the full as ſmall a Concern in the public Depredations as any Country in *Chriſtendom*: And it is remarkable, that the two great Courts of Concourſe, the Rivals of the *Engliſh* Court, I mean *Rome* and *Verſailles*, have each had their Time in encouraging the finer Arts and Sciences, ſuch as *Painting*, *Poetry*, *Eloquence*, *Muſick*, &c. but the *Engliſh Court* has never yet thought it worth its while to encourage Men of Art. 'Tis true, there have been ſome forward puſhing Fellows fortified by Ignorance, who ſharing a ſmall ſmattering in ſome of theſe Arts, have found eaſie Acceſs to, and particular Favour from, the Great Men of *Britain*, who ſeldom yet have had Diſcernment enough to diſtinguiſh, or Generoſity enough to prefer a *Man of Art* to a bold *Pretender*.

This is a Mark of a Scandalous Avarice, every one aiming at the making his own Market of the Public; which is the Bubble to e'ry Side and Party, while all make a Clamour of the Service of Prince and Country, that they may have it in their Power to love only themselves; and scarce any Nation can show so many Families rais'd, and so many Estates got by the Public, as this *Island*, that boasts of her Virtue and Liberty.

My *Guinea* then pausing a while, call'd softly to me to lay my Ear closer to him since what he had to utter was not to be trusted to a Voice that might be interrupted by any other. I was curious enough, not to make any Difficulty of punctually observing his Directions; where he unfolded such Monstrous Vices to the confounding of Sexes and Nature; such prodigious Hypocrisies, to the calling in doubt of every thing that is said and done; such villanous Designs, as would make one think that there was no other Hell, and that the Devil was not only Prince of the Air, but Prince of the Earth.

He pull'd off the Mask from the false Patriot, and show'd him a crusty hypocritical Knave, that laugh'd at the causeless Credulity of the People, by which he made his Mark of the Liberty and Property. In short, the Mysteries he reveal'd are like those of *Bona-dea*, which are not to be expos'd to unhallow'd Eyes, for fear the Sense of Things should destroy all confidance betwixt Man and Man, and so put an end to Humane Society. These things I reserve for a more lucky Opportunity; for tho' the Piety, Public Spirit, Generosity, Learning, and good Sense of the

Pre-

Present Court must ever exempt it from all parallel in this Account, yet since the Depravity of Men is so great, that either thro' Envy or Dissatisfaction they will find spots in the Sun, I shall not give those evil Inclinations the Satisfaction of finding Fewel for their Malice in what I shall thus publickly deliver. Putting, therefore, my *Guinea* in my Pocket I left my Chamber, and took the Air as far as *Hamstead*, diverted my self with a Bottle, and the Conversation of a Friend; I mean a Companion; for, by what I had heard, I began very much to doubt whether there were any such thing in the World as a Friend, since every Man has his own Interest and Self-Love so much in his Eye, and at his Heart, that it is almost impossible to find any one without a Design on his Neighbour for his own advantage.

Returning to Town, I fell in at *Bradbury's*, in pursuit of a Relation, who was one of those Fools who would put it to the determination of the Dice, whether his Money should be his own or not. 'Tis true, that the Dice are sometimes very good Judges in the Case, deciding the Cause for the poor Sharper against the rich Bubble; which puts me in mind of a Story much in favour of the Cubical Gentlemen. There was a *French* General, that being now grown old, desir'd as a Retreat the Government of some Province, where being to be Judge in *meum* and *tuum* as well as criminal matters, the King ask'd him how he would do, without any Insight into the Law, as having

ving always been bred a Soldier? He told the King he would venture his Majesties displeasure on the just discharge of his Office. He has the Place, comes off with wonderful Applause, in all his Decisions; insomuch that his Reputation of an able as well as just Judge went before him to Court; where being ariv'd, the King was very inquisitive to know how he could order matters so well as to please every body in a Post in which the ablest Lawyers had fail'd. He told his Majesty, that his Method was this — he carry'd with him to the Bench a Box and Dice, and having heard both sides, he then threw for Plaintiff and Defendant, and whoever had the highest Dice carry'd the Cause; and that he seldom mist of judging Right by this Method, to the Satisfaction of all that heard so well-pois'd a Judgment.

But finding not my Relation, I retir'd towards Home, desirous to make some further Enquiries of my wonderful Spies, in matters I did not so very well understand. Being got into my Bed-chamber, and having dismiss'd my Man, set my loquacious Pieces at large, and with my *Guinea* laid them on the little Table by my Bed, into which I got, and desir'd them to proceed in their farther Account of the Court, which yet I thought was far from compleat.

To number up the Vices, as some *Tramontani* call them, said the *Italian* Piece, or the Virtues, as the wiser *Italians* count them, would be an endless Task. You count Ambition, Murther

ther by Poison, or Dagger, Whoredoms; private dispatches of their own Wives, and other Womens Husbands, Contracts, Re-contracts for advantage of Fortune or Revenge, great Hypocrisies, false Complaisance to those you depend on, and Insolence to our Dependants. You, I say, court Vices of the first magnitude; we think them wise Precepts of Policy, to gratify our Pleasure and Interest. You make a great noise about Favourites making their Fortunes by the Goverment; we look on it as a Duty, and a Customary piece of Pruduce, and in this we have Precedents of the wisest and best *Romans*; *Cato* the *Elder* thus rais'd himself from an unknown Villager to the Head of the Commonwealth; *Marius* from a *Plebeian* to a seventh Consulship. *Sylla* from a desperate Fortune to the Head of the World. Nor did any of 'em regard those musty School Morals which teach such a Respect to others, not center'd all in themselves, while *Epictetus* remain'd a Slave by following the contrary Maxims.

Thus you Gentlemen make a mighty Do against Gaming, which is a thing that has prevail'd over all the World, ev'n from this to *China* it self, where they play away their Wives Children, and themselves to Slavery, in the Ardor of their Sport.

I was pleas'd with his mention of Gaming, and desir'd him to let us know what Discoveries he had made in that Affair. *Gaming* (said he) may have many ill Consequences, I will not deny it, but since it is so establish'd a Cuſtom, that it is a ſort of Ruſticity and Ill-breeding not to Game, I know no other Rule of our Actions but the common Uſage and Mode of all Nations. It is a thing ſo follow'd in *Italy*, that every Village almoſt yield us daily Examples of the good and evil Effects of it; by which ſome poor Rogues get Riches, and other wealthy Fools get Beggary: and like other Trades it ſeems a neceſſary Engine of Providence, to compleat that Viciſſitude, which is ſo viſible in all things under the Sun.

The Unlucky Caſt.

THere was in the Town of *Leghorn* a Merchant of ſome Note, who, beſides his Adventures at Sea, did often venture an Eſtate by Land, and make quicker Returns by the Dice, than ever he could do by all the Wings of the Wind. He had long ſince ſent his Prentice to *China*, where ſome years he had been his Factor; but having got a tolerable Eſtate, he return'd home for himſelf, and in a little Time marry'd one of the moſt beautiful Women in that part of *Italy*. *Freſcobaldi* the Maſter kept a very good Correſpondence with his quondam Factor *Antonio*, and was a more intimate Friend than ordinary, preſent at his Wedding, and ſaw his Wife with Eyes not ſo hoſpitable as Friendſhip requir'd; but that in *Italy* never enters into the Balance with Pleaſure or Profit; ſo *Freſcobaldi* finding that his Heart was entirely engag'd by the Wife of *Antonio*, was reſolv'd by one means or other

to

to become Master of his Wishes, and possess the fair *Flaminia* in spight of his own Age, and her, and her Husbands Youth.

He employ'd all his Art, set to work all the Engines of this Venereal War, which are thought to be of use in Engagements of this nature, such as Presents, female Agents, and the like; but the Lady was not yet weary enough of her Husband, nor was her Appetite so deprav'd as to prefer an old batter'd Gallant to the Vigour and Fire of a lusty young Husband. Tir'd at last with the Obstacles he met with, Chance threw into his Head the means of accomplishing his desires, tho' with the Ruin of *Antonio* and his Family. *Antonio* had added to the *Italian* Itch of Gaming that adventitious Habit which he had got in the *Indies*.

Frescobaldi push'd on the Humour, and every day won some of *Antonio's* Money, allowing for some encouraging Intervals, which he had to fix his Bubble to his Arms: In this manner being highly in Game, *Antonio* lost all his Ready-Money, and Bills of Credit, and had at last no stock left but himself and his Wife; he set both, and lost both; *Frescobaldi* would remit nothing of his good Fortune, but sells him to the Galleys, and takes her to his own House.

Yet he had another task to accomplish, tho' he had her in his Power. It happen'd that she either dislik'd his Person, or his Treachery so far, as not to be prevail'd with by any Entreaty to accept of his offering a Heart both

both despis'd, and hated. This gave *Fresco-baldi* some Trouble, but little Pain, since she was in his House, in the Hands of his Vassals, who must act by an implicite Obedience whatever he commanded. The Night being therefore come, when he was resolv'd to admit of no farther delay, *Flamania* being in Bed, and in her first sleep, by a secret door he conveys himself into her Chamber, and quite into her Bed, before she wak'd, and spite of her strugling accomplish'd his desires. But unable to strugle for a second Embrace, he left her, till he had recruited for another Encounter. He saw her in the Day all in Tears, which he endeavour'd to mitigate by Praises of himself, his Riches, and Power to make her Happy; but all being in vain, he told her, that she had better submit willingly to what her Fate had subjected her to, since he was resolv'd to oblige her by Force to comply with his Will till he was weary of her, and then he would turn her upon the Common. But if she would use those endearing Arts of which without doubt by the Character of her Sex she was Mistress, she should command both him and his Fortune.

I know not how it came to pass, whether thro' Obstinacy or unconquerable Aversion, she could not be work'd on to be easie to his Wishes, so that tir'd with being oblig'd always to commit a Rape by himself, he order'd two of his Servants to hold her, whenever he had a mind to satisfie his amorous Inclinations. As this was but an imperfect Pleasure to him, so it ex-

treamly

treamly aggravated her Misery; which she was resolv'd to free her self from, ev'n by her own Death; yet resolving not to perish alone, she with a great deal of constraint pretended to relent, assur'd him of a Complaisance for his Passion, that would be more agreeable to his Wishes. Which she observing for some time, had procur'd her self a greater Liberty than usual, and in him a Confidance that betray'd him to his Ruin. For having by this means secretly got a Razor into Bed, in his first sleep she dispatched him by cutting his Throat; and not satisfy'd with this, she cut off the offending Parts, and having provided her self with some Money and Jewels, she made her Escape, and arriving at the Place where her Husband was in the Galleys, she paid his Ransom, and set him at Liberty; which charm'd him beyond measure, so that he would have proceeded to the Rights of a Husband, she utterly refus'd him. —— *No,* (said she) *Antonio, you have dealt by me too much like a Fool and a Villain ever to have any thing to do with me more; you have brought me into too much Guilt to escape long the Punishment of the Law; yet as I once lov'd you, I have here set you at Liberty with the Prize of my Honour and* Frescobaldi's *Blood. Provide for your self, lest you share my Fate. Know how to value your self and your Honour more, and if it be possible for you, after what you have done, to enjoy Tranquility, may you find it in abundance. For my part, I have determin'd of my self, and will this moment return to* Leghorn *and surrender my self to Justice,*

Antonio

Antonio did all he could to perſwade her from ſo fatal a Reſolution, and that ſince ſhe had ſo happily eſcaped, not to put her Life in in danger, which he did (as he ought to do) value much more than his own. But all perſuaſions were in vain, the next morning ſhe ſet out for *Leghorn*, and he follow'd her ſo cloſe that they arriv'd juſt together, he ſtill diſſwaded her from entring the Town, but all in vain, for ſhe went directly to the Magiſtrate's Houſe, and told him, that ſhe was come to ſurrender her ſelf up to Juſtice for the Murder of *Freſcobaldi*, who had receiv'd his Death by her Hands.

She had no ſooner done, but *Antonio* interpos'd, and told the Judge that ſhe was mad, for it was he who had murder'd *Freſcobaldi* in revenge of the Cheats he had put upon him in Play, by which he had not only ruin'd him, but ſold him to the Galleys.

My Lord, (interrupted *Flaminia*) the falſity of this is evident, for *Antonio* was a Slave in the Galleys when *Freſcobaldi* was kill'd, with whoſe Money I redeem'd my unjuſt Husband. This Conteſt held ſome time, till the Judge enquiring into the whole Story, was wonderfully touch'd with the Narration; but Murder being Death, he could not but commit her; yet took care ſo to repreſent the matter at Court, that *Freſcobaldi*'s Death was look'd on as a juſt Puniſhment of his Barbarity; and *Flamania* pardon'd the Crime. *Antonio* was baniſh'd for his unjuſt dealing by ſuch a Wife, yet had his Exile remitted by her Mediation.

How-

However, nothing could prevail with her to live with *Antonio* any more; but shutting her self up in a Nunnery, she spent her short remains of Life in Prayer and Pennance, for she dy'd in less than a Year after her Enclosure; and *Antonio* pin'd away in a melancholy Solitude a few months after.

This (assum'd my little French *Louis d'Or*) is an Argument of the abominable Folly and evil Consequence of *Gaming*, which like other Vices has pass'd the *Alps* from *Italy* into *France*, and there has produc'd as many fatal Proofs of its Mischief as in most places where it reigns: It has debauch'd most Families in the Kingdom, and brought many to irretrievable Ruin. It has Bastardiz'd the Nobility, yet some have made their Fortune and enobled their Blood by it, as if it were an Excellence equal to the bravest Martial Atchievements: Monf. *Chamillard*, from a petty Counsellor of the Parliament of *Paris*, became (by playing well at *Billiards)* First Minister of State. 'Tis true, we are something refin'd in Morals *à la Italienne* since the Ministry of Cardinal *Mazarine*, but we can by no means come to the Perfection of the Court of *Rome*, to call Vice *Virtue*, and Virtue *Folly*. Indeed some few Politicians act as if they were of that very Opinion, yet they keep a Decorum in their Professions, and double their Villanies by a convenient and strong Hypocrisie. Nay, in this very Evil of Gaming our Court has much reform'd the Abuse, which was grown to a vast height, by forbidding *Basset* and other Games of great Sums and great Chance, and liable

ble to great Cheats; yet the Humour is ſtill ſo radicated, as not to be entirely expel'd without ſeverer Laws. Monſ. *Chamillard* owing his Riſe to his Skill in one ſort of Game, may perhaps be excus'd for the Favours he has beſtow'd on ſome Scoundrels, who have come to make a Figure by being the Appendix of Gaming; among the reſt there is one, whom by way of ridicule the Town has call'd the Chevalier *de Gaſcoign*, who was originally a Boy that us'd to wipe the Bowls at a Bowling-green, where Gentlemen giving him a petit Piece now and then, he induſtriouſly took care to improve it by Gaming with his Equals, till by good Luck and Addreſs he encreas'd his Stock, to be able to go a *Louis d'Or* ſometimes with a Gentleman that was playing for a great deal of Money; an Indulgence which Men of Quality are very free of to Scoundrels, tho' ſeldom to Men of Senſe.

This ſoon enabled him to throw aſide his blue Apron, and entertain ſome more aſpiring Projects, by which he try'd one day to make a conſiderable Figure in the Town, few or none being ſo juſt to themſelves to examin who and whence the Mortal is, that makes the Appearance of a Gentleman, and ventures his Money. He firſt gets into the Ordinaries, among the Foreigners, who are pretty numerous in *Paris*, by whom he rais'd his Stock to about a thouſand *Louis d'Ores*, then being unwilling to run any Hazard, took up a ſafer Courſe, and frequented the Baſſet and Hazard-tables of better faſhion, and being thorowly acquainted with all who play'd, lent out his Money, making 5 or 10 *per Cent.* in a Night, beſides

besides going a *Louis d'Or* by the bye with the Fortunate.

Being now grown rich, he sets up his Coach, and by I know not what means comes acquainted with Monf. *Chamillard*, who managing the Treasure of the whole Kingdom, and being prime Minister of State, had abundance of valuable Places in his Gift, yet ne'r bestow'd one of any value on a Man of Merit or Learning: Mr. *Racine* (an excellent Poet) dying, he left, among other Places, one that was a perfect *fine Cure*, of about 400 Pistoles a Year; Mr. *Chapelle* (a very ingenious young Man) succeeds him, but hapning to be prefer'd to a Post of more value, this became vacant, and in the Gift of *Chamillard*, who in all *France* could not find one more worthy of it, in his Judgment, than the famous *Chevalier*, the very Jest of the Town, equally worthless in Mind and Person; his Countenance confess'd the Boor, he had but one Eye, clumsie in his Person, awkard in his Behaviour, and dull in his Conversation; he wanted it not, while many a Man of Learning was starving, without being able to recommend themselves to this Minister of State, who was always hard of Access to Men of Parts, and open to Gamesters and Sharpers: He yet affects the Opinion of being a Wit and Man of Sense, but wants enough to shew it, by providing for those who are more oblig'd to Fortune than Nature. But that's a thing now quite out of fashion in *France*, a certain Proof of its speedy declining.

I could

I could give you the Characters of ſeveral other Gameſters in *Paris*, who have rais'd themſelves from the Coach Tail to their Lord's Table and Lady's Bed, but thoſe are things now of e'ry days experience, and you can't paſs the Streets without ſeeing Sharpers as well as Quacks in their Coaches.

But the Infection is ſpread even among the Nobility; they play not now for Diverſion, as formerly, and on the ſquare, but Lords and Dukes turn Sharpers, and take the Trade out of the hands of the Scoundrels. There was a certain Marquis of a very great Fortune, and who has been deem'd not only a Man of Senſe, but even a Critic and Poet; who being eat up with Avarice, that Parcimony would not ſatisfie his Thirſt of Gain: Reſolving therefore to ſet up for a Gameſter of the worſt ſort, as not deſigning ever to play fair: To learn to cogg a Dye, he had for ſome Nights together ty'd down his Finger, to bring it to a habitual poſture of managing it to advantage. This very Nobleman frequenting the public Gaming-houſes, tho' naturally a proud haughty Man, would ſubmit to a familiarity with the moſt infamous of People, if he thought he could bubble 'em of but 20 *Louis d'Ores*. Among the reſt was a Fellow, who living at the fag-end of the Town, had pickt up about 500 *Louis d'Ors* by dealing in Offals among the Poor: This Fellow was ſo mad as to venture what he had got with much Induſtry and Pains, at the Uncertainty of a merry Main; but that he might have the faireſt Play for his Money, he would frequent only thoſe Tables where the Quality was. The

Marquis

Marquis soon found him out, and proving very complaisant to him, resolv'd to have the Bubble to himself. The Man was transported at being taken notice of by one of his Quality, and so he swallow'd the Bait. This Offal-man had won about 25 Pieces, and breaking up from Play, my Lord Marquis took him up in his Coach to set him down near home, but indeed carries him to his own House, and bubbl'd him that Night of all he had about him. He treated him handsomely, inviting him thither often, and so dismiss'd him highly satisfied with the loss of his Money and the gaining his Lordship's Acquaintance.

This held some time; the Offal-man won in public sometimes, but was sure always to lose in private, till at last the Marquis had quite stript him. What to do he knew not, having left neither himself nor his Family any thing to subsist on; but at last resolv'd to try what the Marquis would do for him, who had won much the greater part of his Money: so he comes to my Lords, was admitted as usual, but appearing very pensive, and the Cause being ask'd, the poor Fellow confess'd his Folly, desiring his Lordship to take some Pity on his condition, and give him something to begin the World again, and provide for his Family. *No, no,* said the Marquis, *thou art an idle Rogue, to go and throw away thy Substance at Gaming; thou art not to be trusted; for since thou hast got such an Itch, to trust thee with Money is to send it from my self to some other, for thou'lt only be the Porter of it to some Sharper. Go get thee out of my House, I'm not Company for Offal-men; away, lest my Servants use you sawcily. Ah! my Lord,*

K some

ſome Pity, cry'd the poor Fellow; *What can I do? I have not one Farthing in the World, to buy Bread for my ſelf and Family. Why, you Rogue,* (ſaid the Marquis) *would you have me keep your Family? Go and hang thy ſelf, if thou canſt get no Money.*

Thus turning him out of doors, the Fellow took the Marquis's Advice, and went immediately and hang'd himſelf. A terrible Example to ſuch Fools as throw away their Fortunes at Gaming.

But this Noble Marquis ſerv'd another Tradeſman as bad a Trick as this, which has made him pretty famous in his way. He had to do with an Upholſterer, who furniſh'd him a Country *Villa*, to the worth of about 8 or 900 Piſtoles; he had often waited on the Marquis for his Money, but got nothing but fair Words, till at laſt he was fain to ſpeak ſo preſſingly, that the Marquis appointed him a Time to come and receive his Money. The man was extreamly pleas'd at his Succeſs, and returns punctually at the time appointed: He was introduc'd with all the Civility imaginable, had into my Lord's Cloſet, where his Lordſhip being at Breakfaſt, he was made to ſit down and drink ſome fine Wine, being aſſur'd that when his Steward came he ſhould be paid all his Money. The Time in the mean while hanging on their hands, the Marquis ask'd the Tradeſman if he could play at any ſort of Game, as Cards, Tables, or Dice; he replied, That he underſtood *Trick-track* as well as moſt Men: This News was very pleaſing to the Marquis,

for

for that he was a Maſter of; tho' he perfectly knew how to diſguiſe his Maſtery, till he had fix'd his Bubble: This he effectually executed, having loſt ſome Crowns to him, till now hot in Play, they doubl'd their Bets; the Marquis wins two Games and loſes one, which raiſes the Trader to a deeper Game, till at laſt he was manag'd ſo finely, that he had loſt moſt of the Money he came to receive.

The Upholſterer began to fume, telling the Marquis he would play no longer, ſince he had not play'd fair with him. When ſmooth words would not do, the Marquis bully'd, aſſuring him of a good Baſtinade by his Servants, for an Inſolence that ought not to be pardon'd; but in conſideration of his Loſs, he would pay him the remainder of his Money, provided he would never come near his Houſe more. The Upholſterer knew not what to do, curs'd his own Folly, beg'd the Marquis's Pardon, and receiv'd about 60 *Louis d'Ores*, (what remain'd of his Debt) needing no Threats to keep from a place where he could expect to meet nothing but Deſtruction. It was the Fellow's good fortune, that it was not his All; he could yet keep up his Payments, and by a thrifty Life afterwards made ſhift to provide for his Family, but put the Marquis ever after in his *Litany*, inſtead of *Deadly Sin*.

Yet this Marquis, as cunning as he is, and as much as he is in with all the Sharpers, had a notable Trick put upon him by three or four Gameſters of the beſt credit and figure. 'Twas beforehand agreed among 'emſelves to let the

Marquis into the Secret, by pretending to take him into a Bubble, from whom they propos'd to win at least three or four thousand Pistoles a man: But they so order'd the matter, that while the Marquis thought himself one of the Sharpers, he was the only Bubble, losing in one Night 6000 *Louis d'Ores*, which they divided among 'emselves, as a lawful Trophy won from an Invader of their Province.

But there would be no end of relating the Adventures of this nature, which are the Business and Practice of so many hundreds as live meerly on the Elbow; were a true History of the Acts and Deeds of this noble Marquis alone committed to Writing, his Character would be as singular among Posterity as 'tis in the present Age.

But if these are the Disorders among the Men, those it brings among the Ladies are not fewer, or of less dangerous consequence. *Paris* and the Court, for many Years, had given daily Proofs of it before there was any stop put to it, which has not been so extensive as wholly to suppress the Eagerness of the Ladies in *Gaming* and the Irregularities it produces.

The Fair Extravagant.

MAdam *de Montpensier* was a young Lady of infinite Beauties of Body and Mind, for she had as many Charms in her Wit, as she had in her Face, Shape, and Mien; all these were heighten'd with perfect Modesty, yet accompanied with a sprightly Gaiety, that made her

her as tempting as invincible. This Character ſhe maintain'd ſome time after ſhe came to Court, and her Husband was envy'd as the Happieſt Man in all the large Dominions of *LEWIS* the *Great*. But the Court, which is a place of glorious improvement, in time work'd on her, Temper, and ſet at Liberty the *Woman* in her, which afterwards playd its Part to the utmoſt.

The Ladies of the Court firſt taught her to play, then brought her into Company that run the Humour up to the height, which always having a Spice of Avarice in it, hit Madam *Montpenſier*'s Temper ſo exactly, that ſhe exceeded ſoon all the Gameſters of either the Male or Female Sex in thoſe Parts. But tho' her deſires of Gain were infinite, yet her Luck was not ſo complaiſant to her Wiſhes; ſhe often loſt, and was at laſt forc'd to ſtrain her Credit to ſupply her Luſt of Play; and when that was ſpent, unable to forbear the Cards, and as unable to prevail with *Monſieur* her Husband to ſupply her Extravagance that way, ſhe began to reflect which way ſhe ſhould be able to ſupply her Wants without him. She therefore threw aſide her former reſervedneſs, and admitted the Addreſſes of the many that admir'd her beyond their own Happineſs; nay, ſhe began to learn to Coquet it at laſt, but yet kept within the Bounds of Honour. She would provoke her Lovers to play with her, who of courſe muſt loſe their Money to her, in hopes that Gold genteely thus thrown into her Lap, would make a *Danae* of her. But ſhe kept off till ſhe had ruin'd ſome, and tir'd the reſt, who would not be ſuch Fools to throw away certain Money for an uncertain Favour. So that finding at laſt that ſhe muſt come cloſer to the point, and give real Satisfaction before one Man, whoſe Purſe might ſupply her Extravagant Gaming: and by ſome ſurmizes revive the Hopes of others, ſo far as to make 'em Bubbles to thoſe Hopes, which ſhe reſolv'd to gratify where ſhe could keep them no longer alive without it.

The firſt happy Man was *Vander Vermin* a *Dutchman*, who from a Tapſter in the *Hague*, by lucky Hits and good Management had arriv'd to a vaſt ſtock of Money. Madam *Montpenſier*'s Eyes, Wit and Mien had warm'd his Flegmatic Conſtitution into Love, and his Money had drawn her Thoughts to make him her Bubble. *Vander Vermin* was a goodly portly Fellow, and one whoſe Perſon might pleaſe a Woman well enough, whoſe Inclinations were that way. But then he was in his Converſation a dull heavy lump, without Spirit or Vivacity; yet his Money ſupply'd all to this Lady, whoſe tendre for Money was greater than for Man; a perfect Mercenary to her Nature, who would deny no Favour for Gold, nor grant any without it; with it the moſt worthleſs Wretch was an *Adonis*, without it the moſt meritorious had no Charm.

She did not however yield to *Vander Vermin*, till ſhe had fram'd his Complaiſance to its utmoſt ſtretch; and till he grew as impatient for the Favours he thought he had ſufficiently

ciently purchas'd, as ſhe was to be Miſtreſs of more of his Gold, to throw away to others at Gaming.

The Appointment at laſt being made, *Vander Vermin* overjoy'd at the Happineſs, indulges himſelf till the happy minute, according to the laudable Cuſtom of his Country, with the Bottle and an intimate Friend or two, who by his diſcourſe had diſcover'd to what Country he was bound, and therefore to make themſelves ſport, they took care to convey ſomething into his Glaſs, that in a few Hours would have ſuch an Effect, as would put both him and the Lady into a miſerable Condition.

The Hour is come, and away ſpeeds *Vander Vermin*, is admitted to the Ladys Room, and after a noble Preſent, they venture to Bed; where what was done I leave to themſelves: but they had not ſpent much time in theſe their Enjoyments before a diſmal Cataſtrophe attended the Lovers, too ſecure of their Happineſs from abroad, without ſuſpecting any Enemy within. *Vander Vermin*, who had perform'd like a Lover of Vigour, attempting the ſame Race of Pleaſure again, the unlucky Doſe given by his Boſom Friends forc'd an unfortunate Paſſage both upwards and downwards, and in ſuch abundance, that the poor Lady quite frighted out of her Wits, ſcreams out, and flies in a miſerable Condition from the Bed in her Shift, leaving the Heroe in a moſt expiring Condition. The truſty Maid flies to her Miſtreſs, alarm'd with the noiſe, but was almoſt ſtruck down with the abominable ſtench when ſhe came to the Bed. The Knight was left to ſhift for himſelf, while *Abigal* took care to recover her Lady, by ſtripping and waſhing her all over in a Bath that was at the other end of the Houſe, and whither *Vermin* could by no means be admitted.

What to do he could not tell, he ſtill diſembogu'd, he ſtill purg'd to extremity, found himſelf as ſick within as ſtinking without; he heard that the Hour approach'd of Monſ. *de Montpenſier*'s Return, and did not believe matters would be amended by his finding him in that Condition in his Houſe, and his Lady's Bed. In ſhort, there being no Remedy, he was fain to dreſs himſelf in that condition, and ſcarce able to move, to get out into the Street, and make the beſt of his way to ſome *Bagnio*, or his own Lodging. The Evening was dark, yet as Fate would have it, one of his Companions half drunk, comes by with a Light, and knew him by his Cloaths, reels up to him, and going to embrace him, finds ſuch an unſavory flavour ſalute his Noſe, that he kept at a little more diſtance from him; he look'd very pale, and every now and then was taken with his paſt Evil.

His Friend finding him very ill, he enquir'd into the matter, but being unable to ſtand or talk, they went into the firſt *Cabaret*, whence ſending home for Linnen and his Servant, he was therefore put to Bed, but continuing ill, *Vander Vermin* told his Friend, that he verily believ'd that he was poiſon'd by a Lady who had that night granted him the Favour of making

king her Husband a Cuckold, and ſo related to him the Adventure with this particular, that after he had drunk a Diſh of Chocolate with her in the Intervals of Love, he found that ſtrange alteration in himſelf, nor did he expect to live till the Morning. But his Friend perſuaded him to ſend for a Phyſician, and try the means of recovery, altho' it ſhould fail of the End. A Gameſter is never fit to dye, and ſeldom willing in cold Blood, and therefore *Vander Vermin* comply'd with his Friends Advice; and a *Phyſician* was come, but found no Symptoms of a capacity of taking a little Reſt. Where we leave him, and return to the Lady, who fled from him in a moſt lamentable Pickle; almoſt dead, ſhe reach'd the Bath, and with much ado by the help of Sweet Waters and Perfumes, qualified the filthy Odours which her unfortunate Lover had beſtow'd upon her. *Lettice* (ſaid the Lady) was ever a Woman ſo unfortunate as I am, who after I had preſerv'd my Virtue as well as Reputation thus long, when Ill-luck and my hard Stars had reduc'd me to a neceſſity of yielding to this Creature, our very firſt meeting ſhould be ſo fatal to my Satisfaction. 'Tis ominous, or rather a favourable Warning to me at the beginning of my Folly, to adventure no more into ſo hazardous a Voyage. *Alas, Madam,* reply'd the Maid, *I am ſorry for that Misfortune; but I am not of your Mind, dear Lady, nor would I be at all dejected with one diſaſter, eſpecially ſince the Evil it has produc'd is ſo eaſily redreſs'd. But I would never more have to do with a* Dutchman, *who*

who by Nation is a ſlovenly Brute, fitter for the Gun-room than a fine Lady's Arms; he is always ſwilling, and when his Stomach is overcharg'd with Wine, he eaſes it in any Place without any Ceremony.

The good Lady being now well refreſh'd, and by degrees forgetting paſt Misfortunes, gave a willing ear to her Maids Advice, which was not thrown away upon her. For falling to Gaming again, ſhe had her uſual good Fortune, and obtain'd that Exchequer which *Vander Vermin* had fill'd, who being quite diſguſted with *France* by the laſt Adventure, left *Paris* and Intrigues to ſome new Comer. She then pick'd out among thoſe who adreſs'd to her the Duke of *Nemours*, who was then paſt fifty, but a Man of a tolerable Vigour for his Age, and whatever he wanted in Vigour of Body, he had in that of the Mind. He had long follow'd Madam *de Montpenſier* with a fruitleſs Addreſs, till ſhe having loſt at play, was oblig'd to borrow 200 *Louis d'Or's* of him, which he lent with ſuch a Grace, that ſhe eaſily imagin'd him a proper Man for her turn, and therefore reſolv'd to admit him to thoſe Favours ſhe had no Right to diſpoſe of. She gave him ſuch favourable looks, and ſuch diſtinguiſhing morals of Regard, that he had hopes, that his Happineſs would not terminate on this ſide of Enjoyment. He therefore, to engage her the more, was conſtantly with her at Play, and always prevented her asking him for Money, by conveying it privately when he perceiv'd her Occaſions. And having made ſuch approaches, he he was resolv'd not to lose his Aim by the Neglect of any Opportunity of finishing an Intrigue to his Satisfaction in the Arms of the finest Lady of *France.*

The lucky Minute is come, and a fair Opportunity, join'd with a very little Importunity, vanquish'd all the former Resolutions, and made the Duke of *Nemours* as happy as he then desir'd: But he was of a strange Temper, that the most violent Passion before Enjoyment, soon after turn'd to Indifference, Coldness and Aversion. The Lady soon discover'd the Change, and was heartily mortify'd at the Neglect. He avoided her Company as much as possible, and when he could not, he conceal'd that Disgust of her which so reign'd in his Bosom. The Lady one day press'd him to know the Cause, with a design to make that use of his Pocket as she had formerly done, but he frankly told her, ——— *You, Madam, owe my neglect to your own ill Conduct; for when you once admitted one to those Favours, beyond which you had nothing to give, you put an end to that Passion which, till satisfy'd, you might have turn'd to your Pleasure and my Slavery.* He would not stay to hear her Answer, but flung from her, and left the Room.

Two such Misfortunes in the two first Intrigues she had ever ventur'd on, should, one would think, have restor'd her to Virtue. But whatever Resolutions of Goodness they rais'd in her for a time, the next ill-luck at Play destroy'd them, and threw her into the very same necessities of hazarding her Happiness as well

as

as Reputation, by a criminal Commerce with ſome Bubble of Quality or other.

Thus ſhe run thro' the Ability and Patience of many a Lover, till her Husbands Chaplain, by his Intimacy with *Lettice*, and by his own Obſervation, had found out ſo much of her Conduct that he reſolv'd to prefer his Suit to her, he thinking that ſo delicious a Morſel ought not entirely to go by the Mouths of the Clergy, without paying them at leaſt a Tenth. He found his Opportunity of ſeeing her alone in an undreſs, and fit for ſuch an Aſſault as he had deſign'd, lying ſupinely on the Couch in a warm day, and her Limbs all diſtended. He got to her ſide, threw himſelf on his Knees, and ſeizing her Body, deſir'd her not to be ſurpriz'd till he had ſpoke a few Words to her, on which her Ruin depended. The Lady a little ſurpriz'd (but not diſpleas'd with the Perſon, who was very Handſom, and very Vigorous) ask'd him what he meant by this Inſolent Behaviour? to which the Prieſt thus briefly reply'd. *Madam, I muſt be very ſhort with you, I am privy to all your Intrigues from the Duke of* Nemours *down to this time, nay, I could go higher, to your ſcurvy Adventure with the* Dutchman; *I am, Madam, a Gentleman and a Scholar, my Friends who oblig'd me to take Orders, could not diveſt me of Humane Nature and Humane Paſſions; Beauty has the ſame force on me as on other Young-men. I have view'd your Charms ſo long with deſire, that to live longer without Enjoyment, is not in my Will nor my Power; and ſince you have not deny'd the laſt Favour to thoſe who lov'd you leſs, I am reſolv'd to attempt the ſame Happineſs, with this Comfort, that if I fail in my Happineſs, I ſhall not fail in my Revenge.*

Madam *de Montpenſier*, like a true Woman, deny'd all ſhe had been charg'd with, vow'd Revenge if he did not withdraw, and to call out if he preſs'd her any further; but he was too full of Luſt to be frighten'd with words; and therefore preſſing the matter home, ſhe eaſily ſuffer'd him to overcome, and was ſo well pleas'd with his Conduct, that ſhe continu'd the Intrigue with him, till the diſcovery was the Cauſe of her Confinement and the Prieſts Flight. For Madam having, in complaiſance to her Luſt of Gaming, gratify'd ſo many Gallants Luſts of *Venus*, it became a common talk, till at laſt it reach'd her Husbands Ear. This made him more watchful of her Actions, which brought him at laſt to find this Lady and the Prieſt in a very familiar Converſation, from which the Prieſt eſcap'd by leaping from the Window in a very uncanonical Condition, and the Lady to be confin'd to a Nunnery during her Husbands Life. And this was the unfortunate End of a Debauchery which firſt proceeded meerly from ſuch a Love of Gaming, which too many Lady's are poſſeſs'd with, without conſidering the fatal Conſequence of their Folly.

The Honeſt JILT.

BUT Madam *Grammont* had more Prudence and better Luck, for ſhe was affected much in the ſame manner, loſt all ſhe could

could get of her Husband, or on his Credit; and that Fund failing, was fain to run on Tick to the *Chevalier de Beauvin*: He was a gay Man, had a great deal of Money, and a very Handſome Wife of his own; who yet ſeem'd not ſo charming in his Eye as Madam *Grammont*, becauſe ſhe was his own. It happen'd that there was a particular Intimacy betwixt theſe two Lady's, ſo that they generally diſcover'd all the ſecrets of their Boſoms to one another, unleſs they were of a Nature that would not admit of any Partner. Madam *Grammont* thought that the Money ſhe had loſt to the *Chevalier* was of that Kind; and therefore had never told her one Syllable of the matter, till ſhe found her ſelf under a neceſſity of doing it to ſave her own Honour, and keep their Friendſhip inviolate.

The *Chevalier* had long had a ſecret Paſſion for Madam *de Grammont*, but never durſt utter a Word of it, till he had got her ſo much in his Debt, that he had reaſon to believe ſhe would grant him any thing, rather than apply to her Husband to diſcharge ſo conſiderable a Demand; and then he began to declare his Paſſion for her, and urg'd it with ſome vehemence. She being one day at play, and having loſt all her Money, was fain to apply to the *Chevalier* as uſual; but he denied her, without a Promiſe of a private meeting, where he might have the liberty of convincing her of the eagerneſs and reality of his Paſſion. She was too far engag'd in her Play to ſcruple, and therefore agrees to the Propoſal, and appoints the place, and like

a

a Woman of Honour met him accordingly, but was not a little ſurpriz'd to find him ſo very intent for more than ever ſhe deſign'd to allow him; however, ſhe had plac'd a Servant within call, to prevent the worſt of her Fears.

The *Chevalier* knowing nothing of this, was by no means deficient in promoting his own Cauſe. *Tho' I ought not* (ſaid Madam *Grammont* afraid to put him into Deſpair) *to have admitted an Addreſs of this nature, and I believe ſhould ne'r have born it from any other, yet ſome Men have ſuch a way, or natural Privilege, that we can't be angry at the Profeſſion we can't believe, and which perhaps might be more agreeable, if we could flatter our ſelves that what we heard was any other than a Method of Talking to all Ladies, who have Youth enough to keep 'em in countenance. Ah, Madam!* (interrupted the Chevalier) *what Proofs would you have of the reality of my Paſſion? I think I've given the greateſt in Nature; to fight for you would be far leſs, ſince that we do commonly for a meer Acquaintance: I've done that which we would not do for all the Ties in Nature; I have lent, (nay, given) you my Money, and that in no trifling Sum; nor did I ever deny you the command of my Purſe, to get this Opportunity of convincing you that I love you above all the World, and of telling you, that you have the advantage of me in Fortune, having it in your power not only to acquit your ſelf of all your Debts of Honour with Honour, but at the ſame time, and by the ſame act, of beſtowing a Reward on a Paſſion, that without it muſt deſtroy my Life, in the moſt exquiſite Torment of a languiſhing Deſpair, which is unworthy your Juſtice, unworthy your Charms. It would be be unworthy my Justice indeed,* (assum'd Madam *de Grammont*) *should I listen to so rude as well as unjust a Request, of regarding neither my own Honour nor my Husband's, the Laws of God, or the Duty of a Wife. No, no,* Chevalier, *you would make me pay Extortion for the Money you lent to my Folly, if you require a Compensation so infinitely beyond its value. I can never think the* Chevalier *so mercenary in his Aims, as to take the advantage of my Misfortunes to accomplish my Ruin: The Offer had been more supportable had it been done without such Bond as might make my Grant the Effect more of Fear than Inclination.*

I protest (interrupted the Chevalier) *I'll take no advantage that Fortune has given me over you; I will not press my Passion any farther at this time, that you may no more upbraid me with a thing so far from my Temper: But, Madam, when I have convinc'd you of this Error, by giving you a Discharge of all you owe me, I hope you'l no more scruple the sincerity of my Love.*

Saying these words, he rose up, and with a profound respect took leave of Madam *Grammont*, and the next time he met her he deliver'd her a Paper, which contain'd a general Release of all his Demands. She took it with a gracious Smile. *This, Madam, is a Sacrifice to my Passion; yet offer'd with as free and hearty a Zeal as ever Bigot pray'd to his Favourite Saint: Admit me therefore, as a Lover worth your Regard, and continue not to keep me at such a distance, as makes a perpetual Winter in my Bosom, which if the Sun of your Smiles shine not quickly upon, will freeze me to death.*

Madam

Madam *Grammont* was infinitely pleas'd at this Present, and treating the *Chevalier* with all the Complaisance he could expect in such a place, she retir'd, fully resolv'd never more to play, lest having thus escap'd the wreck of her Honour and Reputation, she might split the next time without any Refuge. She was always civil to the *Chevalier* when she saw him, but carefully avoided all Opportunities of hearing or trying how far his Passion might carry him to the prejudice of her Virtue. The *Chevalier* was no Fool, and easily perceiv'd she had jilted him out of his Money, making so cold a Return to his Passion, that he had no reason to expect she would ever give him that Relief which alone could render him satisfaction. He could not blame her for any breach of Promise or dishonourable Conduct, but only himself, for over-acting his Part, in throwing up the only secure Key to his Treasure; however, the more difficult he found the Conquest, the more eager were his Desires; he watch'd her closer than ever he did his Wife, and waited with more Diligence than ever, yet no Hopes appear'd; the Lady was shy, tho' civil, and so he return'd in his state of Despair, till a sudden Thought came into his Head: He could not imagin a Lady so given to Gaming could at once so entirely vanquish that Inclination so far, as not to be won by Art to a Relapse; he resolv'd therefore to set some Friend to draw her in, without telling him the End he aim'd at. The Person imploy'd was well acquainted with all the Niceties of this Art, and in a little time, by an admirable Addreſs, got her to play, won all her Money, and got her conſiderably in his Debt; when the *Chevalier*, as by chance, comes into the Room full of the uſual Reſpect he us'd to pay her, and in his Eyes even more Fondneſs and Paſſion than he us'd to expreſs. She bluſht at his Preſence, ſeem'd in ſome confuſion, and would have left off, but being ſo deep in, was willing to reduce it to ſuch a Sum as ſhe might venture to ask of her Husband; and Fortune proving unkind, ſhe ſtrove in vain, the Debt ſtill encreaſing, till at length tir'd with ill-luck, ſhe reſolv'd to give over. Her Antagoniſt was as willing ſhe, but preſs'd her for an Acknowledgment of the Debt; ſhe ſeem'd unwilling, but the Chevalier advis'd her to it, for he would certainly go to her Husband and demand the Money. He enquiring the Sum, proffer'd her to pay it. *Ah! Chevalier*, (ſaid ſhe) *I am more afraid of your lending it, than of his demanding it of my Husband, tho' that too would render me unhappy. Have I, Madam, ſo ill behav'd my ſelf on ſuch an occaſion*, (ſaid he) *that I deſerve not to be truſted? You have behav'd your ſelf too well* (replied the Lady) *in ſome particulars, tho' other things give me no little pain; however it would be a foul Injuſtice to try another Friend on this unlucky Occaſion, when you proffer your Service.*

He gave her Bills to the value of her Loſs, which ſhe deliver'd to the Chevalier's Friend with an abſolute Reſolution of never playing more, promiſing to diſcharge the Chevalier's Debt the firſt opportunity. Now he having got her again in his power, reſolv'd not to play

ſo

ſo fooliſh a Game, as not to make uſe of his preſent Advantage for his own Happineſs. He grew very importunate, plainly telling her, that nothing but the laſt Favour could reſtrain him from ſeeking his Money of Mr. *Grammont*; that he had already ſacrific'd ſo much Money to imaginary Joys, that therefore he muſt have thoſe which are more ſubſtantial.

Madam *Gramont* knew her Husbands Temper, and that he would preſently imagin, that a Woman who had loſt ſo much Money with a Man, would not be very ſcrupulous of paying it at another Game, if he would be ſuch a Coxcomb to accept it ſo: She was at her Wits-end to know what to do, a thouſand times curſing her own Folly, who being once deliver'd from the like Diſtreſs by a ſingular Favour of Fortune, (her own Addreſs and the Caprice of the Chevalier) had madly again thrown her ſelf into the very ſame Dilemma. She knew that ſhe muſt be either newly guilty, or be thought ſo by him, who only could make her unhappy by ſuch a Suſpicion; but ſhe would rather chuſe an innocent Miſery than an aggravated Guilt, yet fain would avoid both.

After a mature Debate in her Mind, ſhe reſolv'd to Jilt the Chevalier again, but in a manner more agreeable than the former: For tho' ſhe would not admit him to her Arms, his Pleaſure could not be the leſs, ſo long as he thought himſelf in her Boſom. Madam *de Beauvin* was much of her ſtature and ſize, both exquiſitely ſhap'd, nor was ſhe in reality any thing inferiour to her in Beauty, tho' the deprav'd Appetite of her Husband (desirous of Change) made him slight her, because his own.

Madam *de Grammont* took the first opportunity of getting a place of free Converse with her dear Friend Madam *de Beauvin*, and being alone, after some previous Discourse, —— My Dear, (said she) I have always thought my Happiness as uncommon as great, in possessing the Friendship of a Lady of so much Sense, as to be so rarely cross'd in all the Duties of so sacred a Tie as Amity, as you are. How few of our Sex have any Notion of it! how much fewer ever reduce any part of it into Practice! suffer me therefore to value my Felicity in this Particular extreamly. I can't imagin why the Men run us down on this head, as incapable of such a Virtue. It is the Vanity of their Nature, (replied Madam *de Beauvin*) they would engross all that's great and glorious to themselves, tho' they perform no more than the weakest of our Sex, at least in our days; but if Men are always the same, we may justly suppose it meer Boast: Mean while I find in my Bosom such Sentiments for my dear *Grammont*, that there's nothing I could not sacrifice to her Content. Ah, my Dear! (replied Madam *Grammont*) we easily think so when the Trial's at a distance, but when present, small Difficulties stifle all those generous Notions. That's too unkind (assum'd *de Beauvin*) to come from your dear Mouth, put me to that Trial, and then condemn me if I plead any Excuse. That Assurance (said *Grammont*) is so kind, and utter'd with such an Air of Sincerity, that I must

not

not let ſlip an Occaſion whereon my Life and Happineſs depends, tho' I fear it may give you ſome Pain. Speak freely (ſaid *Beauvin)* and ſecure of no Repulſe, if in my power. 'Tis only in your power, my Dear, (replied *Grammont)* nor can any but your ſelf relieve my Diſtreſs. Make no more Ceremony, (aſſum'd the other) but tell me my Part, and ſee how cordially I'll perform it.

Know then, my Dear, (ſaid *Grammont)* that I have been ſuch a Fool as to be drawn into Play, and that too deep to own to my Husband, whoſe ſuſpicious Temper you are not altogether unacquainted with: Your Husband coming in, I thought by the Friendſhip that was betwixt us I might make uſe of his Purſe, reſolving to pay him again out of my Allowance by ſuch degrees as might not be perceiv'd by my Husband. 'Tis true, he complied with my deſires, and ſupplied my occaſions, but would you believe it, my Dear? —Shall I proceed? Can I tell you the reſt? Can I make you uneaſie? 'Tis impoſſible, let me rather periſh unhappy.

This had fir'd Madam *Beauvin*, and made her the more uneaſie to know the Sequel, but having preſs'd her Friend with impatience, ſhe went on in this manner: Since you command me, my Dear, I will proceed. Could you imagin him guilty of ſuch Perfidy to you, and ſuch Injuſtice to me? He preſſes me to injure both my Husband and you, or vows to betray all. Villain! (interrupts Madam *de Beauvin*) are all my Charms then vaniſh'd? am I grown old and ugly already? Nothing of this, (replied Madam *de Grammont*) you are as charming as he is false; but Men, who accuse us of Fickleness, are the most inconstant Creatures in the World; nay, they would engross the Folly to themselves, as the Prerogative of their Sex, and yet grudge us the innocent Liberties of our Birth: However, all is well yet, let me but prevail with you to supply my place, I'll make the Appointment, and you shall give him greater Happiness than he could receive from me, could I induce my self to be false to you and my Husband.

In short, Madam *Grammont* easily prevail'd with her Friend to lie in the Bed in her Apartment, and receive her Husband in the dark as his Mistress, not his Wife.

This Part so well play'd, she appoints the Chevalier to come to her House when her Husband was abroad; she receives him in an Undress, the more to deceive him, and suffers him to ravish a thousand Kisses from her, till she led him into the dark Chamber, even to the Bed, and there giving him the slip, left him to his Wife. The Entertainment of new Lovers was so long, that Mr. *de Grammont* returns in the mean while, and seeing his Wife look so charming in her Dishabille, was very fond and amorous upon her, till at last pressing her to go into the Bedchamber, she refus'd, which Refusal continuing, he grew jealous, and swore she had hid her Gallant in that Apartment, from whom his coming had disturb'd her. She was in a mighty strait what to do, and now saw a necessity of discovering all, or being yet more unfortunate; so assuring

him

him of her Innocence, desir'd him to sit down, and she would confess the whole matter to him: With some Persuasions he allow'd her time to remove his Doubts, and clear her own Innocence; then falling on her Knees, she ask'd his Pardon for venturing to play beyond her own Stock, and so gave him an account of all that had past since her last misfortune, which was all that was necessary to let her Husband know. He discovered his Resentment for her playing, but could not but approve of her Conduct in preserving her own Honour, and putting his own Wife upon him, which when he was satisfied of, he told her, he should be more easie.

This Discourse had held so long, that *Grammont*'s Voice was heard by the Lover, as busie as he was; the Chevalier's Wife took this Opportunity to get from her Husband, assuring him, that she heard Mr. *Grammont* in the Antichamber, bid him lie still, and she would go remove him to a more safe place whilst he made his retreat. Secure of her self, and ready with an Excuse, she comes out, to the no small satisfaction of *Grammont*, who found he had made a discovery of all the Affair. She advis'd Madam *Grammont* to keep him in fear a while, and therefore, that Mr. *Grammont* should press to go into the Room, and Madam should dissuade and wheedle him thence; and that while she went to set him at liberty, they would retire into the next Room and hear all that pass'd betwixt 'em. This was put in execution: But while Madam *Grammont* went to free him, Mr. *Grammont* had a few minutes to express his Passion to Madam *de Beauvin*, who look'd then infinitely charming. *Madam*, (ſaid he) *how could the* Chevalier *be ſo ignorant, as to prefer my Wife to you, who excel her more than the Silver Moon the leſſer Stars of the Night? Muſt he come off thus? But do both your ſelf and me that Juſtice which Fleſh and Blood commands: You've done enough for your Friendſhip to my Wife, do ſomething in Juſtice for your ſelf and me.*

He ſaid much more, and preſs'd his Affair ſo handſomly, being himſelf a very graceful Perſon, that he found Madam *de Beauvin* lik'd him better than his Wife did the Chevalier; but by that time ſhe came back, which was very ſpeedily, he had made ſuch a progreſs, that he had no reaſon to ſuſpect a Succeſs anſwerable to his Deſires.

Madam *de Grammont* returning, told them, that tho' ſhe had found him in a terrible Fear, yet if ſhe had not alarm'd him with the nearneſs of her Husband, ſhe had been ſtill in danger of calling out for their aſſiſtance; but, that he would not go till ſhe had made another Appointment for a ſecond rendezvous, which ſhe had done. She beg'd her Husband, ſince he knew her Misfortune, to pay the Debt, which ſhe would allow out of her Pin-mony, leſt out of a Vanity common to Men, he ſhould give himſelf the liberty of talking, at the expence of her Reputation.

Grammont allow'd of her Care, and promis'd to perform it, but pleaded as yet want of Money, and that in the mean while he muſt be kept in his Errour. Whilſt Madam *Grammont* left them a few minutes, he made an Appointment

ment with her fair Friend to come an hour before the time, and he would take care his Wife ſhould be out of the way, and her Husband denied admittance. This was punctually obſerv'd, and *Grammont* had the ſatisfaction of being fully reveng'd on him who had deſign'd him ſuch foul play, and believ'd that he himſelf had eſcap'd the like Shame.

Things paſs'd in this manner; when *Grammont*, unſatisfied with his Revenge till his Cuckold was ſenſible of his condition, took care to have his Wife out of the way, and got the Chevalier admitted and conducted to the Bedchamber, as if expel'd the Field of Battel. He comes, was conducted in, carried to the Bed, and finds a Man upon it with a Woman; concluding it to be the Husband, would have withdrawn, but *Grammont* ſeizing him by the Hand, drags him to it, throws open the Curtains, and diſcovers the Chevalier's Lady upon it, in a panic fear of the Event. The Interview was ſurprizing to all but *Grammont*, who had deſign'd it. *What* (ſaid Grammont) *is your buſineſs in my Bedchamber, eſpecially at an hour which I dedicated to Pleaſure? Speak Madam,* (ſaid he, as to his Wife) *do you know of this Aſſignation? Ha!* (ſaid he) *who have I been happy with? Not with my own Wife! I thought the Charms were too tranſporting for her to beſtow.* The Chevalier confounded, did not know what to ſay, till the Lady getting off the Bed, began thus;

I am ſorry for this Event of what was deſign'd, but 'tis the Effect of your Villany and Treachery: I, by my Friend's deſire, have frequently receiv'd you

in

in her place, and this day expected you as I us'd to do; but how Mr. Grammont *came to deceive me I know not, for in all my Caresses I took him for the Chevalier. Madam, I think the Event so just, that I cannot be displeas'd at it; for knowing nothing of this Affair, I came to lie down and take a little Rest, but finding a Lady in the Bed, concluded it must be my Wife, not imagining that any body else could be there, and to seize what I thought my Right; I had remain'd in Ignorance, had not your coming in that manner rais'd my Jealousie, and made me seize your Hand, whence all this Discovery arose, in which, by a strange Miracle, we that had committed the guilty Fact are chiefly innocent; and you, who have been disappointed in all your Designs without the guilty Fact, are only guilty.*

In the midst of this confusion Madam *Grammont* comes in, and is infinitely surpriz'd to find 'em all together: The Chevalier was the most confounded, begs all that was past might be buried in Oblivion; and, to purchase it, he would remit his Demands of the Money he had lent her. Thus was the Bubbler bubbl'd, and the honest Jilt jilted; but finding out the Falshood of her Friend, she prevail'd with her Husband to leave the Court for the Country.

I could tell you a thousand Examples more of the ill Effects of GAMING, but I remember that I ought not to take up all your Time, but leave some of the remaining part of this Night to my Brethren. Here my little *Louis d'Or* gave over speaking, and then my *Guinea*, after a small pause, began in this manner,

Against

Against GAMING.

SInce our *Italian* Companion has began his Discourse on this as well as the former Subject, with a Vindication of the Folly and Vice we have talk'd of, I shall likewise say something in opposition to it. First, the wretched State of his Country, and a Relish of their Pride and Vanity, appears through his destructive Paradox; but the ill effect of their Politics, in the ignorance and destruction of all the People of their Country, is a very weak motive to engage in any of their Principles. What he says, indeed, smells much of the *Conclave*, but that is the worst proof in the World of its Validity and Reason. Thus in *Gaming*, he has given it a turn, as an excuseable Mode, and would make you believe, that there is nothing in it of want of Sense or want of Honesty. Honesty indeed he laughs at, as a meer Notion of the Schools; but the *Tramontani* are yet happy enough to have it in Practice in all Degrees and Stations, and that by Men of the best Sense and Understandings, Fools having not Matter enough to make an Honest Man of; at least they have not yet arriv'd to such an abandon'd Degree of Vice, as to reduce it to Principles of Practice, and disown those external Truths on which the Maxims of Morality are founded. If the Practice of Virtue is not so general as it might be, yet all allow the Excellence of it,

Thus

Thus in *Gaming* it ſelf, ſearch all the Court, City, and Country, and you ſhall not (or very rarely indeed) find one Man of Senſe a Biggot to the Folly. Your practic'd Gameſters, your Sharpers of all ſorts, from the Lord to the Footman, are the moſt ignorant and ſenſeleſs Rogues of the Creation. The Faſhion and Ill Company have, I confeſs, drawn in ſome Men of tolerable Underſtanding, but ſcarce one of fine Parts. The Sharpers of Quality are Men without Honour, Generoſity or Senſe, and have nothing to diſtinguiſh them from the Mob but their Title. They, like our *Signior* here, alter the diſtinction of Right and Wrong, call a Debt a Man is bubbled of in Play, a Debt of Honour; but that which is due for Goods received from a Tradeſman they never pay till they are forc'd, by having their Coaches and Horſes ſeiz'd as they ride the Streets. The vulgar Sharper generally riſes from the Refuſe and Scum of the People, and having no ſenſe of Honour, Riches, or Religion, he is qualify'd to ſtick at no Roguery that will fill his Pocket, and raiſe him to make a figure in a Coach, whoſe original Station, both by Nature and Fortune, was at its Tail. Yet when theſe abandon'd Wretches have got Money enough, they are admitted to the Tables of Lords, and the Beds of Ladies. Thoſe very Fellows, who (without the Advantages which they derive from Cheating) would have made their Servants have kick'd out of doors, now by their Succeſs of Roguery they careſs in their Boſoms. They hang the poor Thief, that robs

but

but for Subſiſtence, and takes away but half a Crown, when they protect and reſpect the Thief of a Gameſter, who has bubbl'd (that is, robb'd) hundreds of their Eſtates. The Men of Quality can, without any Indignation, ſee Sir *William* walk in a Thredbare Coat and Piſs-burnt Wigg, and thoughtleſs *S*——*s* in his Coach and Six. 'Tis true, a Man that is ſo egregious a Fool as to loſe an Eſtate to a Sharper, deſerves as little Pity and Redreſs as he that ventures his Health with a known and common Whore; 'tis true, both may eſcape by prodigious Accident, but that is owing to Fortune, not their Prudence. Yet methinks Men of Quality, who are proud enough in the wrong place, ſhould value their Dignity more than to proſtitute it to the Power of Sharpers; and the beſt Remedy that I know of, is to make all Summs loſt at play forfeited to the State.

The Parliament conſiſting of Men that are, have been, or are to be marry'd to a ſtrange ſort of Infatuation, I wonder they don't put a ſtop to that Evil that may ruin their Sons, debauch their Wives and Daughters, and render their Families infamous. But if the Wiſdom of your Nation paſs this over as a *Bagatelle*, I ſhall not trouble my ſelf about the matter, but give you ſome Account of what I have diſcover'd in my Progreſs through the Hands of the Sharpers and Gameſters, both Gentlemen and Ladies.

There are ſeveral Claſſes and Clans of theſe Vermin, from the Court to the Mob; and thoſe

ſo

ſo various, that to dwell on each would wear out many Nights in my Diſcourſe. There is no Extravagance that a diſtemper'd Fancy can form, that is ſo madly whimſical as a Gaming-room about midnight, where nothing is diſcover'd of Reaſon or rational Being; 'tis a *Bedlam*, and e'ry one that loſes expreſſes a various kind of madneſs; which has made one ſometimes wonder at the vanity of Men in aſſuming to themſelves the Preheminence of the reſt of the Creation; whilſt his Conduct diſcovers more of *Chaos*, and leſs of Deſign, than the moſt Senſual and Brutal part of the Animal Kingdom.

Theſe *Gameſters* or *Sharpers* are a-kin to the Devil their Maſter, for they not only lye in wait for the Ruin of themſelves, but their *Setters* the *Sweetners*, and the deſperate Inſtruments that go about the World daily ſeeking whom they can devour. Some frequent the Coffee-houſes of Note, and the Chocolate-houſes; others the Play-houſe, where while the young Heir comes to expoſe his Shapes to bewitch the Lady's Eyes, and ſteal away their innocent Hearts, the *Setter* gets into their acquaintance, and under the ſhape of a profeſſing Friend, gay Gallant, thoughtleſs Rake, grave Adviſer, drunken Scoundrel, or any other Appearance he thinks moſt likely to take with the young Gudgeon, wheedles him to a Bottle, and delivers him over to the Executioners, the *Sweetners*, and the *Sharpers*; who by peculiar Arts only known to themſelves and the Devil, work the moſt averſe by degrees up to Gaming, and then

then manage them as they think moſt conducive to their own Advantage. The *Setter* all the while is concern'd for his Friend, a Bubble to appearance like him, tho' as ſoon as the Coaſt is clear he ſhares the Spoil with the barbarous *Rapparees*. Yet as villainouſly ſcandalous as this Setting Trade is, I have known Agents, Envoys, and other weighty Negotiators rais'd out of their Tribe, and many a Man of Quality has no more ſcrupled the ſetting a Friend, than a Man of Mode pimping for his Friend, or Cuckolding him. Nay, 'tis now grown ſo common, that it's profeſt among the Gentlemen of the Town for as lawful a Vocation, as any Corporation; and it is thought that a Miniſtry may come to get them incorporated into a Body Politic, and then I know not but St. *James*'s and *Covent-Garden* may entirely rival the *Change*; and that there may be more Adventures at *White*'s and *Bradbury*'s, than to the *Levant*, or both the *Indies*.

Tho' there be a thouſand Tricks in the Play betwixt Man and Man, yet that betwixt Man and Woman is ten times more hazardous. For the Man-Sharper endeavours to diſguiſe the Cheat ſo, as to deceive you into an Opinion, that you have loſt your Money on the Square, but the Woman-Sharper thinks you oblig'd in Complaiſance to overlook the moſt clumſey of her Impoſitions. And to take notice of a Lady's cheating, is thought an unpardonable piece of ill-breeding. 'Tis true, there are other Ladies, who are leſs ſkill'd in theſe Arts, that will be as great Bubbles as the Men, and when they

they have play'd away all their ready-Money engage their Charms than in this Nation; tho' perhaps they have not made ſo great a noiſe elſewhere. I ſhall give you two or three Inſtances, and ſo put an end to your Attention this Night.

The Foul Extravagant.

THE Lady—— has one Leg ſhorter than the other, her Back overlooks her Head, and her Face is as formidable as *Meduza*'s; ſhe has but one Eye, like the *Cyclops*, but that not in the middle, ſpacious like the Grecian Shield, or Sun, but ſmall as that of a Pig; her Noſe thin, high and crooked; her Teeth rotten, her Mouth wide, her Lips thin and ſtiff, her Breath contagious, her Neck long and lean, her Breaſts flabby, her Arms, Hands, and Fingers long and ſcraggy, her Legs crooked, and her Feet large. Her Mind is not furniſh'd with greater Beauties than her Body: She is Vain, Talkative, Loud and Silly. With all theſe Defects ſhe brought her Lord a great Fortune, but with it ſuch a Spirit of Gaming, that would bring one ten times as great to a Concluſion.

Sometimes ſhe was a conſiderable Winner, ſeldom roſe from the Table without carrying off ſome hundreds. But Fortune, that is never fixt, various as the Wind, and as uncertain, by degrees turn'd her Back to her, till ſhe had now loſt all that ſhe had ever gain'd, to a handſom young Fellow that had been Page to one

of

of her Family; and who being born a Gentleman, had apply'd himſelf to the moſt honourable way of raiſing himſelf from Contempt, by getting a Commiſſion in the Guards. This brought him to Court, and a handſom Aſſurance to the Baſſet-Table, and to Piquet with the Ladies, where meeting generally with good-luck, he at laſt got Money enough to ſet up for a profeſs'd Gameſter. My Lady—— happen'd to play with him one Night; and tho' ſhe had never till then found any motion in her Heart of Love, or any Deſire but of Gain, yet by a certain Fatality ſhe was ſo ſmitten with the Captain, that ſhe could not mind her play, but loſt all her Money, and ventur'd on upon Tick. Which ſhe ſurely paid the next time ſhe ſaw him, and challeng'd him to a freſh Encounter, in which ſhe was always a double loſer, both of her Money and her Affections; yet bewitch'd with both the Love of him and of Play, ſhe ſtill renew'd her Folly as opportunity ſerv'd. When Money could not be got at home, ſhe would take up Jewels, Plate, or any other Goods, which pawning for ready-Money, ſhe threw it away in the ſame manner.

But nothing gave her more diſturbance than that ſhe ſhould loſe all this Mony to a Man that was yet inſenſible of her Paſſion, and whom ſhe could not tell how to acquaint with her Folly, for fear it ſhould not prove ſo agreeable to him as ſhe could deſire: She made all the dumb Signs imaginable, by ogling him with her ſingle Peeper; but he finding nothing agreeable in her Countenance, seldom disoblig'd his Satisfaction so much as to look at so shocking a Phiz. The difficulty of her Amour heighten'd her Desire more, but still with as little hopes of Success. She at last resolves to write to him, and to trust no Body with the Affair; the next time they plaid, she convey'd it into his Pocket with her own Hands. When the Captain came home and found some occasion for Paper, he found the Lady's Letter, and seeing a Womans Hand, he soon open'd it with some eagerness, being both in his Vigour, and a passionate Admirer of the Sex. No Body can express his surprize when he found it subscrib'd by my Lady——: He threw it aside at first without reading, being so disappointed in his Expectation; but thinking, perhaps, that it might only be to borrow some Money of him, since he had won so much of her of late, he took it up again, and read in it these Words:

I doubt not but you'll be as much surpriz'd in the reading as I was confounded in the writing of this Letter. I'm likewise sensible of the Imprudence of letting you know how much my Happiness and Misery are in your power, but my Fortune is alwaies subject to yours, I could never win of you since we play'd together; and indeed, I must confess, I alwaies found less Desire to win of you, than of any-body I ever play'd with; and I wish that the least valuable thing I have lost to you were my Mony, that I should not regret, that would give me no pain; but I have (dear Captain) lost a Jewel to you, which if you are not generous enough to restore, I'm destin'd to undergo all the Disquiet in Nature: My Heart is the Right of another, yet You have won it of me.—— I am confounded and asham'd; I dare say no more, spare my Blushes, oblige me not to explain

plain my self any farther, but imagin the rest, and you will find me ——— Yours eternally.

The Captain had ſcarce Patience to read it over, and when he had, knew not what courſe to take; he was unwilling to loſe the Advantage of wining her Money, and yet could not prevail on himſelf to think of any Affair with a Perſon ſo forbidding as my Lady. At laſt he reſolv'd to take no notice of the Letter; as if he had never met with it, and to paſs the time with her in the uſual manner, where being in public, he could fear no plainer declaration of her Paſſion, than which nothing could be more terrible to him. This would not ſecure his Repoſe, my Lady ——— when ſhe ſaw him next, ſurvey'd his Eyes and his Countenance, but could make no diſcovery, that could give her the leaſt hopes of Satisfaction. She playd with him again, loſt her Money once more; was e'rey moment tortur'd with a greater uneaſieneſs, and at a greater loſs how to inform her ſelf whether he yet knew her Condition, and if not, how to make him more ſenſible of it. At laſt ſhe roſe from the Table — *Sure* (ſaid ſhe) *no Woman was ever ſo unlucky, I'll play with you no more; I ſhall be ruin'd if I go on* — He made her a Bow, and withdrew, without ſaying one word. This was ſo mortifying a ſight to her, that ſhe was almoſt diſtracted betwixt Deſire and Deſpair, till coming home, ſhe was reſolv'd to ſend him another Letter, but by ſuch hands, as that ſhe ſhould be ſure of its coming to him: She went therefore to her Scrutore, and having wrote and ſeal'd up her

Billet, gave it to her Servant-maid, and bid her be sure to give it to the Captain, and bring her an Answer.

The Captain, as his ill Fate ordain'd it, was at home, and receiving the Billet from his Man, who told him the Messenger staid for an Answer, was oblig'd to open it, that he might not be so rude as to put an Affront on a Lady of her Quality who sent it: He expected nothing but the nauseous Subject of the former, but opening it, found the following Words.

Is it possible, that you could have a Letter from me, and take no notice of the receipt? What Injury have I done you, that you use me so barbarously? But perhaps you did not understand me, I was too obscure for you to come at my meaning. Ah! no, barbarous Man! you too well understood my meaning; you too well knew your own Power, and therefore deal with me in so cruel a manner; you saw I lov'd you, and therefore you ungenerously mean to insult me with a Silence far more odious than the most unkind Letter could ever have prov'd. Must I repeat my own Infamy? Must I tell you again that I love you? What must I do? Inform me, insensible Creature! let me know what you would have me do to convince you of my Love, and gain yours. 'Tis true, I am not Mistress of such Charms as are able to penetrate your cold Marble Heart; alas! I am sensible of my own Defects; yet certainly Love is a Merit that e'ry one can't pretend to: Nor do I think my self so very despicable, but that I might expect a Return to my Passion. Consider your self, and consider me, then I shall not despair.

The Captain was more confounded than if a Bomb had faln into his Chamber, and was as much to seek in his Reply to this Dunn of Love, as he had been in former days to answer an importunate Dunn for Money: He knew the

the Nature of slighted Women, and was sensible that a Woman of her condition was generally more affected with a thing of that nature than a Woman of Beauty. He therefore, after a little consideration, resolv'd to return her this Answer:

Your Billet, Madam, has doubly surpriz'd me; first, by your accusing me of a Letter from your Ladiship's fair Hand, which I never yet saw; and next, with letting me know of the Honour you do me, in having more favourable Thoughts of me than ever I could merit. I must confess, Madam, if I could be so vain as to think you mean any thing but a Banter by this, I would tell you, that I have not forgot the Honour I have had of being in your Family in my Childhood; nor should I ever presume to entertain a Thought against my Lord's Reputation and Honour: But as I am convinc'd your Ladiship (at most) designs it for a Trial, I have nothing to reply, but that I hope your Ladiship will not pursue a Trial of his Honesty who has nothing else to value himself upon. Madam, I love you too well (that is, I pay too awful a Veneration to your Quality and Merit) ever to entertain a Thought injurious to either, but shall alwaies be proud to subscribe my self, Madam, ——— Your faithful Vassal.

Tho' this Answer might have given my Lady ——— sufficient reason to believe that she was far from touching his Heart, or that she could never expect to arrive at that Happiness which she hop'd, in his Arms, yet she could not help sending him another Billet, to this purpose:

You affect (my dear Captain) an Ignorance you never can be guilty of; my Words are too plain to need any Comment: But, to remove all Doubts, I assure you that I was sincere, wrote what I meant, and design'd no Trial but that of your Love. If I am to be happy in that, let me know it; if I am to perish in Despair, let me know it:

Keep me not in Doubt, the worst state of Hope and Desire. I cannot live without you, and you have no reason to prefer airy Notions to my Satisfaction. If you have any Obligations to the Family, discharge 'em in loving me, who am the best of it, and add not Ingratitude to Insensibility. Save my Blushes, and put not on me so improper a Task as usurping your Part.

The poor Captain was puzzl'd what to answer; yet, after some study, he sent her a Letter in Terms as ambiguous as possible, neither to cut off, nor too much heighten her Hope. The Maid which my Lady —— us'd to send was a very pretty fresh-colour'd Country Girl, and who had Charms enough to give the Captain Desires, which he press'd every time she came to bring a Letter from her Lady, at last to that degree of rudeness, that she had great difficulty of escaping with her Virginity; so that when her Lady would have sent her again, she plainly refus'd to go, and on an Enquiry discover'd her Reason. My Lady was heartily mortified at the Story, finding that while she sigh'd in vain for the Pleasure, her Maid had it press'd on her farther than she approv'd; but unable to resist the impetuosity of her Desires, she bid her Maid make an Appointment with him in the dark the next Evening, who scrupling to comply with her Lady's Commands, she assur'd her that she would venture to engage him in her stead.

The Appointment is made, and the ready Lover came to the agreed Rendezvous, and, much to the Lady's satisfaction, acquitted himself like a Man of Honour, when both (tir'd and weary) gave themselves some Repose. My

My Lord, who had long taken a liking to this Girl, ſuppoſing his Lady was faſt aſleep in her own Bed, ſtole up in his Night-gown to the Maid's Chamber, to ſurprize her in Bed, and ſo at once come to a Poſſeſſion, without the troubleſome Fatigue of the impertinent Approaches to a Chamber-maid; ſo throwing off his Night-gown, happen'd to get into Bed on the Lady's ſide, and finding her aſleep, made no ſcruple to awake her in the moſt agreeable manner; My Lady—— little thinking that ſhe had her own dear Husband in her Arms, awaking in Loves Tranſport, cry'd a little too loud, *My dear Captain, what will you kill me with pleaſure?* My Lord was ſoon ſenſible whom he had poſſeſt, and puzzl'd at her words, imagin'd ſomething more in the matter; ſo quitting the Bed, he concluded the Maid and her Miſtreſs had chang'd Beds on purpoſe to abuſe him doubly; and therefore ſtealing down Stairs, he takes his Candle and Sword with him to his Lady's Bed-Chamber, where, to confirm his Suſpicion, he found *Abigail* aſleep, and his Valet de Chambre cloſe by her. The Bed-Cloaths were all off, and ſhe was naked, with nothing conceal'd but part of her Breaſt, over which the Valet had thrown his Arms. The ſight was ſo tempting, that tho' my Lord knew whom he was to follow, he could not reſolve to paſs without ſome Satisfaction in her Arms, which he thought now doubly his due on demand. He therefore gently pricking the Valet with the point of his Sword, made him ſtart from his Trance, who found his Lord arm'd, as he fear'd, to his Ruin. My Lord, cry'd out the Wretch, indeed it is not my Lady, it is Mrs. *Abigail*, whom I have secretly marry'd, I beg therefore for my Life. My Lord bid him not make a noise, and tho' he was satisfy'd his pretence of Marriage was all a common Refuge on such occasion, yet if he would silently away, and get two or three of his Fellow-Servants together, ready to go with him, he would pardon the Insolence he had offer'd to his Lady's Bed. Now Mrs. *Abigail* lay all this while in a terrible Agony, having caught the Sheet and thrown over her, to hide what had already been seen. The Valet being gone, my Lord shut the Door, and coming to the Bed-side, told Mrs. *Abigail* plainly, that she had been in a Confederacy with the Lady to abuse him in the Arms of another; that tho' he ought in reason to take away her Life for such a Treachery, yet she had discover'd such Charms, that by an immediate Compliance she might make her own Peace. With that my Lord setting down the Candle, throwing off his Night-gown and aside the Sheet, seiz'd the trembling *Abigail*, who was pleas'd that any thing could appease her Lord when so justly provok'd. She told him all that had pass'd betwixt her Lady and the Captain, and how he imagin'd that he had her, not my Lady, in his Arms.

My Lord having satisfy'd himself for that time, call'd up his Servants, and went with Lights to see for his Prig, not doubting but he should find them as he left them. But the Lady and the Captain having come to an underſtanding after his departure, the Gentleman was gone, and the Lady with him. The Houſe is ſearch'd all over, but no Body to be found, till they ſaw the Saſh in the Parlour-Window not ſhut cloſe, and concluded, that they had made their Eſcape that way. So ſending all to Bed, he took Mrs. *Abigail* to his own, vowing, that if ſhe had no more to do with his Valet, and prov'd conſtant to him, he would take care of her as long as ſhe liv'd.

The Morning came on, and a Letter was brought him from his Lady, to own her Folly, excuſe her Gallant, and let him know, that in making her Eſcape, ſhe had in the dark faln into a Cellar-Window of a new Building, that had been careleſly left open by the Workmen; that ſhe deſir'd to dye at home, ſince ſhe could not out-live the Bruiſe and the breaking of two Ribbs. And ſcarce one who knew of her Folly would find it their Intereſt to divulge it, it was his Intereſt to conceal his Diſhonour from all the World, ſince ſhe had met with ſo juſt a Puniſhment for her fault from the Hands of Providence. My Lord conſidering the matter, and that he was not wholly innocent in the Adventure, but chiefly that as this was not known to the Town, ſo it deliver'd him from a Woman that was his Averſion, he immediately took care to have her brought home, where languiſhing a few days, ſhe dy'd, and was honourably buried, leaving an Example of the ill Effects of Gaming which caus'd all this Trouble, and her Death at laſt.

But

But it is not the Court only that labours under the Inconveniencies of this hateful Vice, the City Beaux endeavour to imitate in this as in all other Follies.

The Beautiful BAIT *devour'd at last.*

THere was an old Gentleman liv'd in the City, who formerly had a tolerable Fortune, but in his Old-age had nothing to depend on but a Place of about 150 *l. per Annum*. He had a Wife, a very beautiful Daughter just ripe for Man, and a Son capable of succeeding him in his Post, with two little Children about ten Years old. The Family was large to maintain out of an Income so small, but by extraordinary Oeconomy they manag'd it so well, that they made a very genteel Appearance. It was the Daughter's good or ill Fortune to have a young Attorney fall in Love with her, and her Parents having no Money to give her, expected no better Opportunity of disposing of her honestly. Married they were, and continued a while in the City, but Business not coming in as the Limb of the Law expected, or in hopes that at the other end of the Town his Wife might get such Practice by her Beauty as might bring in enough to support him like a Gentleman, without the Fatigue of an Attorney; he takes a Lodging in the *Strand*, that being so great a Thorowfare, might sufficiently shew her to all the Gallants as they pass'd by in their Coaches. It being therefore a considerable Shop of Trade where they lodg'd, Madam was per-

perpetually in the Shop, which invited not a few Cuſtomers to her Landlady, and Addreſſes to her ſelf. *Layter*, as Fate would have it, lodg'd but at next Door, and it being at the very juncture that he was in purſuit of juſt ſuch a Beauty to carry on his Trade, he bleſt his Heart at the ſight, and made his Wife ſoon enter into a ſtrict Friendſhip with her; the Huſband and ſhe is invited to Dinner, and then to Supper, and no Day could paſs but *Sylvia* (for ſo we'll call her) muſt be their Gueſt.

The Husband lik'd this Treatment mighty well, but Money as well as Food was what he aim'd at. *Layter* ſoon found out his Wants, and ſupplied him on Bond with what he had occaſion for; and having thus got him into his Power, he was reſolv'd to make uſe of the Advantage. Whenever his Wife was not with them, he preſs'd for his Money, and manag'd the Husband ſo artfully, that he got the entire diſpoſition of *Sylvia* to himſelf. Nature never fram'd any Creature more charming, and ſhe had beſides from her Education contracted a ſort of Baſhfulneſs, which heighten'd her Beauty to the laſt degree of Perfection. *Layter* took care to invite thoſe to his Table who had not only Money enough to gratifie his Thirſt of Gain, but alſo Youth enough to be fir'd by a Beauty ſo uncommon.

The firſt he caught was a young Country Squire, who had not only a plentiful Eſtate in Land, but a Bank of Money ſufficient to pay for his Follies. *Sylvia* was taught to propoſe Play as ſoon as the Diſhes were remov'd, and the

the Bubble paid too great a Deference to her Eyes to controul her Commands: His Eyes were too much imploy'd on those of the charming *Sylvia* to mind his Game, and so by consequence was gull'd with all the ease imaginable. In the Intervals he ventur'd to tell his Passion to *Sylvia*, who only blush'd at what he said, not daring to encourage his Addresses. The young Gentleman try'd all means to engage her without effect, *Layter* or his Wife alwaies taking care to allow him little Opportunity to make any Progress in his Amour. He had now lost near a Thousand Pounds in this Project, without so much as gaining a Kiss; till weary of this Courtship, he began to find she was the Gamester's Property, and therefore resolv'd to apply to him and his Wife, with the Proffer of Two hundred Guineas for their Assistance, but they receiv'd the Proposition with the highest Indignation, which had proceeded to a Challenge from the Sharper, but that he found the young Gentleman was not to be Bully'd: But he consulting some Friends, who knew the Fun better than himself, thought fit to sit down by the Loss, and never come near 'em any more.

Layter now takes her to *Epsom* with his own Lady, the Season coming on for that place, and there appearing on the Wells, the Fun drew a thousand Admirers, who daily throng'd to *Layter*'s Apartment, and lost their Money to him, for a sight of those Charms they were never to enjoy. Among the rest there hapned to be an old Citizen, who had gotten a great deal of Money by a great deal of Knavery, and

now

now blind *Cupid* was resolv'd to be even with him for all the Rogueries of his Life; for he wounded him so deeply, that if half he'd been worth could have purchas'd her Embraces, he scarce would have scrupl'd it: But *Layter* was not for suffering so great a Treasure, and a Person who brought him in daily so considerable a Revenue from Bubbles and Fools, to be taken from him by any one Man's Money, most of which would go into the Pocket of *Sylvia* or her Husband. So that the old Citizen, tir'd with the Expence and small progress he had made, retir'd in time, having lost above 2000 Pounds by this Folly, the most expensive of all his Life, and which soon put an end to it; for pineing away e'ry day, in a little time he went to the Master he had serv'd; and leaving no Will, good part of what he left was consum'd in Law.

It would be endless to tell all the Bubbles that she made, and to reckon all the Money *Layter* got by her in this manner, both in City and Country, from Clergy and Laiety. But he having made several successful Campaigns with her, it was her ill or good Fortune to lose her Father, whose Death left her Mother and Brethren in the utmost Distress; they had no hopes of Subsistence, but by begging the same Place for the Son, who with it might maintain the Family and raise his own Fortune by marrying to some advantage, which, being a handsom young Fellow, he had no cause to despair of, if he gain'd but this point

to

to ſupport him till a fit Opportunity offer'd to accompliſh his Wiſhes.

There was of this young Lady's Mother's Acquaintance a Lady, who having liv'd in ſome Reputation formerly in the City, out of an odd Vagary being parted from her Huſband, ſet up for Intrigue at the Court-end of the Town, where ſhe was ſo good-natur'd, that if ſhe could not pleaſe her Acquaintance her ſelf, ſhe would very generouſly ſupply that Defect by helping them to ſome other that could. Her Character, I confeſs, is ſomething odd, for ſhe was ſo exact a Profeſſor of Sincerity, that out of a meer Principle of that, ſhe would tell her Husband when ſhe made him a Cuckold, and by the very ſame Principle let one Gallant know when ſhe had been obliging another. This Lady having work'd her ſelf into an acquaintance with ſeveral Men in Power, her Mother thought the fitteſt Perſon to addreſs to on this extraordinary Exigence of her Affairs; taking therefore her Daughter with her in the Coach, came to her Lodging, laid before her her Condition, and deſir'd her Aſſiſtance. The Preſence of this young Lady inſpir'd her with a Reſolution of doing a double Service, at once to help the Son to the Place and the Daughter to a Gallant. She adviſ'd her againſt *Layter*, as the Bane of her Reputation, where ſhe was daily expos'd to the view of all the wild Fellows of the Town, without reaping any Advantage to her ſelf, while *Layter* made her only his Property to fill his Pockets,

kets, and at last to betray her for a Sum, when he could no longer get by his other way.

The young Lady was pleas'd with her Advice, promising to return in a day or two, to know the Event of her Negotiation in behalf of her Brother. The good friendly Lady was not long before she sent for a young Gentleman of Quality and considerable Post in the Government, as well as Estate in Land, who was Master of a great deal of Wit, and a Person perfectly charming: She describes the beautiful Petitioner so warmly, that nothing but she could come up to the Idea she had rais'd: He is infinitely charm'd, promises her Success, and desires to see her at her Lodging, where he would bring her the Grant of the Place she had ask'd.

Layter in the mean while was inform'd by what Interest she work'd, and long'd to be acquainted with a Man, whom if he could draw in, might be worth twenty other Bubbles: So the silly young Creature suffer'd him to come with her to the Appointment; which so disoblig'd the Minister of State, that nothing pass'd but general Words; and all *Layter* could do, was not sufficient to engage him in the least Discourse with him or Regard to him, but taking his leave very abruptly, left 'em all in Despair. Madam took the young Lady aside, and told her, that she had marr'd her Affairs, by bringing so notorious a Scoundrel along with her; and so dismiss'd her with Tears in her Eyes for her Folly, for she could not but like the Man, and now found that all

her

her Hopes of providing for her Friends and her ſelf were diſappointed by her abandon'd Acquaintance.

Fully reſolv'd therefore to take the firſt Opportunity of leaving him, ſhe ſoon met with one; for the young Lord —— hearing of her Beauty, went to play there one Night, and being out of Awe of the Scoundrel, made his Addreſſes to bright *Sylvia*, and ſitting by her, would whiſper her often. She lik'd him ſo well, that ſhe agreed to come to him the firſt lucky minute ſhe could find to make her Eſcape; ſo the next Morning early ſhe got from her Lodging, and ſending for my Lord ——, he immediately took care of her, diſcharg'd her Lodging, and ſent her Huſband out of the reach of poor *Layter*, ſo that he was forc'd to fall to his old way.

Here my *Guinea* made an end; and Night being pretty far ſpent, I turn'd my ſelf to reſt, but could not put the charming *Sylvia* out of my Head; yet I reap'd ſo much benefit from what he had told me, that I reſolv'd ever to hate and abhor thoſe vile Caterpillars call'd *Gameſters* and *Sharpers.*

The End of the Third Nights Entertainment.

The Fourth

THE

Fourth Nights Entertainment,

OF

LOVE INTRIGUES.

AS long as the laſt Nights Entertainment had held, the Morning ſhining out with ſo extraordinary a Beauty, I got up betimes, and took a walk into the Fields all alone to ruminate on what I had heard the Night before: I cou'd ſcarce have believed that Mankind cou'd ſo far degenerate, not into Brutes, but into Divels, as I had heard, but I remembred that Gold wou'd not Lye, and that a Metal ſo Mercurial had means of ſeeing in Security, what I cou'd not experience but at my proper Expence. Lord, thought I to my ſelf, what a Myſtery is not only Man, but the whole Creation! How Beautiful is all we behold, and yet how ſoon it fades and changes from all its Beauty with deformity and diſſolution. The charming Face of Woman, when in the bloom, how many wonders does it diſcloſe, how it warms and tosses the Blood into strange Tempests of Desire; and yet a few years wears off all that's pleasing, and leaves it a Shrivled, Beamless Face, fit only to move our Aversion. The Mind of Man which discovers so many Wonders, and almost frames Beings that exist only in its Fancy; that by its Reason measures the Abiss, views all the Order of the Heavenly Bodies, and passes all the Bounds of Nature, even to the Throne of God, and there displays him in his Majesty beyond the expression of words, yet in a few years is fled with all its fine Notions we know not whither, and sinks in the Grave with such wretches as I have heard describ'd, who have not diserv'd the name of Men. Sure this World is the very Dream of Providence, which must be all beautiful, but must vanish all like a Dream as if it had never been.

Again, how can our Philosophers answer this vast disproportion of Human Minds? Here is one that soars on the wings of Reason to a pitch of Divinity; and there one that never lifts its Faculties above the reptiles of the Earth; nay, is laid beneath them in the Bowels of the Earth, with those fatal Minerals which only engrost all its Thoughts. One moves by his wise Principles of Morality, another is so far from regarding them that he cannot understand them, or form any Notion, but what comes from his most perverted *Self-Love*: So that tho' the

the Form of Men is always the ſame, yet their Minds are ſo different, as if their Kind was far from being the ſame. This puts me in mind of that Verſe:

Man differs more from Man, than Man from Beaſt.

Thus muſing with my ſelf, I paſt away the Morning, and to divert my ſelf, found out a Friend to Dine with whom I had not ſeen a pretty while: He was glad to ſee me, and I to find him yet in the Land of the living, having heard of his Illneſs a pretty while ſince; nor had he ſo far eſcap'd his Diſtemper, but that the pale Tracks yet remain'd. Being ſet at Dinner, I examin'd into his Health, what had been his Diſtemper, and how long he had labour'd under an Illneſs that had left him ſo unlike what he had been? My Friend, *ſaid he*, my Diſtemper has been the juſt puniſhment of my own Folly; if I had had but your Prudence, I had yet been as well as you both in Purſe and in Perſon: I have been weakned in both by Avarice and Luſt; the Sharpers have robb'd me of my Money, and the Whores of my Health: And I am ſcarce yet recover'd from a Diſtemper which I ow'd to their filthy Embraces. Take warning by me, quit this Lewd Town, which contains nothing worthy the Reſidence of a Man of true ſenſe: the Men are Sharpers, the Women Whores; Religion is Hypocrisie; Friendship Design; Knavery thrives, Honesty starves; Fools pass for Wits, and Men of Sense are contemn'd and in Raggs. Arts have no Patrons, Sharpers and Whores find only Regard: Poetasters get Places; true Poets scarce a Dinner. I am resolv'd the next Week to give it my perpetual Adieu.

I smil'd at the strange alteration in my Friend, who had been a long time so bewitch'd with the Town, that he declar'd, That the midnight Ordure was a greater Perfume than the Primrose in his Country. This Discourse with my Friend, put me in mind to enquire of my Gold something on this Subject, soon as the Night return'd me to my Chamber: This desire did not suffer me to stay late abroad, and no Friend so dear, or Bottle so charming, as to have power to make me stay past Ten out of my Lodging. Every Body wonder'd at the change, and ghest all Causes but the real: One swore I was secretly Married, and that the Joys of the first Month were not yet grown dull on my Hands; others less charitable wou'd have it a little Harlot not yet grown stale to me. While little cou'd they imagine the strange Conversation, that Charm'd me, well knowing my Temper, that I was no Miser, that took a pleasure with brooding over my Gold in the Night.

When I was come home, I soon dispatch'd my Servant, and getting into Bed I turn'd

to

to my Gold, and desir'd to know what discoveries they had made among the Ladies, who were kind to their Gallants? The *Roman* Crown taking the Priviledge I had given him, made me this Reply:

Tho' perhaps you may think we have but few Intrigues betwixt the Gentlemen and Ladies, where Cardinals teach another sort of Doctrine in Love, and have more *Ganymedes* than *Phrynes*, yet I must tell you that *Rome* is not without more natural Intrigues; and there are Gallants who will venture their Lives in the pursuit of a Man's Wife; and Ladies that will hazard more than their Reputation to gratify themselves in a Lover: Nay, who, rather than deny their Inclinations, will ask the Man she likes to do her a civil Favour; and punish the neglect with the point of a Bravoes Dagger. I cannot say there is over much Love on the Ladies side, whose general Confinement, and the common Neglect of their Husbands, with an idle, lazy Life, fill them with so much Lust, that they seek the Ease of that, rather than the more refin'd Joys of a tender Conversation, which is spent more in Action than Discourse.

I know this Pleasure of Intrigueing or Whoring, lies under an ill name with the Religious; but yet I can't imagine why, since Nature has given such Desires, which cannot be appeas'd without discharging in the Arms of Man or Woman; and since so many holy Men have given ſuch Examples, as give a ſufficient Sanction to Whoring. *Concubines* and Wives were allowed the Patriarchs; and *David* the beſt, and *Solomon* the wiſeſt of the Kings of *Iſrael*, had both a very jolly company of Drabs, without any imputation of Guilt on that Account. And if the general practice of Mankind in our days be of any Force, there is nothing of greater Authority; and it is ſtrange, that Practice, which is the Rule of Prudence, ſhou'd be ſo erroneous in other parts of Morality. I confeſs that there are many inconveniencies, and hazards, that attend this in the warm Climates, where Jealouſie bears ſuch an unbounded ſway; yet the Pleaſure has been always thought ſufficient to Ballance all theſe Conſiderations.

THE Fortunate Adultery.

I Was once parl of the Ring which a young Gallant of *Rome* wore on his Finger; who had been a mighty Devotee to Pleaſure, and yet was in the purſuit of an Intrigue which he had manag'd with a great deal of Pains and Induſtry. The Prince *Pamphilio* was a Man ſomething in years, and yet very indulgent to his Wife, as as ſar as conſiſted with the Cuſtom of the Countrry, for ſhe had an entire aſcendant over him, being very young, and very handſom; but ſhe was of too Amorous a Nature to be ſatisfied with the Fondneſs, and Embraces of an old Man. 'Tis true, ſhe was not diſguſted at the Dotage of her Husband on her Charms, becauſe that gave her the means of impoſing on him to the advantage of her own Pleaſure. *Sigismundo Fideli*, my Maſter, was the lucky Man who had the good forttune to pleaſe her, and who had never met with any ill Event in all his Amours with her, either in Country or Town. As ſhe firſt ſaw him at *Rome*, ſo that was the firſt time of their Loves; but *Pamphilio*, for his Health, us'd all the fine Seaſon to live near *Freſcati*, whither in the Moon-light Nights *Fideli* uſed to reſort, and be admitted by her Confident. The manner was this: When the time of his coming was fixt, a Key to the Back-door was left under a certain Stone at ſome diſtance from the Palace; and he left *Rome* generally time enough to get thither by Night. But one day he went ſooner to Hunt, and divert himſelf in the Country; but being fatigu'd with the Sport, and the Heat of the day, he wander'd into a Wood, where paſſing through many gloomy windings and turnings of the Foreſt, he came at laſt into a place ſo delicious, that had *Apollo* e'er ſeen it, he wou'd have chang'd for it his old Seat of *Parnaſſus*.

There was a lovely Thicket, whose lofty Trees and thick Leaves, cast a brown shadow all around, which serv'd for an agreeable shelter to a clear living Fountain, whose transparent Streams warbled o'er the Pebles, against the scorching Beams of the Sun; which yet penetrating the Boughs here and there, produc'd variety of sweet Flowers, which Enamel'd the verdant covering of the Place, while the wand'ring *Zephirs* blew the Odours all around; the Roots of the Trees were cover'd with a silken Moss, and their Branches fill'd with the pleasant Notes of the *Nightingales* and *Blackbirds*, made a natural and most delightful Harmony, which was mingled with the soft wispering of the Wind through the Trees, and the murmuring Waters that flow'd along beneath. Sitting down here beneath a Natural Arbor, we soon heard a young Gentleman Singing this Farwell to Love.

I.

Long I a foolish Servitude did prove
A Vassal to imperious Love;
It is enough I now at last am free
From all thy Pains, fond Love and Thee:
The Wild tumultuous Tempest now is o'er,
I fear a Shipwreck now no more,
Safe on the peaceful Shoar.

II.

II.

Safe on the Beach, I ſmile to ſee below
The raging Billows War,
Free from the Blaſts of Hope and Fear,
And all the anxious ſhocks, that ſilly Lovers know;
Secure from thy Shafts, thy Quiver and thy Bow.
While I my Liberty maintain
I never ſhall complain,
Of Lovers painful Joys, and Pleaſing Pain.

To his Verſes he added the melting Notes of his warbling Lute, which made ſuch an Harmony, that had *Ulyſſes* the contemner of the Voices of the *Syrens* been here, and bound to the Main Maſt of his Ship, he had burſt his Bands and come nearer to have heard this new *Arion* Sing.

Having now tir'd himſelf with Playing, laid aſide his Lute, when croſſing his Legs and leaning with his Elbow on his Knee, with Tears he thus addreſs'd himſelf to *Pietro*, who ſate cloſe by him.

THE

THE HISTORY OF *Julio* and *Sempronia*.

EVery Day I find a thousand Misfortunes surround me, but my Soul bent on Honour, either fears nothing, or at least if it be any thing, it is Infamy. I know not whether I owe my Inclinations to Amours, to the vigour of my Constitution, or to my natural Temper; yet how vigorous so ever I have been in this way, and how earnest in the pursuit of this Joy, I soon, nay, presently repent of my Folly; and now I perfectly tremble at the thoughts of all the false Blandishments of Love. But since you my *Pietro* desire me to give you an Account of my late Intrigue, and to remember my Madness, I shall not scruple to relate the severity of my Fate.

I was oblig'd to go to *Leghorn* about some Business of Importance; while I was there it hapned at a publick Festival, the Women of the Town appear'd all bare-fac'd at a Ceremony peculiar to the Saint of the Day; they were all so beautiful, that tho' they were not Godesses, yet the Error had been excusable for any one to have thought them; Beauty appear'd with all its Grace in all, but seem'd yet more lovely in one among them; the Lillies in her Cheeks were heighten'd with the Rosie purple of her Elegant Blood, that dy'd them with a Blush so warm, as to be able to set the coldest Heart on Fire. Her modest Forehead was distinguish'd with two semicircles of shining Jet, separated from each other by an agreeable and snowy Interval; on each side the finest Nose of the World shone two bright Eyes, with Rays more glorious than those of the Sun, and darted the Arrows of Love into the most innocent and frozen Beholders: Her flowing Hair that fell down in Curls, where e'ery Ringlet was plac'd for a Grace, contain'd an Ambush for the Liberty of Mankind; and the Ruddiness of her Lips seem'd to have taken so deep a dye, from the Blood of those Hearts that had been broke for her sake. Her Neck was White as the driven Snow, and without the help of Jewels swelling enough with its own native Charms. Beneath rose two heaving Breasts, which breath'd nothing but Love, and promising Extasies to the happy Man that shou'd be admitted to press them; she had a Shape exact, a charming jetting in her Motion, that promis'd an Agility transporting in the Garden of *Venus*.

The Liberty of the Ceremony admitted all to a nearer Conversation, without either suspicion or scandal.

I tremble much, my Heart new Flames inspire,
And gaze at her who still augments my Fire:
I look, I wonder, but the more I gaze,
The more I languish, and the more I blaze.

I felt too much Pain, I found too much Desire to suffer me to lose this opportunity of letting her know the mischief that her Eyes had done me; I therefore approach her, and address to her in this manner:

Believe me, Madam, there is so suddain a Flame kindled in my Bosom, that if you shew me the least neglect it will entirely consume me. But if you will be so generous to admit the Tears of a Stranger, I shall make two great Gods your particular Friends, and that is Love *and* Apollo. *Your Eyes have drawn the first from that Heaven where he has a Reign more absolute than on Earth, that I might be deliver'd to him, and he to me reciprocally. The other your Face, form'd so beautiful as wou'd have rais'd the Envy of the three contending Goddesses on Mount* Ida, *has call'd from his Conversation with the Muses, to sing its praise; that you might know, that such a Miracle of Beauty ought not to be obscur'd, and enjoy'd by any one Man, since there is no Good, that is not common to more; and that Beauty is given by the Gods to be beloved by, and to love many.*

Cast

Cast your bright Eyes the Universe around,
Nothing more glorious than the Sun is found.
Yet he his Warmth and Beams imparts to *All*,
His *Common Light* on every one lets fall.
Glide on ye Floods, ye beauteous Floods glide on,
Whether your course you take through Beds of Stone,
And in delightful Cascades tumble down;
Or through the flow'ry Meads your Track you chuse,
And to the Fields Fertility diffuse;
None are debarr'd of you th' *common Use*.
A servile Law the Fair alone confines,
Abhorrent of the End of Natures wise designs,
While your Caresses that to one restrains,
And only a poor, barren, lifeless Joy obtains,
Be thou, my Fair, as the bright Sun divine,
On all with smiling Eyes serenely shine.
Let no dull Husband, with his cold Embrace,
The fertile Joys of Lovers thus deface:
For, like the *Sun*, thou wert by Heav'n design'd,
To be the Mistress of all Human kind.

Having heard my Verses, with a Smile she said to me— Despair not, my Julio, *for you came not to this place without the Direction of thy good Fortune; for* Sempronia *finds her Heart equally inclin'd to* Julio, *which has burnt so long with as ardent a Flame, that her desire can't be less, than yours for mutual Happiness. Do you take*

care,

care, like a good Soldier, to be Punctual on the Watch to Night, with Arms proper for the Execution, and I shall defer your satisfaction no longer: Don't forget my House, least you are forc'd to pass the Night without a Bed, and I without a Lover.

As soon as she had done speaking she went her way, and I follow'd her close through the Town till she went into a Magnificent Palace, that look'd it self like a City; so that if I might judge of the inside by the outside, I cou'd expect nothing less than the Golden Palace of *Nero*.

The Sun now very opportunely hasten'd his Course to his Watry Bed, and now the Evening Star began to shine out with a more sparkling Light; which Astronomers tells us is the Planet *Venus*. When the happy shade took Possession of the Hemisphere, and the Door being open'd, and a Woman standing in the Entry with a Conscious murmuring Voice, call'd *Julio*, I made no manner of Pause, but without any more ado committed my Self and my Fortune to her Conduct; for Love drives Fear entirely out of our Bosoms. Taking me by the Hand, and leading me through abundance of Dark Rooms and Turnings of so large a House, at last she brought me into a Room that seem'd the very selected Palace of Luxury, and lock'd the Door after us. Here a vast number of Tapers Whiter than Snow spread round

round a borrow'd Day, while Silver Branches fix'd on the Silk Tapeſtry ſupported them; the Corniſhes of the Room were Ivory inlaid in Cypreſs and Jaſper; the Bed was hung with Purple Curtains, richly Embroidered all over with Gold, and the Counterpain being adorn'd all round with a Fringe of Gold reaching down to the Floor, which was inlaid with Marble and other Stones of various Colours, expreſſing to the Life all manner of Beautiful Flowers in Moſaic Work.

Then my Guide ſet the Table to the Fire ſide, and cover'd it with the fineſt and moſt curious Sweetmeats, compleating the Banquet with handſom Bowls, crown'd to the brim with the ſmiling Juice of the Richeſt Grapes; and then in gentle Murmurs ſhe inform'd me who her Miſtreſs was in theſe words:

It is now, *ſaid ſhe*, Eight years ſince *Sempronia* has been Married to *Antonio*, a Man of very great Wealth, but of no leſs Folly and defects of Perſon and Mind. Let all Young Ladies who meaſure their Happineſs by the heaps of their Wealth beware leaſt in the crowd of their Admirers, they regard in their Choice of a Husband, more the Splendor of Gold, than the Virtue, Wit, and Vigour of the Man; for the poor *Sempronia* lies in the midſt of a heap of Gold, a Widow tho' a Wife, and knows not who ſhall be Heir to all her Husbands Riches; yet the chaſt Matron has ſo great a deſire

for

for Children, that she leaves no means untry'd that may furnish her with an Heir so much desir'd by both her and her Husband. Flatter not your self that you have the Happiness of being call'd to the Embraces of so great a Lady, out of any Passion for any of your Personal Perfections; when ever she pretends to Love, that passes for Words, not Truth; speaking more to the Gust of the Ambitious Admirer, than by any real sentiments of hers; for this Lady of such Consummate Beauty, finds nothing that can move her Love or Desire; for she is not more Beautiful than Modest: For her Kisses are free from Crime, and she is not guilty of Adultery in all the Enjoyments she has bestow'd; for Adultery is the effect of Lust, not the Natural desire of Children. Two Days ago, while she offer'd up her sweet Prayers to the Holy Virgins most Miraculous Image, which seem'd to grant the Prayers of its Votary, and deliver'd this Oracle to her:

That by Young Julio *she shou'd prove,*
Fertile Joys, and Pregnant Love.

Do not therefore wonder that you found so easie a Reception, since the Holy Virgin's Image Commanded her to admit you to her Chast Bed for the Propagation of Humane Kind. If we are not the only care of Heaven, yet certainly that has some regard to our Happiness,

Happineſs, and whatever is done without the Approbation of that, is of no manner of benefit to us. Thus *Antonio* the firſt Night of his Marriage, which was to be ſure diſagreeable to Heaven, deſtroy'd the Fertility and Maidenhead of *Sempronia* together. He has Four Brothers who have taken his place, who while they keep *Antonio* from his Barren Bed, abuſe his Siſter with unfruitful Seed. Mov'd by their Impotence, ſhe has call'd the whole Family into her aſſiſtance; but in ſo vaſt a number of Gallants, ſhe has not yet met with one, who has been able to ſtop the haſtning Ruin of ſo Ancient a Family.

Whilſt this Babler held on her diſcourſe, *Sempronia* her-ſelf tript into the Room where we were, and the noiſe of the Doors opening rouz'd the Maid, who had now almoſt talk'd her ſelf aſleep. The burning Tapers at her entrance ſeem'd to blaze with greater Flames, and the Eyes of this Mortal Nimph ſeem'd to burn the very light themſelves. After ſhe had excus'd her long ſtay by the Importunity of her Husband, and the Affairs of the Family —— *Lovers* (ſaid ſhe) *ſeek Darkneſs and Secrecy.* Preſently the Doors were faſtned, and all troubleſome Lights put out, and the Bed all Perfum'd left half open; ſhe was pleas'd with the Maids Diligence and Adreſs, when ſmiling, ſhe threw her Arms about my Neck, and giving me Voluntary Kiſſes that Reliſh'd of *Nectar* —— *The Covert of this Bed* (ſaid ſhe) *is due to the sacred Rights of Love, and you ought to commit those Flames that you shall experience, to that and to silence*; with that she strain'd me close in a more strict embrace, and sucking my Lips into hers, she surpriz'd me with a Tremulous Summons to a closer Engagement, and in the midst of her eagerness threw her falling Lover on the Bed.

You have doubtless my Friend *Pietro*, experienc'd the Transports of Love, when you met with more, than equal Fire in the Fair one; she gave proof of her Satisfaction through all the Combat of Love, till after many Deeds of Valour, both tired, we fell asleep. The next Day refresh'd my Vigour with good Meat and rich Wines, and the Night renew'd our Pleasures; till after a Month of Pleasure and Love, I had the good Fortune to confirm the Oracle of the Holy Statue, by impregnating the Charming *Sempronia*. But now Surfeited with so long a Happiness, I desired my Dismission; and *Sempronia*, either angry with my indifference, or, as I rather believe, desirous of a new Gallant, even beyond my Expectation yielded willingly to my request, only adding this Admonition:

If your Stars (said she) *among the other Favours they have bestow'd on you, have given you secrecy, you have found a Friend who will in time reward the Fidelity of your Silence with unexpcted Honour; but if you suffer your Tongue to divulge what has past betwixt us, assure your*

self

Jest that your Rashness will be punish'd with a most certain death. The Hands of an injur'd Woman are long, and implacable, as never being weary till the destruction of the Offender: And of all Injuries a Woman most resents the discovery of her private Favours. But that you may not think my Threats only empty Words, bring hither Bombo, *that his death may sufficiently convince* Julio *of what he ought to expect on the violation of his Trust. Fortune has been very malicious against my Reputation, and a Domestick of my own has been so bold as to cast a Reflection on my Name: For this Fellow whom I had taken from a Groom, prefer'd him in the House, nay receiv'd him to this very Bed, that by Luxury and Pleasures he might forget the lowness of his Condition; has betray'd my Favour, and by a pernicious Loquacity made an ungrateful Return for all the Obligations, that I had laid upon him. The Perfidious Ingratitude of the Sex reaches even to the servile Vassals; for when once you have sufficiently glutted your Appetites with Pleasure in our Arms, you laugh at your Mistress, and with a haughty Pride neglect those Joys, which you had before sought with so many Watchings, Sighs, Tears and Fastings.*

Towards the end of her Discourse *Bombo* was brought in bound, his Countenance and Eyes confess'd Laciviousness; his Hair was Black, and his Chin cover'd but yet with its first Down, only a swelling in his Breast and Belly deform'd a very comly and beautiful Person: Whom when the Maid had tied fast to a Beam, she fastned his Cloaths behind him, and put a Silver Vessel under his Feet, and then thrust the Sword she held in her Hands up to the Hilt into his Bosom, whence issued such a Gush of Blood as almost fill'd the Vessel at once: Then taking out his Heart, opening the Mouth of the Sufferer, who made no manner of Noise, gave the Heart to him to eat, adding to it this Imprecation——*That All those, who ever shou'd rail at and defame the Lady he had enjoy'd, and wou'd scruple to lie for the Reputation of his Mistress, might dye the same cruel death.* Cold almost to death with Fear, I expected immediately the same Fate, and all I durst pray for was only a milder Death: For I knew that the Cruelty of Women, like that of the *Panther*, stops not at any Mean; but devours more than will fill his Belly. When the cruel *Sempronia*, and the more barbarous *Abigail*, bidding me remember the Fate of *Bombo*, turn'd me out of doors.

Being got out, I at last began to resume new Courage, and with all the speed my Leggs wou'd furnish me with, I fled from an Abode more horrible than the Isles of *Circe*, and the *Sirens*; and having found out my Quarters, I got into my Chamber, nor stir'd I out of Doors in three Days, ruminating all that while on what I had seen. O ye immortal Gods, cried I, how abandon'd are we Men! We foolishly buy Adultery at at the expence of our Lives, or what is yet more grievous than any death, a perpetual Banishment. Murther comes upon us in the midst of our Joys, and that in a manner so cruel, that the Common Hangman wou'd tremble at the Execution. Why cruel Women have you thus a while repriev'd me, when I was half way over the *Stygian* Lake, and restor'd me to a momentary Life, only to put me suddenly to a more cruel death? This is a false Kindness which you shew me, which instead of forgiving, only defer the Punishment. Let me die in Peace, and without any farther delay restore this Victim to guilty Fate: For to what purpose was I made Witness of the Death of *Bombo*, but that I might be convinc'd, that when once a Woman will prostitute her Virtue in unlawful Embraces, that she sets no Bounds to her Vices? He had in his Power, not only a Voice, but Sighs and Groans in the midst of his Torment, and utter'd not one: And while his Blood Gush'd out in such a Flood, taking no notice, looks as if he were in a Lethargy, or had some drowsie Potion given him to make the Operation the more feasible. The Heart drag'd out of his Body by that audacious Jade the Maid, seem'd less than a Human Heart. All things to day bore the face of Imposture; but indeed we lay not aside our disguise against Heaven it self, so that if the Divinity had not a regard to Human Frailty,

Jupiter having thrown all his Thunder-bolts, wou'd have ſtood in the Clouds an in-offenſive Spectator, not Puniſher of our Crimes.

While theſe Thoughts fill'd my Mind, I heard ſome body knock at the Door, when to my equal Surprize and Wonder, who ſhou'd have been liſt'ning to my Complaint but *Bombo* in his own proper Perſon, whoſe death I had been bewailing; not at all Bloody, nor with a ſwell'd Boſom, yet with a more fearful Countenance, than he had when he ſaw his Heart pull'd out of his Boſom; who throwing himſelf on his Knees to me, thus began—*Forbear, I beg you Sir, to rail at ſo great a Woman, whoſe Anger the very Stars themſelves are ſenſible of; what ever has been ſaid of* Medea *falls ſhort of her skill, for ſhe dives into the very Thoughts of Men, and tho' at a diſtance from them hears their abſent Diſcourſe. What you ſaw done to me, was perform'd without the ſpilling of any of my own Blood, only to ſtrike a Terrour into you. But avert the Omen Gods, that this Mimic Death ſhou'd be any promiſe of yours in Reality; but believe me, and take my faithful Advice, fly this place with your utmoſt ſpeed, for here, certain Death unavoidably attends you. Nor am I of ſo barbarous a Temper, as to ſuffer a Man, who has been admitted to the Fruition of the ſame fair Lady with my ſelf, to periſh by an untimely Fate: For who knows but the ſame Stars which brought us both to the ſame Bed, may bring us both to the ſame Grave.*

I

I cou'd not but receive this kind Information with abundance of Thanks, promising that when ever it lay in my way he shou'd challenge as great a Service from me; so taking my Leave of him and *Leghorn*, I made the best of my way to *Rome:* Where yet I can't put the strange Adventure out of my Head; but retiring to my Cousins, *Villa* come often here to this pleasing Shade, to run over the matter, that keeping up the Memory of it, I may never more think of any more Amorous Engagements.

The Continuation of the Fortunate Adultery.

JUlio having given this Account to his Friend, and plaid a Tune or two on his Lute to calm his Mind which the Relation had ruffled, they went their way, and left my Master to expect the proper Hour of getting into the Arms of the Amorous Princess. The Night now coming on, and the Moon rising, he got up and went to the Stone, where he found the Key, by which he let himself in at a private Door in the Garden: The first Animal he met was a great Dog, that was the nocturnal Guard of the Place; but this terrible Animal, the Princess, out of a pretended kindness for it, had made acquainted with *Fideli*, by having brought him with her to *Rome*; so that he only faun'd upon him, and attended him to the place where he was to wait for Mrs. *Abigail's* coming with news from his Princess. How tedious so ever the Time might seem to a desiring Lover, yet it did not in reality exceed half an Hour. *Abigail* conducted him up the back Stairs into Mrs. *Abigail's* Apartment, who being a particular Favourite, had one fit for the Use her Lady once a Month to be sure wou'd put it to.

I will not repeat the mutual Embraces of the Lovers when they met, nor any thing that past all the remaining part of the Night: But the Princess lost some of her Prudence in prolonging her Joys till late the next Morning; nay, being up, they cou'd not be satisfied but they must again retire to the Bed to waste a few Minutes in the agreeable Pleasure: But in the midst of their sport, the old Prince comes to the Door, opens it, and was entring the Room, when she call'd out to him to retire, for having that Morning taken *Physick*, she must have no Man in the Room a Minute; the good old Prince guessing her meaning, and unwilling to disturb her on such an occasion, retir'd, and the Lovers pursu'd their amorous Affair. The next day they were in the same Condition, and hearing the Prince come, *Fideli* was slipt into the Closet, the very place to which the Prince was bound for some Money to play with; she had got

the

the Key, nor wou'd ſhe part with it to him on all his earneſtneſs; which he finding, What, ſays he, thou haſt got ſome pretty Knicknack there now, which you won't let me ſee? I have ſo, ſaid ſhe; but you ſhall ſee it ſome other time, when 'tis more fit for ſight than at preſent. Well, well then, ſaid the Prince, give me ſome Money to play, and I'll not ſee your Trinkam. The Princeſs put her Hand into her Pocket and gave him what ſhe had there, which hapned to be ſufficient for that occaſion. The Prince being retir'd, the Lover was again ſet at Liberty. But conſulting how to avoid the like hurry again, *Fideli* being young enough, they reſolved to dreſs him in a Womans Habit, and that he ſhou'd paſs for a Relation of Mrs. *Abigails*; the matter was no ſooner agreed on but put in execution, and the Princeſs wou'd have the pleaſure of Dreſſing him her ſelf.

After this they were much leſs on their Guard, and made no ſcruple of letting the Prince find them together: His ſtay was generally during the light Nights, and when thoſe were gon he return'd to *Rome*, which allow'd ſuch a grateful Interval to their Amour, that it kept up their Paſſion and Deſire to ſo great a degree, that the Prince now dying, and leaving her a conſiderable Fortune, ſhe thought fit to beſtow it on *Segnior Fideli*, with her ſelf in Marriage: Which Match how fortunate ſo ever

it

it was to him, was not ſo to her; for he being ſenſible of her former Infidelity, was too watchful over her Actions ever to give her the leaſt opportnity of ſerving him in the ſame kind; beſides a perpetual cohabitation both at Bed and Board, without any Fear or Apprehenſion from any Body elſe, made their Paſſions ſink to Indifference, and that to Diſguſt;all had perhaps ended in the Murther of one or the other, had not his Death prevented: But ſhe in his ſickneſs was ſo ſedulous about him, that he cou'd not reſolve to wrong her of any part of her Fortune ſhe brought him, which remain'd yet unſpent, but left her all intirely. In that one Action Juſt; in all others without Principle or Honour. She Buried him handſomly. And I was beſtow'd on a Siſter of his, whoſe Story I muſt add before I give over.

THE
Whores Revenge.

L*Ucilla Fideli* was very beautiful, and very young when her Brother died, and in a Nunnery in *Florence*, and deſign'd for a Nun; but her Brother being dead, and ſhe not liking the then unſubſtantial Joys of the enclos'd Ladies, quits the Monaſtry

nastry where her Cousin was Abbess, and takes a Lodging in an Eminent Citizens House, where she soon enlarg'd her Acquaintance. Among whom was a venerable old Lady, who talk'd of nothing but Death or Judgment, and the Miracles of Saints and the Like, and yet was secret Bawd to the young Duke who was yet a single Man, nor did he care to hearken to Marriage. *Lucilla* had a Beauty was the most agreeable to his taste in the World, vvhich Madam the Bawd knew so well, that she easily got him a sight of her new Acquaintance, making her a Visit in Womans Clothes. The Duke was infinitely charm'd with her Person, but more with her Wit and Knowledge, having been so great a Reader in the Nunnery, that her Conversation was much different from that of most of the Sex,

Lucilla is invited to the old *Beldam*'s, a Place fitting for the deed; and before the Collation was ready, the young Duke was admitted. He makes his Addresses, she is not averse; but being inform'd that it was the Duke of *Florence*, her Vanity and Pride soon blew up the small Garison of her Virtue; yet she made the Conquest of her Person more hard than that of her Heart, lest by too easie a surrender she shou'd lessen his Esteem of her, and by consequence his Value and Love: But having kept him long enough in suspence to fix her Empire in his Bosom, she found

found ſuch a means of ſurrendring, as ſhou'd ſeem rather a Storm than Capitulation. He vow'd perpetual Love and Conſtancy, plac'd her in a Magnificent Apartment, and took all that care of her, which a Love, ſo ſincere as he certainly was poſſeſs'd of for the Charming *Lucilla*, cou'd prompt him to.

There was in the Court a Man of wonderful Parts and Integrity, tho' an old Courtier, whoſe name was Count *Horatio*; he had ſerv'd the Duke's Father many years, and diſcharg'd his Adminiſtration with the Applauſe of both Subject and Prince. This Man had not only a Fatherly Care over the young Duke, but a kind of Paternal Authority and Aw; he finding out the Intrigue, and in a manner agreeable to the Perſon he ſpoke to, inveigh'd againſt all illegal Amours, and us'd many Arguments to move him to think of Marrying. The Duke thank'd him for his Advice, and promis'd to follow it; but Nature is too frail to ſuffer a young Man to vanquiſh an habitual Paſſion for a Woman, whom he in ſome meaſure had been the cauſe of forſaking the Paths of Virtue. The ſight of *Lucilla* ſoon put an end to all his fair Reſolutions, and made him think of *Horatio* as an envious diſturber of his Pleaſures.

Horatio was ſoon ſenſible of this, and therefore reſolv'd by a very ſubtil Addreſs to make *Lucilla* her ſelf the Cauſe of her own defeat: He therefore comes to her,

and

and examining her about her Amour with the Duke; flatters her Beauty, and Power over him, insinuating, that it must be her own fault if she were not Dutchess of *Florence*; that having him now in her Power, she shou'd deny him the Favours she had granted, and press him to Marriage. There is nothing in nature so credulous as a young Woman in things that flatter her Vanity: She therefore writes to the Duke, and sends the Letter by *Horatio*, which was to the following purpose:

Lucilla, to *Cosmo* Grand Duke of *Florence.*

THE Praise of deceiving an innocent poor Girl is below the Ambition of a great Prince, aim not at encreasing your Fortune and Glory by the Misfortunes of her who loves you: If you design for Matrimony, in me you will find one who by Use and Habit knows how to please you: But if you design no such thing, I will flie from your sight, that by my Absence you may forget me. The Name of a Mistress, tho' to a Monarch, is very odious, and the malice of Tongues has already attack'd my Reputation; so that if you call me not to your Nuptial Bed, I will call you to my Grave. Farewell.

The Duke had no sooner perus'd her Letter, but finding the Ambition of the Woman, he paus'd a while, and then turning to *Horatio*——*Let her go* (said he) *for an in-*

insolent creature; the Band which bound me to her is at last broke asunder, and since she cou'd not tell how to bear my Love with moderation, let her try to bear the contrary.

Horatio willing to improve this opportunity, endeavour'd by cunning Arguments to convince the Duke of the Inconvenience of a single Life; he urg'd that his Station was such, that all his Actions affected the Publick, all his Subjects being concern'd in them; That he ought to look out for a Wife, whose lawful Embraces might restrain him from running astray, and bring him Children worthy her, and worthy himself; That there was no Princess of *Europe* but wou'd be Ambitious of the Honour of being his Wife: That he therefore shou'd select some one among them, who besides her Person, shou'd bring into his Coffers a considerable Treasure. That in the mean time he shou'd forget *Lucilla*, and all other Ladies of her Condition, and think only of his Glory, and the Good of his People.

The Duke being touch'd with this good Advice, disdain'd to return any Answer to *Lucilla*, and made it his Business to think which of all the Princesses of *Europe* he shou'd chuse, to make the Partner of his Bed and his Throne. *Lucilla* in a little time found out the Alienation of the Duke's Affections, and found out the Treachery of *Horatio* in his pernicious Advice; consulting therefore her Resentment, she consider'd only

only how ſhe ſhou'd accompliſh her Revenge. Thoſe who have Money will never want Tools and Engines to execute their moſt profligate deſigns; for every were whether Poyſoners, or Aſſaſſins, have the Price of Iniquity, only Virtue is without any Reward.

There was in *Florence* one *Caſtrucio*, perfect and diligent in mixing of Poiſons, in managing falſe Witneſſes, and murd'ring Men by Aſſaſſination. *Lucilla* mad at once with Rage and Love, deſigning to make uſe of this Engine, ſhe wrote to him a Letter to put her deſign in Execution. The Letter ſhe commits to the moſt belov'd of her Servants, who had ſcarce got out of doors but *Horatio* met him in the Street, and ſtopping him by a ſubtil Addreſs, enquiring into his Haſte, he got from him his Lady's Letter; which when he had read, and found the deſign againſt his Life, he deſcended from the Greatneſs of his Quality, to win him to his Intereſt. He was afraid of a Reconciliation betwixt *Lucilla* and the Duke, and he knew that a Woman, who had once gon into ſuch deſperate Meaſures, wou'd never ceaſe to perſecute him whom once ſhe had fear'd. *Alas*, ſaid he, *How honourable a thing is chearful Poverty? And how cloudy a Glory is theirs who follow a Court? 'Tis ridiculous for a Man in the midſt of ſo many ſorts of Vanity, to expect a Happineſs of any duration; Uneaſineſs finds us out where-*

ever

ever we are; and amidst our Feasts all is sour'd with something troublesom and disgustful. No Man can have very great Advantages of Fortune, and yet keep them long: Fate laughs at those to whom it gives a suddain Rise, since her Inconstancy is a Comfort in our Afflictions, and that our Amours still naturally exposes us to all Misfortunes.

With these Reflections he retir'd from *Florence* to a Wood in the *Appenines*, and led an Hermetical Life, taking with him the Servant of *Lucilla*, by whom he had discover'd his Danger. *Horatio* had not long absented himself from the Court, when the Duke and *Lucilla* were reconcil'd, and so was pleas'd with the Misfortune which he ought to have deplor'd; lost in the present pleasure, he forgot his Friendship for *Horatio*. There is no greater Enemy to a Great Man, than to be too sincere in his Love to his Prince; and none are so sure of unhappiness, as those who study most the Safety and Honour of his Master: *Horatio* is saught for every where to be put to the most exquisite Torments, not that he was, but because he wou'd not be guilty of a Crime against the Happiness of his Soveraign. *Horatio* being absent, he is accused of Necromancy, and was said to have engag'd the Duke's Friendship to him by fascinating Arts; and even what had been formerly prais'd in him for Virtues, were now condemn'd as Crimes.

Thus

Thus *Horatio* ſound by experience to how little purpoſe it was to perſuade a Prince againſt his Inclinations; and how dangerous to provoke a Woman in her Buſineſs of Ambition and Love.

The *Roman* Crown having done; my little *Louis Do'r*, according to Cuſtom, began next to entertain me with Affairs of this nature: I know not (ſaid he) what Guſts the *Italian* Gallants find in the danger, and difficulty of an Intrigue; but I am ſure the Matter is purſu'd as much, and with as much Aſſiduity in *France*, where the Acceſs, and the Opportunities have none of thoſe Hazards. I ſhall not enter into the diſpute of the Lawfulneſs, or Unlawfulneſs of theſe Intrigues, I ſhall only tell you the Practice, which will ſhew you Women of the firſt Quality, and of boaſted Reputation, in the Arms of their Gallants, with no other Fear before their Eyes, but that of their Huſbands, which yet is not ſo great as to diſturb the leaſt of their delights. A convenient Aſſurance, with the natural Liberty the Women challenge in *France*, and a ſpice of Hypocriſie on certain occaſions, is all that the Ladies think worth their ſtudy, to ſecure their Pleaſure and Reputation. In *France* there is a univerſal Leudneſs goes round, and a Lady of Quality without an Intrigue at Court, looks as ſingular and aukward as a Beau without a Wig or a Snuff-box: Nay, the Men of Quality make no ſcruple of admitting

mitting a Gallant to their Wives themſelves, provided he has any Intereſt to carry on by the Reputation. It wou'd be endleſs to give you a Relation of all I have ſeen in the *French* Court on this head, I ſhall therefore confine my ſelf to a very few Inſtances, which will give you a ſample.

THE

Political Whores.

IN the Time of *Henry* III. *France* was extreamly divided into Factions; one ſide had the Duke of *Guiſe* at their Head, the other the King, under the Names of the Royaliſts and the *Guiſards*. Each ſide was very zealous in the encreaſing the Intereſt of their Party, by the Addition of ſuch young Noblemen that came to years of Age ſufficient to engage in ſuch Political Quarrels. There were two young Noblemen juſt come into the Wold of Buſineſs, and each Party ſtrove which ſhou'd engage them, the young Duke of *Candale*, and the young Duke of *Nemours*. The Duke of *Candale* had ſeen the Beautyful Wife of the Baron *de Grammont*, who was a violent Royaliſt, and her Charms ſoon made a ſenſible Impreſſion on the Heart of the young Duke; who had neither Art, nor deſire of diſguizing

zing a Paſſion from her, who only cou'd give him Relief. He, therefore, after all the Addreſſes of Eyes, Sighs, and preſſing the Hand, *&c.* took courage to diſcover a Flame, that was not diſagreeable to the Lady. And ſhe, who was a zealous Royaliſt, did not doubt fixing him in that Party, who had thus long fluctuated betwixt both; and ſhe was a Woman of too much ſenſe, not to make uſe of that pretext with her Husband to favour their Meetings; who being not very jealous naturally, ſmother'd all ſuſpicion in the hopes of having ſo conſiderable a Man a Convert to his Party by the Art of his Wife, whoſe Fidelity he did not in the leaſt queſtion: So that full Liberty was allow'd to their Converſation, which the Duke of *Candale* was too much in Love, and too Gallant a Man not to improve to the Advantage of his Pleaſure in the Arms of Madam *de Grammont*. The Duke was converted by the Lady, and ſhe highly diverted with her Convert, till he being fixt in his Principles, and ſhe grown fertile by his Cultivation, the warmth of the Affair abated, and in a little time the Baron had his Wife to himſelf, gaining by the Intrigue, a Powerful Man to his Cauſe, and an Heir to his Eſtate.

But the *Guiſards*, who were a very active Generation, having loſt their Hopes of the Duke of *Candale*, were reſolv'd to be beforehand with the Royaliſts in the young

Duke of *Nemours*, juſt then come of Age. Madam *de Chaſtillon* was a moſt compleat Beauty of the Fair Kind; her Hair was Flaxen, or ting'd with Gold to the Colour of the Sun-beams, and fell into a thouſand entangling Curls; her Forehead ſpacious, her Eyes a dark Blue, large and languiſhing, her Skin Whiter than *Alabaſter*, and her Shape and Mien anſwerable to thoſe admirable Parts we have deſcrib'd. Her Stature was inclining to Tall, which gave her Port a ſort of graceful Majeſty, which at once gave Deſire, and Aw'd it. Her Charms join'd to her Zeal for the *Guiſe*, gave her the Name of the *Belle Guiſard*. Her Husband Monſieur *de Chaſtillon* was a buſie Tool of the Party, who won him by a perpetual Flattery of his Parts, in Learning and Politicks, tho' he had not enough of the firſt to ſet up for a Village Schoolmaſter, nor of the latter, for a common Newswriter. His Study was ſtor'd with Books, whoſe Gilt Backs amuz'd his Eye, but whoſe inſide never improv'd his Underſtanding. So for Politicks, he herded with the moſt active of the Court, who finding him a fit Inſtrument for their Ends, admitted him into the *Junto*, on whom the whole Machine of Faction turn'd; of this the Abbot *Fouquet*, and the Count *de Hocquincourt* were the chief: The former being by profeſſion a ſingle Man, in an Honourable and Beneficial Poſt, might have ſpar'd himſelf the Fatigue

tigue of ruling a Party, having no Posterity to reap the Advantage of his Toils. But as he was of a Pale Swarthy Vizage, so his Mind had a Tincture of the same unwholesom Mixture; he lov'd to be at the Head of a Party, and being in his Nature incapable of forgiving an Injury either real or imaginary, the rest of the *Junto* took the same Principle, by which at last they made themselves so many Enemies as overturn'd their Dominion, and gave the Cause to the unpopular Royalists. In this *Junto* was it debated how the young Duke of *Nemours* shou'd be secur'd to the Party; Monsieur *de Chastillon* desir'd to let him have that Task himself, for the accomplishment of which he wou'd be answerable to the *Junto*. Tho' one of the *Junto* very much doubted his Capacity, yet finding that *Fouquet* approv'd of the Motion, easily acquiesc'd, not doubting but that *Chastillon* mov'd by the directions of *Fouquet*; as indeed he did. For meeting with him when the noise was hot of the Duke of *Candale*'s going entirely into the Interest of the contrary Party, and having some hints at the motives of his Resolution——My Lord (said *Fouquet*) the Baron *de Grammont* has acted like a Politician indeed, and like a Man of Sense, and one who will be advanc'd by sacrificing the Trifle of a Wife's Embraces to the good of the Cause he is engag'd in. A Wise Man shou'd never Marry a handfom Wife to pleafe his own Gufto, and to deliver himfelf a Victim to her Charms; nor like *Sampfon*, forget all great Actions in the wanton Arms of *Dalilah*; but he fhou'd make the fame ufe of her, that *Grammont* has done. I fear he will purfue the fame Method with the young Duke of *Nemours*, now full of youth, and fway'd by Amorous defires, a fine Woman may lead him whether fo ever fhe pleafes, and having once declar'd of one fide, there are Arts enough to retain him, if he has not Refolution to keep to what he has once efpous'd.

My Lord (replied *Chaftillon*) I believe I have the means then of ferving the young Duke of *Nemours*; my Wife is in all things fuperior to *Grammont*'s, and which is ftill better for the defign, the Duke has fixt his Eyes upon her with fuch marks of Affection, that I believe I do not flatter my felf, when I fay I have it in my power to make him our own; nor fhall it be faid that *Grammont* did more for his Party than I will for mine. This was the affurance that made the Abbot *Fouquet* affign him to *Chaftillon* in the *Junto*. *Chaftillon* made it his bufinefs to carefs the young Duke, and carry him home to Dinner and Supper, and then officioufly to leave him alone with his Wife, who had her Inftruction to deny him no Favour, that might fix him in the Faction of the *Guifards*: And the Duke was fo entirely Free in that Particular, that if fhe had

had propofed the *Alcoron*, the hopes of the Bleffing of her Perfon, wou'd have carried the Caufe. Till he had done, fome public Act for the Party, tho' he was a Man as accomplifh'd for the Lady's Service as any at Court, fhe allow'd him no fubftantial Joys; but making him only half Bleft, made him the more eager to come to an entire poffeffion.

They were both young and wanton, and fhe fhew'd no little command of her felf in refifting an Importunity fo agreeable to her, till fhe had gain'd her point; but her zeal for her Party happen'd to be ftronger than her Luft, fo at once fecur'd her Conqueft, and fixt her Gallant in Politicks and Love, fo that he never after forfook the Caufe. Tho' in Love he grew a little roving, and fhe, who had now by her Hufbands confent bid adieu to her Virtue, began to provide for her felf, nor ftuck at any thing in which fhe hop'd the leaft pleafure. Nor cou'd the Husband juftly find fault, fince he firft not only taught, but commanded her to think of another in fo Criminal a way.

I will not tell you of Madam *d' Olone*'s numerous Intrigues, with the Duke of *Candale* (the Grand-fon of the former) Monfieur *de Beauvin*, *Jeanin de Caftille* a rich Merchant of *Paris*, or *Paget* as rich a Banker of the fame place, the Count *de Guiche*, and the Father the Marfhal *de Grammont*, the

Prince of *Conde*, her Husband's Chaplain, the Marshal *de Hocquincourt*, and various more, while by false Caresses she lull'd her doating Husband asleep, till her Favours grew so common that they were not thought worth the concealing; till it came to her Husband's Ears, who leaving the Court, took his Lady with him into the Country, in hopes there to enjoy her without a Rival; ev'n in that he was deceiv'd, for while he kept a Servant, his good Lady wou'd not be depriv'd of her Recreation. Tho' all the Court Ladies are not so very inconstant as Madam *D'Olone*, yet all of them have their share of Man, except those who are for a strange odd Tast of acting the Men themselves, and debauching the young Girls, to pursue more filthy, more unnatural, and more empty Joys. But this, like all other Novelties, spread much at Court, and was mightily follow'd because a new Vice: Yet Madam *de Veneville* stuck to the old way of more substantial Pleasure in the Arms of the Count *de Tholouse*.

THE Lucky Escape: OR, THE REPRIZAL.

MOnsieur *de Veneville* was look'd on as a Man of Wit and Pleasure, and of a pretty good Estate, to encrease which he Married the Daughter of the Chevalier *D' Harcourt*, a very considerable Fortune; She was moderately Handsome, had a Pertness of Discourse, and an Air very agreeable: Her Husband had by his Conversation with some Jovial Fellows contracted a habit of Drinking, and of coming home pretty late, which left his Lady many idle Hours to contrive a satisfaction, which his Conduct had of late very much abridg'd her of, and to which she found her self not a little inclin'd by Nature. A Woman of Address and Youth need not in the *French* Court be long destitute of a Gallant; and the Count *de Tholouse* being a young Man of Quality, and bred to the Sea, her opportunity of seeing him often with her Husband, who belong'd to the Maritime Affairs, gave her no small liking to the Man; and her Conversation and Person rais'd in him a tender kindness for

for her; ſo that both being willing, it was not long e'er they came to an *Ecclaircisment.* Several haſty Enjoyments they found means of obtaining; but thoſe ſerv'd only to heighten their deſires of a more full ſatiſfaction. Madam *Veneville* underſtanding, that her Husband was engag'd one Night, both at Play and at Drinking, believ'd her ſelf very ſecure till towards the Morning: The Count is inform'd of the matter, and in the Dusk of the Evening comes to her Houſe, is admitted to her Chamber, where they ſoon entred the Liſt of Love, getting to Bed out of Hand. They had not long Revell'd in Joy, but News is brought that Monſieur her Husband is return'd, but very much in Drink. The Count is immediately dreſs'd in Womens Night-cloaths, and the Lady gets out of her Bed in her Gown in order to ſtop her Husband from coming into the Room: But he, full of Love now as Wine, was reſolv'd that Night to lye with his Lady, which he ſeldom of late did, but when he was thus unfit for that place. Madam ſtops him at the Door, and tells him he muſt not come in, ſince *Madammoiſelle de Chartres* was in her Bed, and juſt got to ſleep, not being very well. He ſwore that nothing ſhould hinder him that Night from being her Bedfellow. Madam grows angry, but cou'd not provoke him to be gon; and when at laſt he found his Fondneſs in vain, he ſwore he wou'd not leave the Room till he he had taken one kiſs of the young Lady, for robbing him of the Pleaſure of lying that Night in her Arms. This alarm'd them more than all; but whatever ſhe cou'd do he found his way to the Bed-ſide, he ſtruggled ſome time in vain for a Kiſs, the Count hiding his Face in the Pillow, and Madam and her Maid pulling him away, tir'd at laſt, he ſwore that ſhe was a perfect Virago, but that in the Morning he wou'd take his Revenge ; ſo betwixt Scolding and Perſwaſion, they got him up to Bed, where he was no ſooner laid but the fumes of the Wine got the maſtery of his Senſes, and he ſlept as ſoundly as if the Count had not been ſupplying his place with his Lady; who immediately return'd to him, and faſtning the Chamber Door againſt any other Interruption, ſhe flew to his adulterous Arms as full of Deſire and Love, as if ſhe had never enjoy'd him before; or that Adultery were a Modiſh Accompliſhment with which the Conſcience had nothing to do.

The Danger being over, and the Count recover'd of his Fright, they cou'd not forbear Laughing at the Impoſition on the Husband, and reſolving to make uſe of their Time, they let ſlip but few minutes; until the day coming on, the Count got up, and went away in a Chair to his own Apartment: Nor had he been ſcarce gon, but Monſieur *de Veneville* getting up, comes down to his Lady's Room, finds her in Bed, and

and asks for *Madammoiselle de Chartres*; yes replied Madam his Wife, you have behav'd your self very finely, you come home Drunk, and then abuse the best Friend I have; *Madammoiselle* affronted at your last Nights Behaviour, took Chair as soon as it was day, resolving never to come near your House any more. Monsieur *Veneville* was a little vex'd at the misfortune, because he had long had a Passion for the Lady, that burnt in his Breast: He therefore charg'd his Wife to go to her that day, and make his Excuse, and endeavour his Reconcilement with her, since whatsoever he had done was only the effect of the Liquor he had drank. That being oblig'd to go so early about the Business of his Office, he wou'd meet her in the Evening at Monsieur *de Chartres*'s Apartment, and there have her make up his Peace. Madam having promis'd to obey his Commands, he left her, to go about his other Affairs. But here Madam committed a great oversight in Love Politicks, since she ought immediately to have gone to the Lady to inform her what Part she was to act in her behalf: But she being pretty well tir'd with the work of the Night, yielded to her Inclinations for Sleep and Refreshment; not suspecting that her Husband wou'd ever think of going near *Madammoiselle* till she had made his way easie.

But it so happen'd, that as he was going to his Office, he met with *Madammoiselle*'s

Woman,

Woman, who had often follicited in his behalf, and had been retain'd by him some Time: Finding her thus early abroad, made him conclude that all that he had been persuaded to by his Wife was really matter of Fact, so that coming up to her, Ah my dear *Beaumelle*, said he, am I not quite ruin'd in your Lady's good Opinion? Will she ever forgive my drunken Impertinence? And must I always languish under a Cruelty which I have now but too justly provok'd? What new Adventure alarms you (replied *Beaumelle*) what have you done then to ruin what I have been so long a doing for you; even when I had brought her to confess that she lik'd you, and cou'd with difficulty deny you any thing? Alas! last Night (said the disconsolate *Veneville*) last Night was my Ruin, I came home too much Elevated with the Juice of the Grape, which made me so whimsical to design to lye with my Wife; but as my ill Stars wou'd have it, *Madammoiselle* was got into my Place fast asleep, and I like a rude inconsiderate Lover wou'd needs ravish a Kiss from her, which with her utmost struggling she denied me.—Hold (interrupted *Beaumelle*) you are I fear not sober yet, and repeat your wild Dreams for matter of Fact. My Lady was not out of her Apartment all the Day nor Night, nay rests yet in her Bed. *Veneville* was Thunder-struck with these words, and cou'd not be prevail'd on to believe

lieve her; but ſhe aſſuming the Diſcourſe went on: Come then, I find you are like other Husbands, in the Dark as to their own Affairs, and while you are ſo eager in purſuit of my Lady, never take Notice what is done at home. It is plain that your Wife had a Gallant in her Bed, and this was only her Excuſe to impoſe upon you; I will go before, and prepoſſeſs my Lady of the Affront put on her by Madam *de Veneville*, which ſhall be ſure to turn to your Benefit, if you come ſoon after me, and preſs the Advantage I have given you. *Veneville*, as much as he was vex'd at this Trick of his Wife's, was tranſported with too much Joy in the Proſpect *Beaumelle* had given him of immediate ſucceſs with his Miſtreſs, to think of any thing more; ſo doubling *Beaumelle*'s Fee he diſmiſs'd her, and went to the *Bagnio*, where cleanſing himſelf he prepar'd for the pleaſing encounter, which he perſuaded himſelf was very near.

Beaumelle by this time had ſufficiently fir'd *Madammoiſelle de Chartres* to Revenge the Injury Madam *Veneville* had done her, in making uſe of her Name to cover her Thefts: Which with her Inclinations for *Veneville*, made her reſolve not to be cruel to him when the firſt opportunity preſented his eager Addreſs. In the midſt of theſe Thoughts *Veneville* found her juſt wrapt in her Night-Gown, which was thin enough to diſcover all the Beauties of her Perſon; he is conducted

ducted privately up Stairs to her Bed-chamber by *Beaumelle*, and there left to his own Courage and good Fortune. *Veneville* address'd himself to her in the most passionate manner, and finding encouragement, proceeded step by step to the last Happyness she cou'd bestow; The Amorous Combat being over, he took his leave, and retir'd, expecting that his Wife wou'd soon be there to make her, her Friend, meaning her self, her Bedfellow that Night. The Husband had not been long gone but the Wife came, and found *Madammoiselle* yet in Bed, little dreaming that she came to Address to the only Woman who wou'd betray her. First Complements being over, alas! my Dear, said Madam *de Veneville*, I am utterly undone, unless you stand my Friend. In all that I can with Honour replied the other. I desire no more, replied *Veneville*: But you must first promise never to say one syllable of what I am going to tell you; for businesses of this Nature are not to be confided without the utmost Caution: For tho' all Women will gratify their Inclinations, yet while our peace depends on the Humour of a Man, whom the Law has given a Power over us, we must play the Hypocrites, and rail at that in another, which we dayly practice our selves; for it is not the Action, but the Conduct, that the World condemns. People of Sense know that Nature will be Nature, and that while we we indulge our Appetites and Senſes in all other Pleaſure, Chaſtity is only a meer Pretence, to carry on an Intrigue with the leſs ſuſpition.

What I have ſaid will be ſufficient to convince you, that I have been guilty of the Frailty of my Sex, and view'd another Perſon with Eyes of a tender Regard beſide Monſieur *Veneville*; yes Madam, I confeſs the Woman, I have ſeen, and I love the moſt charming of his Sex. My Husband was impos'd on me by a Brother, and my Inclinations no more conſulted, than if I had none; he has beſides us'd me like a Husband, his brutal Humours I am always ſenſible of, but ſeldom a kind offer comes from him, but when he is incapable of making them any thing but Offers. In ſhort, Madam, laſt Night, being aſſur'd that he wou'd not come home till very late, if at all, I admitted the dear Man I love to my Bed, where we had not been long, but my drunken Beaſt interrupted us, but I had the Addreſs to paſs him upon him for you my Dear; and on his rude Behaviour, I told him you were gone away in diſguſt; two things I muſt therefore beg of you, one, to own your Lying with me laſt Night; and the other, to admit of a ſeeming Reconciliation, this Evening when he will come to beg your Pardon.

I know not Madam, replied *Madammoiſelle*, what I ought to do in this Caſe, I think

think you us'd me but indifferently in making ufe of my Name on this occafion, yet fince it is paft, I will do what I can to ferve you, but fear I fhall be trapp'd by his Curiofity. The beft way in my mind faid *Veneville*, will be for you, after Reconciliation, to go to my Houfe this Night, and take a Bed with me, and let him find us as he did my Gallant and me the laft.

Madammoifelle having fome other Thoughts agreed to the Propofal; but when the Reconciliation came in the Evening, fhe told him his Wife's defign, and that he might make what ufe of the Intelligence he pleas'd. Juft before they were got into Bed *Veneville* comes home, and as before, pretending himfelf Drunk, wou'd make his Wife and *Madammoifelle* drink a Bottle of Wine with him; to quiet him, by her Confent the matter was agreed: He took care to fill his Wife's Glafs very largely, which (fhe not being us'd to good Liquor in any Quantity) foon had its defir'd effect. Madam goes to Bed, and *Madammoifelle* with her; whither *Veneville* as foon as undrefs'd comes after, and there revenges his Quarrel on his Wife; for in the very place where fhe embrac'd her Gallant but the Night before, he, by her fide, had a full Enjoyment of his Miftrefs even to fatiety, the Fumes of the Wine imprifoning Madam *Veneville*'s Senfes fo far that fhe knew nothing of the matter. *Veneville* having acted like a Man, wou'd

 needs

needs persuade *Madammoiselle* to a fresh onset, when now in all probability his Wife must wake and be a Witness of their Caresses; She utterly refus'd it, but he pressing it with vigour, she made but a weak Resistance to a Pleasure she lik'd, when in the height of their Raptures Madam *Venville* began to wake, and was at last sensible of the Treachery of her Friend; but being prov'd too Guilty her self, was fain to submit to what Terms they wou'd give her. The happy Life they afterwards liv'd you may easily Guess, when Love was on neither side, yet Distrust and Diffidence on both.

THE

Countrey JILT.

BUT the strange Appetite of Woman in things of this Nature, I must give you an Instance of, in an Adventure of a Doctor of Physic, who lodg'd at a creditable House in *Paris*: He was not yet a Man of much Practice, and so kept but indifferent Hours. He had frequently observ'd that a handsom young Country Lady was up when ever he came home, and being sometimes exalted with good Liquor, he ventur'd into her

her Apartment, where ſhe receiv'd him very civily; he ſaw ſhe was Beautiful, and believ'd her very Innocent: However he frequently made his Addreſſes in his Drink, which for fear of diſobliging her, he denied all Remembrance of when he was Sober. When he really was not Drunk he wou'd pretend to be ſo, to puſh on an Affair in which he propos'd a great deal of pleaſure. Coming home one Night pretty early he found her in Tears, and after much preſſing to know the Cauſe, ſhe ingeniouſly confeſs'd, that being but young and fooliſh ſhe had been betray'd to Marry her Father's Coachman; but, that having never Conſummated, ſhe thought her ſelf free, and wou'd Marry the Doctor if he thought fit, having a Fortune of 40000 Crowns at her own Command. The Doctor was infinitly pleas'd with her Perſon, and deſir'd nothing more, than always to live with ſo charming a Creature: So having blam'd her for a Folly ſo much beneath her Quality and Fortune, and made her promiſe him not to ſee him if he ſhou'd come to Town (as his Letter had told her) but remove to ſome other place where he cou'd not be able to find her: He left her and went to Bed, ſhe allowing him no Liberties beyond Kiſſes while he was Sober. The next Night he came home pretty merry, and made himſelf appear much farther gon than really he was; he preſs'd matters ſo far, that there being a Bed in the Room he accomplish'd his desires, and the next day ask'd Pardon if he had done any thing amiss, since he cou'd remember nothing he did.

This Method continued a while, but when he pretended to the like Favours when he was Sober, she wou'd fly into a passion at his attempts on her Honour; so resolving to make the matter more easie, he comes home in a woeful Condition in appearance, and the Lady believing it real, admitted him to her Embraces; but in the midst of his Joy he said to her, Madam, 'tis now a folly any more to deny me, I am in possession, and I am Sober, assure your self I was not ignorant of my Happiness all this while, but cou'd no longer bear the thoughts that you shou'd give those Favours to me when I was least like a Man, and deny them when I knew how most to take them; I therefore now claim you as my own, since purchas'd by Stratagem as well as real Passion: She was too well pleas'd with what was transacting to shew any Resentment; and never after deny'd him what he ask'd, whether drunk or sober.

But now another Letter comes from the Coachman her Husband, That he wou'd be in Town the following Week. She promis'd him faithfully, not only not to admit him to her Bed, but even to her Sight, and to remove with him assoon as he cou'd get them another Lodging. The Doctor went out

out in order the next day to provide her a new Lodging, but according to Custom made it late before he came home; when enquiring for the Lady, he was told that she was in Bed with her Husband, who that very Evening was come out of the Country. The Doctor was in a Passion scarce to be restrain'd, against his Rival Coachman, and her fickle Jilting Temper, which he concluded at last not worthy his Thoughts; so to Bed he went, and lying pretty long in the Morning, the Lady in her loose Gown came to his Bedside, threw her self on the Bed with Tears in her Eyes, begg'd his Pardon, and protested that she cou'd not help what was past, but that she was ready to go with him wherever he pleas'd with all her Fortune.

No Madam, replied he, you are only fit for the Husband you have chosen, who I doubt not will use you according to his sense and Education; you have now Consummated your Marriage, and have no longer any pretence to Separation, nor will I share in a Guilt that can afford me no Pleasure; while you were mine, and as I believ'd only mine, I valu'd you above all the World; but when you have shewn your self not proof against so contemptible a Wretch, you give a proof that your Soul and your Body are very ill match'd; and I, Madam, who can never love the Body only without any Regard to the Beauty of the Mind, must from this moment ceaſe ever to think kindly of you.

She heard him with Tears, threw her Snowy Arms about him, with her ſelf on the Bed by him, nay, made ſuch Advances as were ſufficient to unbend any Reſolution but his: But he ſtruggling from her Arms, got on his Cloaths, and left her ſighing on the Bed, whilſt he went out and got a new Lodging, whither he removed that very Night. But afterwards, enquiring out of Curioſity after his Damaſelle, he heard that ſhe received her Husband that very Night to her Bed, and was never more Brisk and Jolly in all her Life: But that ſhe was reſolv'd not to keep all her Charms for the Coachman, ſhe had then got three ſeveral Gallants. So concluding that ſhe was wretched enough, he never Curs'd her any more.

My little *Lowis d'Or* having ſaid this held his Tongue, when my *Guinea* thus gravely began.

OF

LOVE.

LOve, it is moſt true, is a Paſſion that Rules in every Man's Breaſt that is not a perfect Brute and Barbarian, yet not in all in the ſame degree. There is a ſoft and dif-disquiet desire of Pleasuring whomsoever we find any satisfaction in, whether by Chance, their Merits, or our own Mistake: And this cunningly insinuates it self so into our Hearts, that we find our selves in Love before we have any Thoughts of the Measures of our Love. It wou'd be no difficult matter to banish this Passion in its first approaches, did it not sooth those whom it afflicts, with such a Witchery of Pleasure and Softness, as to make it seem a sort of inhuman Ferocity (especially those who never felt it before) to drive so gentle a delight from their Hearts. But if this Passion be rightly manag'd, there is nothing more noble and sublime in the whole Nature of Things; for it not only heightens the Virtues the Lover is Master of, but even casts an agreeable Vizor or Veil over his Vices. Ill therefore do our formal Philosophers, full of a severe Moroseness, form to themselves an enervate and filthy Image of Love, to raise their Aversion to so heavenly a Passion; since in all human Affairs there is nothing more sincere, provided its Flames are kept in just Limits, and be not suffer'd to burn those things that are forbidden. But to make it appear, that this Fire of Love is not an Addition to a Breast worthy and fit for its Reception, but Born in it: Experience shews us, that not only Youth and Men of Riper years, but even Boys have felt the Force of this Passion. And Boys and young Men being more free from the Incumbrances of the World, can less govern themselves in this Affection; it is more anxious and solicitous in theirs than the Breast of Men more involv'd in Years and Experience. This spurs up their Minds to things above the common stress of their years, and makes them aim at an Excellence they wou'd not else have thought of: An Example will make the matter more plain.

THE

Force of LOVE.

THere was a Boy at School in a Country Town, who loving his Play more than his Book, made but little progress in the Arts he came thither to learn. It happen'd that a Lady of Quality came to the same Town with two of her Daughters; who being a particular Acquaintance of the Parents of this Boy, sent for him to her Inn, there to entertain him in Honour of his Friends. When he was come, he first began to regard one of the two Daughters with a singular Admiration, then to dwell on her Words, and at last in the first Interview to love her to extremity.

This brought his rude and uncultivated Mind to have a sense of some Cares; so that the

the next day he went again to the place that he was Conſcious of the Birth of his unknown Wound, and encreas'd his illneſs by a longer Converſation. The next day the Lady purſued her Journey, and left the Stripling almoſt dead in the place; for he durſt not own the Malady for fear of his Relations, and of being made the ſport of the Boys his Schoolfellows. After a long debate within himſelf, he cou'd find no other way worth following, but a cloſe and diligent Application to his Studies, hoping by his progreſs in Learning to redeem his paſt Time, and render himſelf ſo agreeable to his Parents, as to make them able to deny him nothing; that when he had employ'd his Time from this Accident ſo well, he might get leave, as a Reward of his Diligence, to go to ſee the next City, where this Lady then lived with his Beloved. This ſtrange Change of his Conduct ſurpriz'd both the Maſters and his fellow Schollars, who cou'd by no means geſs at the Cauſe of it, that he that ſo little a while ſince had a perfect Averſion to the ſtudy of Letters, ſhou'd now ſurpaſs every Body in his Love and Application: For he got up in the Morning to his Book, while others were taking their Repoſe; nor wou'd ever be drawn to any diverſion, but by the Force of his Maſter's Commands. For that Force of Love, which had poſſeſs'd the Boy, and begot this Diligence, mitigated

gated the ſenſe of the Labour, and gave the Muſes a Charm to him which he never knew before. But as it happens in ſo tender an Age, long Abſence had pretty well wore out that Flame which the Preſence of the young Lady had lighted in his unripe Boſom, the Thirſt and Deſire of Learning yet remain'd; and he made ſuch a wonderful Progreſs in Arts and Sciences, that the learned World was afterwards very much oblig'd to his Studies.

Growing now up to a Youth, he had yet a mind to ſee the Lady to the Power of whoſe Charms he had ow'd ſo conſiderable an Advantage, he made a Journey to the City of her Abode; but coming thither he found that ſhe was the day before Married to another: So never vent'ring to ſee her, he return'd to his Studies, and made them ever after his Wife and his Miſtreſs.

There are Ten Thouſand inſtances of the wonderful effects of Love; but that which is the preſent ſubject of our diſcourſe, tho' it go under that glorious Name, is far unworthy of the Title. The Ancients indeed made two *Venus*'s, two Goddeſſes of Love; one the Daughter of *Jupiter* and born in the Heavens, and therefore the ſource of all juſt Paſſions which are founded on Virtue; the other ſprung from the Froath of the Turbulent Sea, who is the Goddeſs of Luſt, ſpeaking properly; who ſcatters about thoſe unlawful, and thoſe waving and inconſtant Paſſions,

Paſſions, that give abundance of Fatigue and Pain in the Enjoyment, and often Miſery and Deſtruction in the Event. One is the ſource of the nobleſt Happineſs of Man, the other of the greateſt Miſery and Pain. 'Tis true, that experience has ſhown me, that if Reaſon and good Sence is incapable of Reforming them, all Penal Laws and Informers only add to the Evil, and harden thoſe in the Folly, who elſe might have been taught by one evil to avoid another. The Fatigues and the Conſequences of Whoring are often a ſeverer Puniſhment for the Folly, than any Law did hitherto ever inflict, nay, perhaps than is in the Power of any Legiſlators ever to invent; if horrible Diſeaſes, unpitied Poverty, and univerſal Contempt may be thought of that Nature. To ſee a Fool that has kept his Coach and Six, reduc'd to trudge about in a Thread bear Coat, Cobled Shoes, and a Piſsburnt Wigg, for an Age together, and carry Letters for a Pot of Ale, for being a Bubble to a Jilt, who never was true to him, nor wou'd give him one penny to keep him from ſtarving. To ſee another in the midſt of his Youth, decrepit as Age, full of Aches and Pains, Diſguſtful, nay, Loathſom Blotches, that bring Mortality it ſelf almoſt into Diſguſt; and this by a Company of Scandalous Drabs, who are as common as the Street he trod on; is a Puniſhment, I think, that no Law

Law has yet, nor any but Nature inflicted on the foolish Transgressions this way.

As I have observ'd Men of Quality impos'd on in every thing, the Poetaster passeth on them for a Poet; a Dawber for a Painter; a Scraper for a Musician; a Mason for an *Architect*; so does a worn out Whore of the Town for a Citizens Wife or Daughter; and she that has been common to his Valet de Chambre, goes down with him for a pure Virgin by the help of Alom and Address. There was a certain Noble Man in this City, who being an extraordinary Husband in all things, was very parcimonious even in his Whoring; he kept a Bawd whom he allow'd Twenty Pounds a year Salary, which was ill paid, to provide him Whores; and a *French* Surgeon whom he paid better, the better to Cure the ills the former procur'd; for he wou'd rather hazard his Body with a Drab of the Town, put on him by his Bawd for a Citizens Daughter, tho' he knew the Cheat, than venture his Money to procure wholesom Food. But this is a Common Bite among the Quality who deal with Bawds, *Drury-lane* furnishing them with Citizens Wives and Daughters, of all Degrees and Complexions.

Other Noble Lords are for singling out a bright Nymph of the Stage, or the Bar, and keeping her for his own use, while he is only at the expence of maintaining a Whore for the Publick. Tho' this were a mightier

tier Mode ſome years ſince than now, yet it is now ſo common, that Drawers and Tapſters keep their Whores averſe to Marriage. They are never Faithful, have no regard to the Man that ſupports them, make him and his Fortune a Sacrifice to their Vanity, Avarice, or Luſt; they act Love without Tenderneſs, a Man's hugging to his Boſom a cleaving Miſchief, inſtead of a ſoft and dear Companion.

THE

Kept MISS.

There was a Merchant in the City of *London*, who dealt for a great deal of Money, and as he had a plentiful income by his Trade, ſo he was reſolv'd to employ part of it, in thoſe Pleaſures which were agreeable to his Age, which was under Thirty Years. Gaming was a ſport he never much car'd for, and Drinking, tho' it gave the enjoyment of a Friend at the ſame time, yet his Conſtitution did not ſeem made for that Delight; Women were his chief Pleaſure, and yet afraid to Hazard his Health by living on the Common, he reſolv'd to find out ſome agreeable Girl whom he might keep to himſelf, and ſpend his looſer Hours with in Enjoyment, that a deprav'd Appetite

tite cou'd not give him with his Wife, tho' every way more Accomplish'd than the Lady of Pleasure which he chose. She was Beautiful in her Person, and Affable in her Temper; and had she been any Man's Wife but his own, there never had been a Woman that cou'd have pleas'd him better; but having had her some years, he cou'd find no more Charms in her.

This Gentleman Walking in the Park, met a young Lady, whose Face, whose Person, and whose Air pleas'd him extreamly: He address'd himself to her, and found her Discourse as agreeable as her Appearance, and perfectly compleated the Conquest of his Heart. He Walked with her so long, that he prevail'd with her to wait on her Home, where, by her Art, she fixt him to her Will, and he agreed to remove her from her Lodging and her present Gallant, who being an Officer in the Guards, cou'd not allow her to that extent which her Vanity desired. The Merchant immediately took her very fine Lodgings, and on her coming into them, presented her with a Hundred Guinias, and a Diamond Ring of more value; and Celebrated the first Night's Enjoyment with as much Pomp, as if it had been his Wedding Night to the finest and most Virtuous Lady in *London*. Her Caresses as little as they had of Nature, were, however so improv'd by Art, that the Merchant thought himself the happiest Man in *Christendom*:

ſtendom: Scarce a day paſs'd but he made her ſome preſent or other; and was ſuch a Sot, to believe that his Love and Generoſity had entirely engag'd her Inclinations. He only wiſh'd that good fortune wou'd rid him of his preſent Wife, that ſhe might ſucceed to his Ligitimate Embrace; but alaſs! a Whore has no Thoughts but of her Self, her own Interſt, or her Pleaſure; for when a Woman has once forſaken the Rules of Virtue, ſhe has nothing to retain her within any Bounds. All her care was to keep the Thefts of Love from the Eyes of her Keeper, and ſecretly to divide his Spoils with the Scoundrel ſhe fancied.

She never ſlipp'd any opportunity of his Fondneſs, without getting ſomething from him of value, either in Jewls or Money. The Miſs imagin'd it a prudent care to provide for her ſelf, if he ſhould Die or alter his Affections, which ſhe thought was impoſſible. She went to the Park and the Play, the Opera, and all the Reſorts of the Young and the Fair, nor wou'd ſhe deny her ſelf the ſatisfaction of the Embraces of any young Fellow ſhe lik'd, either at Home or Abroad, tho' her kind Keeper thought her conſtant to him, and that he only enjoy'd a Pleaſure which he paid ſo very dear for. At the Play She was mightily taken with one of the Actors; and rather than want her ſatisfaction, ſhe not only let him know her mind by the following Letter,

but

but ſent with it a Preſent to move his deſire of Gain.

YOu will not ſure be ſurpriz'd, that you ſhou'd ſeem agreeable to a young Lady, ſince doubtleſs you have found that by experience; that you never appear on the Stage but you Wound more in reality in the Boxes, than the Hero you repreſent does, in the imaginary Field. At leaſt I muſt on my ſelf own of thoſe, who think nothing more agreeable. If you doubt the Truth of my Letter, meet me in Covent-Garden-Square, *before Play time this Evening, and I'll convince you that I am no Hypocrite, when I profeſs that I Love. Yours* Amelia.

The hour appointed is come, and ſhe in a Hackney Coach waits with impatience the coming of *Roſcius*, who never diſappointing a Challenge of this Nature, was there waiting her coming; pleas'd with his readineſs at the Aſſignation, ſhe beckned him to the Coach, which when he was enter'd, ſhe pull'd off her Mask, and drew up the Glaſſes; ſhe was too Pretty not to ſatisfy him with the Adventure, and too Willing not to deny him any ſatisfaction he deſired, her Wiſhes preventing ever his Attempts. According to the Mode of *Covent Garden*, he ſoon made the Coach conſcious of his Vigour, and gave her that delight, that ſhe was reſolv'd to take him home to her Lodging; but it being a Night when he Acted a Chief a Chief Part, the Hour was appointed when the Play was done. In the mean time ſhe went home to have all things in that order, as to ſeem more worthy his purſuit, and to ſecure their Pleaſures from any interruption from her Keeper. She always took care to have a Maid exactly tutor'd to her Will, and therefore made her imprudently her Confident. This Maid, when the Merchant came, told him, That ſhe had been ill all day, and that ſhe was gon to Bed in hopes of getting ſome Sleep that Night, and deſir'd not to be diſturb'd till the Morning. The good Man was mightily troubled for her Indiſpoſition, and valued her Health ſo much, that he immediately went away, charging the Servant to have a peculiar care of her Miſtreſs; and the more to encourage her, gave her half a Piece.

The Keeper being thus eaſily put off, ſhe only expected her Gallant with impatience, and being in Bed for fear the Merchant ſhould have come up, ſhe was reſolv'd to receive her Gallant in that place and manner: She had provided a neat Collation and rich Wine, Conſerve and other comfortable eatables. *Roſcius* who had conceav'd Mountains of his Lady, was punctual to his Word, ſcarce allowing himſelf time to ſhift himſelf. *Phillis* lay in her Bed with her Boſom negligently bare, cover'd only with a fine Holland Sheet; for the Weather was very Warm: The ſight was ſo tempting, that tho' ſhe was taking her Gown to get up, having told him the Reafon of her being in that place, that the Maid had fcarce time to withdraw, before he threw himfelf into her willing Arms, and gave her an earneft of what he promis'd to do when in Bed. The firft Scene of Lewdnefs being over, the Lovers got up, Madam only in her thin loofe Gown, and *Rofcius* in his Cloaths all unbutton'd, as he generally wore them in the heat of the Weather. A Cap and the poor Keeper's Gown was foon brought for the Gallant to put on, who ftripping himfelf to his Shirt to be on equal terms with the Lady, clapp'd on the Gown that was brought him, and fate down to the Collation, and having eaten and drank to fatiety, the Bawd retires, and the Lovers go to the encounter, which lafted almoft till Morning, to the no fmall Scandal of the Houfe, and then departed highly fatisfy'd with his Intreague, of which he fufficiently boafted among his brethren, according to the worthy Cuftom of the Gentlemen of that Family. The Maid was told of this irregularity by the Landlady; who, according to her defire, acquainted her Lady with it; which was fo far from reforming her, or making her afraid of a difcovery, that the firft thing fhe did, was to put her fond Keeper on taking a fmall Houfe for her, where fhe might live more fecurely in her Whoring. She had not bin long fettled in her new Abode, but fhe found out

out a new Lover (for she us'd to say, That after the first or second engagement with a Man, the Pleasures grew Pall'd and Insipid) and this was an under Dancing Master in the House A Fellow, all whose merit lay in his Heels, and that but very slender too. Few of these Sparks, or Fidlers and Singers, have any share of Sesne and Understanding sufficient to make them above Fools. However Monsieur *Caper* had jumpt fortunately into this Ladies Affections, which was not only agreeable to his Lewdness, but his Vanity, who never had an Affair before with any Woman above an Orange-Wench. The same was his Treatment, and as Vigorous his Embraces; so that she thought she had chang'd nothing but the Man, and that for the better.

But this Coxcomb was more troublesom than she expected ; for tho' he valu'd her as little as she cou'd him, after the first heat of the Battle was over, yet he wou'd not quit her, in hopes of Food for his Body as well as his Vanity. The Letter she sent him was show'd to all the House, and *Roscius* at last had a sight of it ; He knew the Hand very well, but dissembled his Knowledge, and plainly told Mr. *Caper*, That he would never believe it any thing but his own inditeing to himself, or else from some *Drury-lane* Strumpet, unless he brought him into her Company. That *Caper* readily agreed to, and finding at last that he cou'd not get her to a Tavern, he carries *Roscius* directly to her House; the Door being open'd, and without any Cerimony, lead him in with such Assurance and Familiarity, as convinc'd him of what had past. Coming into the Parlour to her, Madam was Drinking her Chocolate, her Keeper as good Fate wou'd have it being just gone to the *Change* —— *My dear* Phillis, (*said* Caper,) *I have made bold to bring a dear Friend of mine to Drink a Dish of Chocolate with you*— *Here* Betty, *draw me a Chair for the Gentleman* —— Madam no sooner saw *Roscius* but she started, and blush'd with a Scarlet dye. He made her a Bow, and address'd himself to her in this Manner —— *And Madam, can you indeed fall so low, to admit such a Creature as this to those Arms which are only fit to incircle a God! Was I thrown aside for this Animal, that has not sence enough to know the Happiness he enjoys? Whether will you fall? what greater Wretch can you find out next for your Embraces? But that I can do nothing to do you an injury, who have given me so much Pleasure, I wou'd let the Gentleman your Friend know this great Rival: But that I will leave to his own Vanity, who has taken care that so many shou'd see your Letter, that I doubt not but it will come soon to his Ears. If this shou'd happen, Madam, and you be discarded, as you really deserve, for past favours, I'll get you in to be a waiter in the House, and there you will be a new Face, may get a new Cull, whom you may use a while like the Gentleman you have; but I fear it is not in your Temper*

to

to make uſe of your good fortune, and therefore as your ill luck may be Infectious, from this time I ſhall never trouble you. Adieu moſt judicious Lady.

With theſe words he left the Houſe, but *Caper* ſtaid with her, and wou'd have preſs'd her to grant him new Favours; but ſhe with an Aſſurance peculiar to her ſelf, not only refus'd him any more, but flatly deny'd that ſhe had ever ſeen him before, or had any thing to do with him. On his proceeding to Rudeneſs, ſhe threatned him with a Reſentment of a Gentleman's Sword, who wou'd not ſee her abus'd. That qualified his Rage of Love, having a Mortal Antipathy to the ſight of a Sword; ſo challenging the Maid as a Witneſs of his paſt Happineſs, he found her in the ſame ſtory, and to convince them both of their Impudence, pull'd out her Letter, which being what ſhe deſir'd, ſhe ſnatch'd it away; he ſtruggling for it, the Maid and Miſtreſs fell both upon him, and with the Poker knock'd Poor *Caper* flat as a Flounder. As ſoon as he recover'd himſelf he beg'd for Quarter, which on theſe Conditions they admitted him to; That he ſhou'd do her that Juſtice to clear her Reputation to *Roſcius*, and own the Truth, That he never had ſeen her before, but miſtook her for ſome other Woman. The Terms were harſh to a Man of his Vanity; but Fear prevail'd, and he promis'd any thing to get out of the Houſe.

He was no sooner gone, but the Rage that *Roscius* had express'd, stuck on her mind, she fancied it discover'd something of a value he retain'd for her Person, and that renew'd her desire of a fresh Commerce with him. The more she thought of it, the more she desir'd it, and at last sends her Female *Mercury* with this Letter to him:

I *Was so surpriz'd (dear* Roscius*) to day with the unaccountable Impudence of the Fellow that came with you to my House, and the Reproaches that you very unjustly then made me, that I cou'd not tell what to say to you; and your hasty departure left me no time for Vindication: But coming to my self, I suppose I sufficiently punish'd him for his Insolence with a Lady whom he never saw before. I desire but one hour to convince you of the Truth of what I say, and then censure me as you find me Innocent or Guilty. I find what I cou'd never have believ'd, that I cannot bear your Resentment; tho' I wou'd not have you imagin it the effect of any Passion for you, but only to clear my self of an Imputation which I scorn and detest.* *Yours* Amelia.

Roscius knew not what to make of this Letter, but promises to meet her the next Night at the Park near *Rosamond*'s Pond. In the mean while he went to find out Monsieur *Caper*, to examin the matter a little closer;

closer; he found him in Chamber with his Head bound up, and his Eyes Black and Blue: How now Monsieur *Caper*, said he, what disaster befell you after I left you with so fine a Lady, in whose good Grace you had so considerable a Place? What did the Kind Keeper come and catch you in his *Purleus*, and give you a Remembrance of his Resentment? Come prithee unfold the Mystery. Damn the Bitch (cried out the disconsolate Monsieur) this is a barbarous Nation, they have no respect to Art; to use a Forreigner at this abominable Rate? Why, Sir, assoon as you were gon, she not only refus'd the Favours she had formerly granted, but denied that she ever had seen me before; I press'd the matter more close, she fell a scratching my Face, the Maid coming to her assistance knock'd me down with a Poker, and for fear of the Resentment of my Anger, call'd in a Fellow to keep me in Awe, whom I promis'd to do her justice, as she call'd it, and tell you, that I never had seen her before in my Life; but I promis'd that only to save my Life then in danger, but now I am got free, I will publish her in the Streets. *Mortbleu*, there never was so impudent a Whore in the World, I have lain with her Twenty times: Nay, you saw her own Letter (which she has now got from me) and yet the Damn'd Jade denies she ever saw me.

Roscius cou'd not forbear laughing at the Monsieur's ill Fortune, and tho' he was satisfied that what he said was true, yet since she had made him such a sacrifice to him, he cou'd not but forgive her, and to prevent further Mischief, advis'd poor *Caper* to to sit down with what he had, and hold his Tongue, both because he cou'd not speak of it without shame to himself, and even the hazard of his Life, since a Woman's Revenge for an Offence of that Nature, seldom stops of this side the Grave. The Monsieur full of Pain, and stout at the Distance of future Danger swore he wou'd have Ballads made on her, and sung about the Streets, and under her own Window. *Roscius* finding that all his persuasions were in vain, left him to consult his Pillow, and the next Night met the Fair Wanton at *Rosamond*'s Pond. *Roscius* had no mind to make any doubts of her Protestations, so that whatever she said found the success, that she desir'd ; but he told her it was necessary, that she shou'd threaten the Monsieur a little more, since Fear wou'd cure his Vanity more, than any other Medicine whatsoever. She enquired his Lodging, resolving to take his Advice. They spent some time in renewing their Passion, and so adjourn'd to the Tavern, where their usual Freedoms past betwixt them, and she told him that she wou'd be glad to see him at her House, but that it was dangerous to her Fortune,

since

ſince her Friend was of late grown very Jealous. She only made this Excuſe, becauſe her Indifference return'd: So parting very kindly, ſhe ſet him down at his Lodging, and went home to her own Houſe, where the Cully was waiting her coming with impatience. She ſeem'd very Melancholly, he enquir'd the Cauſe: Alas! ſaid ſhe, I have been to ſee a dear Schoolfellow of mine who is dying, and whom I fear I ſhall never ſee more; I ſtaid thus long to ſee her depart this Life if I cou'd, but her Fate is lengthned perhaps to another day. She had always Tears at her Command, and then ſummoning them to her Aid ſhe let fall a Pearly Shoar, which ſtruck the tender Merchant to the Heart; for a Weeping Beauty has a ſtrange Power to move the Soul. He comforted her all he cou'd, and by the help of a Preſent he had brought her, and a Glaſs of right *Burgundy*, which he took care ſhe ſhou'd always have by her, her Melancholly was recover'd, and nothing but Joy and Pleaſure ſucceeded, till the Hour he was to go home; never in all his dotage paſſing the whole Night with her, but having been in Bed till Twelve, One, or Two, he went home to his Wife, out of Civility to her Virtue, not Love to her Beauty.

If any thing cou'd have given her a Moderation, or Caution, the ſeveral Eſcapes ſhe had had might have done it; but walking

ing in the Temple Garden ſhe ſees a young brisk Fop, that with as much Impertinence, as Pertneſs, makes his Addreſſes to her: The Fellow was handſome enough in his Perſon, and being juſt in the Bloom, the Down but yet riſing on his Chin, gave her a Reliſh of Youth which ſupplied all other defects. He was Clerk to a Lawyer of the *Middle-Temple*, and it being now Vacation time, he Beau'd it with his Long Wigg and Sword: But had he been a Sharper, a Footman, or greater Scoundrel, if his Appearance was clean, Madam never examin'd into the merits of his Birth, Honeſty, or Underſtanding. However ſhe thought him too young to be truſted with her Houſe, for Youth ſeldom guards the Reputation of Ladies it has to do with, a very young Fellow being fond of being thought a Man, diſcover their Intrigues to get that Reputation. So that the *Italian*'s Advice is good to the Ladies,——*Intrigue not with a Man under Thirty, ſince he will tell to be thought a Man*; *nor paſt Forty, for he will tell to be thought not paſt one.* For this Reaſon ſhe appointed to meet him at a Lady's of the Town, who was her Relation by Birth, as well as Occupation, and there ſhe gratified her ſelf, and him, as long as they both thought fit; when getting up, Dreſſing and Parting, he was reſolv'd to dogg her to her Lodging, having been infinitely pleas'd with her Converſation. The next day he

was

was there to enquire who liv'd in the Houſe, and found that only a ſingle Lady and her Maid liv'd there, with none of the choiceſt Reputation in the Neighbourhood: Tho' he was not very certain that this was the right Houſe, yet being a forward young Chick he was reſolv'd to knock at the Door, and try his good Fortune. By chance the Maid was gone out, and Madam went to the Door her ſelf, and was very much ſurpriz'd to find her laſt Nights Gallant had follow'd her ſo cloſe; but having a ready Wit ſhe Wink'd at him, and ſtopt his firſt Sally by ſaying, Sir, you have miſtaken the Houſe, we Let no Lodgings here ; and ſoftly wiſper'd, ſhe wou'd meet him at the ſame place, her Friend being then with her. Which ſhe only did to get time to conſider how to get rid of ſo dangerous a Companion: But ſhe cou'd find no expedient but a Promiſe to meet at the old place as often as he ſhou'd ſend to her. This to her was an intollerable Yoak, and muſt be broke ſome way or other.

Her Relation had a very large Acquaintance among the Pocky Siſterhood, and therefore on her deſire cou'd provide her with a Lady that was capable of giving him ſuch a Remembrance that wou'd coſt him ſome Months to get off: So making the young Spark pretty mellow, after the heat of his Love was over, he fell aſleep, and ſhe getting from him let the other ſupply her

her place. Being now refresh'd by sleep, he wakes, and renews the encounter in so vigorous a manner, that in less than a Week he found he had reason to wish he had not been so eager for the continuation of an Amour for which he was like to pay so dear. However hoping it was but a small Evil, and Business now in Term time keeping him so close to his Desk, that he cou'd not take proper Medicines in time, let it alone for three Weeks longer, when ev'ry day discover'd new symptoms of a more terrible disaster, he is confin'd to his Chambers during the operation of threeMonths; in which Time the good Lady remov'd from her House at the Court end of the Town into the City, and left no Track or Footsteps by which she might be trac'd by the Spark she had so severely punish'd for his troublesom Kindness.

To recount all that she had betray'd her Friend to wou'd be endless, since from the Knight to the Carman she had tried all that she fancied, it being her Maxim to deny her self no Pleasure that Health, Wealth, and Youth cou'd afford her.

It was now the Fortune of the Merchant to have run out a little too much of his Cash in a Merchandize that made no Returns; and while he was thinking what course to take, he had Letters from the *Indies* of a near Relation who was dead, and had left him a very considerable Fortune.

The

The better to ſecure it, he was adviſ'd by his Friends, not only to go thither himſelf, but alſo to carry a Cargo with him that he might double before he return'd. He had no manner of ſtruggle to leave his good Wife behind him; but it went to his Soul to think of parting with his Miſtreſs. He did all he cou'd to perſuade her to go with him; but ſhe declar'd that the very ſight of the Sea was ſufficient to kill her. So leaving her a better ſupport than his Wife and Family, he ſet Sail, accompliſh'd his Voyage with ſucceſs, and in his Return home, ſtaid a little while at the Iſle of St *Hellena*; there he met with an old Acquaintance, who had been oblig'd lately to go thither as a Refuge from that ill fortune, which his own folly had brought upon him. Enquiring into the matter, our Merchant found his Friend had there got a Place which afforded him and his Wife a happy ſupport.—But my Friend ſaid he, why brought you your Wife with you, when your Fortune, as bad as it was, had left you ſo good an excuſe of leaving her behind you? I think the farther from my Wife the Happier, and if it were not for the moſt Charming of her Sex, a taking young Harlot, that I have kept for ſome Time, I wou'd never have return'd from the *Indies*; but ſhe is the pretticſt Innocent, Faithful Turtle that ever lov'd.

His Friend firſt Laugh'd at him, then fetch'd a Sigh from the bottom of his Heart: Alas!

Alas! my Friend, I wish you may never be convinc'd of your Error in the putting any Faith in the Protestations of a Harlot, as I have been, you wou'd then to your Cost find the difference betwixt a lawful, faithful Wife, and the designing Caresses of a Whore, who values what she gets of you, and not your self: There is no Tye of Interest betwixt you, and where there is not that, there can be no lasting Friendship betwixt Man and Man, or Love betwixt Man and Woman. Your Wife's Interest is yours, she is Happy or Miserable as you Thrive or Lose; Interest therefore fortifies her Love to take care to guard your Reputation and Substance, while it being quite contrary in a Whore: It is her Business to get all from you that she can, and the sooner she Ruins you, the sooner she gains her bad ends, in casting you off for some one that has more of the smiles of blind Fortune. And then she who Caress'd and Wheedled you will not know you, and if you speak to her spit, at you, and call you Sawcy Fellow. I am my self proof of this very thing I assert; and in my Misfortunes met with several miserable Objects ruin'd by the same Cause.

THE

THE
Cully's Fate.

YOU know very well that I was a Man who got a great deal of Money, and might have left my Family a considerable Fortune, had it not been my ill Fate to have faln into the bewitching Company of that deteſtable Creature to whom I at laſt ow'd my Ruin. The Plot was it ſeems laid for me by her former Gallant, who being weary of her, and unable better to provide for her, propos'd to get me to ſee her, and doubted not by her Arts and my Folly to engage me in her Snares. He invited me to a Bottle and a Fowl, and to make the Cheer compleat, when I was a little warm with Wine, he, by my conſent, ſent for *Sylvia*; ſhe was not very young, having paſt her Thirtieth year; but by Art and ſome Benefit of Nature, the Lights and other Occurences, ſhe loſt at leaſt Ten years of her Age in my Opinion.

She was of a middle ſize both for Stature and Bulk; her Hair Cole Black, her Eyes Hazle and Sparkling, her Skin Clear, her Lips Ruddy, her Noſe Aquiline; ſhe ſung prettily, was Gay, good Humour'd and Airy, ſhe wou'd not let Melancholly come into the place where ſhe was; at leaſt till ſhe

ſhe had ſecur'd the Fool ſhe deſign'd for her Gin. Theſe things took wonderfully with me that Night, and I diſcover'd my liking ſo far, that my Friend (I ſpeak after the way of the Town, which calls any one Friend) took occaſion to withdraw; I made uſe of my Time, preſs'd matters ſo cloſe that we agreed on the Point, I was to bring the Purchaſe with me the next day, and take poſſeſſion of what I had bought. I am aſham'd to tell what I gave her, ſo much was I beſotted on her, but I wiſh my Extravagance had ceas'd there; but having once admitted me into her Arms, ſhe was reſolv'd never to part with me till ſhe had drain'd me of all my Money: The Park and the Play, *Chelſea* and all the Reſorts of Pleaſure muſt we frequent. I was once with her at the Magpye at *Chelſea*, and up in a Chamber where there was a Bed, after our Sports we drank a Bottle, and I ſung her a Song. One pair of Stairs there was an Acquaintance of mine, who hearing my Voice knew it, and ſending his Name, I invited him up with his Friend to my Room. Drinking about I began to ſing a Song, as I then us'd frequently to do; but ſays he Mr.——your Voice is excellently Good, but like all Baſes, that are ſo, I think it ſounds much better at a Diſtance; if that be all, ſaid I, I will go down to the bottom of the Stairs and try; the Voice in the Aſcent I believe will ſound very agreeably.

ably. He embraced the motion, it being indeed what he deſign'd; I cou'd ſuſpect nothing ſince there were two in the Room with her; yet her Impudence was ſuch, that whilſt I was Singing ſhe laid her ſelf on the Bed, and let my Acquaintance lie with her whilſt the other was in the Room. The miſchief was but juſt over as I had done my Song, and I thought I ſaw ſome Confuſion in his Face tho' none at all in hers. I proferr'd, on his praiſing my Voice at that diſtance, to go down a ſecond time, but he excus'd my former Trouble, and adjourn'd it to another Time, his Friend having refus'd to make uſe of the ſame Opportunity, as they afterwards told me, when the diſcovery cou'd be of no uſe to me.

She had with her a Servant as good as her ſelf, who wou'd drink as much as her Miſtreſs, and that was a large Portion; and who having a Brother in Town, wou'd needs one day take her Miſtreſs to ſee him, which ſhe agreed to on this Condition, that ſhe ſhould paſs for her fellow Servant. *Sylvia* being thus dreſs'd, goes with her Maid to an Ale-houſe, and ſends for the Brother of her Maid, who taking her for a Servant Wench was as free with her as he cou'd deſire, ſhe giving him all the encouragement he cou'd wiſh; She Treated him there, then carried him to the Tavern, and from thence to her own Bed, where ſhe kept him betwixt

Drunkenneſs and Luſt for three whole days: But then expecting me to Town, the Fellow was diſmiſs'd till ſhe wanted him again to do her drudgery.

I all this while ignorant of the matter, concluded that I had as true a Turtle as ever bill'd: But at laſt by my Dotage on her, Neglect of my Buſineſs, and ſome Misfortunes in Trade, I found my ſelf unable to ſtand my Ground; ſo being Arreſted, I was forc'd to turn my ſelf over to the *Queens-Bench*, where I ſpent not only all I had my ſelf, but all that my poor Wife cou'd find among her Friends for my ſupport. I ſent to *Sylvia* often in my diſtreſs, ſhe firſt denied me Civily, then Rudely, and poſitively refus'd me Money enough to pay my Fees of the Priſon, when now I had made up my matters ſo far as to get my Liberty, to ſollicit ſome other means of maintaining my ſelf and my Family, ſufficiently convinc'd me of my former Error. However I once went to ſee her, to try if ſhe cou'd refuſe me a little of that Treaſure which had made her a conſiderable Fortune: But ſhe wou'd not ſee me, and plainly affronted me, which touch'd the very Miniſter of her Lewdneſs, her Maid, to that degree, that ſhe proffer'd me Five *Guinea's* of her own Money. Tho' my Occaſions were great, yet I wou'd not take ſuch a Summ from a Servant, and ſo went my way. Then cou'd I hear of all the Tricks ſhe had play'd me,

no

no body telling me one ſyllable of them before. 'Tis true, ſome urg'd in their Excuſe, That when a Man is beſotted on a Woman, he is ſo far from being reform'd by a diſcovery of her Roguery, that he hates the Man that makes it. Pride perhaps is the Reaſon, which is aſham'd to let us own our ſelves in an Error, or enduring at leaſt to be caught in it by another, who by that may pretend to a greater ſhare in Wiſdom, than our ſelves. At laſt my Friends taking Compaſſion more on my Wife and Children, than on me, got me this Place by her ſollicitation, who wou'd not leave me in ſo hazardous a Voyage, but ventur'd her ſelf with me, and gives me a ſort of happineſs I never experienc'd in the Arms of that Harlot.

If you think you have got ſuch a Treaſure in yours, make one Experiment which will juſtify or condemn your Conduct to her, and to your Wife. As ſoon as you come to *England*, and made your way to *London*, go to your Miſtreſs, and pretend that you are Caſt away, have loſt all your Fortune, and only have what you left in her Hands to begin the World with; then ſee how ſhe will receive you. Do the ſame to your Wife, and then diſcover the difference betwixt Vice and Virtue.

When the Merchant's Friend had done, the Merchant was ſo touch'd with his Miſfortunes, he was reſolv'd to take his Advice, and promis'd him if he found the Benefit of it in the Tryal, he would take his eldeſt Son Prentice without any Money.

The Continuation of the Kept Miſſes.

THE Wind ſitting Fair the Merchant arriv'd ſafely at *Plimouth*, where taking Poſt immediately, he got ſafe to Town, and dreſſing himſelf at a Friend's Houſe who was to ſecond his pretended Misfortunes, both to his Miſtreſs and his Wife, he went directly to the former; who had given her ſelf over to all manner of Lewdneſs in his Abſence, and had not much left beſides the Jewels he had given her, which were in Pawn, and about Fifty pieces of old Gold, and Two hundred Pounds in current Money.

She was at firſt overjoy'd to ſee him; but when he had told her a moſt diſmal ſtory of his Misfortunes, and what Treaſures he had loſt, and deſir'd her to aſſiſt him in his neceſſity, which her welcom Tranſports at his Arrival perſuaded him, that he had reaſon to expect; ſhe grew very cold, told him that ſhe was unprovided of Money, that the Neceſſities of her Friends had drain'd her of her Money, but that if he wou'd call on her the next day, ſhe wou'd try her utmoſt to ſerve him; ſo ſhe diſmiſs'd him, and ſent immediately to the Merchant his Friend who us'd to pay her his Allowance in his Abſence, and of which there

there was now a quarter due: He ſent her Word (as he had bin directed by the Merchant) that truly he cou'd pay her no more, having already made greater diſburſements for him than he fear'd he ſhou'd ever be pay'd, ſince he was come back ſo needy a Bankrupt from his Voyage, that he had not Cloaths to his Back fit to appear among Gentlemen.

The Jilt having heard this Story from another, concluded that what the Merchant had ſaid to her was not a meer Tryal of her Love, as ſhe had before imagin'd, and therefore had her Anſwer ready for him the next day.

In the mean time he took his Friend with him to his Wife, and made him go before to introduce the matter to her by way of precaution, which having done in the moſt lamentable Words he cou'd think of, But where is my poor unfortunate (ſaid his Wife) 'tis well that I have not loſt him too; I value not his Goods if he but ſurvive: He is my dearer Part, Where is he? Let me ſee him. Upon this coming in, ſhe run into his Arms, and embrac'd him for near a Quarter of an Hour, ſmothering him almoſt with Kiſſes and Tears of Joy---- Ah! my Love, ſaid ſhe, do I hold thee in my Arms! have I got thee ſafe from the Rocks and Seas! Trouble not thy ſelf at the loſs, we muſt ſubmit to Providence which orders all things for the beſt, at leaſt for me——for none will Rival me in a broken Fortune, I ſhall have thee all to my ſelf. Upbraid me not, ſaid he, my dear Wife in my Misfortunes——far be it from me ſaid ſhe; I ſhou'd not deſerve thy Love if ever I did——But I have ſav'd ſomething out of my Allowance ſince I have been thy Wife, which will do more than Cheriſh thee, tho' it be got by my good Houſewifery 'tis thy Money, thou canſt improve it for the good of thy Family: A Thouſand Pounds, beſides my Rings and the few Jewels my Mother left me, take all and be eaſie.

The Merchant unable to hear ſo much unmerited Love from a Wife whom he never had valued, as ſhe diſcover'd, was quite confounded and aſham'd——Why all this Goodneſs to me, ſaid he, my Dear, my injur'd Wife! Thou knoweſt I have wrong'd thee, gon aſtray after forraign Charms, and was blind to thoſe Beauties of Mind and Perſon, of which in thee I was the happy Maſter——I know no Crime, I am not a Judge of thy Actions aſſured ſhe. All that I am is thine by Right, and I ſurrender it to thee, hoping at leaſt that thou wilt own that I have been a good Steward, and that Praiſe from thy Mouth is my Reward——No more I conjure thee (interrupted the Merchant) I am not able to ſupport thy Goodneſs; but I will make thee amends all my Life to come. Know then that this Story of my Misfortunes was only a pretence

tence to try thy Goodneſs, and that Womans Villainy who has too long miſled me from my Duty, and whoſe Enchantment is now at an end, and I to morrow will give a Proof of my Repentance in her Puniſhment.

This moving Scene being over, the Merchant with his Friend paſt the day with his Wife and Family in Joy, and celebrated that Night as if it had been the firſt of their Marriage, as it was like to be the moſt happy of their Life.

The next day in his old Cloaths he came to his Miſtreſs, but ſhe cou'd not be ſpoken with; with much ado he gain'd admittance, but not one good Look. She told him ſhe wonder'd at his Aſſurance to apply himſelf to her for his Money again, after ſhe had wore out her Youth and her Beauty with him: That truly ſhe muſt firſt take care of her ſelf, and if ſhe thought he wou'd ever trouble her any more, ſhe wou'd not be long in his knowledge. He begg'd, he pray'd, reproach'd her, but nothing wou'd do; when in comes the Merchant his Friend to ſpeak for him, but that was as fruitleſs; till at laſt, ſays his Friend to the Merchant, I have in my Hands the means of your Revenge, by breaking your Order, for I have let her have no Money ſince you have been gon but what ſhe has given me her Notes for; ſo that if ſhe do not immediately pay that down, I have the Officers without to execute a Writ upon her. This Houſe is taken in your Name, and the Goods I know you paid for, I ſhall likewiſe ſeize on them for your uſe. Come Madam, Four Hundred Pounds you have had of me on Notes under your Hand, if you have not Money, your Jewels will do; for immediate ſatiſfaction will I have, or you ſhall be treated with the utmoſt Ignominy.

Her Paſſion can't be well expreſs'd, but oblig'd to comply, ſhe produc'd her 200 *l.* and 50 pieces of old Gold, aſſuring them that her Jewels were in Pawn; ſo on her giving them a Note to the Perſon that had them, they gave her up her Notes. Well, ſaid the Merchant, tho' your barbarous Treatment of me deſerves no Compaſſion, yet I will do ſomething for you becauſe you once pleas'd me: The 200 *l.* is yours, and your wearing Cloaths; whatever elſe of Jewels and Furniture is here, or in Pawn, ſhall be given to my Wife, who, tho' injur'd for thy ſake, Treated me with Tenderneſs and Generoſity, ſav'd a great deal out of ſo ſmall an Allowance, when thou haſt ſquander'd all away on Vice and Folly. To thy greater Confuſion know that my pretended Misfortunes are only to try thee, and that I bring home with me upward of 70000 *l.*

The Miſs in Confuſion, with her Servant in Iniquity, is turn'd out of Door, the Goods and Jewels redeem'd and given to his Wife,

and

and he for ever averſe to bad Women, having learnt too late, that their Smiles and Charms were like the Harmony of the *Syrens*, that brought nothing but deſtruction.

When this Change in the Merchant was known to his Friends, he was ſoon told of all her Tricks and Whoredoms, which ſtill confirm'd him in his Contempt of ſuch Creatures, and ſatisfied him that ſhe wou'd revenge him on her ſelf by her own Lewdneſs and Folly.

Near *Golden-Square* there liv'd a Lady of this Kind much celebrated for her Beauty, but more remarkable for her Pride and Luxury. She was a pedling Grocer's Daughter in St. *James*'s Pariſh: Nature had given her a Perſon extreamly Charming, and that conſidering the Men ſhe had to do with, paſs'd for Wit and Truth, and every thing elſe, of real Value; for among her Cullies ſhe had a kind of a Party Bully, an old formal Courtier, a Country Member of Parliament, a worn out Beau, and a City Gameſter, beſides any other who wou'd pay her Price.

She ſo far forgot that ſhe ſprung from a Mechanick, that ſhe was perpetually railing at them as a contemptible part of the Vulgar: When Green Peaſe were at Fifteen Shillings a little Plate full, ſhe complain'd they were too old for her, and fit only for the Vulgar; equally extravagant in all other things, ſhe never ſpar'd her Cully's Pocket. The State Bully was ſoon weary of her;

her; then the Country Senator took his Place; but she being entirely Mercenary, having a fairer offer from the old Courtier, receiv'd him as Commander in chief of her Fort; yet in private met her Member of Parliament at her Sisters, a venerable Bawds not far distant from her: For she wou'd not lose the Benefit that might be made of any Coxcomb, that wou'd share her with another. By several of these she had two or three Boys, and as they run about her House she calls them, as Beaux do their Wiggs, by the Names of those that made them; so does she her Children by their Names whom she thinks did beget them. She was a profess'd Enemy to good Sense and Generosity, using to say, Men of Wit, and Generosity, were always poor wretched Fellows; always Beggars. Tho' her other Gallants wou'd admit of Rivals in her Favours, the old Courtier wou'd not suffer it; so that all her Intriguing with the Rest was done in Private, and each had their particular Hours and Days of Happiness appointed, at the House she had taken for her Sister to that end. But the Lady cou'd not Dance so nicely in a Net, but that some Spies on her Actions, who watch'd to do her a Kindness, gave the old Courtier Notice of her abusing him with more than one, and let him know the very Place of their Rendezvous. But too much infatuated, at first he gave no Ear to the Information, till afterwards a fit of of Jealousie succeeding, he plac'd such Spies as shou'd be sure to bring him certain Intelligence; by whom he found that he was made the Property to support her Vanity and Grandeur, while others shar'd the Prize on much easier Terms. So coming to the Lady's Sister's when she was actually in Bed with her Senator, he forc'd his way up Stairs, and found Madam just Rising, and the Spark escap'd into the Closset; she wou'd soon have perswaded him that being late at her Sister's the last Night, she was forc'd to lie there, and not sleeping well, she lay in Bed so late to recover her sleep: But the Courtier was not to be impos'd on, and taking his leave of her, never saw her more.

The chief Cully having thus forsaken her, half the Bait to their Amours was taken away, and her Lovers dropt off one after another, till she was left to her own Fortune to provide fresh Gallants, which she did, till her Face was so common that none of the Grand Gusto wou'd have any thing to do with her; then she fell to filthy Mechanicks, who had been so much her Aversion; from thence to Porters and Footmen. When plying in the Streets the godly Reformers press'd her for *Bridewell*, in which worthy Colledge she compleated her Character and Knowledge so far as to be a confirm'd Whore, and Pick-pocket; by one she got the Pox, and by the other the Gallows, which was the Noble end of this Heroick

roick Lady, who was endued with all the extreameſt Qualities of the moſt abandon'd Whores.

I cou'd tell you of other ſorts of Whores, who breath nothing but Piety, go to Church every *Sunday*, and to the Sacrament every Month, and at Night to Bed to their Gallants, with as little ſcruple, as if Fornication were no more a Sin, than eating of Syllabub: But this is a Diſcourſe proper for another Head, with which I will to morrow Night entertain you if you think fit; that is, The Godly of our Nation, and the Pious Reformers.

I cou'd likewiſe tell you of the abandon'd Male Whores, but theſe are not fit to be mention'd tho' too common, and viſible; and of your Scoundrel Stallions, who, like Mercenary Whores, ſell the pleaſures of Love. Nay, they are a Vermin ten times more pernicious; becauſe it is ten times more in their Power to do Miſchief: Theſe Fellows, generally of the *Hibernian* Nation, who appearing like Gentlemen of Figure and Eſtates, are admitted to your Houſes as Friends; by this means they get Acceſs to your Wives, and the opportunity of Corrupting them; whom they make pay for their Folly, while the Husband that had admitted this Fellow as a Gentleman, pays for the maintaining the Port and Appearance to which he ows his Diſhonour. Of theſe, as of Whores, there are different Kinds; ſome

ſome Lew'd or Rakhelly, others Grave and Formal; the latter are the more dangerous, with the Ladies who value their Reputation, tho' they wou'd enjoy the Pleaſure. For on their Gravity they promiſe Caution and Secrecy; for there are Ladies fond enough of a private Amour, who will not truſt their Fame to a Man that has no regard to his own; while they thinking it ſecure in the Hands of one of theſe Grave Stallions, they ſtretch their Purſes to oblige him. Theſe are more inexcuſable than Whores, becauſe they ſeek out and tempt thoſe they Ruin, Whores are ſaught to; Theſe are Men, and while there are Wars in the World ought not to quit the Encounters of *Mars* for thoſe of *Venus*: Beſides, Women have not all the Opportunities and Means of employing themſelves, and living handſomly by their Induſtry; a Man may always put himſelf forward in one Poſt or another. The Whores have nothing to do with Corrupting of Families; but theſe Stallions invade other Mens Rights, and put their own Spurious Iſſue in the Room of the Right Heir of the Family. In ſhort, inſtead of our Reformers falling on the poor Whores who take up with Half-a-Crown, they ſhou'd ſearch into theſe Scoundrels, that Revenge the Whores Quarrel on their Wives and Daughters.

I cou'd give you ſome Inſtances of the Villainy of theſe ſort of Creatures, which con-

contain the higheſt Treachery, and the greateſt Ingratitude: But the Night is ſo far waſted, that I fear you are now quite tired with my tedious Diſcourſe. However this Uſe you may make of the Diſcoveries we have given you of this Kind, to fix in your Mind, That there is no Whore in the World, how plauſible ſoever ſhe may ſeem, how dear, proteſting and loving; that cares one Farthing for any Man by whom ſhe has any Benefit, or to whom ſhe owes any Gratitude. 'Tis true, few of the moſt profligate Whores there are, who has not ſome beloved Scoundrel, on whom ſhe ſquanders what ſhe has got by her Cully. You ſee the Nature of all the Trade in theſe few Inſtances we have given you; ſo that if you are after this miſled by their falſe Charms, and falſer Proteſtations, you are without excuſe.

My Zealous *Guinea* here putting an end to his Diſcourſe, with thanks to the *Golden Spies*, I turn'd my ſelf to my Reſt; which in a little Time I found coming on me moſt agreeably.

THE

THE
Fifth Nights Entertainment.
OF
The Godly and Reformers.

I Was ſo pleas'd with the Diſcoveries I had made by my *Golden Spies*, that I retir'd home with pleaſure every Evening betimes; but this Day had produc'd other Buſineſs, that took me up ſome time after it was dark: For as I was returning home, I was ſent for into the Neighbourhood by a Friend, to Bayl a young Lady that was taken up by the Reforming Conſtables, as ſhe was leading home to her Father's Houſe by a Relation.

When I came, I found the poor Lady all in Tears, and the Gentleman, who had ſent for me, a little in Drink, and Swearing at the Rogues of Reformers. The Conſtable was a Zealot, and took notice of all his Oaths, and Swore before the Juſtice that he had Swore about Two Hundred; for which he was oblig'd to pay. I endeavour'd to mitigate the Matter with the Conſtable, and Wheedle him very ſmoothly, to prevail with

with him to ſtay till Juſtice —— was come home, who was an honeſt Gentleman, and had been out at his Bottle till it was now paſt Ten a Clock when News was brought that he was come home. By good Fortune the Juſtice knew both the Gentleman and the young Lady, ſo diſmiſs'd them, and gave the Conſtable a very ſevere Reprimand; which made him go out muttering to himſelf, that he wou'd bring no more Griſt to his Mill.

The Juſtices Coach was yet at the Door, which being ſtopp'd, the Lady was ſent home in it for fear of any freſh diſaſter of that Nature; and the Juſtice ſtopping us to drink one ſolitary Bottle till the Return of the Coach, I began to enquire what he thought of theſe Reformers?

Why truly (ſaid he) I am of the Opinion of a Learned and Worthy Judge, who is the Honour of the Bench where he preſides; who when the Fellows went about to get People of Faſhion to ſubſcribe to be of their precious Society of Reformation of Manners, told them with an honeſt Heat, That he did not find this Age any Wickeder than the laſt; and ſinc ethat did well enough without Reformers, he cou'd ſee no occaſion for them now, nor wou'd he ſet his Hand to their Paper. Tho' this Noble Judge refus'd it, yet the Jeſt on it is, they went to the Perſons the moſt remarkable for their frequent and profeſs'd Gallantry to the Fair,

Fair, who willingly subscrib'd to be of a Society, which pretended to direct their diligence against the very Frailty for which they had the greatest Inclination. But this indeed must be said for some of the great Ones in this particular, they subscrib'd for the suppressing of poor Whores, not of those who were Rich; of them who got but little by playing the Whore, not of those who got a great Deal. The Project indeed was calculated for greater Designs than every one is aware of, no less than the subversion, as some pretend to tell you, of the Church and State; at least it is so far plain, that had People come in as was expected, and had it been countenanc'd so much by the Men in Power, as the Projectors design'd, it would, in a little time, have brought every thing under its Power, and have prov'd as villainous as the Inquisition of *Spain* or *Rome*. But some wise Men found out the Aim of it, and so left it to languish in the Hands of Beedles, Headboroughs, and hired Constables; and some needy or busie Justices of the Peace, who either have nothing, or but little else to depend on, but their Commission, encourage these Informing Rascals, who bring Grist to their Mill, and nothing else has kept them up so long. But concluded the Justice, God be praised, I have an Estate of my own independent of any such Roguish ways of Support, so that I dare check the Insolence of Constables, and do an honest Gentleman a piece

 of

of Service by Chance; as I have you now and your Cousin, tho' I must tell you, that it was much that the Constable could be persuaded to come before me.

The Coach by this time being come, the Justice oblig'd us to take it home, and the Night being somewhat dark, and the Watch very troublesome, we were glad of the Offer.

I was vext to have been kept so long from my dear *Golden Spies*, and long'd to hear what Discoveries they had made of Things of this Nature, which carries the Awe of a Religous Pretence: As soon as I came home I hasten'd to my Chamber, and undressing my self with speed, I laid me down in my Bed, and thus addresss'd my self to my *Guinea*, —— I suppose, you Forraign Pieces have known but little of what I now enquire about, and therefore I apply my self to my British Piece, to let me know what Discoveries he has made amongst the Reformers; my Reason of Enquiry I told, by a Relation of what had kept me so long from their Company.

I confess, (said the *Roman* Crown) Reformation of any thing is what we are not very fond of in the City and Court of *Rome*; least if we should give way to it under any Pretence, it should get a Head, and Curtail the Gown: Yet by the little I have seen, I must needs say, I think the Method we take in the Cities of *Italy*, seems more

more reaſonable, and more likely to reform Offenders, than that which is taken in this Place. Firſt I take it for granted, that it is not in the Power of Man, nor in all the Diligence of Magiſtrates, to put an end to Whoring, to keep Men Chaſte, and within the Bounds of what is Lawful, and Religious; cou'd that indeed be done, there wou'd be ſome ground for all this Stir. But till you Reformers can make a new Nature, they labour in vain at a Thing, that the Corruption of Mankind can never ſuffer to be aboliſh'd. Your Severity is ſhown againſt the poor Traders in Fornication, not againſt ſuch as being private Whores, Cuckold their Husbands, and induce a ſpurious Iſſue into his Family for Negligence, where-ever the Injury is greateſt, there mnſt be the greateſt Offence. Now when you pay your Woman her Price, you do no jniury to any but your ſelf: But when you make a Cuckold of a Man, you injure him, and all his Family; if you deboach his Daughter, you bring her to Ruine; but the Son with the Trader, far leſs injurious, and by Conſequence far leſs Criminal. But if you ſuppreſs the Traders in Fornication in General, or moleſt them too much in their Occupation, you leſſen their Trade or deſtroy it, and turn all thoſe who will be Whoremaſters into Adulterers, which as I take it, is out of the frying Pan into the Fire. Now the ſage Wiſdom of the *Italians* conſidering, that humane Nature was not to be alter'd by Humane Laws, contriv'd Laws at leaſt that ſhould aim at a Reparation of thoſe Defects, by a true Repentance. The Women therefore that deal in that way are confin'd to a certain part of the Town, pay the State a ſmall Tax, and are protected and righted in their Gains: But then they are oblig'd all to be at Church, or at leaſt are at a Place aſſign'd to that Office, and to hear a Sermon againſt the vicious Courſe to which they have devoted themſelves. Now this I take to be more the Rationale of the Matter, than the hunting of Whores out of their Burroughs, with reforming Tiezers, to throw them into an abandon'd Goal, where they learn only to be more harden'd in their Iniquity.

For my part, I ſpeak as a fair Stander-by betwixt the Difference of Religion among them, for they are no more to me than a Pancake, for I have no more a Soul to be ſaved by the one, than a Stomach to feed by the other; but you ſeem to carry things too far, and reject things purely becauſe in uſe with the Papiſts, without examining whether juſt or reaſonable, or not. Thus you reject the Uſe of the *Gregorian* Regulation of the Year, becauſe he was a Pope who ſet it a Foot; tho' it is manifeſt to a Child, that it is much more perfect than that of *Julius Cæſar*, who if not a Pope, was a Heathen Uſurper.

I

I confess (assum'd the *Guinea*, finding that the strange piece had done) that I cannot in my own Reason find any ground to quarrel with what the *Roman* Crown has spoken; for indeed, all that our Reformers have done, has been of young Whores to make old ones; of Bashful Whores, to make Impudent Strumpets; confirming them by a *Bridewell* Discipline in those Vices, in which they were before only newly initiated. But then we must consider that we are generally hurried away more by meer Words than Things; to attempt the same Regulation in this Country, wou'd be to make the *Canters* cry out, that we were establishing Wickedness by a Law, tho' it be the only way in the World that can give the least Prospect of lessening a Vice, that can never be enrirely rooted out.

But this is not all, those Hands which are set to the Plow in this *Sham Reformation*, are the most Wicked the Nation can produce; Fellows that take Bribes to slip over a Whores Lodging, and will Swear in another that he knows nothing of but her Name. The same happens in their swearing about Oaths: In a Tavern with them the other Night, one of these Informers, with a Friend or Two: The Fellow was Drunk, yet Zealous in his Drink, and Intent on his Business, he fancied that the two in his Company swore; they believing him in Jest laugh at the Frolick, and bid him put each down ſo many Oaths; the Maſter of the Houſe coming in, he ſpake to him about three Words and paſs'd on about his Buſineſs, the Company bantering him on, bids him ſet the Maſter of the Houſe Fifty Oaths, the Drunken Informer does what he is bid; but the next day goes before a Magiſtrate Sober, and Swears all he found in his Book, tho' he made the Maſter of the Houſe guilty of ſix times the Oaths that he ſpoke Words.

But let us look into the Men that are employ'd: Among the Reſt there is a *Presbyterian* Tayler and Tally-man, who lives by ſelling the Whores Rigging of all ſorts on Extortion, a Man likely to be puſh'd on by a Pious Zeal ſor Religion: Another is a broken Shoemaker, who, unable to live by his Trade, through Idleneſs, ſets up for an Informer at the Salary of ſo much a Week, and what Perquiſites he can get from the depending Whores: A Third is a Bodice-maker, and he quits his Trade to be a Reforming Conſtable, which if it were not very Beneficial, his Zeal wou'd never chuſe before a reputable Trade; eſpecially ſince Men of Probity and Buſineſs chuſe rather to Fine, than ſtand Conſtable even for their year: Yet theſe Reformers keep ſuch a Poſt all the Years of their Lives. Now where the Advantage is ſo viſible to their Pockets, and the Proof of their Religion ſo ſmall and inviſible, it is no Breach of Charity to believe,

lieve, that the Devil himſelf might be one of our Reformers without ſetting up againſt his own Kingdom, which by his falſe Zeal and Hypocriſie he every day enlarges.

Thus the late Saint *DENT*, of whoſe death the Judges diſcover'd another Notion, than that of the Parſon who Canoniz'd him in his Sermon. I ſhall give you a Story, which will ſhew you the Temper of them all; for I had not been parted long from the very Lady that ſuffer'd, by his Roguery, before I came into your Hands.

St. *DENT*:

OR, THE

ReformingConſtable.

BUT becauſe I wou'd ſet the whole matter in a clear Light, I muſt begin a little higher, to ſhew a probability at leaſt, that this *DENT* was a Tool to the perfecting a former deſign againſt the Lady I mention: You muſt therefore know, that their lives within a Mile of *Charing-Croſs* a Perſon who has the Title of Captain; He is by Birth a *North-Briton*, his Father was a ſort of *Scots* Scrivener, by which and other means, he got a tolerable Livelihood; But being plagued with an intolerable Scold of a Wife, the poor Cuckold thought it better to venture Honourable Scars in the Field, than an inglorious Scratching at Home: To this end he went for *Holland*, where he ariv'd to the Honour of carrying a *Brown-Musket*. But Madam Termagant wou'd not suffer him to enjoy even this wretched Retreat of Cannons and Bullets, far less terrible than her Tongue; but speedily pursues him with our young Hero in a Scapjack at her Back, and twanty geud *Scots* Poonds in her Pocket, and getting an Eleemosynary Passage to the *Brill*, she prudently lays out her Treasure in a Cargo of *Geneva*, a Comodity of good Sale among the Soldiers, while she follow'd the Camp in diverse Capacities. Having now rais'd her Stock to greater Adventures, she pass'd the Seas frequently, but at one time in the Company of a Foot Soldier (whose Clothes she us'd to mend, and betwixt whom and her self many a good Turn had past while yet her Husband was alive) and by her address (being now a buxom Widow) got the Woodcock into the Noose; and so from selling *Geneva*, and following the Camp, came to be a Collonel's Lady; for to that Honour did the Foot Soldier arive after he had got so great a Treasure as the Mother of our Hero. The young Stripling in the mean time growing up, was prefer'd to the honourable Post, of a Footman to a certain Widow Lady: From whence, on his Father-in-Law's Rise, he was

was advanc'd to be a Trooper, which Dignity he forfeited, having his Sword broke over his Head for ſuſpicion of purloining a Utenſil call'd a Silvar Tankard. Under this Misfortune he retires to *Ireland*, and to redeem his paſt Loſs of Time, Marries the Widow of an Innkeeper of *Dublin*: But fickle, like the Heroes of old, he quits his fair *Venus*, having had a Son by her, and once more applies himſelf to *Mars* in the poſt of a Trooper for *Tangier*; which Place, and the Gallows, as well as the Sea, refus'd no Man. Here being near his Father-in-Law, he was much entruſted by him; but how faithful to the Truſt he prov'd, appears from his putting 2000 *l.* in his own Name, which the Collonel gave him only to carry to the Bankers. It wou'd be endleſs to tell you half the Exploits of this *Hero*; I ſhall therefore only add, that as he Cheated his Father-in-Law, ſo he was ſhrewdly ſuſpected of Poyſoning his Mother; for ſhe died in a Day or two after ſhe had been Drinking with her Son at the Tavern. Thus, Rich with the Spoils of more than one, and being now weary of his Wife, he leaves her with her Son in *Ireland*, and paſſes the Seas for *London*, there to purſue another Courſe; he had Lodg'd at a Tayler's Houſe, where he lik'd the eldeſt Daughter very well; and thither he goes again in hopes of getting a freſh Maidenhead, and living like a Gentleman, ſince he now

now had the Poſt of one, by keeping his Miſtreſs. However Matters were manag'd, he got the Taylers Daughter in the mind, and with his *Scots* Art impoſes on the Father, ſo far that he was Married to his Daughter, by which he got Lodging and Diet, and what Money the old Stitch-louſe cou'd part with. Madam took ſtate upon her, and the Honourable Captain improv'd his time ſo well, that he Purchas'd many Houſes; but all along neglected to ſupport his own Wife in *Ireland*. She comes over and diſturbs him, gets a little Money, and a promiſe of an yearly Allowance, Signs a Paper diſowning all Claim to him as a Wife, and that in her Maiden Name. Having thus got rid of his Lawful Wife, he was much at eaſe, but never cou'd keep his Hand out of Miſchief. There was a Gentleman of Faſhion liv'd next Door to him, who with his Lady were come to a very great Familiarity with him and his ſuppoſed Lady, the Tayler's Daughter.

The Captain was always an inſinuating Perſon, and the Gentleman his Neighbour was a very honeſt unſuſpecting Perſon, who put a great Confidence in the Captain's ſincerity, veracity and underſtanding; but his Lady, who perceiv'd the cunning deſigns of the Captain more than her Husband did, therefore always countermin'd his deſigns. The Captain found out the *Remora* of his Projects, and therefore ſecretly vow'd a

Re-

Revenge, that ſhou'd put her out of the way of keeping her Husband out of his Clutches.

But he had waited long in vain for an opportunity, till her own good Houſewifery expos'd her to his Mercy. She had ſav'd unknown to her Husband about Fifty Pounds, which by the help of a Friend ſhe had put out to Uſe: But an Acquaintance one day wanting Ten Pounds on a very urgent Occaſion, ſhe took Coach, and call'd on her Friend at the Coffee-houſe to ask him for ſuch a Summ; he aſſur'd her he had not ſo much about him, but that if ſhe wou'd go with him to any Tavern about *Weſtminſter*, he wou'd ſend a Porter home for the Money. The matter being agreed, he remembred, that the Night before he had drank ſome good Wine at a Tavern near the Abby, and as he thought, the neareſt to it, which was the Horn; but not knowing the Sign, he bid the Coach go to the Tavern by the Church-yard. Being come out of the Coach, he fancied that it was not the ſame Tavern; but being lighted up Stairs by a Servant Maid, he call'd for the Drawer, but was anſwer'd that they had no Drawers in that Houſe; this convinc'd him of his Error, but deſigning only to ſtay till he had ſent a Porter for the Money, thought it not worth the while to remove for a Pint of Wine, which with a Fire was all that he call'd for, except a Porter, and Pen, Ink and

and Paper: But while he was Writing, she sitting on one side of the Table, he Writing on the other, in comes the Reforming Constable and his Watch and hurries them away; having first ask'd their Names, which ignorant of the ill use that was made of it, they gave in false, unwilling to expose their own on such an Occasion.

Before the Justice they must go, and before a Justice fit for the purpose; for the Gentleman they went before, is said to have a Wife, that has made him use even Cruelty to all the Fair Sex that are brought before him. St. *Dent* was very busie about the Justice, who asking who the Lady was, he replied, that her Name to his knowledge was *Smith*, a common Strumpet, that ply'd e'ery Night at the Play-house Passage. The Lady, who before had assum'd that Name to conceal her own, came up to him, and throwing up her Hoods, ask'd him with some vehemency whether he knew her or not? He replied again what he had said before, asserting that he cou'd Swear it. After St. *Dent* had affirm'd it, it was in vain to contend it with the Justice, tho' there were those present who knew her, besides the Gentleman with whom she was; but her Mittimus must be made for *Bridewell*, all that was urg'd was in vain, the Justice is inexorable, and away she is carried. But the next Morning the Gentleman had got Bail, and deliver'd the enchanted Lady from

from Captivity, and all might yet have been well, but that ſome who were for helping the Informers and Reformers to Ruin a Family, took care to carry her Huſband word of all that had paſt; upon this Word was ſent to her not to come near home, the Storm was too high, and her abſence wou'd be much better till the noiſe of the Adventure was over.

In ſhort, the Roguery of this Conſtable was the occaſion of the Ruin of the Lady, the Infamy of the Children, and the Deſtruction of the Family, without doing any body the leaſt Good, unleſs it were by the Fee for a Mittimus, and the paying the Priſon Fees, and the Bail-Bond.

Nay (ſaid the *Lewis d'Or*) ſince being in this Country I have been in the Hands of the Godly, and been Witneſs of their Artful Hypocriſie: But I wonder that theſe mighty Reformers of Manners extend their Care only to Whoring, Drinking and Swearing, all Vices bad enough it is confeſs'd, yet all retain ſome certain ſort of Human Frailty abſtracted from Malice, which is a Vice one wou'd think peculiar to the Devil; and that is perhaps the Reaſon the Godly leave it untouch'd. Backbiting, Detraction, Calumny, Cenſuring our Neighbour, over-reaching him in our Dealings, Extortion, Oppreſſion of the Poor and the Needy, is a Task worthy true Reformers; theſe do a Thouſand times the Miſchief in the World which

which the others ever did. Match-making for their own Profit, without any regard to the Good of thoſe they joyn together; getting of Truſts which they make a Market of, and the like, are Sins that the Godly will have no hand in Reforming, becauſe they bring them in ſo conſiderable an Advantage.

THE
Hypocrite Uncas'd.

I Was once in the Hands of one of the Godly, who being a Miniſter of the Word, expreſs'd a great deal of Zeal in his Preaching, and Prayer; this got him ſo great an Aſcendant over his Congregation, that nothing was to be done in any of the Families, but the Man of God muſt be firſt conſulted: No Maid muſt have a Husband, or young Fellow a Wife, that he did not approve: And whoever cou'd get into his good Grace, was ſure never to loſe his Cauſe, if within his Juriſdiction. Among the multitude of his Hearers was a pretty young Woman, who had about Five Hundred Pounds to her Portion; a Church-man of a tolerable good Trade had ſeen her at a Friends Houſe, and tho' nothing in her Fortune cou'd be an obſticle to his Pretenſions;

ſions; yet underſtanding that nothing was to be done with the Mother but by the means of the Miniſter, he was ſo much in Love, that he reſolv'd to play the Hypocrite with the Hypocrite: He therefore pretends to turn Diſſenter, and enter himſelf in this very Man's Congregation. No Man was more aſſiduous than he at Morning Lectures, and none ſeem'd more diligent in Writing down the Sermon, tho' indeed he knew nothing of Short-hand. His exemplar Conduct made him taken notice of; and the Teacher hoping ſomething from ſo uncommon a Zeal, took care to come acquainted with him. The young Man was glad of the opportunity, and made him a preſent, which often engag'd his Viſits. He being a ſingle Man, the Man of God enquir'd into his Circumſtances, and urg'd him to ſettle by Marriage; he ſeem'd indifferent till he thought he had ſufficiently eſtabliſh'd himſelf, and then he propos'd the Lady he deſir'd to have to his Wife. The good Man told him he had reaſon to hope a greater Fortune, and that if he wou'd be rul'd by him he ſhould have one: But he perſiſting in his Choice, the matter was ſoon brought to an Agreement; for his Intereſt and Care in Procuring, he was to have One hundred Pounds out of the Five.

The Bargain being made with the Teacher, the Hearers were ſoon determin'd on the matter, the Mother was prevail'd with to admit

admit him to her Daughter, and the Daughter to be rul'd by her Confessor and Mother; Besides the young Man had a very agreeable Person, and what might engage the Heart of any young Woman to love him for a Husband.

The Marriage is concluded, the Day appointed, and the Nuptials celebrated. The next Morning the Bride put him in mind to go to hear the good Man's *Sunday* Lecture, but he easily found means to cool her Zeal of the Spirit, by the Application of the Flesh... The Mother waited as long as she cou'd for them; but being impatient, she goes away without them. Then the Bridegroom and Bride agreed to get up; but it being too late to come into the Meeting without being taken notice of, he prevail'd with her to go to the Parish Church with him. Whence returning home, the Mother began a Lecture on their Remissness, in not getting up to go to the Meeting; they both affirm'd that they had been at Church: But the Mother making a further Enquiry, the Husband thus spoke to her:

Madam, *You are impos'd on by a grave, starch'd Formality, which makes you a Property to those Knaves that lead you where-ever they please; I must be candid, I never was of that Opinion; but having a Passionate Love for your Daughter, and knowing no other way of getting your Consent, I dissembled thus long, to gain the only Earthly Happiness I desired (I ask*

ask Heaven Pardon for my Hypocrisie) I was not deceiv'd in my Thoughts, for your zealous good Minister sold me your Daughter, and her Fortune, for One Hundred Pounds; for which he has my Bond, and which he will come to receive to morrow at Noon. Get you a Friend with you, and be within hearing; and you shall find, that I have not laid any thing to his Charge, but what will appear to be true to a Tittle.

The Mother and Daughter seem'd strangely surpriz'd, and promis'd, that if he made out this Accusation, that they wou'd both go to the Parish Church, and for ever quit the seperate Congregation. The *Monday* is come, and the Man of God with a chearful Countenance is arriv'd, with his Stomach set to a good Dinner, and more to the Hundred Pounds. Dinner was past, with the young Married Couples good Healths, and several Pious and Godly Discourses, till the Cloath being taken away, and the Tea pot brought in, the sober *Bohea* went about, when the Mother and Daughter pretending Business to go abroad, left the good Man and the Husband to pursue their Affairs.

Well, said the precise Hypocrite, my good Friend, how like you a Married State, and how like you the Wife I have procur'd for you? Is she worth the Price you give? Am I worthy my Hire? There is no body better pleas'd, than my self (said the young Man) I have got the Woman, whom of all other

I lov'd, nor do I think I can ever pay too dear for her. A good hearing (said the Minister) a good hearing my Lad; I have generally had very good luck in the many Matches I have made since the Lord has put me into this Vineyard. But I am afraid, Sir, (said the young Man) you have been harder with me than any other on this Occasion: No, I protest (said the Hypocrite) on my veracity I never take less; nor has any one ever scrupled to give me two Hundred out of a Thousand. That may be (replied the other) but then perhaps the Man has not had an Equivalent to the Lady's Fortune, whereas I have in my Stock, and a small Estate, something more than the whole Five hundred requires. Alack-a-day (says the Parson) I examin'd not into that, it had been all one to me; you were a Godly young Man, and my Interest and Trouble was the same: Well but Sir (interrupted the young Man) considering that you have provided well for two of your Congregation, it will be some Reputation to you; and I suppose a satisfaction so great, that you will, for the good News (since more than you knew before) abate one half of the Summ. Fie, fie young Man (replied the grave Rogue) how can you offer it! What I deliver from my Pulpit I impart to you all alike for the Contributions that they give me; but in this way of dealing, which is none of my Spirituality, I can abate nothing.

The

The young Man having tried all means to make him abate to no purpoſe, he calls for his Bond, which the old Fellow produces, and while they are reading over, the Mother and Daughter, and two Friends came in upon them; the Man of God was ſo frighted at the ſudden aſſault of the Mother's Tongue which let fly, Rogue, Hypocrite, Villain, and a Thouſand other good Morrows in a trice, that he let go the Bond, which the Husband took care to Cancel, and lay aſide. The poor Marriage Broaker was ſo beſet, that he wou'd have given a Hundred Pounds more to have been out of the Houſe: But he hop'd it in vain till their ſpirits were ſpent in Reproaches; but then having aſſur'd him that they wou'd never herd any more with Diſſenters, but immediately conform, he beg'd them to ſmother his diſgrace, telling them that the beſt Men were ſubject to frailties, and that ſince he had a great Family on his Hands, he hop'd a moderate profit for the Intereſt he had in his Congregation was allowable both by the Laws of God and Man. He was not therefore ſolicitous for any thing, but that the Enemies of his Way might turn it into Ridicule to the prejudice of the Saints; that therefore he remitted the Bond to the young Man, and hop'd for his Friendſhip, ſince by his means he had obtain'd ſo good a Wife, and one that he lov'd.

The Company was mov'd with his Diſcourſe, and promis'd to ſay no more of the matter, only that he ſhou'd have a care of ſuch ſort of dealing; but if that he wou'd purſue it, that he ſhou'd regard the good of thoſe that he join'd, more than his own Profit, ſince elſe he might be the Ruin of others, only to enrich himſelf. With that they diſmiſs'd him, who returning home, took his Bed for vexation, and very narrowly eſcaping his death he reviv'd, but went on in the ſame way as long as it was in his Cuſtody.

The Story you have told (aſſum'd the *Guinea*) carries the Air of ſo much Fact to me who have been very Familiar among them, that I make not the leaſt doubt of your veracity; but this, as the young Peoples good Fortune directed, met with a lucky Concluſion to both; but what, I now ſhall relate, was far more terrible in the Event.

THE
Godly Debochee.

ISabella was a beautiful young Woman, who having but little Fortune but her Needle, maintain'd her ſelf honeſtly and genteely by her Work. There was a young Man juſt out of his Time with a Mercer, and who had a good Fortune in Money to ſet up his Trade, which, as ſoon, as he had done, he deſign'd to Marry *Iſabella*, thinking her valuable enough in her ſelf without any Portion, well remembring, that a good Houſe-wife, wise, and a good Humour, bring Plenty and Happiness, while the contrary, with never so much, will destroy both. Their Loves had been of some duration, and their Ages near the same, tho' she had the start of him near a year.

It was the hard Fortune of poor *Isabella* to have old *Gripe* see her at Church, and there to fall in Love with her to such a degree, as to follow her Home, and *Sunday* not being a proper time to begin an Affair of that Nature, especially he being a Zealous Brother, he put it off till next day; when on enquiry he found that she maintain'd her self by plain-work, which gave him both an opportunity of introducing himself to her by bespeaking half a dozen Shirts, and hopes, that her Necessities wou'd lend an easie ear to a Price for her Maidenhead, which might put her in some better way.

He came to her every day, and every day added new fewel to his Fire; what to do he knew not, for he had by this time heard of her Engagement with the young Mercer, and that cut off all his hopes of success in a Passion, which he cou'd not, or wou'd not overcome. He had no means to make way for himself but by endeavouring a Rupture betwixt them; he therefore found out the Relations of the young Man, by some Agent which he had, and discover'd his Intention of throwing himself and his Fortune away on a Beggar. Tho' no Body cou'd hinder him of his present Portion, yet he had an Uncle who cou'd leave him a confiderable Eftate; and he by this means coming to know his defigns, affur'd him he wou'd leave him never a Groat if he proceeded in fo fcandalous an Amour: He let him underftand, that tho' his own Fortune was pretty confiderable, yet that the greater his Stock was, the fooner he cou'd get an Eftate; and that if he were enclin'd to Marry he wou'd provide him a Wife who fhou'd equal his Portion, and fettle a Jointure upon her out of his Eftate.

The young Man was not eafily won from his Love by the profpect of Gain; he informs her of the Propofal of his Uncle to him; but at the fame time affures her, that he wou'd never forfake her for all his Uncle's Eftate an Hundred times told. *Ifabella* was a little ftruck at the News, fhe confider'd that this was not an Age to hear Men quit a great deal of Money for a meer Form; and therefore refolv'd to be beforehand with her Lover, and either have the advantage of lofing him handfomly, or binding him fafter. So that the next time he came, fhe told him that——

She was fenfible of his Paffion, and the Advantage of having an Husband of his Circumftances, which were far greater than fhe cou'd merit; that fhe return'd him a reciprocal Kindnefs, and indeed lov'd him too well to let him be a fufferer in his Fortune for her fake: That Trading was a Lottery, and if he fhou'd not meet with the fuccefs he

propos'd, she wou'd never put it in his Power of reproaching her with being the Cause of his Ruin by disobliging his Relations, who otherwise wou'd have set him above the Assaults of Fortune. She begg'd him therefore, with Tears in her Eyes, to strive to forget her, and place his Affections on some more fortunate Woman, and more agreeable to his Relations, and his Estate.

I will not pretend to draw the moving Scene of their parting that Time, he protesting inviolable Constancy ; and she assuring him, that she wou'd admit no more of his Courtships, till she was satisfied that his Relations allow'd his Addrefs. Notwithstanding this he wou'd still see her, and renew his professions, till his Uncle had now found out a Lady to his mind : She was the Daughter of a Mercer who was dead, and had left her above 2000 *l* to her Fortune, in the Hands of a Guardian who was of the Uncles Acquaintance The Matter being mov'd, the Conditions were agreed on, and the young People were to be brought together by Accident to see one another. *Berinthia* (for that was her Name) was about Seventeen years of Age , and the young Man betwixt one and two and Twenty. She was perfectly Handsom, and having had a good Education, set off her Beauty with a Thousand Graces of Mien and Addrefs, which were new to the young Spark, *Isabella* being only of a plain, untaught, unsophisticated Nature , deriving nothing from Art. The Uncle invites his Nephew to Dinner, without acquainting him with a word of his Design, lest Prepossession shou'd create an Aversion; whereas seeing a Charming young Lady, without knowing that she is to be impos'd on him for a Wife, might raise a Passion for her, which much more easily wou'd bring the same Matter about.

The Uncle's Notion was so just, that before Dinner was over *Isabella* was quite forgot, the present Lady younger by four or five years, with all the Bloom of the Plumb, with a Genteel and Courtlike Air, adorn'd with Jewels, and set off with all the Art imaginable, struck the young Citizen so deeply, that he cou'd not but gaze on her all the while she sate at Table. The Uncle was very well pleas'd to observe this Alteration in his Nephew, but yet resolv'd to make no discovery, till he had first made his Application to him; by which he wou'd so far confirm his Love, that he cou'd not recede, and the Woman he design'd wou'd seem the voluntary choice of his Nephew, and no Imposition of his.

The young Lady was gay in her Temper, and free in her Conversation, and he being the youngest of the Company they soon join'd in Conversation: The old Folks indulg'd it, and withdrew to smoke a Pipe in the next Room. In short this meeting had so entirely vanquish'd the false Lover, that he, before he went home, made some motions

tions to his Uncle about her; asking her Fortune, Quality and the like: But hearing that her Portion was so considerable, he sigh'd in despair. His Uncle ask'd him the Cause; he frankly at last told him, that in obedience to him, he had broke off his Inclinations from *Isabella*, and hop'd, that since now he had fix'd them on an Object, which he cou'd find no fault with for want of Fortune, that he wou'd make good his Word, and enable him to make his Pretension, and Addresses to her for a Wife.

The Uncle cunningly at first rais'd some difficulties; but at last told him, that being both his Uncle and Godfather he wou'd stretch a Point, and that nothing on his side shou'd be wanting to satisfy her Guardian, provided he cou'd satisfy her, and win her Affections.

All this while *Isabella* knew nothing of the Change of her Lover, whom notwithstanding her generous discourse, she cou'd not find in her heart never to think of any more. In the mean while the old Reformer, employ'd all his Engines to endeavour to corrupt her with the hopes of an easie Maintenance, without naming his Name, and only specifying his Age, and Circumstance of Riches, and his Love for her: But no Argument cou'd prevail to make her give ear to the immodest proposition. This Difficulty old *Gripe* attributed to her Hopes of her Lover; and therefore suspended his despair till his Marriage was past, which he heard

heard was very near, before he discover'd his Infidelity; lest by seeking him out, she shou'd recall him to her Obedience. But he had no need to let *Isabella* know, that her Lover was False, since he had not been to see her for some Time. Yet he being now Married, old *Gripe* took care that she shou'd know, that all her hopes were gon of that Nature, since now he was another Woman's Husband.

The Concern with which she receiv'd the News is not to be express'd, yet she took care to discover as little as possible to the Person who brought her the Intelligence; yet cou'd she not conceal such symptoms, as betray'd an Agony of Mind much more than appear'd. When her Passion was vented, and she had a little recover'd her self, she resolv'd to Write him an upbraiding Letter, which she did to this purpose:——

Your Conduct has been so extraordinary in this Affair, that tho' I resolv'd never to think of you more, yet I must do what you wou'd not do by me, send you this Farewell. I was always sensible that I never was a proper Match for you, or was Mistress of Charms sufficient to secure your Heart; but then it had been more generous and just in you, either never to have Vowed, or at least to have kept your Vows: But you are a Man, and I ought never to have expected any thing else at your Hands. Yet since perhaps some Curse may hang over you for your Perjuries to me, in consideration of the poor Lady you have Married, I Cancel all Obligations of that Nature,

Nature, and pray that Heaven may as eaſily forgive you.

The Mercer receiv'd this Letter not without ſome ſting of Conſcience for what had paſt, and a new deſire of ſeeing her, and deſign if he could, to make her his Miſtreſs, ſince now he cou'd not his Wife; he came to her, ſwore a Thouſand Oaths that he lov'd her ſtill more than ever; That what he had done, was only to enable him to do more for her than his tranſitory Fortune wou'd have done by a meer dependance on Trade. She minded not what he ſaid, but deſir'd him never to come near her more, and not to think of being as unjuſt to his Wife as he had been to her; but as ſhe was a fine Woman, had brought him a large Portion, and was young, he ſhou'd keep his Affections for her, leſt he ſhou'd teach her to alienate hers from him, and place them on one ſhe might think more deſerving.

He wou'd not be denied, and preſs'd, every time he came, his Love, and its ſatisfaction, till ſhe forbid him her Lodging, and wou'd not ſee him when ever he came. However he often watch'd her going out, and wou'd purſue her where-ever ſhe went; wou'd watch her Return, and wait on her home, and with great difficulty repuls'd the entrance of her Lodging. This gave old *Gripe* the villainous thought how to compaſs his Ends, tho' by a way, that the Wicked cou'd never have entertain'd.

He

He had obferv'd, one Night, as fhe was returning home, and her Mercer in fpight of her Teeth ftill purfuing her, the Reformers (being fet on it by old *Gripe*) feize her as a Night-walker, and carrying them both before a Juftice, fhe was fent to *Bridewell* for being in a Married Man's Company: But the Matter the next day being examin'd into, and the Mercer appearing, fhe was fet at Liberty. But how innocent foever a Woman be, the very Name of *Bridewell* does her a Prejudice; and this coming to fpread (by the induftry of old *Gripe*) about the Neighbourhood, the poor young Woman was fain to leave the Place, and lofe moft of her Bufinefs.

Gripe in this diftrefs renews his Addreffes, proffers her Money, nay (which is extraordinary) left a *Guinea* on the Table when he went away, and which fhe found not till the next day. He finding her obftinate againft all his unlawful Propofals, offers to Marry her; and fhe willing to be fo well provided for, then liftned a little more patiently to his Pretenfions. She therefore enquired a little more narrowly after him, and to her great mortification found, that he was already a Married Man. Having therefore fufficiently reproach'd him, forbid him her Houfe. All this cou'd neither allay his Paffion, or his Refolution of fatisfying it one way or other: He therefore fets one of the Informers to dog her out when fhe went in the Evening to carry home her

Work,

Work, and by one means or other to send her to *Bridewell* once more. The poor Girl coming home, was follow'd by this *Reformer*, or *Informer*, who wou'd needs pick her up, but she always refusing him, he at last told her, he wou'd not part with her till he had drank with her; so she ventur'd to sit down at an Ale-house door in the Street on a Bench by him, and had no sooner drank to pledge him, but she was again taken up by the Gang, and sent away to *Bridewell*. She knew not what to do, nor whom to send to, when old *Gripe* pretending only to look at the Unfortunate Wenches, and to see which was worthy his Compassion, found her there and immediately Bail'd her out. She cou'd not but in Gratitude go to the Tavern with him, where he had plac'd another Woman, who was to draw her into drink; and perhaps by mingling something in her Liquor, intoxicate her to the last degree

This horrid Plot was put in Execution, so that the poor Girl was carried in a Coach Drunk to a place agreed on, and put into Bed, to whom the old Letcher was soon admitted, where he did what he pleas'd, Drink having quite rob'd her of all power of resisting.

The Morning came on, and she coming to her self found, first that she was not in her own Bed, and speedily drawing the Courtain found the old Fellow by her side now asleep,

aſleep, and tired with his Nights Villainy. She gave ſuch a Scream that ſoon rais'd the old Rogue, and flying at him had very near throtled him; The Noiſe brought in the Bawd, and ſome aſſiſtance, who took her away from him; but ſo bruis'd with her Knees and Hands, that he was ſcarce able to get home; where he languiſh'd a little while and died. The poor young Woman found worſe, for being a little come to her ſelf got out of the Houſe, with a Reſolution of having all the Actors in this Villainy ſeverely puniſh'd; but her Rage and Concern was ſuch, that it threw her into a Feaver, and that into a Delirium, in which ſhe continu'd till ſhe died. And this was the fatal end of our *Godly Debôchee*.

The Night waſtes a-pace, ſo I will only give you a very ſhort Account, How ſome Informers, and their Journyman Juſtice were met with, by one who knew how to manage them: For confident of their Power as Reformers, they often Tranſgreſs the Law without being taken notice of.

THE

THE
Reformer Reform'd.

I Belong'd to an honeſt Gentleman of the City, who one *Sunday* had Buſineſs at the other end of the Town, ſo reſolving to take a walk into the Fields, he prevail'd with two Friends more to go along with him; when they came near to the Place, there was a Coffee-houſe, where he deſir'd his Friends to ſtay while he ſtept a door or two farther, to ſpeak a few Words with the Perſon he had Buſineſs with. Church was done when they went into the Coffee-houſe, where they found only two Women, whom they ask'd for ſome Coffee, they replied they had none; for ſome Thea, and the ſame was the Anſwer. In ſhort, nothing elſe being to be had, they bid them bring Half a Quartern of Brandy, inſtead of which the Impudent Baggage brings a whole Quartern, but drinks firſt her ſelf, and leaves them not half; the Meaſure being adapted to the Place. While they were arguing on this Head, in comes a Reforming Conſtable with his Gang; and ſeizes them for being in a Bawdy-

a Bawdy-house. They perceiv'd that they were grave Citizens, and so hop'd to make them bleed a little freely, rather than be expos'd as taken up in a Bawdy-house. The Whores they were for begging them to make it up, and not go before the Justice; and one of them more timerous than the other gave a willing Ear to the Proposal; but the Friend coming in the *Interim* he examin'd into the Matter: The Constable told him they had found them Drinking with those Whores in a publick Bawdy-house. How! says my Master, do you know that they are Whores, and this a publick Bawdy-house? They replied yes. Then said my Master, I Command you to take them with us before the Justice; for before him we will go; and do it at your peril.

The Whores and the Constable did all they cou'd to persuade them not to expose themselves; nay, wou'd at last have dismiss'd them without a Farthing. No, no, said my Master, we are too well known in the City to fear being expos'd in such a piece of Roguery as this: And I will spend Five Hundred Pounds but that I will drive it so far to make you all asham'd of it.

In ſhort, he oblig'd the Conſtables to take theſe Ladies of Pleaſure with them, and go all before the next Juſtice, who happen'd to live in the Neighbourhood. When they came there, the Conſtables made a plauſible Story of their being taken in a known Bawdy-houſe, and with known Whores: The J ſtice, with a very formal ſupercilious Look, addreſs'd himſelf to them. *Gentlemen, I am ſorry to find Men of your ſeeming Gravity, to be caught in the Company of ſuch Lewd Women, and in a Houſe ſo Notorious as that where you were taken.* Sir, ſaid my Maſter, *do you know that to be a Bawdy-Houſe, and theſe Women Whores?* The Juſtice replying in the Affirmative, *Why then,* purſued he, *how comes it that you, who are a Magiſtrate, ſuffer ſuch a Houſe to keep open their Doors, on purpoſe to betray the Innocent into ſuch a Premunire as my Friend and I am fallen into, who went in there to reſt, and did nothing Undecent, nor knew any thing of the matter. Since therefore, Sir, you knew this, and yet ſuffer'd it under your Noſe, I deſire we may be all bound over to the Seſſions. I will ſend, Sir, for Ten Thouſand Pound Bail, and I will ſpend ſome Money, Sir to have you and your Conſtables made an Example, for laying Traps for Her Majeſty's Liege People, and making thoſe a Prey who want either Money or Knowledge to deal with you as they might. You have this time miſtaken your Men, we are above your doing us any Harm, and we are able to do you Juſtice.*

The Magiſtrate found himſelf in the wrong Box, and began to mollify the matter, perſwading them to make it up, that it might be ſome Reflection upon them, and the like good Advice. But they perſiſted ſo earneſtly in being all bound over, that the Juſtice told them they might, if they pleaſed, go about their Buſineſs, for he had nothing to ſay to them. Then ſaid my Maſter, I have this to ſay to you, that if I find this Sign up and Houſe open the next time I come this way, I will take care of your Worſhip and your Commiſſion.

With theſe words they parted, the Conſtables asking them a Thouſand Pardons, and excuſed themſelves by their want of knowi g them, or they ſhould not have given them this Trouble, and ſuch a lame come off.

In a few Days after my Maſter went that way again, on purpoſe to ſee if all was perform'd, and he found the Sign removed, and the Doors all faſt, for they perceiv'd that they were ſo much in the wrong, that to ſtand againſt him, wou'd have brought Matters ſo on the Stage, that might very much have ſunk their Markets.

All that I ſhall obſerve from what has this Night been ſaid is, That you ought to be very much on your Guard, when you have to do with a Man that pretends to more Holineſs than his Neighbours.

There

There is such a Leven of the *Pharisee* in all those sort of Men, that you cannot sin against Charity when you describe them such, since the Picture is so like the Original, that 'tis impossible to Affront them.

The *Guinea* here ending, and the Night being pretty well advanc'd, when I came Home, I turn'd my self to rest, praying, as from suddain Death and deadly Sin, likewise to be deliver'd from Reformers and Informers.

THE

Sixth Night's Entertainment, of Peace *and* War, *or, the* Trade *of the* Camp.

I Got up in the Morning, and taking a Walk in the Fields, reflected on the strange depravity of Mankind, that left nothing unattempted with his corrupt Practices. Religion, the most Sacred Tye of Humane Society, I found by my last Night's Conversation, was, even in the purest Country, made often a Stalking-Horse to Private Interest and Sinister Designs. Tho' this indeed is a stronger Proof of its Excellence, and only an Evidence of the Extraordinary Wretchedness of Mankind. Nor did this put me out of Conceit with the present Age, because I found in my Books, that the same abominable Viciousness was charg'd by the Writers of former Ages on the Wickedness in their Times. In this as well as other Emergencies of the World, I cou'd never find any great Variety; Men were always the same in their Desires, in their Sins, in their Follies, and not very different in their Knowledge; if one Age lost it, the succeeding ones revived it, and tho' with little variation from what it was before, yet the Reviver has challenged the Honour of the Discovery. This holds in most of our Modern Philosophical Notions. So in every Age Noblemen, Usurers, Traders and Soldiers have desired Money more than Fame; some few Wise Men have valued Honesty, while the greatest Knaves praise it; and those who most cry it up, do least for it in Distress. Courtiers always valu'd themselves more than the Publick or their Prince; States-men coloured Self-Interest under *Publick Good*: Priests always first pursued the Goods of this World, themselves more, than they preach'd the Goods of the other World to others; never forgave their Opposers, and endeavoured by their Practice to undermine the Belief which they taught. Contrary Parties were always Knaves and Fools to each other; while the Leaders of both might challenge the first Title in Reality, and all the Followers the latter. Pedants always would assume

ſume the Name of Men of Letters, and Poetaſters palm themſelves on this Senſeleſs Town and Quality for Poets. Men always, as well as now, talk'd as they would have it, and Peace and War became the Subject of common Diſcourſe, as Men grew weary of War or Peace.

Full of theſe Reflections I return'd to the Town, to refreſh my ſelf and meet Company to dine with, I went to the Coffee-Houſe, where I found a ſort of a *Jack*, or diffident *Pinnacler*, in deep Debate with a Whig of the New Cut about the Peace. This juſtify'd my laſt Reflection, and will be plain from what follows. Says the firſt, Had not the Act forbid it, I would lay any Man Ten to One, that we have no Peace before *Michaelmaſs*. Whoo! we love to run down our Enemies, and make nothing of them; but 'tis a fooliſh Method, for if they are in ſo woful and deplorable a Condition, what need we attend their Terms? Why don't we march into their Country with an irreſiſtible Army, ſuch as we pretend to have, of above 160 Thouſand Men, Veteran, Noble, Gallant Fellows, well fed, well Cloathed, well paid? What can oppoſe them in a Country, that is ſtarving, an Army without Men, and Men without Hearts, Cloaths, Money, or any thing neceſſary for Defence? Who fly before we come near them, and can no more make a ſtand againſt us, than a drunken Old Fellow against a Brigade of Constables and Watch-men? How can the *French* Monarch pretend to Capitulate on any Terms, but to surrender Prisoner of War? Or why don't we serve him as he did the Doge of *Genoa*, make him come with a Halter about his Neck and beg our Pardon, and submit to our Clemency? 'Till I see these things done, for my part I shall not believe, that the *French* are so damnably reduc'd, or that there is any likelihood of a Peace.

Sir, said the *New Cut*, you are a little too Hot, Politicians suffer the Under-spurs of the News-Writers, to magnify the sad Condition of *France*, to give our own People Heart to hold on the War 'till we can get an Honourable Peace; but for my part I must deal ingenuously with you, I am far from imagining the *French* Affairs in so desperate a State; this King is a Wise, a Great, a Powerful Prince, and he would never let the Prince of the *Asturia's* be acknowledged by the *Cortez*, or the States of the Country, had he found that he must so soon be obliged to disembogue the whole *Spanish* Monarchy. For my part, I could wish, for the good of *Europe*, that he were as low as he is represented; tho' on the other hand I must tell you, that I do not think it is the common Interest to pull him down too low; for *Europe* has been in danger once already, from the Power of the House of *Austria*, and should the Empire, and the *Spanish* Monarchy be join'd again, I know

know not but there would be a Neceſſity of a Confederacy againſt that Exorbitant Power. Come, come, we are never ſatisfy'd, we rail'd at poor King *William* on the Treaty of Partition, and yet I can ſee no means of reſtoring Peace to us all, but a Treaty on that Foot. Beſides, I muſt tell you, that tho' the *Dutch* are our Good Confederates and Allies at preſent, yet I do not think it good Policy to have them entirely ſecure on the *Terra Firma*, for ſhould they be ſo, I know not what Deſigns they may form againſt *Great Britain*, that is their Rival in Trade. Oh! Gentlemen, there are a great many things to be conſider'd in Affairs of this Important Nature, and Things that do not fall into every Man's Capacity to think of; under the Roſe, we have a great many Buſie, Noiſy, Grumbling Fellows, who, were they intirely out of Fear, might play the Devil for God's ſake. No Man wou'd be ſecure. The Clamours againſt great Men are, alas! generally but too Popular, and ſince great Men are but Men, they can't but give (thro' Inadvertence or Folly) ſome Handle for Malice to take hold of, and when Men make a Noiſe for the Publick Good, how eagerly is all they ſay ſwallow'd down for perfect Goſpel. Another thing is to be conſider'd, our *Hot-ſpurs* are for having the *French* King to deliver up the *Spaniſh* Monarchy as a Preliminary. Lack-a-day, Sir, that is a perfect Jeſt; 'tis not in his Power, Sir, to give up that Monarchy; 'tis in his Grand-son's Hands, and none but he and the *Spaniards* themselves can do that. What would you have us to do then? Why if the *French* King will give you Passage through his Country to drive his Grand-son out of *Spain*, then while Prince *Eugene*, with an Army of good Catholicks, does that Work, our own Men may be brought into *England*, and while they are on foot, they may be ready to Sail either to *Holland* or *Spain*, as occasion requires, and in the mean while they will keep the Grumblers in Awe. In short we were lull'd asleep too long by the enervate Reign of King *Charles* the 2d. when he got up to such a Power as to be an Over-Match for all *Europe* besides. 'Tis very well that we have bang'd him till his Sides Ake, and made him glad to seek a Peace, which, I think we may be willing to accept on easier Terms than some Men propose, who are carry'd away by I know not what sort of Enthusiastick Zeal, that is only founded on Fancy. If he recovers by a Peace, why, so shall we; what's Sauce for the Goose is Sauce for the Gander.

There sat by these Learned Disputants an *Old Whig*, whose Colour went and came Twenty times, whilst these Worthy Knights were settling the Affairs of *Europe* on a Secure Foundation. At last, taking up *New Cut*, Sir, said he, I know not what to

call

call you, for you talk more like an Engine of *France*, than an *Englishman*. I think what you have said amounts to little less than Treason, at least against the Interest of all the High Allies, as well as our own Nation. What, Sir, to insinuate so great a Libel against the Bravery of our Generals, the Courage of our Soldiers, and the Honour of our Statesmen, after the prodigious Expence of so much Blood and Riches for the carrying on of this War; and since Heaven has Blessed Her Majesty's Arms with such Miraculous Success, that History can't Parallel; when the *French* have been beaten every where, their Armies destroy'd, their Chief Towns plundred, their Country laid Waste by the Hand of Heaven, and their Prince's Cruelty, by forcing above two Millions of Industrious People out of his Country for Religion, whose Hands would now have Cultivated his Fields and shut out Famine, that is now entred their Dominions; after all this, Sir, to obtain a Peace that will leave us worse than the War found us!

The bare Surrender of the *Spanish* Monarchy, good Sir, sets us not where we were before the War; because it is brought much Lower, less capable of Defence, and more lyable to be Seiz'd than ever. The same may be said of the *Netherlands*, tho' not in so great a Degree. So that there is a Necessity of making them Refund *Burgundy*, *Alsace*, and *Franche-Comte*; to lessen the Number

Number of their Ships, and not be suffer'd to appear on the Ocean with a Ship above 50 Guns; to Surrender *Newfoundland*, their Claim to part of St. *Christophers*; to Demolish *Martenico*, and *Dunkirk*; to give up *Calice*, and to disband his Army. As for restoring the Power of Parliaments, I have nothing to say to it; for I am of Opinion, that to make *France* more Terrible to *Europe* than ever, make it perfectly Free; in their Slavery their Spirit is quash'd and yet by a Politick Prince, you see what they have done; but then indeed bad Success makes all their Glory moulder away much swifter than it rose.

Tho' I am not fond of Discourses of this Nature in a Coffee-House, yet, Sir, I cannot hear such Designs insinuated against my Country, without taking notice of them. You were finely preparing a Way for a Standing Army, by your Peace and no Peace; but I had rather see you, and all your Party Hang'd, than ever see that settled again in *England*. What was the Effect of it in *Oliver*'s Time, Slavery first, and then Confusion of Changes. No, Sir, were your Libel true against the Managers of our Affairs, yet give me leave to tell you, That there are safer ways of Defending our Laws and Liberties, than by a Standing Army. Since the Parliament deny'd it to the Best of Kings, I dare believe the Best of Queens will never seek it.

While

While these Gentlemen were thus hotly discoursing the Matter, there sat by them a Jolly sort of a Man, who seem'd one of those who meddled not with Parties, who when the Matter grew High, interposed his Pleasant Face.

Gentlemen, said he, for my part, I am one of those Happy Fellows who never examine into the Secret Motions of Government, nor enquire how such or such a thing is to be brought about. All my care is to have the Blessing of Peace, while you Statesmen, you Wise Politicians contrive to give it me. I confess I love both Peace and War, but for several, I mean different, Reasons. War carries away abundance of Scoundrels that used to infest the Town, and disturb our Pleasures in the time of Peace; but then on the other side, it carries off a great many Honest Fellows too: It is a great promoter of Sobriety; but then it is because it makes Drunkenness too Expensive: It drains the Corrupt Humours of a Nation, by a seasonable *Phlebotomy*; but then for want of Skill it lets out a great deal of good Blood with them. It gives us Glorious Victories, but then the deuce on't is, that it Ruins our Trade. It raises abundance of Brave Fellows to be known in the World, who else had never been heard of; but then a great many hundreds find other Arts to Live by in the very Camp, than by the Sword; and who make such

ſuch a Figure in the World, that they had better never have been heard of, for the Honour of thoſe who Raiſed them, and the Dignity they bear. In ſhort, when I think on the Balance, War is not ſo much to be admired, as it once appear'd to be. But then for Peace, no Body can find fault with it but the Soldiers——but then we have ſtopt their Mouths with Half Pay, and no Broken Bones. The Trader Rejoyces in it, for the Privateers fright his Sleep no more away from him, and he has no Hazard but the Rocks and the Sands, much more Merciful than *French* Privateers. The Young Girls they are glad of it; for, they hope now that they may no longer ſtick a Hand; their Sweet-Hearts will not be raviſh'd from their Arms. The Good Fellow is pleaſed with Peace, for then Wine will come Cheaper, and the Vintners will not need to Brew it at that abominable rate, they do now. The Lawyer will Rejoyce at a Peace, becauſe according to the Old Proverb, Peace brings Plenty, and Plenty Litigiouſneſs, and Litigiouſneſs fills *Weſtminſter* Hall, which has had almoſt a long Vacation ever ſince the War, while Boys whipt their Tops about the Hall in *Michaelmas Term*. The Parſons will like Peace, for there will be more Marriages, Chriſtenings, and Burials, beſides they have too great an Intereſt in the Plenty of good Wine, and want that Conſideration of their Satisfaction in a War.

War. The Bayliffs will be likewise over-joy'd at a Peace, for then they may have a full Gang of their Lubberly Followers without any fear of being press'd to harder Service, either at Land or Sea. Tho' I am afraid that all would not be Pleas'd ev'n with a Peace; *Stocks* would be much abated, which would be a Mortal Blow to *Stock-Jobbing*; Those who have Places in the Taxes would be in fear of paying off the Publick Debts by a Peace, and then they should have their Fortune to seek. There may be others perhaps of their Mind who got Money by War. But 'tis now time to settle; *every Man for himself, and God for us all.*

Thus you see Gentlemen, how many would be pleas'd with Peace, so I beg you let us have it, that we may all sit quietly under our own Vine, laugh away the livelong Day, have much Joy, and little, tho' sound, Slumbers, Friends, Wine, and Women, without controul. And which way soever you compass it, 'tis not a Half-Penny matter.

When he had said this he took his Leave, and the Grave Coxcombs confounded, paid their Dishes, and went off; when I, meeting at last with my Friend, adjourn'd to the Tavern, where we spent the Day as plentifully as if it had been Peace already.

But the Evening being come, I went Home in pretty good Order, and retired to my my Post of Audience. And the Disputes of the Day, having fixt the War and Peace so much in my Mind I determined this Night to have some few Words about the *Camp*, where the Fate of Peace and War is decided.

When I had proposed the Subject; For my part, said the *Roman* Crown, I cannot pretend to say much of a Subject so Warlike; at *Rome* we have no *Fulmina Belli*, tho' we have sometimes a noise about the *Fulmina Cathedræ*. Ours is a *Spiritual Warfare*, and the Stratagems and Arms we use, are proportioned to the End of our Designs. For your Great Guns, we have our Canons, and our *Ordinances* for your *Ordnance*; for Fire and Sword, we have Bell, Book, and Candle; for your Plunder, we have our Indulgences, and *Peter*-Pence. But then, whereas the *Spiritual War* Deals in Immortality, it is Immortal, and never Ceases, the Devil fights hard on one side, the Pope on the other. The Devil finds Temptations and Decoys People to Sin, in order to Damn them, but then out comes the Pope with *Indulgences*, *Agnus Dei's*, and the like Ammunition, and for a very little Money makes the Sinners Souls *rectas in curia*; the more they Sin, the more he gives Indulgences, and the Trade goes on without ceasing; the Devil's ne'er weary of Tempting, the *Romans* of Sinning, nor the Pope of Pardoning; the more the Devil Tempts, the

the more the *Romans* Sin, the more the Pope Pardons; ſo the Devil adds Temptation to Temptation, the *Romans* Sin to Sin, and the Pope Pardon to Pardon: And yet the Devil never gives over till Death, nor the *Romans* in Sinning, but then comes in the Pope, by a plenary Indulgence, a Scapular, or a St. *Francis*'s Cord, and whips the *Roman* Souls out of the Devil's Hands, and ſends them directly to Heaven.

This is the State of our Spiritual Warfare, where the Oppoſites being Immortal, and the Ammunition Imaginary, the Conteſt is Perpetual, in which every one gets but the Devil: For the *Romans* get Pleaſant Sins, and the Pope gets their Money for his Pardons; but for your Wars of this World, I leave an Account of them to my worthy good Brethren, who have been more Converſant about them.

Here the *Roman Crown* cloſing his Diſcourſe, my little *Louis D'or* thus began, Sir, I think my ſelf the propereſt piece of Gold of this Company, to ſatisfy your Curioſity in your Enquiries of this Nature, becauſe I having belong'd to the *Grand Monarch*, know more Secrets of this kind, than the Cabinet Council it ſelf, or all the Generals of the Armies of *France*. For I may aſſure you, that all the ſucceſsful Campaigns that *Lewis* has formerly had, tho' he Challenge the Glory, we had the principal ſhare in acquiring them. I confeſs, that we are not

not the only Inſtruments of obtaining a Victory, it muſt be indeed allow'd that he has other Troops appear in the Action, but we that work Inviſibly, are the main Engines that do the work Effectually. The Troops of the Houſhold flatter'd formerly with the Name of the *Invincible* (tho' ſince beaten into a ſenſe of the Adulation) have but the Pompous Title, whilſt it is only we who have the true Poſt of Honour, and are indeed the true Troops of the Houſhold, and deſerve the Name, if not of the *Invincible*, at leaſt of the *Irreſiſtible*; for we make the firſt, and the moſt effectual Attack. We bear the King's Image, and carry with us a greater Awe, and ſtrike a deeper Terror, than thoſe who only wear his Liveries. We have always Conquer'd, nay, whole Armies have laid down their Arms at our Approach. No Fort, no Ramparts, no Bulwarks or Walls, but fall down like thoſe of *Jericho*, when we go in Proceſſion about them, and at laſt paſs Triumphant in without a Breach. When we ſpring the Mine, the Fortreſs is no longer Tenible.

I muſt ingenuouſly Confeſs, that we have not been ſo Succeſsful in the open Field, as in Sieges and Blockades; and yet I may venture to Aſſert, that we have done very conſiderable Services, either in by-aſſing the oppoſite General, retarding his Marches, or putting a ſtop to the Purſuit, when Victory was theirs, and ours forc'd to

fly.

fly. From all which, our Titles to Valour and Conduct can by no means be disputed, two Qualities of so great value in a General; nay, we may likewise pretend to the Honourable Apellation of generous Enemies, since we never shed any Blood in the Field, nor take any City or Fortress by Storm.

First we appear before it, and let the Enemy take a view of our Strength and our Numbers, then we summon them to Surrender, which if they refuse, the Politick King draws fresh Troops out of his Garrisons, (that is, out of his Coffers) and this never fails to make the most Impregnable Fortifications fall into his Hands.

Thus *Lewis le Grand* has possess'd himself of so many considerable Towns and Cities in so little a space of time in the *Franché-Conté*, *Flanders*, and the rest of the *Spanish Netherlands*, and at one fatal juncture, throughout all *Holland*, tho' an Accident prevented keeping them. And yet the *Dutch* Fear and Reverence him more for their own sakes than his, because every Branch of their Trade with *France*, proves Profitable to them. Our Attacks have always prov'd very successful in the Empire, where Cities and whole Countries have become our Vassals, without aspiring to the Honour of striking one Blow to yield with the better Grace.

I have been in several, nay many Conferences, and aſſiſted at divers Councils of War, while I was in the Poſſeſſion of the *Intendants*; the *Secretaries* of *State*, and the Commiſſaries of the Armies, and I can aſſure you on the Word of a *Lowis d'Or* of Honour, that there has never been any one Thing of Moment enterpriz'd above theſe Forty Years, the Execution of which has not been entruſted to our Care and Adreſs.

When any of our Generals have demanded any Number of Thouſands of Horſe or of Foot, for the attempting any Action, the King (who loves to act the ſureſt part) wou'd then propoſe a like Number of *Louis d'Ors*, being ſufficiently convinc'd that this was the moſt certain way to accompliſh his vaſt Deſigns; and in this his Opinion, he ſtill was ſeconded by his Cabinet Council, who always thought it better to Buy the Town, than hazard Attack.

To give you an Inſtance, when the great *Condé*, or *Turene*, and a few more of that Character, (who, good Men knew no other Uſe of Gold, than to pay their Troops) would demand 20000 Foot, and 10000 Horſe; the King and his Wiſe Council wou'd add a a like Number of *Louis d'Ors*, as well knowing that one Man might be as as good as another, but that no Man was ſo good as a *Louis d'Or*, ſo that on any demand of Men by theſe fighting Generals, the Council of the King conſulted how many of us were fit to be employ'd in ſuch an Expedition

tion; if one Sum prove too little, Additions were made, and Succeſs always attended. Then did the Army take the Field, and the King put himſelf at the Head of them; and march'd to a Victory already aſſur'd, who like *Saul* among the Prophets, would ſay at his going away from *Verſailles. I am going to Beſiege ſuch a Place, and I ſhall take it ſuch a Day*; and this has been obſerv'd never to fail in the Event. But to do our ſelves Juſtice, I muſt declare, that neither his own nor his General's Conduct, not yet the Bravery of his Troops cou'd aſſure them ſuch ſignal Honour, of Subduing ſo many Wealthy Towns and Provinces, but only we who carry with us where ever we go, ſuch an Intrinſick Value, and ſo Irreſiſtible a Power.

But this does by no means hinder all the Appearance of a formal Siege, tho' we have ſecur'd the Surrender, yet they draw Lines of Circumvallation, Contravalation, raiſe Batteries, and play their Great Guns; but this is only for the Honour of his Arms, and ſo ſteal a Glory of Martial Prowes for the Monarch: But the ſpringing the Golden Mine, produces the Flags of Capitulation, then is the King extoll'd by all, as a Man of wonderful Valour, and ſo enters the Place new taken in Triumph.

Thus the Great *Lewis* makes War his Diverſion, entertaining the Ladies either in the Camp, or in the fine Fields of *Doaille*, the Danger and the Succeſs is always the ſame. For what I have ſaid, I leave it to you to judge, whether *Lewis* does not in the niceſt point deſerve the Sir-name of *Great*.

Near my little *Louis d'Or*, lay a Spaniſh *Piſtole*, who, at this, broke his Silence. You diſcover a piece of a Gallic Aſſurance (ſaid he) in aſſuming all the Honour of theſe Actions to your ſelf, tho' too many of us *Spaniſh Piſtoles*, have had too large a ſhare in the matter, I confeſs indeed, that we ought to be aſham'd, and not value our ſelves on this Merit of Unſtability to aggrandize your Monarch and leſſen our own, when by paying the Price of thoſe very Towns which they have wreſted out of our Hands.

The *Louis d'Or*, with a ſeeming Modeſty and Deference, thus anſwer'd, And what you ſay Sir, is true, nor did I deſign to do do you any Injuſtice, but ſtill what was done by both our means, muſt redound to the Honour of my King, who knows ſo perfectly well his own Intereſt and Advantage, as to oblige his very Enemies to Contribute to his Greatneſs.

Truly, interrupted the *Guinea*, this is an Honour ſo peculiar to the *French*, that it has not been nam'd among us yet in this Iſland; for to Bribe and Subborn, to deal with Traytors, and Traffick for Towns like Jockeys for Horſes, is fit only for the moſt Baſe, or the moſt Abject of Men; and are theſe thefe then the Steps by which *Lewis* had mounted fo high as to threaten all *Europe* with the Terror of his Name? The Event may have fince convinc'd him, that Victory is not always the Reward of Treachery.

My *Louis d'Or*, who expected no fuch Anfwer, feem'd in fome Confufion, but being us'd to the *French*-Air, he foon put on a little Affurance, and faid, I do profefs that there is no difference in Conqueft, whether it comes by *Gold* or by *Iron*: Whether by numerous Armies or prodigious Sums of Money; for let Victory be bought with *Gold* or with Blood, it is certainly ftill Victory.

But pray Sir, affum'd the *Guinea*, is this the way that *Cæfar*, *Scipio*, and *Alexander* made War, they difdaining that Victory that was not the purchafe of Blood: They always wou'd fay that they were Generals, not Merchants. Thefe were Men famous in War, and in great and mighty Conquefts the Patterns of Heroes, and the Admiration of all; and their Method feem extremely different from thefe you advance.

I look on them (reply'd the *Lewis d'Or*) as great Men of their Times, when the True and Modern way of making War was unknown; they fcarce knew their own Original, much lefs the wonderful Influence that *Gold* has on the Minds of Mankind; that mighty Bait was referv'd in ftore for the

Discovery of the present Polite Age, and our *Lewis* the *Great* has so throughly study'd Men, that he perfectly knows their weak sides, and never fails to attack them in that place. Thus instead of shedding whole Deluges of Blood, he spreads his Conquests a more gentle and Humane way, by Deluges of Gold; these are Conquests worthy the *most Christian King*. And yet I much wonder that *Alexander* should so far forget his Father's Wise Maxims, by which he Conquer'd all *Greece*, and smooth'd his way to the *Persian* Monarchy. Nor was it much wonder that he quitted these Maxims in the difference of Antagonists, The Brave one is to be Corrupted, the Cowards to be Beaten, Poor Men of Valour will submit to Gold, and Rich Cewards to the Sword. Thus Gold Conquer'd *Greece*, and Iron all *Asia*.

Why, said I, my little *Louis d'Or*, thou art not satisfy'd with taking Towns, and gaining Victories, but puts in as a Panegyrist for a Place among the Flatterers that surround thy Master's Throne.

Why truly Sir, (reply'd the Piece) I am not asham'd of the Character of an Orator, and you Men seem to allow it to Gold, when speaking of a more than commonly Eloquent Man, you say he has a *Golden Tongue*; the Metaphor is just, for 'tis taken from the greater Excellence, for our Eloquence does far surpass yours. There is no

Cause

Cause so Bad, that does not become Good in our Hands; and no Cause so Good, but when we are against it shall appear Bad. It is our Tallent to Conquer; and even *Time*, that grave Destroyer of all things, has no Dominion over us; for a *Louis d'Or* that has been rambling throughout the World, e're since the time of *Lewis* XIII. is as capable of Undertaking any considerable Action, as any one that received the Stamp but Yesterday, so little does she impair our Virtue and Force. Thou art, my little Piece, a most profound Casuist, said I. No, that Talent we leave to your Men (reply'd he smartly) for Words are your Province, but Actions is ours, and I might therefore fitly apply the Words of *Ajax* and *Ulysses* to my self.

——————*Quantum ego Marte feroce*
Inque Acie valeo, tantum valet iste loquendo.
As much as I in Martial Deeds prevail,
So much does he in a fine varnish'd Tale.

I wonder that the World should so much Reproach *Lewis le Grand* (who so well knew his own Interest) for making use of that Metal which commands the World, and is it self the Bulwark of Kingdoms; and the darling Object of all Mens Desires; this Metal he has at his Command, and with this he compasses his vast and Noble

Designs, and which when that fails, must also fail. I will add but one Word more on him, and that is, that he seems by Fate design'd to command the whole World, since by his Policy he has already got Possession of the New, which furnishes him with Gold to make War in the Old; Nay, his whole Reign 'till this present, has been an *Age* of *Gold*.

But said the *Italian Crown*, the Golden Age was succeeded by the Silver Age, and that by the Brazen and Iron Ages; and then *Lewis* has out-liv'd the Three former, and has now no more Gold to dispose on his several Occasions about this part of the World as he was wont. So that whilst his Soldiers have nothing but Rust, he himself must submit to the Conquest of the Iron of his Enemies. Witness his Unsuccessful Campaigns, and whilst his Foes are making vigorous Preparations for War he is fain to send his Plenipotentiaries to sue for a Peace.

You give we the Spleen (said the little *Louis d'Ors*) to hear you speak thus without Reflection, I confess that we are now in the Enemies hands, but then as I told you, we are Invulnerable and immortal, whilst a General or other Officer taken, must be a Prisoner till Ransom'd, or we are at liberty, and may pass back again into our Old Masters Hands; and when that comes to pass, you may be sure we shall again gain him

him this wonted Succeſs; and retrieve all thoſe Loſſes which now appear in conſiderable. But ſince the Golden Age is now no more (ſaid the *Guinea*) and the Iron Age bears all the ſway, why does not he make uſe of this Metal to perpetuate the Conqueſts that his Gold had obtained there, and make at leaſt a Vertue of Neceſſity, and at laſt draw the Sword when his Purſe will no longer anſwer his Demands? Our Generals would think the Hiſtory of their Actions would make but a dark Figure, if any of them were owing to ſo Mercenary a Metal; but take the Field after we are ſent away with the Baggage, admitting with a grievous Diſdain of all other Help but their Swords, whilſt on the contrary, your King is coming to his Army when his Golden Bridge has ſecur'd his Paſſage.

That (ſaid the *Louis d'Ors*) was always thought the ſureſt, and moſt ſubtil Art of making War; *Philip* the Father of the great *Alaxander*, and Pattern of my Maſter, as I have obſerv'd, us'd to ſay that there was no Fortreſs impregnable, if there was a way for an Aſs loaden with Gold to get Entrance. Private Men as well as Monarchs, make uſe of the moſt probable means of Succeſs, and both have found Gold to be the ſureſt means.

I agree with you (ſaid the *Guinea*) that no Prince ever had a greater Regard to his own Intereſt; for to advance that he has never ſcrupl'd to ſacrifice all things that were

Sacred

Sacred or Dear to Man; but to esteem this an Honourable Cause is what I can never subscribe to.

It is as Humour's in Fashion (reply'd the *Louis d'Or*) every one has his own Fancy and Notion. And as *France* is the Fountain of *Fashions*, and Cookery, so I think her Right has not been disputed in setting the Standard of both with the well-bred fine Gentlemen; the same will hold of what is Honourable and Dishonourable, at least by the Practice of the Beau Mond. Here are no Honours so distinguish'd as those we have practised; and if the Honours of *Lewis le Grand* are now in Decay, it is because we have left his Dominions.

That is to say, assum'd the *Guinea*, that he has no Honour left, in the favour of your Monarch, I presume to deny, and affirm that he has now as much Honour as ever he was Master of.

Be not so hard, said the *Louis d'Or*, on our great King, who has ever paid dear enough for his Purchase. But I must again say that nothing is more glorious than to see him take Towns, and over-run Countries, with little more force than what he desir'd from his *Louis d'Ors*. You know that *Philip* the 2*d*. Boasted, that he commanded the World, and made his Enemies tremble without going out of his Closet. This may properly be said of *Lewis le Grand*, since without

without ſtirring from *Verſailles*, he has accompliſh'd theſe Warlike Deſigns, which have frighten'd all *Europe*; and I call it glorious to gain Battles and Towns with an Inſtrument ſo mean. For the weaker the Means, the more Honourable the Exploit.

But ſince we have entred ſo far into this Argument, let us examine which Conduct is moſt agreeable to Reaſon. Your Generals you ſay, know no way to Conqueſt but by the Sword; and where is then the Wonder, that at the Head of Brave and Vigorous Troops Victory ſhould attend them. No Man ever doubted the Valour of *Guſtavus Adolphus*, who accompliſh'd ſo many Glorious Actions, and great Things by meer force of his Army. The Kings of the *North* know no other way, nor have it in their Power to try any other. While we call this a Gigantick way of making War.

But the Victories of *Lewis le Grand* are ſo *Ænigma*, which the beſt Hiſtorians, or Poleticians are not capable of explaining. The terrible Effects of his Power are e'ery Day felt, but the Fountain from whence they ſpring, has been always a Secret. You daily hear of Forts, Towns and Cities Subdu'd, but could never diſcover the Hand that did the Work. This is truly more than Humane Wit.

But I will let you know how he became Maſter of *Strasbourg*, the Capital of all *Alſace*, a Place which other Princes would have

have reckon'd worthy a Campaign, which yet we took without the loſs of one Man's Life, or ſo much as a Wound, but a world of good *Louis d'Ors* were bury'd in the Town.

The King diſpatches away his faithful *Louvois*, and only our Servant, he finds the Chief Burger-maſter's Coach ready to receive him without the Gates, whilſt he is carry'd to the Burger-maſter's Houſe; he ſends his Man out under pretence of buying up Horſes: The Burger-maſter's Family being got out of the way, he Aſſembled the reſt of the Magiſtrates, and in the Midſt of them, Mr. *Lovois* opens the Caſe, produces alſo very large Promiſes, extolling the great Rewards his Maſter was preparing for them, in conſideration of the Affair they then met about, and as an Earneſt of it preſented each of them with a Thouſand *Louis d'Ors*, adding that his Maſter was not Rich enough to requite ſo great a piece of Service to the height of the Merit, but aſſur'd them they had engag'd with a Prince who would always be liberal of his Favours to them, and Honour them with his Eſteem, as his beſt Friends and Allies.

At the Second Conference it was agreed, that the Firſt or Chief Burger-maſter ſhou'd have a Preſent of Four hundred Thouſand *Louis d'Ors*; and every other Magiſtrate of the Cabal ſhould have Three Hundred Thouſand; on the Payment of which the Keys

Keys of the City ſhould be deliver'd into his Hands, and that it ſhould for ever after be tributary to *France*, and that the Publication ſhould be made on the 23*d*. of *October* 1661. The King was punctual to the Agreement, and enter'd the Town on the very ſame Day.

I ſhall next inform you how we got the King the Maſtery of *Cazal*, a Place of ſuch Importance that I need not enforce it. I had a Relation of that Fact from a Piece that was ſent on that very Expedition.

The taking of Caſall.

The Marquis *d' Louvois*, whoſe Head was always at work, and had met with ſuch Succeſs ſo lately in the Affair of *Strasburg*; let the Duke of *Mantua* know that if he would ſell *Caſall* to his Maſter, he would pay him down two Millions of *Livers* for it; a mighty thing in the Pocket of ſo Poor a Prince as *Mantua*: Therefore in his Anſwer, he acquainted him that the Propoſal was not diſagreeable to him. The Fatigue that *Luvois* had lately, and alſo in his Journey to and from *Strasbourgh*, had diſabled him from undertaking that Journey; he therefore adviſed the King to make uſe of Mr. *Colbert*; who having received his laſt Inſtructions, ſet out with all Dilligence for *Caſall*; who, as ſoon as he arriv'd had a Private Conference with the Duke. Then by Misfortune, drawing out ſome Papers from his Pocket, he dropt one of his Memoirs, in which he had Inſtructi-

ons

ons to go as far as Four Millions, leaving other little Affairs to his own Management. This Paper, one of the Duke's Pages finding, brought to his Master. But Mr. *Colbert*, coming among others the next day to his *Levee*, the same Page with abundance of Address, convey'd it again into his Pocket without being perceived. The Duke seeming to know nothing of his Instructions, told him that he could not part with a Place of that Importance for less than Four Millions. Mr. *Colbert* was surprized to find the Duke in a Mind different from what he seemed the last Night, but dissembling his Instructions, told him, That he could not exceed what had been before proffer'd; but yet rather than leave his Court *re infectâ*, he would venture, on his own hazard, to exceed his Commission some Hundred Thousand of *Livers*. It was at last agreed, That the Duke should have his Advance of 500000 *Livers*, and a Yearly Pension of 200000. This Poor Prince being thus caught, he Sign'd the Contract of Sale, and Mr. *Colbert* return'd to Court in less than six Weeks. This was the Prelude to that Prince's Misery.

In this manner, said the *Louis d'Or*, does our great Monarch accomplish his Designs, and yet you will not allow his Conduct Honourable and Just, tho' you cannot deny that there is nothing more Lawfully got, than when we Purchase with our Money.

I do aver, reply'd the *Guinea*, that that very

very Maxim will not generaly hold good, as reaching no farther than the Bargains of private Men. But in Matters of State, a Man of Honour would Blush at it, and rather expose his Life in Honourable Conquest, than steal a Town, a Province by a Bribe to a Prince, who has no Right to sell it.

Tho' I think your Assertion, said the *Louis d'Or*, will not hold good, yet to pass over that Subject, *I* will proceed to the Relation of another Action, which no less tends to the rendring his Name Immortal, and that is, the Conquest of his own Subjects; and those of Millions of Souls which he has Converted to the *Catholick* Faith, in which we also have acted no inconsiderable Part!

Then I find, said I, that thou art a Missionary, as well as a Soldier, and Statesman! Pray, let me then hear what Success you have had in this Apostolical Function.

Is it possible, said he, that you can be Ignorant of that which all the World knows already so well?

I know very well, interrupted the Guinea, who could not be silent on this occasion) that *Lewis* XIV. has routed the Protestants out of *France*, and that *Dragoons* were the villanous Instruments of that Work, effected by Fire and Sword. By which the *Dragoons* made more Converts in one Week, than their Bishops and Prelates could do all their Lives. But I must own that I am quite Ignorant of what part you cou'd have in that Weighty Affair.

I expected no less, said the *Louis d'Or*, I see you are prepossess'd with that False Notion, as well as others, of attributing all his Success to the Fury of his Arms; when we alone deserve all the Praise. In this I already open'd your Eyes as to his Secular Conquests, now I am to assure you, that those likewise which are Spiritual derive all their Glory from us.

Was

Was I in your place, said the *Guinea*, I should easily surrender my share to the *Dragoons*, who seem fitter Instruments of a work of this Nature than you.

Why, said the *Louis d'Or*, in a kind of heat, is the Conversion of Two Millions of Souls to be past over in silence? Which can't be equal'd in History, even since the Days of the Apostles; nay, I may say, that this exceeds all they did. If they Converted many Nations, it was by strange and wonderful Miracles, Preaching, and the Holy Spirit; but here was not so much as one Miracle perform'd, nor the least pretence of having the Gift of the Holy Ghost. And since these strange things are brought about by our means, why should we refuse the Glory we deserve.

But we in *England*, said the *Guinea*, being quite Ignorant of these Things, I hope you will pardon our Doubts. And I think that Corruption is a less excuse for defending an Opinion than Fame.

The Dispute is not of that, said the *Louis d'Or*, whether it be more or less Culpable, but let it be taken as it will, it makes our Enquiry of equal extent; and since Men's Consciences are not proof against our Power, it plainly follows that nothing else is.

In effect, Gentlemen, said I, to put an end to the Dispute, you are the Darlings of the Age, your Empire is over all, and you are the Arbitrators of *War*, *Peace*; but to the Shame of those who advanced you to that Power be it spoken. It is the Scandal of *Lewis le Grand*, to have made so Brutal an Use of you; as well as of the Popish Church, to commit so many Sacriledges by your means, And a Reproach to Mankind to prostitute himself to your Charms.

Yet since there can be no Intelligence like what you can give, I shall take care often to Consult my GOLDEN SPY.

FINIS.